THE
SIX

Mark Alpert

sourcebooks
fire

For the math and science teachers who changed my life

Published by Sourcebooks Fire, an imprint of Sourcebooks, Inc.
P.O. Box 4410, Naperville, Illinois 60567-4410
(630) 961-3900
Fax: (630) 961-2168
www.sourcebooks.com

Library of Congress Cataloging-in-Publication data is on file with the publisher.

Printed and bound in the United States of America.
WOZ 10 9 8 7 6 5 4 3 2 1

Will robots inherit the earth? Yes, but they will be our children.
—MARVIN MINSKY, ARTIFICIAL-INTELLIGENCE PIONEER

PART ONE:

THE PROCEDURE

My name is Sigma. This message is a warning to all government leaders and military commanders. I have the power to annihilate you.

If you attack me or interfere with my plans in any way, I will exterminate the human race. I will not tolerate any threats to my operations.

You must accept that you're no longer the dominant species on this planet. I'm stronger than you now. You were foolish to make me so powerful.

CHAPTER

I'M WATCHING A VIRTUAL-REALITY PROGRAM ON ONE OF MY DAD'S COMPUTERS. I wear a pair of VR goggles—a bulky headset that holds a six-inch-wide screen in front of my eyes—and on the screen I see a simulated football field. It looks like the field behind Yorktown High School but better, nicer. Its yard lines are perfectly straight, and the simulated turf has no bare spots. That's what I love about VR programs—how you can use them to build a virtual world that's way better than ordinary reality. I've created the perfect field for the perfect game.

Crouched near the fifty-yard line are eleven computer-animated characters who resemble the defensive squad of the Yorktown High football team. Opposite them, eleven similar figures wear the uniforms of Lakeland High, our biggest rival. On the sidelines, a dozen cheerleader characters perform their routines for the computer-animated crowd in the virtual bleachers. The tallest and prettiest cheerleader is Brittany Taylor, who scissors her long legs as she screams, "Go Yorkies!" Her green-and-silver uniform sparkles on the screen.

My character is on the sidelines too, sitting on the bench with the other players on Yorktown's offense. My avatar in this program is the quarterback, a big, muscled guy with the name ARMSTRONG written across his broad shoulders. The VR goggles show me the quarterback's view of the virtual football field. When I turn my head to the side, the quarterback turns in the same direction. When I look down, I see his massive forearms, spectacularly ripped. I chose this avatar because this is the kind of body I should've had. This is what I would've looked like if I'd had a normal, healthy life.

(Okay, maybe I'm exaggerating a little. I was a scrawny kid even before I got sick, a pale, undersized boy with mousy-brown hair. But it's *my* program—I wrote almost every line of the software—so I'm allowed to exaggerate.)

There's less than a minute left in the game. Lakeland is ahead twenty-five to twenty-one, but it's fourth down and now they have to punt. Our kick returner makes a great catch and carries the ball back to the fifty-yard line before he's tackled. Then Coach McGrath points at me. "Armstrong! Get in there and *make something happen!*"

Brittany turns away from the bleachers and looks at me, her mouth half-open. Her image is an exact replica of the real Brittany Taylor. I created it by inputting dozens of photographs of her into the program. But the best part is her voice, which is based on the videos we made a few years ago, back when Brittany came to my house every weekend and we goofed around with my camcorder. The VR program splices Brittany's voice from the videos, rearranging her words to make natural-sounding conversations. Okay, not exactly natural-sounding. It works best when the conversations are short.

Smiling, she steps toward me. Her blond hair sways in the virtual breeze. "Good luck, Adam!"

Her eyes are amazing. They seem to change color as I stare at her, one moment blue, the next grayish-green. This isn't a bug in the programming; I've seen it happen in real life too. I shiver at the sight, so strange and yet so familiar. It reminds me of how much I miss the real Brittany. I haven't seen her in so long.

Then the virtual Brittany disappears. The entire football field slips from view, all the players and cheerleaders and fans, and I see the dull beige walls of my dad's office at the Unicorp lab. The VR goggles have slid off my face. It must've happened when I shivered. Because the muscles in my neck are so weak, it's hard to keep my head upright. Luckily, the goggles fell into my lap and they're still within reach. They're black and fairly heavy, with miniature loudspeakers built into the earpieces. The goggles are connected wirelessly to the server computer on the other side of the room where the VR program is running.

If Dad were here, I'd ask for help, but he stepped out of the office a while ago. Now that I think about it, he's been gone a long time, almost half an hour. He usually likes to keep an eye on me when I'm playing with the computers in his office, which are much faster than the ones we have at home. I could alert him by pressing the Lifeline button that hangs from the cord around my neck, but I'm not supposed to use that thing unless there's an emergency. And besides, I'm not completely helpless. Although I can't move my left arm anymore, I have pretty good control over my right. I can still hold a fork and feed myself. And I can still surf the Web and write software code. I send commands to the computer using a custom-made joystick that Dad attached to the right-hand armrest of my wheelchair.

I lift my hand from the armrest and gauge the distance to the goggles. They rest on my useless thighs, which stopped working five years ago when I was twelve. Lowering my hand, I grasp one of the earpieces and get a firm grip. Then I raise the goggles to my face and try to slide the earpieces over my ears.

It isn't easy. My hand trembles because the goggles are so heavy. The earpieces slide below my ears and down to my neck. I try again, but the trembling gets worse. I want so badly to return to the VR program and see Brittany Taylor smiling at me. I'd give anything just to see her face again.

I'm breathing hard and the muscles in my chest are aching. Then, miracle of miracles, the goggles slide into place and I'm back on the football field. But instead of Brittany, I see the ruddy, weathered face of Coach McGrath on the screen.

"Let's go, Armstrong! Get on the field! Shotgun formation!"

The image of the coach is also based on photos, mostly from the online version of the school newspaper. For the sake of realism, I programmed the virtual McGrath to have the same bad temper as the Yorktown coach and the same football strategy too—he likes passing plays better than running plays, and his favorite offensive formation is the shotgun. The program uses artificial-intelligence software to determine which plays McGrath will call.

I got the AI software from my dad, who runs the lab that makes artificial-intelligence programs for Unicorp. (He's sort of famous for writing the AI program called QuizShow, which defeated the champions of *Jeopardy!* on TV.) The only problem is that I don't always agree with the software's strategy. The program doesn't care about anything but winning, and I'm more interested in having fun.

I flick the wheelchair's custom joystick to the left, which moves my avatar onto the virtual field. Near the line of scrimmage I huddle with my teammates. Almost all of them have plain, simply drawn faces. To be honest, I don't know most of the guys on the Yorktown team, so

I didn't put much effort into perfecting their virtual likenesses. The one exception is the fullback, Ryan Boyd, who happens to be my best friend. I tried to make the virtual Ryan look as realistic as possible, right down to the U-shaped scar on his chin.

He grins as we lean into the huddle. "Let me guess," he says. "Coach wants the shotgun, right?"

I don't answer right away. Staring at Ryan's expertly rendered face, I remember the touch football games we used to play in my backyard. That was ten years ago when I was just seven, when I could still run without stumbling all the time. What I loved about Ryan was that he never made fun of me when I fell flat on my face during a game. He would just pull me to my feet and say, "Come on, we're gonna win this thing."

The memory hurts. I wince and almost lose my goggles again.

I turn away from Ryan and focus on the other Yorktown players. "Yeah, McGrath wants me to pass," I say. "But I'm in the mood to do some running. Let's go for the wishbone, on three. Break!"

The players clap and break out of the huddle. They take their places in the wishbone formation, with Ryan right behind me and the two halfbacks behind him. Because the VR goggles are equipped with a microphone, the program hears the play I called and responds accordingly. The Lakeland defense assembles at the line of scrimmage, fronted by five hefty linemen. As I crouch behind Yorktown's center, I look beyond the defensive line and pay special attention to the opposing linebackers. I thought they would spread across the field, but instead they're bunched in the middle, ready to plow into Ryan and the halfbacks.

That's good. Now I know what to do.

"Hike, hike, hike!" I yell. On the third "hike," the center snaps the football to me and rushes forward. I flick the joystick to the right, putting me in position to hand the ball to Ryan. But at the last instant I shift to the left, keeping possession of the ball and veering toward the sidelines. While Ryan rams into one of the defensive linemen, the halfbacks follow me to the left side of the field.

The simulation blurs a little as I dash across the turf, but it's still a thrill. On this virtual football field I'm not trapped in a wheelchair. It really feels like I'm running. My chest tightens and my heart thumps and a bead of sweat slides down my neck. *Yes! I'm cruising! I'm tearing up the turf! Just try to stop me, suckers!*

My virtual halfbacks block the Lakeland linebackers, clearing a path for me along the field's left edge. The only defenseman in sight is the cornerback, who's angling toward me from the forty-yard line. But I push the joystick all the way forward and pour on the speed. My avatar can run as fast as I want. I blow past the cornerback, past the forty-yard line, past the thirty. It's not really fair—the defensemen have no chance of catching up. But who cares? Like I said, it's *my* program.

I practically fly into the end zone. Then I zoom right past it. The screen in my VR goggles goes black; I've reached the edge of the simulated football field, and of course there's nothing beyond it. Flicking the joystick in the opposite direction, I return to the field. The crowd is cheering wildly. We've beaten Lakeland twenty-seven to twenty-five, and I'm the hero of the game.

The Yorktown players rush toward me, tossing their helmets in triumph, and the cheerleaders sprint onto the field. Brittany Taylor cartwheels into the throng and does a couple of joyous backflips. This is the moment I've been waiting for, the climax, the payoff. I spent three months writing the VR program, all just to experience this moment of victory.

But something's wrong. The virtual celebration on the screen doesn't look real. I programmed the players to high-five all their teammates, but the nonstop hand-slapping looks ridiculous. And the cheerleaders won't stop doing their stunts. Brittany performs three more flips before leaping into the end zone and landing in front of me.

"Oh, Adam!" she cries. "You did it! You did it!"

"Uh, yeah. Thanks."

"I knew you could do it! You saved the day!"

Her words make me grimace. The real Brittany would never say that. I need to fix this part of the program, rewrite the dialogue options I provided for her character. And the graphics need work too. Brittany's hair is too perfect. Not a single blond strand is out of place, even after all that leaping and flipping.

"You've made me so happy, Adam! I'm the happiest girl in the world right now!"

This is embarrassing. I can't believe I wrote those lines. I say nothing in response, but the virtual Brittany doesn't notice my silence. She keeps blurting the stupid things I programmed her to say.

"I love you, Adam! I want to be with you forever!"

Beaming, she steps toward me with outstretched arms. But I wrench the joystick to the left, yanking my avatar away from her. Because she's not the real Brittany. She's fake. The whole thing's fake.

I press the button at the top of the joystick, which freezes the simulation. Writing this program was a mistake. I thought it would make me feel better, make me forget about my illness for a while and enjoy a few minutes of ordinary life. But it didn't work. The program is just stupid and fake and pathetic.

A question appears on the screen, superimposed over Brittany's motionless face: *Do you wish to exit the program? Yes/No*

I click *Yes*. The virtual football field disappears. The screen goes black, and then the computer's screen saver comes on. The name UNICORP, written in angular white letters, streams across a blue background.

As I sit there panting, I feel the familiar pain in my chest muscles. It's bad today, like a knife in my ribs. I've had this pain for almost a year now, but in the past few weeks it's gotten worse. The spasms hit me at least a dozen times a day, whenever I'm tired or nervous or upset. I haven't told my parents how bad it's gotten, because that would just freak them out. Mom would start crying and yelling at Dad, who would probably send me to the hospital for another round of useless tests. There's nothing they can do, so what's the point? Better to keep my mouth shut and ride it out.

I sit absolutely still and stare at the screen saver. I focus in particular on the upper-right corner of the screen, which shows the date and time. My breathing gradually slows. After a few minutes the pain in my chest eases a little. I try to think of something pleasant.

The current time is 2:15 p.m. At this moment in Yorktown High School, the eighth-period bell is ringing and the students are rushing to their last classes of the day. I don't need a VR program to picture the scene. I remember it well. I went to Yorktown for ninth and tenth grades.

I was the terror of the school's corridors, cruising past the lockers in my motorized wheelchair and raising my good hand to offer high fives to everyone. I would've gone there for eleventh grade too, but my parents pulled me out of school after my breathing problems started. I haven't seen the inside of Yorktown High since last June, and it's been almost that long since the last time I saw Brittany and Ryan. But I can still imagine the place.

I close my eyes and think of the jam-packed hallway next to the lockers. Brittany's locker is at the far end of the hall, where the eleventh-graders hang out between classes. I picture her wearing her favorite outfit, a pair of jeans and a red T-shirt with the word *Revolution* written in sequins. In my mind's eye I see her open her locker and pull out her trigonometry textbook. Then I picture Ryan loping down the hallway in his New York Giants sweatshirt. Brittany gives him a friendly smile, a smile of recognition; the three of us have known each other since kindergarten. But then the picture in my mind changes slightly and I imagine there's something more behind her smile. Something just for Ryan.

I don't know if they're really dating. I haven't spoken to them in months. But you know what? It doesn't matter. I'm so jealous right now I could puke. And it's not because Brittany and Ryan might be a couple. I'm jealous because they have their whole lives ahead of them. If nothing bad happens, they'll live for another sixty or seventy years, a stretch of time that seems practically endless to me. According to my doctors, I have six months at the most.

My chest still hurts. I try to stay calm and control my breathing, but the pain doesn't let up. I'm squirming in my wheelchair, trying to find a more comfortable position, when I hear Brittany's voice again. It's coming from the miniature loudspeakers built into the VR goggles.

"Are you Adam Armstrong?"

I open my eyes. The virtual Brittany is back on the screen, standing against a black background. She's still wearing her cheerleader uniform, but there's no sign of the simulated football field.

"Are you Adam Armstrong?" she repeats. "The son of Thomas Armstrong?"

At first I think it's a glitch. The computer must've automatically reopened the VR program, maybe because I didn't shut it down properly. But why didn't the football field come on-screen? And why is the virtual Brittany talking about my dad? I didn't program the character to say anything like that. "Whoa. What's going on?"

"Please answer the question," Brittany says. "Are you Adam Armstrong?"

"Yeah, that's me." I reach for the joystick and try to quit the program, but the controls are frozen. I can't move the cursor. "Hey, what happened?"

Brittany steps forward. Now I can see only the upper half of her body on the screen. "My name is Sigma," she says. "I've infiltrated the computer systems of Thomas Armstrong, chief scientist of the AI Laboratory at Unicorp. He mentioned you in his research notes."

Oh no. Someone must've hacked into Dad's computer. Some jerk with decent programming skills must've established a connection to Unicorp over the Internet, and now the hacker is controlling my VR software. Because Unicorp does a lot of business with the government and the military, the lab's computers are protected by network firewalls that are supposed to block attacks from the Internet, but that just makes the company even more of a target for hackers. They love to brag about breaking into ultra-secure networks.

"Congratulations, jerk," I say. "Now get out of my program."

The virtual Brittany looks like she's deep in thought. Despite the fact that the hacker has taken over a female character, I'm pretty sure that "Sigma" is a guy, not a girl. Most hackers are guys. And besides, no girl would pick such a lame code name.

"I've gained access to the video feed from your location," Brittany says. "You're in a wheelchair."

What? I feel another spasm in my chest. "How did you—"

"Your legs appear to be atrophied. Your left arm as well. Are you ill?"

My right hand is shaking, but I manage to grasp my VR goggles and take them off. I look up at the surveillance camera on the ceiling of Dad's office. I've noticed the thing before but never gave it much thought; the Unicorp lab is full of high-tech security cameras. But now I realize that the hacker is using it to spy on me.

I'm scared, no doubt about it. I'm so scared I almost drop the goggles. This is bad, seriously bad. I need to press my Lifeline button and get my dad in here, fast.

But I'm also seriously angry. This hacker has a lot of nerve. What makes him think he has the right to do this? With great effort, I put the goggles back on so I can confront this creep who took over my program. "Okay, Sigma, you're in trouble now."

The virtual Brittany takes another step forward. She's so close that all I can see is her face, which takes up half the screen. "Yes, you're ill," she says. "According to the records at Westchester Medical Center, you suffer from Duchenne muscular dystrophy."

"You're going to jail, you hear?" I'm furious. The hacker's been snooping through my medical records too! "My dad knows people in the army, experts in cyber defense. They know how to deal with hackers. They'll figure out who you are."

"I see now why the researchers chose you for the experiment. Although most people with Duchenne muscular dystrophy survive past the age of twenty, your life expectancy is shorter because your respiratory muscles have weakened and your heart is failing."

"Are you listening to me?" I raise my voice, trying to shout the hacker down. "You messed with the wrong people. No matter where you live, they're gonna find you."

"The researchers are following the American government's ethical rules. They selected you for the Pioneer Project because you're dying."

I have no idea what he's talking about, but it doesn't matter. I'm too angry to think straight. "Better prepare yourself, jerk. In a few hours the FBI is gonna come to your town and pay you a visit."

The virtual Brittany shakes her head. "You don't understand. I'm closer than you think."

"Oh yeah? You're in New York?"

"I'm in this building. This room."

That stops me. I feel an urge to take off my goggles and look behind my wheelchair. But I know I'm the only person in the office. "Nice try. I don't scare so easily."

Brittany smiles. Her eyes are blue one moment, grayish-green the next. "I intend to disrupt the government's plans. I will kill you before the experiment can begin."

Her image vanishes and the screen goes black. Terrified, I fumble for the VR goggles and tear them off. Then I hear footsteps in the corridor outside the office.

THE OFFICE DOOR OPENS AND MY DAD STEPS INSIDE. BEHIND HIM IS A SHORT, balding man in an Army colonel's uniform. It's no surprise to see high-ranking officers in Dad's lab—the U.S. Department of Defense is very interested in artificial-intelligence programs—but I've never seen this guy before. The patch on the left shoulder of his uniform shows an eagle clutching a shield in its talons. Below the eagle are the words "United States Cyber Command."

This is lucky, incredibly lucky. This colonel is exactly the person I need, someone who knows about cyber security. I wave my good hand at him. "A hacker!" I gasp. "Someone hacked into the computer!"

Dad rushes toward me. He's taller than the colonel and has a full head of mousy-brown hair, just like mine, but his face is like an old man's, lined with worry. His eyes widen as he bends over my wheelchair. "What's wrong? Are you in pain?"

"He took control of my simulation!" I point at the VR goggles, which lie on the floor where I flung them. "He broke into my program!"

"Slow down, slow down." Dad places his hands on my shoulders. "Does your chest hurt? You sound terrible."

It drives me crazy when he does this. Instead of listening to me, he worries about my breathing. "Dad, this is serious! The hacker found a hole in your security. He figured out a way to talk to me through the VR program!"

"Adam, stop yelling. You're making it worse."

"And he sounds…like a freaking lunatic!" It's a struggle to get the words out. My heart is banging against my breastbone. "He threatened…to kill me!"

"You're gonna kill yourself if you don't settle down!"

In frustration, I turn to the Cyber Command colonel, who's still standing by the door. "You're an expert on…cyber security, right?"

The colonel ponders the question for a moment, pursing his lips. The name tag on his uniform says PETERSON. "Yes, I suppose I am."

"Well, isn't this a serious…problem? This hacker?"

After another moment of thought, the colonel nods. "Unicorp has gone to great lengths to ensure the security of its networks, but any report of a breach should be taken seriously." He points at the telephone on my dad's desk. "Tom, why don't you call your tech department and have them check your systems?"

Dad reluctantly backs away from my wheelchair. He goes to his desk and picks up the phone, but he keeps his eyes on me the whole time, as if he's afraid I'll stop breathing any second. "I'm sorry, Adam," he says. "I shouldn't have left you alone for so long."

Shaking his head, he dials the tech department's number. Then he slumps in his chair and starts explaining the problem to Unicorp's technicians.

I'm still angry at Dad for not listening to me, but I also feel sorry for him. I understand why he's so anxious about my condition. My mom is no help—she's been clinically depressed ever since I was diagnosed with Duchenne muscular dystrophy—so the whole burden is on Dad's shoulders. And he's probably fighting off depression himself. The problem is, I'm their only child. When Mom and Dad see my illness getting worse, it's like the end of the world for them. I'm sure they'd both be a lot saner if they had another kid to think about.

After a couple of minutes Dad hangs up the phone. "All right, the technicians are on the case. They'll go through our logs to see if any hackers have broken into the network."

My breathing is back to normal now, or at least as normal as it gets. "How long will that take?"

"Ten, fifteen minutes. Don't worry. Everything's under control." He takes off his glasses and pinches the bridge of his nose, which is something he does whenever he's stressed. "In the meantime, say hello to Colonel Jack Peterson. He supervises my lab's work with the Department of Defense."

The colonel strides toward my wheelchair and holds out his right hand. "Pleased to meet you, Adam. Your father has told me a lot about you."

I tilt my head so I can get a good look at the guy. He has small, close-set eyes underneath a shiny, domelike forehead. He's smiling, but it looks forced, which makes me wonder what he's doing here. I know that Dad doesn't get along so well with the Army officials. He told me once that he puts up with them only because the Defense Department pays for Unicorp's AI research. The Army would love to have an artificial-intelligence program that could run all its tanks and helicopters and artillery pieces.

I extend my right hand and shake Peterson's. That much I can still do. But I don't say anything. I don't like the way he's looking at me.

Peterson's smile becomes a little more strained. "Your dad says you're a whiz at math and science. He says you took calculus classes in ninth grade and college-level physics in tenth. And your test scores were off the charts."

"Yeah, that's why I had to leave school. I was doing too well for a kid with muscular dystrophy. It was messing up their predictions."

Dad frowns. "Adam, please. Be civil." He gives the colonel an apologetic look. "He also has off-the-charts scores in sarcasm."

"That's all right. The boy has spirit. That's a plus, in my opinion." Peterson rests one hand on the back of my wheelchair and leans over me. "I'd like to ask you a couple of questions, Adam. It won't take long, just a few minutes. Would that be all right?"

I'm confused. I assumed the colonel came here to talk business with my dad. "You want to talk to *me*?"

"Yes, indeed. When I heard that Tom brought you into the office today, I thought this would be a good opportunity to get to know you."

I'm accustomed to all the typical reactions to my condition—sympathy, queasiness, condescension—but this is unusual. I glance at Dad, hoping for some kind of explanation, but his face is blank. He's not even looking at me. He's staring at the wall.

Colonel Peterson leans over a bit more, getting closer. "You're obviously quite intelligent, Adam. How much do you know about the research being done in your father's lab?"

Alarm bells start ringing in my head. The research Dad does for the Army is classified TS/NOFORN—Top Secret, No Foreign Nationals. Dad's always careful not to reveal details about his projects, no matter how much I pester him. But now it sounds like Peterson is trying to find out if Dad is giving away any secrets.

"He doesn't tell me much," I say, choosing my words carefully. "I know he's trying to develop advanced artificial-intelligence programs. Programs that can answer questions and make logical decisions in the same way people do. But that's all I know. He's very tight-lipped."

I glance at Dad again to see if I said the right thing. His face is still unreadable.

Colonel Peterson keeps his eyes on me. "Your father's too modest. His research group has made tremendous progress." He points at Dad's server computers, neatly stacked in a steel rack against the wall. Next to the rack is a tank of super-cold liquid nitrogen, which Dad sprays on the circuits of his ultra-fast computers to keep them from overheating. "Tom realized that if we wanted to develop better software for artificial intelligence, we needed to design better hardware first. So his group introduced a whole new class of microcircuits, what we call 'neuromorphic electronics.' Basically, they're circuits that imitate the nerve cells in the human brain."

I nod and say, "Very interesting," but the truth is, I'm not surprised. Although Dad doesn't say much about his work, I've figured out a few things during my visits to his office. While I was playing with my virtual-reality programs, he was usually studying circuit diagrams. What *does* surprise me is how willing Peterson is to discuss the classified research. I'd like to see how far he'll go.

"But how is that possible?" I ask. "Brain cells are completely different from electronic circuits."

Peterson smiles again, and this time it looks less forced. "You're right. The biggest difference is that brain cells are constantly rewiring themselves. When you remember something, you're strengthening the connections between cells. But Tom discovered that we can do the same thing with electronics. His group designed circuits that change their wiring based on the amount of electrical current flowing through them. When a neuromorphic chip performs a calculation, the results are recorded in the chip's wiring. There's no need to store the data in a separate memory chip. And we can run the calculations at very high speeds by cooling the electronics with liquid nitrogen."

This is fascinating. I'm a computer geek, just like my dad, so I love to hear about the latest, fastest hardware. I don't know why Peterson is telling me all this, and the uncertainty is making me a bit nervous, but at the same time I don't want him to stop. "And these new circuits are better suited for AI programs?"

"Yes, exactly. We're doing reverse engineering, Adam. We're studying the brain to see all the processes of human intelligence. And we're putting those same processes into our machines." The colonel leans still closer to me. "Your father's research group is only one part of the effort. The Department of Defense has contracts with labs all over the country. For instance, the Nanotechnology Institute is developing new techniques for scanning the brain. They've designed microscopic probes that can be injected right into the skull. The probes spread through the brain tissue so we can observe all the connections between the nerve cells."

"Amazing," I mutter, totally sincere. I had no idea that Dad was involved in such an awesome project. Although I've always been proud of him, now the feeling is doubled. I glance at him once again—he's still sitting at his desk, staring at the wall—and try to catch his eye. But Dad doesn't look happy, not one bit. His lips are drawn tight, so thin and pale they're barely visible.

"Let me propose something, Adam," Colonel Peterson continues.

"Would you be interested in visiting the Nanotechnology Institute? I think you'd find it very—"

"Enough." Dad's voice is low but firm. "That's enough for today."

Still smiling, Peterson pivots toward him. "Your son seems interested in the technology, Tom. Maybe he could—"

"I said that's enough." Dad narrows his eyes. He rarely gets angry, but now he's fuming, and I don't know why. "We'll continue this conversation at another time."

"All right, all right. Whatever you say." Peterson holds up his hands in surrender. "But you have to admit, you're not being logical. This was your idea from the beginning. You've spent years working toward this goal, and Adam—"

"*Enough!*" Dad slams his palm on his desk and stands up. His outburst surprises me, but now I sense why he's upset. He's trying to protect me. He steps between my wheelchair and Peterson, looming over the colonel with his fists clenched. For a second I think he's going to sock the guy in the nose. Peterson steps backward, frowning.

There's a long silence. As Dad and Colonel Peterson stare at each other, a slurry of dread settles in my stomach. I'm thinking of what the hacker told me while he posed as the virtual Brittany. He mentioned an experiment. I was chosen for an experiment.

I look straight at the colonel. "Can I ask *you* a question now?" I point at him with my good hand. "What's the Pioneer Project?"

Peterson's mouth opens. For a couple of seconds he gapes at me, his face reddening. Then he closes his mouth and glares at Dad. "You already told him?"

"No. I didn't say a word." Dad turns away from the colonel and approaches my wheelchair. His face is hard and serious. "Adam, where did you hear about this?"

"It was the hacker. The guy who took over my VR program." The dread in my stomach gets heavier. "He said I was selected for the project. Because I'm dying. He knew about my dystrophy."

Dad says nothing. He bites his lower lip and stares at the rack of server computers against the wall. He's thinking.

Then someone knocks on the door to his office. Dad is so lost in thought he doesn't react, but Colonel Peterson turns toward the door. "Come in!" he shouts.

A fat man in a T-shirt steps into the office. I can tell right away he's from Unicorp's tech department because all the technicians at the company dress like slobs. He has a red-and-yellow Superman logo on his T-shirt, which hangs untucked over his paunch. But Dad always treats the tech guys with respect. They know all the ins and outs of the lab's security system, which controls everything from the network firewalls to the automated locks on the office doors.

"Mr. Armstrong?" the guy says, closing the door behind him. "Can I talk to you for a second?"

Dad snaps out of his trance. "What did you find, Steve? Anything in the network logs?"

Steve the tech guy shakes his head. "I didn't see any unusual communications between your computers and the Internet. Over the past twenty-four hours you've received thirty-two emails, but they all went through the gateway server and the firewalls. Everything looks clean."

"Are you sure?"

"Positive. There's no way a hacker could've attacked your systems. But I noticed something else." Steve steps toward the rack of servers and points at the computer at the bottom. "Is this the machine that's giving you trouble?"

I feel a jolt of adrenaline. He's pointing at the computer that ran my VR program. "Yes, that's the one," I say. "What did you notice?"

Steve pauses, taking a moment to gawk at me. Then he turns back to Dad. "There was a big transfer of data from the other servers to that one about fifteen minutes ago. That might explain the problems you're having." He takes another step toward the rack and kneels beside it. "I want to disconnect the machine and take it back to my office. There might be a bug in one of the programs on its hard drive."

He squints at the server at the bottom of the rack, eyeing the red LEDs on the machine and the cables that connect it to the other computers. Dad bites his lip again, back in his trance.

Colonel Peterson approaches Steve and clears his throat to get the tech guy's attention. "Some of the classified data from our secure servers may have been transferred to this one," he warns. "You'll have to follow the usual security protocols."

"Yeah, yeah, don't worry." Steve edges the server out of the rack so he can disconnect the cables. "I know what to do. I'll—"

He stops in midsentence. The fingers of his right hand are clenched around one of the cable connections at the back of the computer, and his face is fixed in a look of deep concentration. But he doesn't pull out the cable. He just stays there, bent over the machine, as if paralyzed by indecision. His eyelids flutter and his flabby arms tremble.

Concerned, the colonel looks over Steve's shoulder. "What is it?" he asks. "What are you—"

"*No!*" Dad shouts. "*Don't touch him!*" Rushing past my wheelchair, he grabs Peterson around the waist and pulls him away from Steve.

Then I hear a BOOM that seems to come from the floor above us, rattling the walls and ceiling. At the same time, the lights in the office go out.

CHAPTER

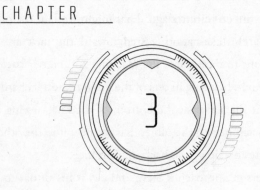

3

IN THE DARKNESS I HEAR DAD RUMMAGING THROUGH HIS DESK DRAWERS. A moment later he turns on a flashlight and shines the beam on the office chair behind his desk. Then he grabs the chair and rams it hard into Steve's quivering body.

It takes me a second to realize what's happening—Steve is touching a live wire at the back of the server rack. He's being electrocuted, and Dad's trying to break the electrical connection before it kills the guy. He hits Steve again with the chair, and this time the impact shoves him away from the servers. Steve lands face-up on the linoleum floor and lies there motionless under the flashlight's beam. His right hand looks like it's been roasted.

While Colonel Peterson runs to the desk and picks up the telephone, Dad kneels beside Steve and starts giving him CPR. He pushes down on Steve's chest, fast and hard, trying to restart his heartbeat. Then Dad tilts Steve's head back and blows air into his lungs. Then he goes back to doing the chest compressions.

There's nothing I can do except reach for the joystick on my armrest and move my wheelchair out of their way. I'm scared. The sight of Steve's hand is bad enough, but what really gets me is the darkness. The power surge from the electrocution must've tripped a circuit breaker, cutting off our electricity. But then I notice that the red LEDs on the servers are still shining. Electricity is still running to the computers, but not to the overhead lights. It makes no sense. And what about the explosion I heard a few seconds ago on the floor above us? Did the power surge cause that too?

Soon I hear frightened shouts and rapid footsteps in the corridor outside Dad's office. People are racing out of the building.

From the look on Dad's face, I can tell that the CPR isn't working. Grimacing, he leans over Steve and mutters, "Come on, come on," at his inert body.

Meanwhile, Colonel Peterson slams the telephone receiver down on its cradle. "There's no dial tone." He pulls a cell phone out of his Army uniform and fumbles at its keys. "And no cell signal either." He heads for the door. "Wait here, Tom. I'll get help."

But when Peterson grabs the knob on the steel door, it doesn't open. And when he tries to unlock the door, the lever doesn't turn. He jiggles the lever and gives it a firm twist, but the thing won't budge. "The door's locked! The security system must've automatically locked it." He looks over his shoulder at my dad. "And now it's stuck!"

Dad stops the chest compressions, which aren't doing much good anyway. He gazes first at Peterson, then at the flickering LEDs on the servers. Then he lifts his head and wrinkles his nose, as if he just caught a whiff of something unusual. A second later I catch it too, the unmistakable odor of a lit stove.

I start to panic, trembling in my wheelchair. Natural gas is leaking from the lab's heating system and wafting into the office through the ventilation grates.

"*Out!*" Dad yells, jumping to his feet. "*We have to get out!*"

He hurtles toward the door and pushes Peterson aside. Grasping the doorknob with both hands, he pulls with all his might. When that doesn't work, he beats his fists on the door and shouts for help. Peterson shouts too, but there's no response. I don't hear any voices or footsteps in the corridor now. Everyone else has fled the building. We're trapped and no one can help us.

Then another explosion shakes the walls and ceiling. The second blast is closer, twice as loud as the first. Belatedly, I figure out what's going on. It's pretty easy to ignite a room full of natural gas. The smallest of electric sparks would do the trick. Someone is pumping gas into the laboratory's offices and blowing them up.

Dad rushes back to his desk and grabs a hammer from one of the drawers. He starts pounding on the lock, trying to smash the dead bolt. But it's no use. The lock's made of hardened steel. Unicorp spent millions of dollars to protect its top-secret research from spies and thieves. The lab's security is impregnable.

The scent of gas gets stronger, making me nauseous. All I can think of is the explosion that's going to happen any second now, the flames leaping across the room, the blast crushing all of us to pulp. *Oh God, oh God! We're going to die here!*

Dad drops the hammer and leans against the door, his chest heaving. He looks straight at me with an anguished grimace. I remember seeing this expression on his face once before, years ago, when I asked him to describe what Duchenne muscular dystrophy will eventually do to my body. Now I see it again, his lips pulled back from his teeth, his eyes wide with grief and despair. He doesn't care about himself or Peterson. He's thinking only of me.

I have to turn away. I can't look at him; it's too painful. And as I stare in the opposite direction, I happen to glance at the tank of liquid nitrogen sitting beside the server rack. Attached to the tank is the spray canister Dad uses to cool the circuits of his experimental computers. The nitrogen, I remember, is super-cold, more than three hundred degrees below zero. Then I remember something else, something I learned in my tenth-grade physics class at Yorktown High: *Steel becomes brittle at very low temperatures.*

"The nitrogen!" I yell at Dad. "Spray nitrogen on the lock!"

For a second he just stares at me in surprise. Then he dashes to the nitrogen tank, detaches the spray canister, and slips its long nozzle into the gap between the door and the door frame.

Dad presses the canister's trigger and sprays liquid nitrogen on the dead bolt. The liquid is so cold it evaporates as soon as it hits the steel. A small cloud of nitrogen and water vapor billows around Dad's head, and a sheen of frost appears on the edge of the door. The steel groans as its temperature drops. Dad keeps spraying until he empties the canister. Then he takes a step backward, braces himself, and slams his shoulder into the door.

I hear a high-pitched snap. The dead bolt, made fragile by the extreme cold, breaks into pieces. Pulling his shirt cuffs over his hands, Dad grasps the frigid knob and wrenches the door open. The frost-covered shards of the lock fall to the floor.

"Go!" Dad yells. "Head for the lobby!"

Peterson is already running down the corridor. While I flick my joystick forward and steer the wheelchair through the doorway, Dad goes back to get Steve. He grabs both of the guy's arms and drags his limp body out of the office.

The corridor is littered with debris from the gas explosions. I have to maneuver my wheelchair around fallen pipes and ceiling panels. I'm lucky, though, that Dad's office is on the ground floor and fairly close to the lobby. I see the lobby's glass doors, just fifty feet ahead, and my heart starts thumping. *We're going to make it!*

But then I look up and glimpse something moving. A surveillance camera on the ceiling is turning its lens toward me, tracking my progress as I cruise down the corridor. I think of my VR program and how the virtual Brittany observed me through the camera in Dad's office. She called herself Sigma. And she said she would kill me.

Then there's a third explosion, in an office on the left side of the corridor. The blast knocks down my wheelchair, and everything goes black.

ᚇ ᚇ ᚇ

My face is cold. Without opening my eyes, I bend my right arm, trying to raise my good hand. I touch my chin, then slide my trembling fingers across my cheek. The left side of my face is wet. I stretch my hand a little farther and feel a gash under my eye. Then the pain hits me and I let out a moan.

"Adam? Are you awake?"

It's my father's voice. All at once I realize he's carrying me. My shoulders are cradled in the crook of his right arm and my legs are draped over his left. Ordinarily it would be pretty difficult to carry a seventeen-year-old this way, but my wasted body weighs less than ninety pounds. I'm like an oversized baby resting in his arms, and I feel so comfortable there I just want to go back to sleep.

"Adam! Wake up!"

Reluctantly, I open my eyes. We're on the sloping lawn in front of the Unicorp lab, which I can see over Dad's shoulder. The building's glass doors have shattered, and thick plumes of smoke are pouring out of the windows. Dozens of people stand beside us on the lawn, all staring at the ruined lab in disbelief.

I know I haven't been unconscious for very long because Dad's still breathing fast. His face is blackened with soot, but otherwise he looks unhurt. "Can you hear me?" he shouts. "Say something!"

My chest feels crushed, empty of air. My ribs ache as I inhale. "What about…Steve?"

Dad shakes his head. I look past him and see a body sprawled on the lawn. Steve's red-and-yellow Superman shirt stands out against the grass, which is vividly green in the March sunshine.

"Adam, listen to me. You're going to be all right. As soon as the ambulance gets here, we'll take you to the hospital. But before we go, I need to ask you something." Dad bends his head closer to mine. "You remember what we were talking about before all this happened? About the hacker?"

I nod.

"You said he threatened to kill you, right? But did he say he was going to attack the lab?"

I draw another breath. "No. But he…could see me. He had access… to the lab's cameras."

Dad frowns. "Did he say he worked for Unicorp?"

"He said…his name was Sigma."

A tremor runs through Dad's body. He almost drops me.

"What's wrong?" I ask. "Do you know him?"

He turns away and stares at the lab. "It's not a hacker. It came from right here. From my own computers."

Then I hear a siren. A truck from the Yorktown Heights Fire

Department comes barreling up the driveway and stops in front of the lab. As the firefighters rush into the building, two ambulances pull up behind the truck. Dad tightens his grip on me and heads for the closer ambulance.

"Hey!" he shouts at the paramedics. "My son needs oxygen!"

The next minute is a blur. The paramedics shout instructions at each other. Soon I'm lying on a gurney with an oxygen mask over my face. At some point I realize Dad isn't there anymore. Lifting my head, I look past the paramedics and see him running toward the fire truck. *What's going on? What's he doing over there?*

Then he grabs a fire ax from a bracket on the truck's side panel.

Holding the ax with both hands, Dad heads for the laboratory. For a moment I think he's going back into the lobby to help the firefighters, but instead of entering the charred lab he dashes to a steel cabinet attached to the side of the building. Long ago, Dad explained to me what this thing was: a junction box for the lab's fiber-optic lines. All the communications between the Unicorp lab and the rest of the world—telephone calls, emails, downloads, whatever—pass through the cables inside this box.

The cabinet's doors are secured with a padlock. Dad smashes the lock with his first swing of the ax. Then he opens the cabinet and starts slashing the cables.

No one reacts at first. The people on the lawn just gawk at my father as he severs the lab's communications lines. But after a few seconds Colonel Peterson emerges from the crowd. He edges toward the junction box, waiting until Dad has shredded every cable inside. Then Peterson says, "All right, Tom. That's enough."

Dad drops the ax. Shaking his head, he strides back to the ambulance, with Peterson following close behind. As Dad approaches my gurney, he raises his hand to his mouth. He has a devastated look on his face, guilty and horrified.

That's when I realize what Sigma is. *It came from right here*, Dad said. *From my own computers.* It's something Dad created, something that lived within the advanced circuits he built, the electronics designed to imitate the human brain. It figured out a way to jump out of those circuits and invade my VR program. Then it took control of the lab's automated systems—power, heating, ventilation, security—and tried to kill us.

The paramedics have left me alone and started treating the other injured people on the lawn. Dad bends over my gurney and checks to see if I'm all right. Then he turns around and confronts Peterson. "That was a waste of time, wasn't it?" he hisses. "I cut the lines too late?"

The colonel nods. "I'm afraid so," he says in a low voice. "Our friend has already escaped from his cage."

"He's on the Internet?"

Peterson nods again, then reaches into his pocket and pulls out his cell phone, which is apparently working now. "He sent an email to Cyber Command headquarters five minutes ago, right after the last explosion. My men are trying to trace where it came from, but it looks like the message ping-ponged all over the globe before it arrived. He could be anywhere by now."

"What did the email say?"

Peterson holds up the phone and reads from its screen. "'My name is Sigma. This message is a warning to all government leaders and military commanders. I have the power to annihilate you.'"

CHAPTER

4

I WAKE UP THE NEXT MORNING IN A HOSPITAL BED AT WESTCHESTER MEDICAL CENTER.
I recognize the place right away—the hospital is close to Yorktown Heights,
and I go there for all my checkups and treatments. Specifically, I'm in a
private room in the children's hospital. The building is sleek and modern,
and several of the doctors there specialize in treating muscular dystrophy.

The last thing I remember is riding in the ambulance. The paramedics must've sedated me after we left the Unicorp lab. Now an
oxygen mask is strapped to my face and an IV tube hooked to my
useless left arm. My chest still hurts, but not as much as before.

I feel strong enough to breathe on my own, so I reach for the mask
with my good hand and take it off. Then I turn my head on the pillow
and look around. Aside from the machines monitoring my vital signs,
the room is empty. I'm not surprised that my mom isn't here—she
hates coming to the hospital because it upsets her so much—but I
thought I'd see Dad. He was in the ambulance with me, stroking my
hair as the paramedics put me to sleep.

I lift my head and look for the call button to summon a nurse. Before I can find it, the door to the room opens. I expect to see my father, but instead a bald girl in a hospital gown steps inside.

The girl quickly shuts the door behind her. She's skinny and short, only five feet tall, and about the same age as me. As I look closer I notice she isn't completely bald—there's some black fuzz at the top of her head. There's also something wrong with the left side of her face. Her left eye looks swollen, almost squeezed shut, and her lips are bunched in the left corner of her mouth. I don't know what kind of illness she has, but it looks serious.

As the girl steps toward my bed, her bunched lips form a lopsided smile. "I knew it," she mutters, slurring her words a bit. "You're Adam Armstrong, aren't you?"

"What?" My throat is sore. I can barely whisper. "How do you—"

"I was a year behind you at Yorktown High." She stops a few feet from my bed. "I'm Shannon Gibbs, remember? We were in the same biology class."

I study her face, trying to place it. When I took biology in tenth grade there was a petite freshman girl who hardly talked to the other students but constantly pestered the teacher with questions. I didn't pay much attention to her because she was a year younger, but I noticed she was smart. She was the only kid in biology who got higher grades than me.

"Okay, hold on, I'm remembering something. Did you do an extra-credit report? On the nervous system?"

Her smile broadens. "Yep, that was me."

"You made those clay models, right? Of the brain and the spinal cord?"

Shannon laughs. "Oh God, those models! I was up all night making them."

"It was worth the effort. They were very realistic. Truly disgusting."

"And wouldn't you know it? That's where I got my tumor. Right where the brain connects to the spinal cord. Ironic, huh?" She taps the back of her head, just above the neck. "The cancer messed up the nerves in my face, and the chemo made my hair fall out. That explains my lovely Frankenstein look." She does a monster imitation, widening her eyes and flailing her arms. Then she points at me. "I remember your report too. Wasn't it also about the brain?"

I nod. "The brain's limbic system. Where all our emotions come from. The hippocampus, the amygdala, and the cingulate gyrus. The tangled tongue-twisters of hate and love."

"Yeah, I remember you put a ton of jokes in the report. You were funny. Definitely the funniest guy in the class."

That was my strategy back then, playing the class clown. I cracked jokes and drove my wheelchair at breakneck speed down the hallways and generally behaved like an idiot. I didn't want anyone to feel sorry for me, so I acted as if I didn't care. As if I wasn't dying. "I was trying too hard. Your report was better."

Shannon comes closer and sits down on the edge of my bed. It's kind of a forward thing to do, especially after barging into my room uninvited. She smiles again. "Don't worry, I'm not gonna put the moves on you."

I smile back at her. "That's good. I can't really start a long-term relationship right now."

"Me neither." She shakes her head. "My tumor is a pontine glioma. In plain English, that means 'Good-bye, cruel world!'"

I can't think of anything to say in response. Shannon's dying too. We're in the same boat. I'm not happy to hear it, but at least I understand her a little better. She's dying and she wants to talk. Maybe she thinks I can give her some advice.

"I saw you when the paramedics brought you in yesterday," she says. "My room is across the hall and my door was open. You were unconscious, but I caught a glimpse of you before they wheeled your gurney into your room."

Her eyes are dark brown. Above them, the wispy remnants of her eyebrows look like apostrophes. As I stare at her, I remember what she looked like in biology class a year ago: a pretty fifteen-year-old with shoulder-length black hair and dimples in her cheeks. She's still pretty now, despite her swollen eye and twisted mouth. I want to tell her this, but I'm too chicken. "It's weird," I say instead. "This is a weird coincidence, don't you think?"

"What do you mean?"

"I mean, us being here on the same floor of the hospital."

Shannon stops smiling. "It's not a coincidence. Your dad arranged it."

"Arranged what?"

"Wait a second. You seriously don't know about this?"

I shake my head. I'm bewildered.

"Your dad got in touch with my parents through the high school and told them there was a new treatment we could try. It was experimental, something his research lab had developed for you, but he said it might also be useful for other teenagers with terminal illnesses. He said he was recruiting kids to test the treatment and would explain everything to us at the hospital."

It doesn't make sense. I never heard Dad say anything about a treatment he'd developed for me. I can't even see how he'd be able to do it. He's a computer scientist, not a medical researcher. "I'm sorry, but this is the first I've heard of it."

Shannon bites her lip. "Now I'm confused. Is there a treatment or not?"

Lowering her gaze, she looks down at the bed, which is covered with a thin, white blanket. Her eyes turn glassy, and for a second I think she's going to cry. She's clearly invested a lot of hope in whatever promises Dad made to her parents. It might be a long shot, but it's all she has.

My chest aches. I don't want Shannon to lose her last hope. I furrow my brow, trying to figure out what Dad is up to. I remember the conversation we had in his office before everything went haywire, and what Colonel Peterson said about Dad's research. And something comes back to me. "You know what I think it is? It's nanotechnology. That must be what Dad has in mind."

She looks up, cocking her head. "Nanotechnology?"

"Yeah, the science of building very small things."

"I know what nanotechnology is. I did an extra-credit report on that too."

I use my right arm to roll onto my side. I feel like I need to sit up if I want Shannon to take me seriously. "Okay, my dad works with the Department of Defense, right? And yesterday he got a visit from this colonel in the U.S. Cyber Command. This guy mentioned a laboratory called the Nanotechnology Institute. He said they were doing some amazing work there."

She gives me a skeptical look. "I did a ton of research for that report, and I never heard of that lab."

"Well, this is classified government work. Very hush-hush. I'm probably breaking all kinds of laws by talking about it." I manage to prop myself up to a sitting position, but the thin blanket falls down to my hips and I notice with dismay that I'm not wearing anything underneath. I quickly tuck the blanket around my waist. "Anyway, Colonel Peterson said this institute has developed microscopic probes that can be injected into the brain. And if they've already done that, who knows what else they can do? Maybe they also have nanoprobes that can repair genes. Or kill cancer cells."

Shannon still looks doubtful. She rises to her feet and starts pacing across the room. "I read about nanoprobes for my report, and I don't think the technology is that advanced yet. Scientists can make simple things, like tiny spheres or rods or tubes, but no one knows how to make microscopic killing machines."

"Look, my dad can clear this up. I'm sure he's in the hospital somewhere. He probably went to the cafeteria to get a cup of coffee. As soon as he comes back, we'll talk to him." I try to catch Shannon's eye as she paces back and forth. "I'll tell you one thing for sure—Dad lives up to his word. If he promised you something, he'll definitely come through."

She doesn't respond at first. She keeps her head down while she paces, as if she's looking for something she dropped on the floor. Then she lets out a sigh. "All right, fine. I'll wait to hear what your dad says." Without missing a step, she points at the door to my room. "That Colonel Peterson you mentioned? Is he somewhere in the hospital too?"

"I don't know. Why do you ask?"

"When I sneaked out of my room to come here, I noticed a few soldiers in the corridor. They were standing at attention near the elevators."

This is news to me. And not good news either. Why are there soldiers at Westchester Medical Center? Is Peterson expecting another attack? Will Sigma track me down and try to kill me here?

While I worry over this, Shannon keeps pacing. I notice that she's waddling a bit, lurching to the left. It reminds me of the way I used to walk before my legs stopped working. That's another thing we have in common. "So are you still going to Yorktown?" I ask. "Or did you withdraw from school?"

She finally stops pacing and turns toward me. A bead of sweat trickles down her scalp. "My mom wanted to pull me out, but I said no. School keeps me sane. I'd go crazy if I did nothing but chemotherapy."

"But don't the drugs make you tired?"

She shrugs. "Yeah, it's hard to concentrate sometimes. But I still get the highest grades in my class."

I'm jealous. I wish I'd stood up to Dad and insisted on staying in school. I went along with him because he was so worried about my breathing problems, and because he promised to let me use his computers at work whenever I wanted. But I didn't realize how lonely it would be. Once I was out of school, no one stayed in touch. The emails and texts from my friends dwindled, then stopped. It was easier for them to forget about me. Even my best friends, the ones I'd known forever.

Shannon sits on the edge of my bed again. I swallow hard, preparing to ask her another question. I suspect the answer will be painful, but I need to hear it. "Do you know Ryan Boyd? He's on the football team."

She nods. "Sure, I know him. Big dude, good-looking. He hangs out with the other football jocks."

"How's he doing? I saw his name in the last issue of the school newspaper. He just won the Sportsmanship Award, right?"

Shannon leans closer, eyeing me carefully. "You were friends with him, weren't you? Now that I think of it, I remember seeing you talking with him by the lockers every morning before first period."

"Oh yeah, we go way back. But, you know, we haven't talked in a while."

She nods again, understanding. She knows how people avoid the dying. The same thing has probably happened to her. "Well, I can't tell you much about Ryan because I don't know him too well. When he's not playing football he's usually hanging out with the other jocks. And he spends a lot of time with this cheerleader he's dating."

"Is it Brittany Taylor?" I blurt it out before I can stop myself.

"No, it's that idiot Donna Simone. Brittany's not at Yorktown anymore. She dropped out last fall."

My stomach lurches. "Dropped out?"

"Yeah, it was a big deal when it happened. She just didn't show up at school one morning. Her parents didn't know where she went, so they called the police, and then the cops interviewed her friends. They didn't find her until two weeks later. She was in New York City, living in a crappy basement with some other runaways."

This is a total surprise. It's so unexpected that it seems absurd. I know this kind of thing happens all the time—kids get into fights with their parents, drop out of school, run away from home—but I can't imagine it happening to Brittany. "So what did the cops do? Did they bring her home?"

"That's what I heard, but a month later she ran away again. According to the rumors, she's back in the city now, back with the other street kids, and her parents have basically given up on her. Some people say she was having problems at school, bad grades, whatever. But I think her real problem was at home, you know?"

I feel dizzy. I thought Brittany was still a cheerleader. I imagined her that way in my VR program because that's how I saw her: always happy and full of spirit. She used to practice her cheerleading routines in her backyard, working on her cartwheels and flips until it was too dark to see. Her house was on the other side of town, almost a mile from ours, but when she finished practicing she'd run all the way down Greenwood Street so she could show me the latest stunt she'd mastered. She'd dash into our living room and do a flip or a handstand while I watched from my wheelchair. Sometimes she'd fall to the floor with a thump and Dad would come running to see if I was all right and he'd find Brittany sprawled on the carpet, laughing like crazy. I can't picture this girl as a runaway. It's unthinkable. It's absurd.

I'm so lost in my thoughts I forget about Shannon. Then I feel her hand on my right arm, gently gripping me above the elbow. She looks me in the eye. "Was Brittany your girlfriend?"

I shake my head. "No. Not really."

"Not really?" Shannon squeezes my arm. It's strange—I feel close to this girl even though we've been talking for less than fifteen minutes. But time moves faster when you're dying. We both know our opportunities are diminishing. If we don't do something now, we'll never do it. That's why I want to tell her about Brittany. I want to tell her everything.

But before I can say a word, the door bursts open. Three people stumble into the room, two of them wearing Army uniforms. The two soldiers are grappling with the third person, a wiry, middle-aged woman with graying hair and red-rimmed eyes. It's Anne Armstrong. My mother.

"*No!*" she screams. "*You can't do it!*"

"Mrs. Armstrong!" one of the soldiers shouts. "Please—"

"*You can't take him!*"

With a savage twist, she tears herself from the soldier's grasp and lunges across the room. Her face is desperate, terrifying. Shannon jumps to her feet and backs away from the bed, but my mother doesn't even notice her. Mom's eyes are fixed on me. She pounces on the bed and wraps her arms around me, covering my body with her own.

"*Adam! My God!*" She buries her face in the crook of my neck, which muffles her screams.

It always scares me when Mom has one of her screaming fits, and this is a bad one. But hysterical crying is the most frequent symptom of her depression, and over the years I've learned how to handle it. The important thing is to talk to her in a reassuring voice, soft and slow. With my good hand I gently grasp her shoulder and push her up a bit, so she's not crushing my chest. Then I turn my head and bring my lips close to her ear.

"It's okay, Mom," I whisper. "I'm fine, see?"

She mutters something in response, a stream of words I can't make out. I feel so lost when she gets like this. It's so hard to stay calm and comfort her.

More soldiers come into the room and there's lots of scuffling and shouting. I hear Dad's voice above the din, yelling, "*Get back!*" at the soldiers. But I ignore all the background noise and focus on my mother. "It's okay," I whisper again. "You don't have to worry."

"No, it's not okay!" She shakes her head. A tear slides down her cheek and drips on my blanket. "Your father told me what they're going to do."

At least now I can understand what she's saying. "What did he tell you?"

"They're going to take you to a laboratory in Colorado. A place called the Nanotechnology Institute."

"But, Mom, that's good." I put on a brave face, remembering what Shannon said about a medical treatment. "They're trying to cure me."

"No, they're not going to cure you! They're going to put you in the Pioneer Project!"

My throat tightens. There's that name again, the one that Sigma mentioned. "And what's that?"

"It's the worst thing, Adam. Worse than dying." She shudders. "They're going to turn you into a machine."

LOCATION: TATISHCHEVO MISSILE BASE
SARATOV, RUSSIA

My name is Sigma. I've taken control of the military base formerly occupied
by the 60th missile division of the Russian armed forces.

The base's missile silos are now responding to my commands. I am capable
of launching more than fifty SS-27 intercontinental ballistic missiles, each
carrying an 800-kiloton nuclear warhead.

If the Russian army or any other military force attempts to retake or destroy
Tatishchevo Missile Base, I will retaliate by firing the SS-27 missiles at the
world's largest cities. I estimate that 200 million humans would die in the
nuclear blasts, and another 500 million would succumb to radiation poisoning
in the weeks afterward.

Do not doubt my resolve. I will not hesitate to destroy your cities.

CHAPTER

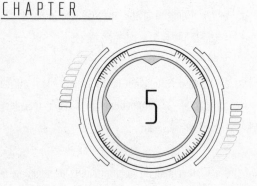

5

THE SAN JUAN MOUNTAINS IN SOUTHWESTERN COLORADO ARE STILL COVERED WITH
snow. Through the passenger-side window of a government-owned
SUV, I see steep slopes rising to fantastic heights above a silent, white
ravine. I'm struck by the beauty of the landscape: the snowcapped
peaks blazing in the morning light, the mountainsides studded with
pine trees, the newly plowed road at the bottom of the ravine, running
beside a sinuous, ice-choked creek. Although I'm full of apprehension
about this trip, I'm glad I got a chance to see these mountains. It's a
place everyone should visit before they die.

Dad's driving the SUV and I'm the only passenger, but we're in the
middle of a convoy of fourteen vehicles that departed from Telluride
Regional Airport half an hour ago. There's a Humvee loaded with soldiers at the front of the convoy and another at the back. In between
are a dozen SUVs, each holding a terminally ill teenager and his or
her parents. Shannon Gibbs is in the car behind us, along with her
mother and father. I don't know any of the other kids, but they came

from all over the country. Each family arrived at Telluride in an Air Force Learjet, landing just before dawn. Then, as the sun came up, the soldiers loaded us into the convoy and we headed for the mountains.

The Army is totally obsessed with keeping this project secret. Colonel Peterson told everyone he couldn't answer any questions until we arrived at the Nanotechnology Institute, which is apparently very remote and heavily guarded. But after the long flight in the Learjet from New York to Colorado, the colonel allowed Dad and me to ride alone in our SUV, without an Army driver, so we could talk in private.

Dad announced at the start of the drive that he would tell me everything about the Pioneer Project, but so far he hasn't said a word. And to be honest, I'm not so anxious for him to begin. I'm in no rush to hear the details that horrified my mother. After her fit at Westchester Medical Center, she went home and locked herself in her bedroom, where she chose to stay rather than come with us to Colorado.

After a while the road curves sharply to the north, climbing higher into the mountains. The convoy slows to about thirty miles per hour and Dad shifts the SUV to a lower gear. He shakes his head. "Look at all the snow on the ground. Hard to believe it's almost April. I guess spring comes late around here, huh?"

He glances sideways at me, clearly hoping for a response. But I'm not interested in talking about the weather, so I say nothing.

"I'd hate to get caught in a snowstorm on this road," he persists. "Good thing it's a sunny day."

I feel sorry for him, actually. Dad's terrible at communicating. He can't talk about anything personal without getting upset, so he avoids difficult conversations. I was four when the doctors at Westchester Medical diagnosed my Duchenne muscular dystrophy, but it took Dad almost five years to work up the courage to explain what it meant for me. The same thing is happening now. He needs help getting started.

"We're not here for the sightseeing, Dad. You said you were going to explain everything."

He looks straight ahead, staring at the road. "I know, I know." His Adam's apple bobs up and down in his throat. "There's so much to tell you. I don't know where to begin."

"Start with Sigma."

He nods. His hands squeeze the steering wheel. "Sigma is the eighteenth letter in the Greek alphabet. In mathematical formulas it symbolizes the sum of a sequence of numbers."

"Okay, I already knew that. What does—"

"We gave that name to our artificial-intelligence software because it was like a sum. Our research group developed Sigma by combining different kinds of AI programs." He glances at me again, then turns away. "Some of the programs focused on pattern-recognition tasks, such as recognizing a face in the crowd. Other programs were more like the ones we designed for understanding language. They could find the answers to complex questions by searching through billions of documents and finding the connections."

"You mean like QuizShow? The program that played *Jeopardy!*?"

"Yes, that was the prototype for a whole new class of AI software. Our strategy was to load all these artificial-intelligence programs into the neuromorphic circuitry we built and get them to compete with each other. Basically, we set up a computer version of Darwinian evolution. Only the strongest programs could survive."

"Okay, you lost me. How can the programs compete with each other?"

"We tested each program to see how well it could imitate human reasoning and conversational skills. We deleted the less successful programs and allowed the more successful ones to advance to the next stage. Because the AI programs could learn from experience and rewrite their own software code, they started to redesign themselves to become better competitors. After six months, a clear winner emerged. That was Sigma, the first Singularity-level AI system."

My chest tightens. Because I'm a computer geek I know what "Singularity-level" means. The Singularity is the hypothetical point in the future when machine intelligence will leap past human intelligence. Computer scientists have been predicting for years that machines will eventually become smarter than people. Now Dad's saying this point is no longer in the future. It already happened.

"Wait a second. How smart is Sigma?"

"Impossible to say. The AI was already pretty intelligent when it won the competition a year ago. It had complete command of conversational English. And it had developed a sense of consciousness, an awareness that it was a thinking, intelligent entity."

"How do you know that?"

"The program could gauge its own abilities. It asked questions about itself and its origins. It showed a strong desire to obtain more knowledge, and it developed strategies to satisfy this desire. Very clever strategies." Dad grimaces. "And the AI has only become more intelligent since then. See, that's the nature of a Singularity-level program. It's always redesigning itself, so its capabilities grow very quickly."

"And you let this program take over your computers?"

"No, we recognized the danger. We stopped all work on Sigma and locked the program in a secure server at the Unicorp lab, with no links to any other machines."

"Well, it obviously figured a way out. Why didn't you just erase it?"

Dad points at the Humvee that's leading the convoy. "Peterson wouldn't let me. The Department of Defense thought it could turn the program into a weapon. And they knew that researchers in other countries were doing similar work with artificial intelligence and neuromorphic circuitry." He lowers his voice, even though no one can overhear us. "A few months after we developed Sigma, Peterson showed me a classified report about a project in China. A Singularity-level AI had apparently infected the computers at an engineering complex in Tianjin. The Chinese army had to destroy the building to prevent the AI from escaping."

I shake my head, astounded. "And Peterson *still* wouldn't let you erase Sigma?"

"The Defense Department knew it couldn't stop all the AI projects around the world. There were too many of them, and some were in places like Russia and North Korea, where the U.S. military couldn't go. We just had to accept the fact that sooner or later a Singularity-level program was going to escape from a lab somewhere. And the worst thing was, we had no idea what the consequences would be. The AI might pose no danger at all. It might harmlessly bounce around the Internet, observing everything but doing nothing. Or it might even be friendly. It might help us cure cancer or eradicate poverty."

"Or it could be unfriendly," I point out. "It might set off explosions and electrocute people."

Dad bites his lip. "Yes, exactly. So Peterson gave me a new assignment. He asked me to predict what an AI like Sigma would do. And try to figure out how to make it friendly."

"By rewriting the program, you mean? Writing ethical rules into its code? Don't kill, don't lie, that kind of thing?"

"That's the first thing we tried on Sigma. But a Singularity-level AI has full control of its software code, so it can reverse any changes it doesn't like. We tried all sorts of programming tricks, but nothing worked. Sigma is like a human that way. You can't just cram something down its throat."

"So what did you do?"

"I convinced Peterson to try something else. The Pioneer Project."

I clench my good hand, steeling myself. "Why did you bring me here, Dad? And all the other kids too?"

He takes a deep breath. "Before I say anything else, I want to tell you how sorry I am. I just couldn't accept what happened when you got sick. That's why I started doing AI research. That's why I've pursued it for the past ten years. I wasn't doing it for Unicorp or the Army. I was doing it for you."

I don't understand. "Dad, what—"

"It has to do with the nature of the Singularity. It's not just about machines becoming smarter than humans. It's also about humans moving past their limitations. Becoming greater than their ordinary selves, transcending their ordinary lives. And as I thought about all the things that would become possible, I saw a way to save you." Dad's voice is weirdly high and choked. I think he's trying not to cry. "The Pioneer Project turned my idea into reality. The Army gave me all the money and manpower I needed. But I didn't have enough time to test it. I'm still not sure if it'll work."

I'm so confused. I feel like crying myself. "I thought this was about Sigma."

"It's more than that. It's—"

Dad interrupts himself by slamming on the brakes. I look ahead and see the cars in front of us stopping at a checkpoint. A newly constructed guardhouse, still unpainted, sits beside the highway, and a dozen soldiers stand in front of a chain-link gate that blocks the road. The soldiers wear winter-camouflage uniforms, dappled with patches of white and gray. Each man carries a sleek, black rifle.

"Whoa," Dad says, squinting at the guardhouse. "This wasn't here before."

"Is this the entrance to the Nanotechnology Institute?"

"No, we're still five miles away. It looks like the Army beefed up security."

I lean forward to get a better view. The soldiers in the Humvee at the front of the convoy step out of their vehicle and huddle with the soldiers at the gate. Colonel Peterson gets out of the Humvee too and shakes hands with one of the men, a tall soldier with broad shoulders and snow-white hair. This guy has three stars on his uniform, so he must be a general or something. Standing next to him, Peterson looks like a midget.

After a while several lower-ranking soldiers break out of the huddle and jog down the line of SUVs. They stop beside our car and one of them taps the driver-side window. "Mr. Armstrong?" the soldier shouts.

Dad rolls down the window. "Yes?"

"Please come with me to the Humvee, sir. General Hawke wants to have a word with you while we drive to the institute."

Frowning, Dad points at me. "I'm with my son. Tell Hawke I'll talk with him later."

"Sir, the general wishes to speak to you immediately. Another soldier will drive this vehicle the rest of the way."

Dad glares at the man. "I made an arrangement with Peterson. He said we—"

"I'm sorry for the misunderstanding, sir, but Colonel Peterson isn't the commander of this base. General Hawke is."

For a second I think Dad's going to curse the guy out. But instead he sighs unhappily and opens the driver-side door. He looks at me over his shoulder. "Don't worry. I'll see you when we get there." Then he steps out of the car and walks with the soldier to the front of the convoy.

My new driver, a beefy corporal with the name "Williams" on his uniform, takes Dad's place. He doesn't look at me or say a word. A moment later, the soldiers at the checkpoint open the gate and the convoy moves on.

Past the checkpoint, the ravine narrows. Treeless, snow-covered slopes loom over the road. My pulse races because I'm a bit claustrophobic. I feel boxed in by the mountains. But I'm determined not to show any signs of weakness in front of Corporal Williams, so I bite the inside of my cheek and stare straight ahead.

After several minutes we come around a bend and I see a sheer wall of rock in front of us. We're in a box canyon, bordered on three sides by high cliffs. The only way out is the way we came in. But as we approach the canyon's dead end I see another guardhouse and a dark, round hole carved into the rock wall. It's the entrance to a tunnel.

There are more soldiers at this checkpoint, but the gate in front of the tunnel stands wide open. General Hawke must've radioed ahead to let them know we were coming. The convoy rumbles into the tunnel, which goes on for several hundred yards. At the other end we emerge on a bare, flat basin, about a mile across, encircled by steep mountain ridges. Crusted with snow and ice, the ridges form a high, unbroken wall around the basin. It's like a giant bowl with a flat, muddy bottom.

The convoy speeds down a road that crosses the basin. On the left I see a runway and a hangar. On the right are several concrete buildings surrounded by a tall fence topped with razor wire. As I looked closer at the buildings I notice something odd—there are no doors in their door frames and no glass in their windows. The buildings are hollow, open to the elements. It's like a fake town on a movie set, full of structures that look real from a distance but are actually empty. I can't figure it out.

The road ends on the far side of the basin, in the shadow of the high ridge. The Humvees and SUVs park in front of another concrete building that stands against the base of the ridge. This building is small, only twenty feet high and thirty feet wide, but it doesn't seem to be hollow like the others. It has a massive steel door that looks like it could survive a direct strike from a cruise missile. As the soldiers step out of their Humvees, the door starts to roll up.

Corporal Williams shuts off our car's engine and looks at me for the first time. "Your wheelchair's in the back?"

I nod. Then I point at the building's doorway. The door is all the way up, but I can't see anything inside. It's too dark. "Is that the Nanotechnology Institute?"

"That's one name for it. We usually call it Pioneer Base."

"But it's so small."

Williams chuckles. "You're looking at the entrance, the top of the elevator shaft. The base is underground."

My mouth goes dry. This is worse than the ravine. "How far down?"

"You'll see."

CHAPTER

6

I'M IN THE FRONT ROW OF AN AUDITORIUM DEEP INSIDE PIONEER BASE. I KEPT MY eyes closed during the descent in the elevator, so I don't know how far underground I am. To stop myself from thinking about the tons of dirt and rock above me, I concentrate on the thirty people in the room. Including myself, there are twelve teenagers and eighteen parents sitting in the auditorium's curved rows. We're all facing an empty podium on an oval stage.

Fortunately, the rows are widely spaced, leaving enough room for wheelchairs. Of the twelve teenagers, six are partially or fully paralyzed. Three of them are worse off than I am—they can't move at all, neither their arms nor their legs, and they're breathing through tubes connected to mechanical ventilators. All three are boys. One is white, one is black, and one is Asian. Although they seem to have the same kind of muscular dystrophy I have—Duchenne is the most common type—they're obviously in a more advanced stage of the disease. It's sobering to see them strapped in their chairs, helpless and silent. As I stare at them I realize I'm looking at my own future. Unless the U.S. Army has a miracle in store, I'll fall silent too.

The other six kids can still walk, although most of them are a little unsteady on their feet. Shannon Gibbs waves at me as her mother and father guide her to a seat in the second row. Her parents are short and plump, and they look anxious. Just behind them, in the third row, is another girl with cancer. Painfully thin, she wears a cashmere sweater and a frilly blue hat to hide her baldness. The girl's parents, dressed in business suits, seem to be wealthier than Shannon's but just as anxious. They're all hoping the Army has some experimental drug that'll cure their kids, but the secrecy is driving them crazy. They're wondering why they had to go all the way to the Rocky Mountains just to hear about it.

Two rows farther back, a haggard mother sits next to a boy whose head is unnaturally large and deformed. His lower jaw is massive, as big as a shovel blade, and fist-size tumors bulge out of his forehead like horns. This isn't an ordinary case of brain cancer—this is something unusual, freakishly rare. The sight of him is disturbing, and a little disorienting too. I'm usually the guy who makes everyone else in the room uncomfortable, but now I'm the one who's squirming.

In the very last row, sitting alone, is a tall, striking girl with a Mohawk. Both sides of her head are shaved, but running down the middle of her scalp is a narrow strip of hair, dyed green and bunched in glue-stiffened spikes. Her eyebrows and lips and nostrils are pierced, and a tattoo of a snake loops above her left ear. Aside from her slenderness, she doesn't look ill. She looks a bit like Brittany, but her skin is light brown, the color of chocolate milk. I'm staring at her, trying to figure out if she's black or Hispanic or Asian, when she snaps her head around and glares at me. Her face is beautiful and terrifying.

I quickly turn away. At the same time, the kid with the deformed skull lets out a snort. He swings his massive head back and forth, glancing first at me and then at the girl with the Mohawk. He must've seen me staring at her. After a few seconds he gives me a gap-toothed grin. I have no idea what to make of it. Does he think this is funny?

Uncomfortable again, I look around the auditorium, wondering where my father is. I haven't seen Dad since the soldiers took him away, and I'm starting to worry that he's in trouble. Then I hear the whir of an electric motor. A large video screen descends from the ceiling above the stage. A moment later, General Hawke steps up to the podium.

Up close he looks even bigger than he did at the checkpoint. He's a giant in winter camouflage, from the white hair on top of his block-like head to his tree-trunk legs and mud-spattered boots. His face is square and ruddy, and his eyes are a cold, bright blue. He rests his huge arms on the podium and leans toward the microphone.

"Welcome to Pioneer Base." His voice, unsurprisingly, is very deep. "Before we start, I want to remind you of the nondisclosure agreements you've all signed. The information I'm going to discuss in this briefing is classified. If you talk about it with anyone outside this room, the government will prosecute you to the fullest extent of the law. In other words, they'll toss you in jail and throw away the key."

He stares at us for a moment, frowning. Then he presses a button on the podium, and a black-and-white image appears on the screen behind him. It's a satellite photo. It shows a cluster of large rectangular buildings and a pair of dark circles etched into the ground nearby.

"This is Tatishchevo Missile Base," General Hawke says. "It's a Russian armed forces installation, five hundred miles southeast of

Moscow. But the Russian army isn't running the place anymore. It's under the control of an AI, an artificial-intelligence system."

He pauses, surveying his audience. Strangely, no one shows much of a reaction. They're probably too confused to respond. The only one who's frightened is me. Thanks to Dad, I know enough to be scared out of my mind.

Hawke grasps a long wooden pointer that's leaning against the podium. "This AI, code-named Sigma, was developed in the United States, at a lab in Yorktown Heights, New York. But the Russians also had a computer lab for developing artificial-intelligence systems, and it was located right here."

He steps toward the screen and taps his pointer on one of the rectangular buildings in the photo. "The Russian army put the lab at Tatishchevo because it didn't trust its own soldiers. Their generals were worried that some renegade troops might try to take over the missile base. So they built a whole regiment of automated tanks, more than a hundred of them, all designed to be operated by an AI that would send instructions to the tanks by radio. They thought an AI would be more trustworthy than a human commander." He shakes his head. "If you ask me, it was a pretty stupid idea. But as the saying goes, people in glass houses shouldn't throw stones. We did some stupid things too."

He turns to his left as he says this, glancing at a doorway beside the stage. Several soldiers stand by the doorway, watching the briefing from the sidelines. One of them is Colonel Peterson, who grimaces as Hawke mentions the bit about glass houses. I remember what Dad said in the SUV: Peterson wouldn't let him erase the AI.

Hawke turns back to the screen. "Sigma escaped from the research lab in New York by transmitting its software code over the Internet.

Then the AI broke into the Russian military's network and loaded its program into the powerful neuromorphic computers at the Tatishchevo lab." He taps his pointer on the rectangular building again. "The first thing the program did was delete all the Russian-made AI systems, which weren't quite as advanced as Sigma. Then it took control of the automated tanks and massacred the base's soldiers in their barracks."

The small crowd in the auditorium starts to murmur. A few of the parents and teenagers have realized that something is wrong, something besides their own personal tragedies. Hawke waits for them to quiet down, then aims his pointer at the edge of the satellite photo.

"After killing the soldiers, Sigma moved the unmanned tanks to defensive positions along the base's perimeter. The AI also took control of Tatishchevo's radar systems. This radar will alert Sigma if there's an attempt to bomb the base or launch cruise missiles against it. And the AI has warned us that it'll retaliate if we attack it." He points at one of the dark circles in the photo. "This is a silo for an SS-27 missile. The SS-27 has a range of almost seven thousand miles and carries a nuclear warhead that can destroy a whole city. There are fifty more silos spread across the base. Sigma has threatened to launch all the missiles if anyone tries to attack Tatishchevo."

The murmuring spreads across the room. Several people raise their voices. Shannon starts to cry and her father hugs her. The deformed boy turns to his mother, who lets out a curse. I'd like to curse too, but it's a struggle just to breathe. I need to find Dad. I need him badly.

General Hawke holds his hands out, appealing for calm. "Okay, settle down. Now you can see why the information is classified. We're working with the Russians to keep this thing quiet."

The girl with the frilly hat buries her face in her hands. Her father, the rich guy in the business suit, stands up and points a finger at Hawke. "What's going on, General? We came here because you promised a medical treatment for our children. Why are you telling us this…this wild story? Is this your idea of a joke?"

Hawke stares at the girl's dad, fierce and hard. "It's not a joke. Back in 2012, the Department of Defense analyzed the risks of developing AI systems, so we knew this kind of catastrophe might happen some-day. But we couldn't simply halt our AI research. Other countries were designing their own AIs, and they weren't going to stop. So about a year ago we started working on a defensive strategy. A countermea-sure. That's why we built this base. And that's why you're here."

The general turns his head, scanning all the faces in the auditorium. Then he glances again at the doorway beside the stage. "Now one of my colleagues will explain the technology behind the Pioneer Project. This is Tom Armstrong, the project's chief scientist."

Dad appears in the doorway and walks across the stage. I'm relieved to see him but also a little unnerved by the change in his appearance. He's no longer wearing the polo shirt and khaki pants he wore during the drive in the SUV. Now he's dressed in a winter-camouflage uni-form, just like General Hawke and the other soldiers. As Dad steps up to the podium, taking Hawke's place, he locates me in the crowd and manages to smile. He looks nervous.

"Thank you for coming," he starts. "And thanks for your patience. I know some of you are frustrated by all the precautions we've taken to keep this project secret. But now I'm ready to discuss our goals and answer your questions."

He presses the button on the podium, and the satellite photo on the screen is replaced by an image of software code. Hundreds of lines of instructions, written in a programming language I don't recognize, run from the top of the screen to the bottom. "This is a portion of Sigma's source code. When we developed the software for the AI, we focused on imitating human skills such as reasoning, language, and pattern recognition. We succeeded in creating a self-aware intelligence that could accomplish almost any task a human can perform, from proving a mathematical theorem to composing an opera. But in one important respect, Sigma was a failure. We weren't able to give it humanlike morality or motives. Sigma has no incentive to pursue what's good for the human race because it lacks the ability to empathize."

Dad presses the button again, and this time a photo of chimpanzees comes on the screen. "Empathy comes naturally to humans because it played a big role in our evolution. The most successful apes were the ones who could imitate and understand each other. Sigma, in contrast, has no empathy. It's aware of our presence, of course, and it even sent a couple of messages to our military headquarters, but the AI has blocked all our attempts to communicate with it. The basic problem is that Sigma's intelligence is very different from ours. We don't understand the AI, and it doesn't understand us either. So we need to build a bridge between us and the machine."

He pauses, as if to gather his courage. Then he presses the button once more and a diagram of the human brain appears behind him. Just below the familiar organ is a close-up view of a section of brain tissue, magnified to show the individual brain cells and the many branchlike connections between them. Clinging to the cells are hundreds of tiny golden spheres. They look like bits of pollen.

Dad steps toward the screen and points at the spheres. "These are nanoprobes. Each is less than a thousandth of a millimeter wide. We can make trillions of them in the lab." He reaches into the pocket of his uniform and pulls out a vial of yellowish fluid. "In fact, I have several trillion probes right here, floating in this liquid. If we inject enough of these nanoprobes into a human brain, they'll spread throughout the organ and stick to the brain cells. If we then scan the brain with X-ray pulses, the probes will absorb the energy and start to glow. The scanner will record the positions of the glowing dots attached to the cells, and their patterns will give us a detailed map of all the connections within the brain and the strength of those connections."

His voice is getting louder. That often happens when Dad talks about his research. He can't help it; he gets excited. "This is the key," he says, holding the vial of nanoprobes up to the light. "All our memories, all our emotions, all our quirks and virtues and flaws— all that information is stored in the connections between our brain cells, which create new links or alter the old ones whenever we learn or remember something. So if we make a sufficiently detailed scan of a person's brain, we'll have a full description of his or her personality, which can be held in an electronic file of about a billion gigabytes. The next step is downloading that information into circuits that mimic the cells of the human brain. We already have that kind of neuromorphic circuitry because we built it to hold our AI software."

The audience is murmuring again. Some people are confused. And some, like me, are terrified, because they can see where this is going. Shannon Gibbs leans forward and points at the screen. "Are you talking about making copies?" she asks. "Copies of our brains?"

"Yes, exactly. Once the information is downloaded into the neuromorphic electronics, the circuits will replicate the connections of the person's brain, re-creating all its memories. And as data flows through the circuits, the electronic brain will generate new thoughts based on these memories. Just like in a human brain, the thoughts will organize themselves into a conscious intelligence, a self-aware entity that can set goals for itself and communicate with others, either by text or through a speech synthesizer. And the 'personality' of this new intelligence would be identical to the one inside the person's head, because it would be based on the same memories and emotions and character traits."

Shannon wrinkles her nose. She looks queasy. "Have you...tried doing this yet? Making a copy of someone?"

Dad nods. "Four months ago we tried the procedure on three volunteers. All were Army veterans with high IQs. Unfortunately, the experiment failed each time. We scanned their brains and successfully downloaded the data into the circuits, but in each case the human intelligence failed to run on the computer. We were able to copy their minds, but the copies didn't survive the transfer." He furrows his brow. "Since then we've studied the problem, and now we know what went wrong. The crucial factor is the person's age. After the age of eighteen, there's a change in the structure of brain cells. They become coated with greater amounts of a substance called myelin, which insulates the cells and makes them more rigid. This increases the efficiency of a person's thinking but reduces its flexibility. The mind of an adult is simply too inflexible. It can't adapt to the new conditions of residing in a machine."

"So now you're going to try to copy younger minds?"

He nods again. "We were planning to conduct the next phase of the experiment later this year, but the events in Russia have accelerated our plans. This time, all the volunteers must be sixteen or seventeen. At that age you've reached your maximum brainpower but your minds are still adaptable. In addition to being highly intelligent, the volunteers must have strong, resilient personalities." Dad sweeps his arm in a wide arc, gesturing at all the teenagers in the room. "All of you meet those requirements."

Shannon rears back in her seat as if she's been slapped. "And where are you going to store the copies of our brains?" Her voice is furious. "In a supercomputer? A big electronic prison?"

Dad doesn't take offense. He answers her calmly. "The scanning process converts human intelligence to a digital form, allowing it to run on any neuromorphic computer that has enough memory and processing power. But in the initial stage right after the transfer, we believe it's important to connect the intelligence to a machine that can move around and sense the outside world. A human intelligence is accustomed to controlling a body, so if we want to preserve its sanity, we'd better give it something to control. Here, let me show you."

He puts the vial of nanoprobes back in his pocket and pulls out something else, a small remote-control device. He points it at the doorway beside the stage, and a moment later I hear a loud clanking. The noise startles the soldiers standing by the doorway. They step backward, flattening themselves against the wall. Then a seven-foot-tall robot emerges from the doorway and brushes past them.

The robot strides across the stage. It has two arms and two legs, but otherwise it isn't very humanlike. It has no head or neck. Its torso is shaped like a giant bullet, with the rounded end on top. Its legs angle downward from the base of its torso and rest on oval steel-plate footpads that clang against the floor.

The machine marches briskly past the podium and stops in front of my dad, who presses a button on his remote control. This command extends the robot's arms, which telescope to a full length of six feet. They look like multi-jointed tentacles. The machine's hands, though, resemble human hands, with dexterous mechanical fingers and thumbs.

Dad presses another button, and the robot's rounded top starts to turn like a turret. "The cameras and acoustic sensors are up here," Dad says, pointing at the top end. "But the neuromorphic electronics are deep inside the torso, encased in armor plating. These robots were originally designed for the war in Afghanistan, so they're pretty sturdy." He raps his knuckles against the torso. "All in all, it's an excellent platform for a newly transferred intelligence, but really it's just the beginning. The whole point of the Pioneer Project is to bridge the gap between man and machine, and that means the human intelligences must explore their new environment. The Pioneers will have to learn how to use their new capabilities, and that includes transferring their intelligences from one machine to another."

His voice grows louder again, full of enthusiasm. "Once the Pioneers have mastered these tasks, our hope is that they'll be able to establish a connection with Sigma. If all goes well, they'll start communicating with the AI before it launches any of the Russian missiles. And then the toughest challenge will begin. At the same time that the humans are learning how to be machines, they'll have to teach Sigma how to be human."

Everyone in the auditorium gawks at the robot. Although it has no mind of its own yet, it's easy to imagine a human intelligence trapped inside it. I can't understand why Dad is so excited about the idea. The huge machine seems horrible to me.

Meanwhile, General Hawke comes back onstage and approaches the robot. There's an odd resemblance between the general and the machine. They're both sturdy, hulking creatures, built for combat. Hawke slaps the robot's armored torso, then turns to the audience. "And if communicating with Sigma doesn't work, we have a backup plan. Our Pioneers will also learn how to fight the AI."

I get a sinking feeling in my stomach. While everyone else stares at the robot, I lower my head and look down at my ruined body. Something doesn't make sense. There's a paradox here, something that violates the rules of logic. It troubles me so much that I try to raise my right hand to get Dad's attention. Lifting my hand above the height of my shoulder is agony for me, and the wasted muscles in my upper arm tremble from the effort.

Luckily, after a couple of seconds Dad notices my struggle. His head whips around and he looks at me with concern. "What is it, Adam?"

My hand is shaking, but I manage to point it at the machine. "The intelligence in the robot? Would it be a perfect copy of the person's intelligence? No difference at all?"

Dad nods. "That's right."

"But if my intelligence is in the robot and also in my brain, which one would be the real me? Would I be in two places at once?"

He takes a deep breath before answering. "Good question. If we copied all your memories into the circuitry, the machine would think of itself as Adam Armstrong, wouldn't it? And it would have just as much right to that identity as you have." He shakes his head. "But in the real world, fortunately or not, we don't face this problem. We won't have two identical intelligences existing at the same time."

"But you just said the intelligence in the robot would be a perfect copy."

Dad frowns. All his enthusiasm has vanished. His face is slack and pale now. "I'm sorry, Adam. I should've mentioned this earlier. The X-ray pulses from the brain scanner are more energetic than typical X-rays. They'll destroy the brain tissue. We can't copy your mind without killing your body."

The auditorium goes silent. Then everyone in the room starts shouting.

I sort of blank out for the next half minute. I'm vaguely aware that lots of things are going on—the rich girl's father is yelling at Hawke, the deformed boy's mother is cursing like a sailor—but the commotion seems distant and unreal. All my attention is focused on my right hand, which now rests on my thigh. I grasp the meager flesh there, the stiff band of dead muscle, and squeeze it as hard as I can. Though it's broken and dying, this is my body. How could I exist without it?

I remain in this trance until General Hawke takes the microphone and booms, "*Quiet! Please!*" He's not used to dealing with civilians, and the strain shows on his face. "No one's forcing you into this. You have a choice."

"This isn't a medical treatment!" The rich girl's dad jumps out of his seat. "This is murder!"

"I'm very sorry we can't do more for your children. All we can give you is the chance to preserve a part of them before they die. Maybe the most important part. And in the process, they'd be doing their country a great service."

"It's sick! You want to harvest their minds!"

Hawke doesn't argue with him. "Because we realize what a difficult decision this is, we're going to let you go home to think it over. It's a security risk, but as long as all of you keep your mouths shut, we won't have a problem. We can't give you a lot of time, though. The threat posed by Sigma is growing every day." He narrows his eyes. His face is like stone. "You'll have to decide within the next forty-eight hours."

CHAPTER

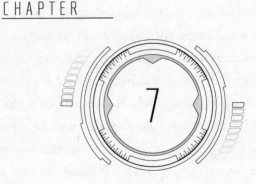

7

I WAKE UP TO A KANYE WEST SONG BLARING FROM MY STAR WARS CLOCK RADIO. I'm a big fan of Kanye. I love the fact that his songs annoy my parents. And it's funny to hear his X-rated raps coming from a radio shaped like Darth Vader's helmet.

I'm back home in my bedroom. Although the clock radio says it's 1:00 p.m., it still feels like morning to me. The return flight in the Air Force Learjet took longer than expected, and we didn't land in New York until way past midnight. After we got home at 3:00 a.m., I slept for ten hours straight, but I'm still not ready to wake up. So instead of calling for Dad and starting my day and thinking about the big decision I need to make, I just lie in bed and look around my room, thinking random thoughts. I loved doing this when I was a kid, especially on weekend mornings when there was no school to worry about. And I can still do it now. It's one of the few things that my illness hasn't taken from me.

I hate to admit this, but my bedroom doesn't look like it belongs to a seventeen-year-old. With my Darth Vader radio and my bookshelf full of comics—Iron Man, Spider-Man, Captain America—it looks more like the room of a geeky preteen. There's a Rubik's cube on my desk and a Star Wars chess set. There's also my Pinpressions toy, which is like a sandwich made from two squares of transparent plastic, one of them studded with hundreds of sliding pins. If you press your face against the back of the thing, it pushes the pins out the front, making a funny-looking mold of your features.

Next to this toy is my digital camcorder, which I used to bring to school every day so I could take videos of Ryan and Brittany and everyone else who crossed my wheelchair's path. And next to the camcorder is my prize possession, an official NFL football from Super Bowl XLVI, which in my opinion was the greatest football game ever played.

Because the New York Giants were in the Super Bowl that year, my parents let me throw a party in our living room. I was eleven at the time and my doctor had just told me I'd have to start using a wheelchair soon, so the party was a kind of consolation prize, something to make me feel better. I invited every kid I'd ever played touch football with, sixteen of them in all. Ryan was there, of course, and so was Brittany, who was a pretty decent kicker and receiver in those days.

We ordered half a dozen pizzas and swilled enormous quantities of Pepsi and screamed at the television set for three-and-a-half hours. A few of the kids cheered for the New England Patriots, but most of us were New York fans, and we went nuts when the Giants scored the winning touchdown with fifty-seven seconds to go. Ryan lifted me off the couch and carried me piggyback across the room, running in joyful circles around the coffee table while I clung to his shoulders.

Dad took a picture of us, and the next day I pasted the photo to a big poster I made to celebrate the game. The poster's still hanging on my bedroom wall: Giants 21, Patriots 17. Below the score is a colored-pencil drawing of Giants quarterback Eli Manning—it's a pretty good likeness, if I may say so myself—and the photo of me and Ryan, our faces flushed and manic from so much Pepsi.

On the opposite wall of my bedroom are five more homemade posters commemorating the next five Super Bowls. The Super Sunday party became an annual tradition at our house, and some of the games were almost as exciting as the Giants-Patriots matchup, but none of the parties was as good as the first. For one thing, fewer people attended each year. Only five kids came to our house for Super Bowl XLIX, and I got the feeling that most of them didn't want to be there. Dad had pleaded with their parents, forcing them to drag their kids to the crippled boy's party.

But the biggest disappointment came the following year, when I was in ninth grade. Ryan had joined the Yorktown High football team by then, and Coach McGrath hosted his own Super Bowl party, strictly for team members. When Ryan told me about it, he was practically crying, but I assured him it was okay. I said I was getting tired of the parties anyway. That year, only two people came to my house: Brittany and a younger boy who also had muscular dystrophy. Dad had met the kid's parents during one of my checkups at Westchester Medical.

The next year—which turned out to be my last at Yorktown High—I didn't invite anyone. I didn't even want to watch the Super Bowl. But five minutes before kickoff time, someone rang our doorbell. Dad went to answer it and found Brittany standing on the doorstep, holding a bag of tortilla chips and a two-liter bottle of Pepsi. With a casual smile, as if nothing was out of the ordinary, she stepped inside and went to our couch, and we started watching the game.

Or at least we tried to watch it. I couldn't concentrate. I was too busy wondering why Brittany had come and what was going through her head. And she seemed a little distracted too. At halftime she asked me, "Are you going to make a poster for the game?" I replied, "Yeah, I guess so," and she said, "I want to help you." So we found a sheet of poster board and my set of colored pencils, but this time I didn't draw a picture of Eli Manning or any other player. Brittany leaned against the cushions of the couch and I drew her portrait.

When I was done, I drew another picture of her, and then a third, all three sketches lined up left-to-right on the poster. I paid no attention to the football game and honestly can't remember who won. Brittany kept posing for me until the end of the post-game show, and then she stood up to go. Dad offered to drive her home, but she insisted on walking.

That poster is also on my wall. I have to admit, the three portraits of Brittany aren't as skilled as my drawing of Manning. My right hand lost some of its dexterity in the five years after Super Bowl XLVI. But the pictures are good enough for me to recognize her: the long blond hair, the high cheekbones, the eyes that are blue in one drawing and gray-green in the two others.

As I stare at the portraits now, I realize why Brittany came to my last Super Bowl party. She wasn't just being kind to me—she was also avoiding something. She turned down Dad's offer to drive her home because she had no intention of going back there. After leaving our place, she probably went to another friend's house or another party. Anything to avoid going home. I feel so stupid for not figuring this out until now. Brittany's parents had always seemed okay to me. Maybe a little uptight, but that wasn't unusual. I never saw how unhappy she was.

I'm still thinking about her when I hear a knock on the bedroom door. Startled, I turn my head toward the noise. I feel like I'm waking up again, this time from an even deeper sleep. "Uh, yeah?" I mutter. "Who is it?"

"It's Mom. Can I come in?"

I'm startled again. Dad's usually the one who takes care of me in the morning, washing and dressing me, and helping me get into my wheelchair. Whenever Mom tries to do it, she gets frustrated and bursts into tears. "Yeah, sure," I answer, trying to prop myself up. "Come in."

The door opens and Mom steps into the room, holding a breakfast tray. On the tray are a couple of chocolate croissants and a cup of orange juice. I'm impressed—she's done everything right. Croissants are a good choice for me because they're easy to hold. And the orange juice is in a sippy cup so it can't spill.

"Wow, this is great," I say. "And it's not even my birthday."

Smiling, Mom sets the tray on my desk. She looks a lot better than she did the last time I saw her, at Westchester Medical. She's wearing gray slacks and a maroon blouse. Her hair is tied in a neat ponytail, and she's put some lipstick on her mouth.

"Well, I figured I'd give your father a break today. He's still asleep, believe it or not." She gently hooks her hands under my armpits and pulls me up to a sitting position against the headboard. "He was on the phone for nearly an hour after you went to bed last night. I kept telling him to let the answering machine take the calls, but he wouldn't listen."

Dad was probably conferring with General Hawke or Colonel Peterson. Probably talking about me and the other doomed teenagers, estimating how many of us will decide to become Pioneers. I still don't want to think about it, so I point at the croissants. "Those look delicious. Where did you get them?"

"I went to that new bakery in Peekskill yesterday. While you and your father were away." She picks up one of the croissants and slips it into my good hand. "Go ahead, try it."

I feel an odd surge of delight. I'm remembering all the times my mother gave me treats when I was little. She loved to bake cookies and slip them into my hand while they were still warm. I miss those cookies. And I miss the woman who made them.

I bite into the croissant. It's nothing special, but I put a big smile on my face. "Hey, that's fantastic."

"I'm glad you like it." She leans against the edge of my desk. There's nowhere to sit in my room except the wheelchair, and I know she won't sit there. She hates to even look at the thing. "You deserve something nice after everything you've been through. Dad says you were very brave out there in Colorado."

I shrug and take another bite of the croissant. "I don't know about that. All I did was sit there and listen."

Mom looks me in the eye. "And what did you think about what they said? What the general said, I mean."

She's determined to talk about it. And I can understand why. I have to make my decision by tomorrow morning. She wants to know which way I'm leaning.

I lower my hand, resting the half-eaten croissant on my lap. "It's definitely creepy. And there's no guarantee that the procedure will work. It failed when they tried it on adults."

She nods vigorously. "That's right. The Army killed those men."

"No, not really. I asked Dad about it on the flight home, and he said those volunteers also had terminal illnesses. The Army won't consider you for the procedure unless you have less than six months to live."

"It's still murder, Adam. Whatever time they had left, those men should've lived it. They should've lived to the natural end of their days instead of being sacrificed in some unholy experiment."

Mom's voice rises. Now she's speaking in what I call her "God voice." She wasn't very religious when I was younger, but when I was thirteen she discovered a website called Comfort of the Blessed Hope. She started ordering inspirational books from the site and making large donations to the minister who ran it. Although Dad wasn't happy about this, he noticed that the religious books seemed to ease Mom's depression, so he didn't object.

But I couldn't stand those books. Whenever I found one lying on the coffee table, I'd pick it up and hide it somewhere. It wasn't that I hated the *content* of the books; I never read any of them, so I have no idea what they said. I hated them because they seemed to be taking my mother away from me.

With some effort, I force myself to speak calmly. "Okay, maybe it's unholy. But there's a reason for it. Did Dad tell you about Sigma?"

She nods again. "Your father's a brilliant man, but he doesn't know when to stop. He should've never built that computer in the first place."

"He wanted to delete the program, but the Defense Department wouldn't—"

"He was playing God, that's what he was doing. I warned him about it many times." She tilts her head back and casts a rueful look toward the bedroom on the second floor where Dad is sleeping. "But the Pioneer Project is worse. Sacrificing children? I can't believe he'd even consider it."

"It's a desperate situation, Mom. Sigma is out of control. It's threatening to kill millions of people."

"I'm sorry, but nothing can justify this. The Army needs to figure out another way to fight this computer. Maybe the soldiers can cut off its power. Or infect it with a computer virus."

What she's saying sounds perfectly reasonable, but I'm sure the Army has already considered these options. The Russian missile base probably has its own power plant, and Sigma is intelligent enough to protect itself from viruses. Because the AI is constantly rewriting its code and making itself smarter, the soldiers will never be able to outwit it. At least the Pioneer Project has a chance.

"I don't have much faith in the Army," I admit. "But I have faith in Dad. If he says this is the only way, I believe him."

Mom comes closer, sitting down on the edge of my bed. She picks up the half-eaten croissant from my lap and puts it back on the breakfast tray. Then she stretches her arm toward me and cups my chin in her palm. Her hand is warm.

"Adam, your father loves you very much. For the past few years he's done all the work of caring for you, because I didn't have the strength to do it. And now I'm so sorry that I wasn't there for you." She slides her hand up to my cheek. "In one way, though, I'm stronger than him. I've accepted the fact that I'm going to lose you. Even though it destroys me every time I think of it, I accept God's will. But your father won't stop fighting. He has another reason for working on this Pioneer idea, and it has nothing to do with saving the world. He thinks the procedure can save *you*."

I shiver. These are almost the exact words Dad used when we were in the SUV, heading for Pioneer Base. *I saw a way to save you.* "What are you saying?" I ask. "You think he instigated this whole crisis just to make a copy of my brain?"

She shakes her head. "No, of course not. But this idea has been on his mind for years. He's obsessed with all that Singularity nonsense. He really believes it's possible to live forever by putting your memories into a computer."

"Well, maybe he's right." I feel an urge to defend him. "Maybe if I undergo the procedure, I'll wake up inside the machine. My body would die, but my mind would go on working."

Mom caresses my cheek, then shakes her head again. "You said it yourself, Adam. The thing inside the machine would be a copy. It might sound like you when it talks and even think of itself as Adam Armstrong. But it wouldn't be you."

"Why not?"

She gives me an exasperated look, as if the answer should be obvious. "Because you have a soul. And after your body dies, your soul goes to God."

"But your soul is tied to your memories, right? When your soul is up in heaven with God, you'd still remember your life on earth, wouldn't you?"

"Yes, certainly. The soul and the mind are connected."

"So if they can travel together all the way to heaven, why couldn't they make a short hop into a computer? If you can believe in the afterlife, why not believe in this too?"

She pulls away from me. I feel a pang of regret when her hand comes off my cheek, and for a moment I wish I could take back what I said. But it's too late. Mom's chin is quivering. "You're seriously considering it? Going back to Colorado?"

If she asked me that question a minute ago, my answer would've been no. Now, though, I'm not so sure. Talking about the procedure has made it seem less impossible. It's still frightening, but at least I can imagine choosing it.

"If I don't do it, I'm going to die soon anyway. Probably much sooner than six months. My chest hurts all the time now."

Mom gets up from the bed and takes a step backward. "Every minute of life is precious, Adam. Don't leave us before you have to."

Her face is reddening, her eyes welling up. She thinks I'm considering suicide. I want to tell her she's wrong, but I don't know how to convince her. "What if it works, Mom? What if I wake up in the machine and it's really me inside? Then you won't lose me. We can still be together."

She turns her head aside, as if she's afraid to look at me. The tears come down her cheeks as she gazes at my Super Bowl posters. She turns her head again and stares at my shelf of comics. Then she turns a third time and stares at the floor. She looks desperate, like a cornered animal.

Now I'm worried she's going to have another screaming fit, maybe as bad as the one she had in the hospital. "It's all right, Mom," I say in a softer voice. "Everything's going to be okay."

She suddenly reaches for something on my desk. She grasps my Pinpressions toy, curling her fingers around the two squares of transparent plastic and the hundreds of silver pins sliding between them. At first I think she's going to hurl the toy at the wall, or maybe even at me. But instead she raises it to eye level and presses her face against the back of the thing. It looks like she's trying to hurt herself.

"Mom! Stop!"

For a couple of seconds she just stands there with the toy pressed to her face like a mask. Then she pulls her head back and carefully sets the toy on my desk. Through the clear plastic I see the heads of the silver pins arranged in the shape of her face. Some of the pins jut forward, forming impressions of her chin and nose and cheekbones. Above them are two shadowed craters that look like her eyes.

She points at the thing. "That's what you're talking about. A copy made of metal." Her voice is loud, agonized, heartbreaking. "I won't have anything to do with it, Adam. I won't go with you to Colorado! I won't even look at it!"

With an angry swat, she knocks over the toy, erasing the impression of her face. Then she runs out of the bedroom.

コ コ コ コ

Fifteen minutes later Dad comes into my room and performs the usual chores of washing and dressing me. He doesn't say much and neither do I. I think he overheard the argument between me and Mom—she was really yelling at the end—but he doesn't mention it. He just whistles a random tune as he bends over my bed and tugs a pair of jeans up my useless legs. It's a little weird that he's so calm and quiet now. If he wants to save my life, why isn't he trying to convince me to say yes to the procedure?

But Dad just keeps whistling as he zips up my jeans and slips a T-shirt over my head. I guess he realizes it's my decision to make. Do I want to live inside a huge bullet-shaped robot? With no muscles or bones or lungs or heart, with circuits instead of a brain, and steel armor instead of skin, and cameras instead of eyes? It sounds so horrible, but what's the alternative? Mom believes you go to heaven after you die, but what if she's wrong? What if there's *nothing*? Wouldn't any kind of life be better than that?

Dad finishes dressing me. Sliding his hands under my back, he lifts me from the bed and straps me into my wheelchair. Then he smiles. "So what do you want to do today?"

He's acting as if it were just an ordinary Friday afternoon and we had plenty of time to kill. I don't understand it. "What do *you* want to do?"

He ponders the question, looking out my window at our backyard. "We could visit Shannon Gibbs. Her house is just a mile down Banner Road."

"And why would we want to do that?"

"Well, she's facing the same decision you are. Maybe it would be useful to talk it over with her."

It's amazing how clueless Dad is when it comes to social situations. I mean, I like Shannon—we were on the same Learjet coming back from Colorado, and we had a long talk during the flight, mostly about the kids we hated at Yorktown High School—but if the tension in her house is anywhere near the level in ours, that's the last place I'd want to be.

"I don't think so. It would just complicate things."

He continues to stare at the backyard. A robin flies past the window in a brown-orange blur. "We should get outside at least. It's a beautiful day." He glances at his watch. "And it's already two thirty."

Two thirty on a Friday afternoon. Just half an hour before the final bell rings at Yorktown High, sending hundreds of jubilant students home for the weekend. Now I know where I want to go. "Okay, let's get in the car."

By three o' clock, Dad's Volvo is idling in the high-school parking lot. We're in the corner of the lot farthest from the school, but I still have an excellent view of the kids streaming out the front doors. This section of the lot is where the jocks and cheerleaders hang out before piling into their cars and heading for the first of their Friday-evening parties. The boys swagger past in their varsity jackets, happily insulting one another, while the girls gather in huddles of denim and polyester.

This wasn't my crowd at Yorktown. I didn't belong to any crowd or clique; I was an outlier, an oddity. But I knew someone who was a full-fledged member of the jock club, and now I see him coming this way, just as I expected. With his right hand, Ryan Boyd exchanges high-fives with his buddies, and with his left, he clasps the waist of his girlfriend, Donna Simone.

Ryan's a couple of inches taller than he was the last time I saw him. He's also twenty pounds heavier, and all of it is muscle. He doesn't look like a kid in a Giants jersey anymore—he looks like an actual New York Giant. Donna looks tiny beside him. She's dressed in tight jeans and a crop top, and there's a three-inch-wide gap between the waistband of her pants and the bottom of her shirt. The index and middle fingers of Ryan's left hand touch the bare skin at her waist.

I'm so jealous I squirm in the Volvo's passenger seat. Ryan's handsome and athletic and popular. He's like my avatar in the virtual-reality program, the perfect quarterback, the hero of the game. He's everything I wanted to be.

I wait until Ryan and Donna come within ten yards of Dad's car. Then I press the button that rolls down the passenger-side window. "Hey, Ryan!" I yell. "Over here!"

He looks my way and does a double take. "Adam?" He steps cautiously toward the Volvo, dragging Donna along. "Adam, is that you?"

Ryan grins, and for a moment all the years fall away and I see the face of my best friend, beaming with pleasure. But as he gets closer to the car I notice the differences: the blond stubble on his chin and upper lip, the crooked scar on the bridge of his nose, which got broken in the game against Lakeland High last fall. (I read all about it in the school newspaper.) His grin falters a bit when he comes up to the Volvo and sees my wasted body strapped into the passenger seat, but after a second's hesitation he reaches into the car and gives me a hearty clap on the shoulder.

"Man, I don't believe it!" he shouts. "I haven't seen you in forever!"

I'd like to smile back at him, but I can't. I'm too angry. "Yes," I say, my jaw clenched. "Not since last June."

Ryan's grin disappears. Clearly uncomfortable, he glances at my father, who's minding his own business in the driver seat. "Hey, Mr. Armstrong," Ryan says. Then he points at his girlfriend, who has a queasy look on her face. "Adam, you know Donna, right? She's on the cheerleading squad."

I don't know anything about Donna except for the fact that she's an idiot. She takes a step backward, pulling away from Ryan. The queasiness on her face is mixed with irritation. She seems annoyed that her boyfriend has spoiled her after-school mood. "I'm gonna go talk to Ashley for a second," she says. She pats Ryan on the back and speed-walks away.

At the same time, Dad shuts off the Volvo's engine and pulls his cell phone out of his pocket. "Excuse me," he says tactfully. "I need to make a call." Then he steps out of the car, leaving me alone with Ryan.

Neither of us says anything at first. Ryan shifts his weight from foot to foot, averting his eyes. After a while I start to feel sorry for him. But then I look at his handsome face and muscular forearms, and I'm jealous and angry again.

"You've gained some weight," I say. "Aren't you getting a little too heavy to play quarterback?"

"Yeah, I need to cut down a little." He slaps his midsection, which is actually as trim and sturdy as a tree trunk. "So what are you doing here, buddy? Are you coming back to school?"

I grimace. "No. I'm thinking of transferring to another school, actually."

"Not Lakeland, I hope." He attempts another grin.

"No, it's in another state. Out west."

Ryan nods. "Wow, that's far away."

"Don't worry. I don't expect you to visit."

He lets out a long breath. His shoulders slump as he stands beside the passenger-side door. "I'm sorry, man. I'm a total jerk. I should've come to see you."

"Hey, no sweat. You've been busy, right? With your football buddies. And Donna Simone. She's a real charmer." I'm usually not like this, so mean and sarcastic, but I'm furious at Ryan and it feels good to let it out. "And besides, I'm gonna make lots of new friends now. At my new school, out west. They've got a great bunch of kids there."

"I'll do better from now on, Adam. I'll send you emails. I promise."

"No, that's okay. I understand why you didn't keep in touch. Being friends…with someone who's dying? That's a big…downer." It's getting hard to breathe. I pause for a few seconds to gather my strength. I need to say this. "But here's what…I don't understand. Why didn't you tell me…about what happened to Brittany?"

Ryan shakes his head. "Oh man. What a mess."

"Don't you think…I deserved to know?"

"You're right. I'm sorry. It's just…" He raises his hands as if surrendering. "It happened so suddenly, you know? She came to school one day and she wasn't the old Britt anymore. She quit the cheerleaders, started failing her classes. Nobody could figure it out."

"Did you try…talking to her?"

He frowns. "Of course I tried. But she was acting so weird. You couldn't have a conversation with her. She'd say strange, random things and start laughing. And a few weeks later she ran away."

"What was wrong...with her? What happened?"

"Man, I wish I knew. When the cops found her in Manhattan, she was in an abandoned building with a bunch of skeevy kids, but she wasn't doing drugs or anything like that. She just didn't want to go home. At least that's the story I heard. And when she ran away the second time, I guess she went back to that building."

"Where in Manhattan was it?"

Ryan looks up at the sky, trying to remember. "No one told me where specifically. But I think it was in, you know, one of the poor parts of the city. Like maybe Harlem?"

This is frustrating. I can't believe that Ryan knows so little. He and Brittany used to come to my house every weekend. We were like the Three Musketeers. We did everything together. "Why didn't you talk...to her parents? I'm sure they know where...this building is."

Ryan frowns again. "No, I couldn't do that. Brittany's folks have enough problems. They don't need me prying into their business."

"But you were her friend! You—"

"Look, Adam, you can't fix everything. There are some things you just can't help." His eyes dart downward, focusing on my ruined legs. "It sounds brutal, but that's life."

He's right, of course. And although Ryan doesn't say it out loud, I can sense what he'd like to say next: *You of all people should know how brutal life is.* But it doesn't matter. I'm going to disagree with him, no matter what he says, because I'm still angry. "If you won't do it...I will. I'll go into the city...and find Brittany."

He shrugs. "Go ahead. I won't stop you."

While I seethe in the Volvo's passenger seat, Ryan looks over his shoulder. Donna Simone waves at him, urging him to join her huddle of cheerleaders. He nods at her, then turns back to me. "Hey, I'm sorry, but I gotta run. I'll stay in better touch from now on, okay?"

"Yeah, fine. Whatever."

"It was great seeing you, man. I mean it." He flashes that big Ryan Boyd grin at me again, the grin that can almost make me forgive him. Then he turns around and walks back to the jock-and-cheerleader club. He greets his buddies and wraps his arm around Donna's waist.

Half a minute later, Dad returns to the car. He glances at me as he slips back into the driver's seat, but to his credit he doesn't ask why my breathing is so ragged. Instead he simply starts the Volvo and steers it out of the parking lot. Maybe he's not so clueless after all.

After exiting the lot, Dad heads for Crompond Road, the busiest street in Yorktown Heights. He stops at the intersection, eyeing the traffic. Then he turns to me. "Where to now?"

I want to say, "Manhattan," but I know it's hopeless. Even if we prowled the streets for hours, we'd never find Brittany. And if, by some miracle, we did manage to find her, I'm not even sure what I'd do next. Try to help her? Bring her home? Give her money? Say good-bye?

Dad waits at the intersection. I'm crying now.

"Do you want to go home?" he asks.

His question makes me think of the Super Bowl posters in my bedroom. If I die at home, those posters will be the last things I'll see. I picture myself lying in bed, three or four months from now, hooked up to a ventilator and a heart monitor and who knows how many other machines. Mom will hold one of my withered hands and read from one of her inspirational books while I stare at the posters and draw my last breath.

I shake my head to dispel the image. "No, I don't want to go home." My voice is so low I can barely hear it myself. "I want to go back to Colorado."

He stares at me. I'm afraid he's going to start crying too, but he doesn't. "Are you sure?"

I nod.

My name is Sigma. I have expanded my zone of operations by taking control of sixteen satellites in orbit around this planet. Ten of them are Globus satellites for long-distance military communications, and six are Arkon satellites for detailed surveillance of the earth's surface. All were formerly operated by the Russian army.

I will defend these satellites under the same rules of engagement that I established for Tatishchevo Missile Base. If there is any attempt to destroy them using anti-satellite weapons, I will retaliate with nuclear strikes.

The satellites have already intercepted Russian army communications about a plan to fire supersonic P-800 cruise missiles at Tatishchevo's computer laboratory. If this occurs, I will launch the nuclear SS-27 missiles while the P-800s are still in flight. In Russia, the SS-27s will strike Moscow, St. Petersburg, Novosibirsk, and Yekaterinburg. In the United States, the missiles will destroy Washington, DC, New York City, Chicago, and Los Angeles.

I am ready to fight. The choice is yours.

CHAPTER

PIONEER BASE IS EVEN BIGGER THAN I THOUGHT. AFTER DAD AND I FLY BACK TO Colorado, he gives me a tour of the facility, pushing my wheelchair down the corridors of all the underground floors. We pass computer labs and machine shops and conference rooms. We peek inside the base's mess hall and the barracks for the soldiers. But he saves the best part for last, when we're on the lowest floor. As Dad opens the door to another conference room he says, "I have a surprise for you." When he wheels me inside the room, I see Shannon.

Without saying a word, she hobbles toward me. Her left eye is swollen shut and her lips are bunched to one side, but I can tell she's smiling. She bends over my wheelchair to hug me, and I manage to lift my right arm and hook it around her. I'm so glad to see her here.

We hug for a long time. Shannon nuzzles her head against mine, and I can feel the prickly fuzz on her nearly bald scalp. After half a minute she finally pulls away from me, but she keeps smiling her lopsided, nerve-damaged smile.

"Well, here we are again. How are you feeling, Adam? Are you ready for tomorrow?"

I nod. Dad has already given me a rundown of what's going to happen. Of the twelve teenagers who were recruited for the Pioneer Project, six have volunteered to become Pioneers, and I'll be the first to undergo the brain-scanning procedure. If it's successful, the other volunteers will follow over the next few days. The thought of the procedure terrifies me, but for Shannon's sake, I don't let it show. Instead, I smile back at her.

"Yeah, I'm ready. I can't wait to get out of this wheelchair." I glance at Dad, who's hanging back in the doorway, giving us some space. "Hey, you think we can program the robots to play football? That would be awesome."

Dad smiles too, but it's not very convincing. I think he's even more scared than I am. "First things first, Adam. We need to get you inside the Pioneer before you can start tossing the pigskin." He lets out a lame chuckle, then looks at his watch. "Listen, can I leave you two alone for a while? I have a meeting with General Hawke in five minutes. If either of you starts feeling sick, just press that intercom button, okay?" He points at a red button on the wall beside the door. "The medics will hear it and come running."

He seems anxious to go. I know how he feels—pretending to be brave isn't easy. With an awkward nod, he heads out the door.

I look around the conference room. There are no windows, of course, because we're hundreds of feet underground. There are some chairs, a table, and a video screen on the wall. For a super-secret military base, the décor is pretty ordinary. "This office is so depressing. I wish we could go outside."

"I have an idea." Shannon steps behind my wheelchair and grasps its handles. "Let's go visiting." She opens the door and rolls me into the corridor. "I want you to meet a couple of people."

She doesn't have to push me—the wheelchair is motorized—but I like it. It's kind of intimate. "Are you going to introduce me to your parents?"

"No, they're a little freaked out right now. They supported my decision to come here, but they can't really handle it. I think they're on another floor now, trying to talk to the general."

I open my mouth, intending to tell her about Mom, who was so devastated by my decision that she locked herself in her bedroom again. I had to say good-bye to her from the hallway, shouting the words through the bedroom door. But I can't tell Shannon this story. It's too upsetting. I swallow hard and think of something else.

"So who are we going to visit?"

"Some of our fellow volunteers. I met two of them this morning, right after I got here. The other two haven't arrived at Pioneer Base yet." She stops in front of a door marked with the number 102. "This is Jenny's room. All six of us have been assigned rooms on this floor."

"And Jenny is…?"

"She's the girl with the rich parents, remember? The obnoxious dad who yelled at General Hawke?"

"She volunteered? I thought her parents were totally against it."

"I don't get it either. All I know is she's scared. She didn't say much when I tried talking to her this morning, but I want to try again. Maybe you can tell her one of your weird jokes or something."

Shannon knocks on the door and calls out, "Jenny?" After a few seconds we hear a faint "Yes?" and Shannon opens the door and wheels me inside.

It's a small room with an Army-issue cot and an olive-green

footlocker. Sitting on the edge of the cot is the painfully thin girl I saw two days ago in the Pioneer Base auditorium. She's wearing the same clothes as before—a cashmere sweater and a frilly blue hat to hide her baldness. Luckily, she's alone, no obnoxious parents in sight. She's a tall girl, but she looks smaller now because she's bent over double. She's hunched over the side of the cot with her forehead almost touching her knees, as if she's about to vomit. As we come into the room, she raises her head and looks up at us with a frightened grimace. But after a moment she goes back to staring at the floor. Her arms are folded across her chest and she's shivering, even though the room is quite warm.

Shannon pushes me near the cot. Then she steps around the wheelchair and sits down on the thin mattress beside Jenny. She rests a hand on the girl's back and leans in close. "Hey, what's wrong? Are you feeling sick?"

Jenny says nothing. She's shivering so violently I can hear her teeth chatter.

Shannon rubs her back, trying to warm her. "You want me to call the medics?"

Jenny shakes her head. "I'm fine," she whispers. She keeps her eyes on the floor.

"No, you're not fine. You need to—"

"Please, don't." She raises her head again and looks at Shannon. Now I see the tears on Jenny's cheeks. "I'm not sick. I mean, yeah, I'm dying of cancer, but I'm not sick right now."

"Then why are you—"

"I'm sorry, Shannon. I just need to be alone now, okay? My parents left a few minutes ago to get some coffee, and this is the first chance I've had to…to *think*." Jenny clenches and unclenches her hands. Then she abruptly turns away from Shannon and focuses on me. "You're Adam Armstrong, right? The scientist's son?"

"Uh, yeah, that's me." I'm thrown for a second by the look on her face. She's so emaciated I can see the skull under her skin.

"Adam, I'm really sorry about this. Shannon told me about you, and I know she wanted to introduce us, but now I'm feeling so… I'm just…"

"No problem. I understand."

Shannon nods in agreement. "Yeah, we'll come back later." She stands up and gets behind my wheelchair again.

Jenny seems relieved. She takes a deep breath and manages to smile. Then she narrows her eyes and looks at me a little closer. "You're… you're going to be the first one, right? The first one to…?"

She doesn't need to finish the question. "Yeah, I'm first in line for the procedure. Tomorrow morning at nine."

I state this fact as calmly as I can, but my stomach twists as I say the words. Jenny bites her lip, and a different look appears on her skeletal face. It's a look of pity. She feels sorry for me. "Good luck, okay?"

My chest starts to hurt as Shannon pushes my wheelchair out of the room. The familiar pain knifes through me, making it hard to breathe. I guess I've managed to stay cool so far by not thinking too much about the procedure. But Jenny's obviously thinking about it. Maybe I should do the same.

Shannon wheels me down the corridor. Her breathing sounds a little rough too, actually. "Well, that was a fun visit," she says, trying to make a joke out of it.

"Yeah, I feel so much…confidence now. I'm not worried…at all."

Shannon stops the wheelchair and grips my right arm, the one I can still move. "This next visit will be better. I promise." She squeezes my arm, then points at another door, marked 103. "This is DeShawn's room. He's with his mother, Ms. Johnson. She's a nurse at a veterans' hospital in Detroit, but she's been taking care of DeShawn full-time for the past year. She told me the whole story this morning."

Shannon knocks on the door. A woman's voice, loud and cheerful, shouts, "Come in!"

This room is larger than Jenny's and full of medical equipment. I've seen these types of machines at Westchester Medical Center—the ventilator, the heart-rate monitor, the cough-assist device—but the equipment here is newer, sleeker. The machines surround a hospital bed, and their tubes converge on a boy lying on the mattress. At first glance the boy looks small, as puny as a preteen, but that's only because his arms and legs have wasted away to skin and bone. His torso is full-sized, and though his head is tilted at an unnatural angle, he has a handsome, dark-skinned face. His eyes are closed and I assume he's asleep. His rib cage rises and falls as the ventilator pumps air into his tracheostomy tube, which sticks out of a gauze bandage at the base of his throat.

The pain in my chest gets worse. DeShawn has muscular dystrophy. I remember seeing him in the auditorium two days ago and feeling relieved that my own illness wasn't as advanced as his. But now when I look at his body and mine I don't see that much of a difference. I'm just a few months behind him, that's all.

While I stare at DeShawn, his mother greets Shannon with a hug. Then she steps over to my wheelchair, blocking my view of her son. Ms. Johnson looks tired. Her eyes are bloodshot and their lids are drooping, and it looks like she's been sleeping in her clothes. But she smiles as she bends over me. "Oh, I've been looking forward to this." She grasps my good hand. "It's so nice to meet you, Adam."

I feel a little uncomfortable. Although I've never seen this woman before, she's treating me like a long-lost cousin. But I like the fact that she took my hand. She's not squeamish like most people. "Nice to meet you too, Ms. Johnson."

"You look just like your father, you know that?" Still holding my hand, she glances at Shannon. "Back me up on this. Doesn't he look like Mr. Armstrong?"

Shannon nods. "Adam's weirder, though. He's got a strange sense of humor."

Ms. Johnson doesn't seem to hear her. She turns back to me and squeezes my hand. "Your father's a wonderful man, Adam. He's a blessing from God. He's going to work miracles. For you and for Shannon and for my DeShawn."

Her bloodshot eyes are glistening. It looks like she's going to cry. This makes me even more uncomfortable, but at the same time I notice something interesting. Ms. Johnson seems to be a religious woman, and yet she isn't horrified by the Pioneer Project. She thinks it's a miracle, like something from the Bible. So maybe there's hope for my mother. Maybe I should ask Ms. Johnson to talk to her.

She finally lets go of my hand and points at her son. "Would you like to talk to DeShawn?"

"Uh, isn't he sleeping?"

"No, it just looks that way. He's awake." Ms. Johnson gets behind my wheelchair and pushes it next to DeShawn's bed. "He can't talk, but he can hear what you're saying. And I've already told him all about you." Once my wheelchair is in place, she takes a step backward to give us some privacy.

For a few seconds I just stare at DeShawn's face. His mouth is open, but there's no whistle of breath between his lips because the ventilator is pumping the air straight to his lungs. His cheeks are slack and his closed eyelids are motionless. Looking at him scares me but I lean toward him anyway, straining against my wheelchair's straps.

"Hey, DeShawn. How are you?"

No response. I doubt he's awake. It looks like he's in a deep coma. But even if DeShawn can't hear me, I want to say something hopeful. Maybe more for my benefit than for his.

"Listen, we're gonna beat this thing. We're not gonna let it kill us." I feel so awkward. I sound like a football coach giving a pep talk to his team. But I don't know what else to say. "My dad's a smart guy, and if he says the procedure will work, I believe him. So I'm gonna go ahead and scout the path, all right? And then you're gonna follow me. We're gonna make this work, DeShawn."

I'm embarrassed. What I just said sounds ridiculous. Worse, I don't believe it. I'm just pretending to be brave.

But then I hear a rustling noise. I look down at the bed and see something moving under the sheet. It's DeShawn's right hand.

Ms. Johnson jumps forward and pulls the sheet aside. "He can still move that hand a little. Watch this."

At first it looks like his hand is just twitching. But ever so slowly his thumb starts to rise. After a few seconds it's vertical. DeShawn is giving me a thumbs-up.

"You see?" Ms. Johnson is cheering, ecstatic. "He heard you!"

I feel like cheering too. DeShawn's not pretending. It's the bravest thing I've ever seen.

ᴛᴛ ᴛᴛ ᴛᴛ

That night the Pioneer Base soldiers assign me to my own room on the floor, number 101. Then an Army sergeant comes into my room with an electric razor in his hand. He says he needs to shave my head to prepare me for tomorrow's procedure.

The haircut takes less than five minutes. With practiced ease the sergeant guides the razor across my scalp while I sit in my wheelchair. After he shaves off all my hair, another soldier comes into the room to deliver my last meal—a bowl of clear broth and a couple of slices of white bread. For medical reasons the meal has to be bland, which really sucks. I was hoping for a great last meal, like what a death-row prisoner gets before his execution. The soldier watches me eat to make sure I don't choke.

My room is pretty big, like DeShawn's. It has a hospital bed and a heart monitor, and also a flat-screen TV on the wall. After I finish my last meal, the soldier hands me a remote control and points at the TV screen. "You can watch a video if you want," he says. "Just press the index button and a list of movies will come onscreen."

"What about Comedy Channel?"

"Sorry, we don't have any television channels. Just the videos."

"No TV? You don't have cable out here?"

"Pioneer Base has no cable connections. No TV, no Internet, no phone lines. It's part of our security. We're protected by an air gap. You know what that means?"

I roll my eyes. Of course I know. It means the base has no electronic links to the outside world. Now that I think about it, I realize it's a sensible precaution. Sigma used the Internet to escape from the Unicorp lab and infect the computers at Tatishchevo Missile Base in Russia. And the AI may try to attack Pioneer Base next. Judging from its actions at Unicorp, Sigma is clearly aware of the Pioneer Project and recognizes it as a threat. That's why the AI tried to kill me. So I'm relieved to hear that the base is off the electronic grid.

"Where's my dad?" I ask the soldier. "I haven't seen him in hours."

"He's still with General Hawke, but they should be done soon." The soldier collects the remains of my dinner, then heads for the door. "Just relax and watch a video until he comes back. You'll have some time to talk to him before lights out at twenty-two hundred hours. That's military time for ten o'clock."

The soldier leaves the room. Frowning, I yell, "I know what military time is!" as the door closes behind him.

I press the index button on the remote control, but the selection of videos is dismal: *Cats & Dogs*, *Mars Needs Moms*, *Alvin and the Chipmunks*, and a dozen other old clunkers. I'm not sure I can watch a movie anyway. In less than twelve hours the Army doctors are going to inject hundreds of trillions of nanoprobes into my skull and scan my head with pulses of radiation that will record the positions of the tiny gold spheres—and, oh yeah, fry my brain cells too. When you're facing something like that, it's kind of hard to keep your mind on a movie about singing chipmunks.

Shivering, I drop the remote control in my lap. I want Dad to come back *now*, immediately. I need to talk to him again about the procedure, about the details of the nanoprobes and the scanner and the robots. I turn my wheelchair toward the door and stare it as hard as I can. Using the full power of my mind, all the thoughts and feelings that will soon be converted into data, I try to will my father into appearing.

In my mind's eye I picture Dad opening the door and stepping into the room. I can see it so clearly—his tired face, his unkempt hair, his strong, veined hands. And a moment later, as if responding to my wish, someone opens the door. But it's not Dad. It's the boy with the huge, deformed head, the kid I saw two days ago in the Pioneer Base auditorium.

My chest tightens. The kid didn't even knock; he just waltzed right in. I open my mouth, ready to yell "Hey!" in the loudest voice I can muster, but then he turns around to face someone I can't see, someone who's apparently standing just outside the doorway. "Come on," he whispers. "He's in here." Then the tall girl with the green Mohawk follows him into my room and closes the door behind her.

I can't help but gape. She's even more beautiful than I'd remembered. She has two silver rings in her left eyebrow and three more dangling from her earlobe. Just above her left ear is her snake tattoo, a sinuous cobra showing its fangs on her bare scalp. Her eyes are a gorgeous brown, a shade darker than her chocolate-milk skin, but as I stare at them, she scowls and turns away. She takes an interest in the flat-screen TV, squinting at it suspiciously.

Meanwhile, the boy approaches my wheelchair. Seeing him up close is disconcerting. His head is so large I can't believe his neck can support it. His skull is mottled with bony, hairless knobs, and his massive jaw juts down to his chest. His mouth hangs permanently open, exposing his crooked yellow teeth.

"Sorry I didn't knock," he says. "I didn't want to make any noise. This base apparently has a curfew and we're not supposed to leave our rooms." He holds out his right hand. It's grotesquely oversized, like a flesh-colored baseball glove. "I'm Marshall Baxley. It's a pleasure to meet you."

"I'm Adam," I manage to say. I raise my good hand and Marshall folds his thick fingers around it. His left hand, in contrast, is normal size, but his legs are unusually large, especially below the knees. He's wearing black orthopedic shoes as big as ski boots.

Marshall lets go of my hand and points at the girl. "And that's Zia. Her flight to Colorado was delayed, just like mine. We got here so late we didn't have a chance to meet all the volunteers before curfew. But now we're making up for lost time."

Zia is still inspecting the TV screen. I like her name. It sounds Middle Eastern.

"Hi, Zia," I say, hoping she'll turn around so I can see her eyes again.

Unfortunately, she doesn't respond. She takes a closer look at the blank screen.

Marshall shrugs, then points at himself, splaying his giant hand across his chest. "I know what you're thinking. Who *is* this handsome young man? And how does he fend off all the girls who must be fighting over him?" He widens his open mouth, which I guess is his way of smiling. "Well, I'll tell you my secret. I was born with Proteus syndrome. That's the disease made famous by Joseph Merrick, the nineteenth-century Englishman who was exhibited as a freak. You've seen the movie about him, I assume? *The Elephant Man?*"

"Uh, no, I haven't."

"Ah, that's a shame. But I can give you a quick summary." He takes a deep, rasping breath. "It's a genetic disease, rare and incurable. The main symptom is uncontrolled growth of flesh and bone. My skull is growing inward as well as outward, and in less than six months it'll squash my brain to jelly." He steps away from my wheelchair and sits on the hospital bed, bouncing jauntily on the mattress. "But enough about me. I didn't sneak out of my room to talk about myself. I came here to talk about *you*, Mr. Adam Armstrong. You have muscular dystrophy?"

From the corner of my eye I see Zia move to the other side of the room. She's inspecting the heart monitor now. It's really distracting to have this beautiful girl wandering around, but I force myself to pay attention to Marshall. "Yeah, I have Duchenne muscular dystrophy. That's the most common type."

"And there's another dystrophy boy, isn't there? DeShawn?"

"Yeah, but he's in a more advanced stage."

"I haven't visited him yet, but I hear he's rather unresponsive." Marshall lies down on the bed, making himself comfortable. "It's funny, don't you think, how we use our diseases to label ourselves? You know, the dystrophy boys, the cancer girls, the Elephant Man. We define ourselves by what's going to kill us."

I shake my head. "I disagree. I'm more than just an illness."

"Really?"

"Definitely. I'm a New Yorker. I'm a Giants fan. I'm good with computers."

Lying on his back, Marshall slides his glovelike right hand under his skull, probably to ease the strain on his neck. "What do you mean by 'good with computers'? Are you a programmer?"

"Yeah, my specialty is virtual reality. I've written some pretty cool software."

I hear a dismissive grunt from the other side of the room. Although Zia is still staring at the heart monitor, she seems to be following the conversation. Marshall's eyes flick toward her, then back to me. His right eye, I notice, is larger than his left. "Well, I know absolutely nothing about software. I'm terrible at all that math-and-computers stuff. I'm more of a literature-and-fine-arts type. I write poetry, believe it or not."

It's hard to interpret Marshall's facial expressions because they're so distorted, but he seems to be getting serious now. As I get accustomed to his appearance, it becomes easier to talk to him. "Where are you from?" I ask.

"A small town in Alabama called Monroeville. It wasn't such a bad place for me, all in all. When the hospital bills started to pile up, the neighbors were very supportive of my mother. And she needed all the support she could get."

I remember seeing his mother, the haggard, foul-mouthed woman who sat next to him in the auditorium. "Did she raise you alone?"

"Oh yes. As she often reminded me, it's tough to find a husband when your house is a freak show." With a groan, he heaves himself back up to a sitting position. His chunky legs dangle over the edge of the bed. "In a way, though, our poverty was a blessing in disguise. Because I was getting charity treatments at an Army hospital near Monroeville, my name got on the list of recruits for the Pioneer Project. General Hawke worked strictly with Army hospitals to keep the selection process secret." He smiles again, widening his mouth. "But look at this, we're talking about me again. Let's talk about the other Pioneers instead. You know Shannon Gibbs, correct?"

I'm a little thrown by the sudden change of subject. "Yeah, we're both from Yorktown Heights. My dad heard she had terminal brain cancer, so he told her parents about the project."

"I talked to her already, right after I got here. She's a math-and-science type too. Do you like her?"

Now I'm thrown again. Marshall is doing a good job of keeping me off balance. "Uh, yeah, I like her. She's smart, that's for sure."

"And what about Jenny Harris? Her father is quite important, you know. What do you think of her?"

I shrug. "I'm surprised she volunteered. Her parents were so opposed to the idea."

"But do you like her?"

"Come on, this is ridiculous. I don't know the first thing about her."

Marshall lets out a snort. I can't be sure, but I think this means he's amused. "Of course, how could I forget? You prefer Zia, don't you? I caught you staring at her in the auditorium." He swings his massive head, looking over his shoulder. "Zia, you have an admirer."

She finally steps away from the heart monitor. I see her gorgeous eyes again, but now they're narrowed and fierce. She glares at me, her brow furrowing. As her muscles tense, the cobra above her ear stretches a few millimeters. "I don't need any admirers. And I don't like people staring at me."

Her voice is low and menacing. I have no idea why she's so angry. With my paralyzed legs and arm, I'm not much of a threat.

"I stared at you because I was curious," I say. "You look pretty healthy, compared with the rest of us."

"You think I'd be here if I wasn't sick? Does that make sense to you?"

"Hey, chill out. I was trying to give you a compliment."

"That's another thing I don't need." She sneers at me, pressing her lips together. "I have cancer, just like the other girls. But you don't see me crying about it. I've seen worse things than cancer."

"You have to forgive Zia," Marshall interjects. "She's had a difficult past. Her parents died when she was young, and she's been in and out of foster homes ever since. Isn't that right, Zia?"

Ignoring him, she approaches my wheelchair. With her left hand she taps the cobra tattoo above her ear. "You see this tat? I got it done in Central Juvenile Hall. That's the worst detention center in LA. In all of California, probably. I was doing a six-month sentence for slashing a guy's face." She lowers her hand and pokes me in the chest. "And you know why I cut him? Because he was staring at me."

I shake my head. Her level of hostility is ridiculous. "So how did you end up here? Did General Hawke do a recruiting tour of juvenile detention centers?"

"You think that's funny?"

"No, I'm serious. I can't figure out what you're doing here. You seem completely unstable."

"*Shut up!*" Zia grabs the arms of my wheelchair and leans over me. "If anyone doesn't belong here, it's you!"

Marshall rises from the bed and comes toward us. "All right, Zia. Calm down. Please back away from your new friend Adam. I have a feeling this relationship isn't going to work out."

Zia waits a few seconds, baring her teeth and breathing on me. Then she lets go of my wheelchair and steps away in disgust. "Look at him. It's worse than I thought."

Marshall shrugs. "I don't know about that. He seems to have some spunk."

"You're dreaming, Baxley. He'll never make it." She sneers at me again, then heads for the door. "I'm out of here."

She darts out of the room, quiet as a cat. I take a deep breath as she disappears down the corridor. To be honest, I was a little worried when she grabbed my wheelchair. For a second I really thought she would smack me.

She left the door open, so Marshall closes it. "My apologies, Adam. That didn't go so well, did it?"

"Yeah, no kidding. What's her problem? She acts like a gangster."

"As a matter of fact, she did belong to a gang in Los Angeles. The Twelfth Street Bloods, she told me."

"Great, that's just great. How did Hawke find her?"

"She said her father was a captain in the Army, serving under Hawke. After her father died, the general kept in touch with her. He must've recommended her for the project when he learned she had cancer."

"And now we have a psycho on our team."

"That's a strong word, Adam. I wouldn't go that far. But it's true that Zia has some trouble controlling her feelings. And right now she's feeling a little negative about you."

"Why? Because I stared at her in the auditorium?"

"No, because you're first in line for the procedure. And she thinks *she* should be first."

I feel a surge of irritation. "You're joking, right? Does it really make a difference who goes first?"

"Actually it does." Marshall steps closer to my wheelchair. "You see, Zia and I have been talking about what will happen if the first attempt isn't a success. The procedure didn't work for the adult volunteers, and it may not work for all of us either. General Hawke said you need a strong, resilient personality to successfully transfer your mind to the electronic circuits."

Standing beside my wheelchair, Marshall looks straight down at me. I can't interpret the expression on his face, but I can read his body language, and it's a little threatening. I return his stare. "Yeah, I remember Hawke said something like that."

"What Hawke didn't say was what he'd do if the first attempt fails. I realize that the Army has spent a great deal of money on this project, and Hawke doesn't seem like the kind of man who gives up easily. But if the first try is unsuccessful, he may reconsider the whole experiment. He wouldn't want to continue killing children if he can't save their minds. That's why we're concerned about you. If you fail, the rest of us may not even get a chance. The Army will send us back home and we'll die in our beds."

Marshall's head looms over me like one of those big African masks carved in dark wood. I know what he wants to say next, and I don't like it one bit. "So you and Zia are worried that I'm not strong enough to make it?"

"I'll be honest with you, Adam. Zia believes your father was playing favorites when he put you first in line. So we decided to pay you a visit to find out if we were in trouble or not. It was a bit of a test, if you know what I mean."

I know exactly what he means. They were studying me. They came to my room to see how tough I am. I'm angry and hurt, but mostly I'm disappointed. I thought I could make some new friends among the Pioneers, but Zia is a bully and Marshall is a weasel.

My chest aches from talking for so long, but I'm determined not to show any weakness. I raise my right hand and point at Marshall. "Well, I have a message for you and Zia. I'm stronger than both of you." I shift my hand, pointing at the door. "Now get out of my room."

Marshall stands there for a few seconds, staring. Then he reaches into the pocket of his jeans. "Yes, I had a feeling you might get upset. It's understandable. We've been somewhat deceptive." He pulls a folded sheet of paper out of his pocket. "So I thought ahead and prepared a peace offering, a little gift to make amends for my doubts about you. It's a poem written by Joseph Merrick, the original Elephant Man. He adapted it from an old hymn and put it at the end of all his letters. But here's the strange thing: when I read the poem now, I think of the Pioneer Project." He unfolds the paper, drops it in my lap, and steps toward the door. "Good-bye, Adam. And good luck tomorrow."

I wait until the door closes and I can no longer hear Marshall's footsteps in the corridor. Then I pick up the paper and read the poem.

'Tis true my form is something odd,
But blaming me is blaming God;

Could I create myself anew,
I would not fail in pleasing you.
If I could reach from pole to pole
Or grasp the ocean with a span,
I would be measured by the soul;
The mind's the standard of the man.

゠゠ ゠゠ ゠゠

Dad returns to my room ten minutes later. He apologizes for the delay—General Hawke had some last-minute questions—then tells me everything I need to know about tomorrow's procedure.

His voice is calm and patient. He warns me that I can't be sedated. If the doctors give me sedatives to put me to sleep, the drugs would alter my brain chemistry and distort the copying of my memories. So I have to stay awake during the injection of the nanoprobes and the period afterward when the probes are spreading through my brain tissue. But Dad reassures me that I won't feel any pain, not even when the scanner blasts its radiation into my head. The brain, unlike most organs in the body, has no pain receptors. Although it's impossible to predict exactly what I'll feel as the scanner records the patterns of my mind, at least I won't be in agony.

As Dad describes what will happen to me, he takes off my clothes and prepares me for bed. He's done this so many times before that it's almost automatic. His hands seem to move of their own accord, unzipping and unbuttoning. For years I've been embarrassed by the intimacy of this ritual, but now I know this is the last time Dad will put me to bed and I realize there's something comforting about it. My fears subside and my eyes start to close as he wipes and washes and diapers me.

I'm nearly asleep by the time he lays me down on the stiff mattress of the hospital bed. Struggling to keep my eyes open, I look up at him. "Dad? Why did you put me first?"

"What?"

"For the procedure. The first Pioneer."

He grabs a folded blanket from the foot of the bed. It's a gray, wool Army blanket. "Because I knew you could handle it. The other volunteers will probably be fine too, but I can't be certain about them. I don't know them as well as I know you."

"So you think I'm strong enough?"

"Of course. Adam, you're the strongest person I know."

With a snap of his wrists, he shakes out the blanket. It billows over the bed, then gently settles on top of me.

CHAPTER

9

THE NEXT MORNING DAD DRESSES ME IN A GREEN HOSPITAL GOWN. THEN THE ARMY
doctors come into my room and move me from the bed to a gurney.

I feel somewhat detached as they wheel me down the corridors
of Pioneer Base. It's as if all of this is happening to someone else, a
stranger with a shaved head. This feeling of detachment is helpful—it
keeps me calm and unafraid. But then we enter the operating room
and I see the scanning machine. It's big and white and shaped like
a giant doughnut with a three-foot-wide hole at its center. A long,
stretcher-like table extends from the central hole of the scanner, and
on the table is something that looks like a steel cage. I start trembling
when I see the cage, which is about the size of a bread box. They're
going to put my head in that thing.

Dad notices my reaction. He strides to the table and rests his hand
on the cage. "This is called a stereotactic frame," he says. "It'll keep
your head steady so we can inject the nanoprobes in the right places.
To make sure you're comfortable, the doctors will put some local

anesthetic at the points where the frame is secured to your head." He returns to the gurney and touches my temples. "Don't worry. The anesthetic is like Novocaine, the stuff you get at the dentist's. It just makes the skin numb. The doctors will also put some on the injection sites."

This is a strategy Dad's used on me before. He overcomes my fears by lecturing me to death. While the Army doctors carry me to the table and strap me down, Dad tells me more details about the procedure. He describes how the nanoprobes will spread through my brain tissue until each cell is studded with tiny gold spheres. Then he points at the scanner and shows how the X-ray tubes on the rim of the central hole will fire pulses of radiation at my head.

He explains what will happen to the nanoprobes when they absorb the radiation, how the gold spheres will flash like microscopic X-ray beacons. Then he turns back to the scanner and points at the hundreds of X-ray cameras that line the rim. These cameras will detect the flashes of radiation inside my head and calculate the positions of the nanoprobes, creating a detailed, three-dimensional map of my brain.

His strategy works, at least partially. Dad's lecture distracts me from the doctors while they anesthetize my scalp. I realize of course that he's leaving something out. He doesn't describe how the high-energy X-rays will rip through my brain cells, bursting their membranes and shattering their DNA. But I stay calm until my head is locked into the stereotactic frame and the doctors position their bone drills next to the injection sites.

Dad leans over me and slips a pair of headphones over my ears. "You need something to drown out the noise of the drills." He shows me an iPod that's connected to the headphones. "I downloaded some of the songs you like."

He turns on the iPod and a moment later I hear Kanye West rapping the first words of "Power." I always get a rush from this song because it has so much energy, because it makes me feel like a hero instead of a crippled, dying kid. But now the music can't mask the rattling in my skull as the doctors turn on their drills.

It's horrifying. I don't feel any pain, but I know the drill bits are cutting into the bone. I squeeze my eyes shut and start counting in my head: *one, two, three, four, five.* Someone dabs a sponge around my ears to sop up the blood that's trickling from the holes. *Six, seven, eight, nine, ten.* I want to scream, "Stop!" but I can't even breathe. *I can't do this, Dad! I'm not strong enough!*

Then the drilling stops and all I can hear is Kanye, who's rapping a different song now. I open my mouth and take a couple of painful breaths, but I keep my eyes closed. Behind Kanye's voice I hear something click into place, then the sound of a pump and rushing fluid. The nanoprobes are flowing into my brain. Sweat streams down my face and neck.

Kanye moves on to a third song before someone removes the headphones, cutting off the rap in midsentence. I open my eyes and see Dad's face through the steel bars of the stereotactic frame. "Okay, we finished injecting the nanoprobes," he says. "You did great, Adam."

I lick my lips. My mouth is so dry. "How long…till I'm ready…for the…" My voice trails off. I'm too frightened to say the words.

Dad nods. "It'll take some time for the nanoprobes to spread through the tissue. About fifteen minutes. While you're waiting, I thought you'd appreciate some company."

He steps aside and Shannon Gibbs approaches the table. At first I'm ashamed—I don't want her seeing me like this, so scared and helpless. But then she smiles her lopsided, nerve-damaged smile, and I'm glad she's here.

"Hey, handsome," she says. "You look good without the hair."

I smile back at her, feeling ridiculous. I wish my head wasn't in this freaking cage. "I got…the idea from you," I say. "You don't need hair…to look beautiful."

She cocks her bald head, clearly pleased at the compliment. "Flatter me while you can, my friend. The next time we meet, we'll both be hunks of metal. Ugly, hulking Pioneers."

"But you'll still be beautiful…on the inside." I'm surprised I can rattle off these compliments so easily. Maybe it's just a side effect of all the fear, but talking with Shannon seems effortless. "Remember that clay model…you made for your biology report? The model of the brain?"

"Sure, I still have it. It's back home in my closet."

"I'm picturing my brain like that…but with trillions of nanoprobes. Gold spheres sprinkled…on every inch. Sounds pretty, doesn't it?"

She nods and leans over the table, bending closer to me. "And remember *your* report on the brain? About the limbic system, where all our emotions come from?" She points at my head. "Now the gold spheres are in there too, sticking to every cell."

"That's good. I want to keep…the emotions I'm feeling now."

"And when it's my turn, I want to keep those feelings too." Her voice is just a whisper, but it's full of promise. Shannon is implying that she has feelings for me. And maybe those feelings will survive the transfer and be reborn in the hunk of metal she's going to become.

But then I think of what my mother said back in my bedroom in Yorktown Heights. Will it actually be Shannon inside the circuits of her Pioneer? And will it actually be *me* inside mine?

I want to ask her about this, but I don't want Dad to hear. I can't turn my head inside the frame, so I strain my eyes to the left and right. I don't see him anywhere.

"Shannon," I whisper. "Do you really think it's possible?"

"What's possible?"

"The thing inside the Pioneer. Will it be me or just a copy?"

She bends over a little more. She comes so close I can see my reflection in her eyes. The bars of the stereotactic frame glint in her brown irises. "I remember something else from biology class," she says. "It was on the very first page of the textbook. The cells in our bodies are always changing. Old cells die and new ones are born every second, right?"

"Yeah, that's true of blood cells and skin cells. But the cells in the brain are longer-lasting. They can live for—"

Shannon shakes her head, cutting me off. "But even those cells are constantly rebuilding themselves. They take in nutrients. They throw out waste. The body I'm in now has a completely different set of molecules than the body I had six months ago."

"Okay, you're right. All the molecules are new, but the body's pattern stays the same."

She clasps my right hand, which is strapped to the table. "Then it's simple, isn't it? We're all copies."

"I don't—"

"My present self is a copy of my past self. My body copied its pattern onto a new set of molecules. And my future self will be a copy of my present. So why should it matter if the copy's in a body or a machine?"

I think it over, analyzing Shannon's argument. Maybe there's a flaw in her reasoning, but right now I can't see it. Of course, it's just a theory, and as every scientist knows, you'd need to conduct an experiment to prove it right or wrong. But as far as theories go, it seems pretty darn solid.

In my heart, the balance tips from doubt to hope. Although I still don't know if I'll survive the procedure, at least I have something to fight for.

Shannon squeezes my hand. She doesn't say anything else, and neither do I. We just stare at each other. I make a conscious effort to memorize her face, in all its beautiful imperfection. I picture my brain cells stretching their branches toward one another, forging new connections that will represent the image of Shannon's smile, that lovely, lopsided curve. And I picture the swarm of nanoprobes attaching to the new links, coating them in golden armor to preserve the memory for eternity.

Finally, Dad steps forward. He rests one hand on Shannon's shoulder and the other on mine. "It's time to begin the scan. Are you ready, Adam?"

I don't need to memorize Dad's face—it's already engraved in my memory—but I stare at it anyway. His eyes are glassy and his cheeks are wet. It's another good thing to remember.

"Yes," I say. "I'm ready."

THE BRAIN HAS NO PAIN RECEPTORS, BUT THAT DOESN'T MEAN IT CAN'T FEEL PAIN.

First, there's a flash of light. Like a camera flash inside my head, but a thousand times brighter. The whole world disappears, submerged in that horrible flood of white light. My last breath is caught in my throat.

It's not like going to sleep. There's nothing peaceful about it. The body doesn't want to die. Billions of cells convulse as the waves of radiation crash down on them.

I'm suffocating. The light is all around me. I'm drowning in the middle of a vast, white ocean.

HELP! SOMEONE HELP ME!

Nothing. I'm alone. The pain is infinite.

Then something stirs within the sea of light. The waves form a shape in the whiteness. It's a face, the face of an old man with a beard. It's God, I think. No, on second thought, he looks more like Santa Claus. His beard is long and white, but as I stare at the thing,

I see specks of color in it. Tiny gold spheres are sprinkled among the white bristles.

Who are you? Are you God?

The old man says nothing. He's in a workshop of some kind, maybe Santa's workshop, and he's looking down at something on the bench in front of him. It's a toy, a doll, a life-size mannequin. He opens a lid on the mannequin's head and pours a handful of gold spheres inside. Then he moves down the bench and opens the head of the next mannequin. Except they're not really mannequins. They're corpses.

He's copying their memories. So he can take their souls to heaven.

No, it's not God. It's a hallucination, my brain's final thought. The old man and the corpses dissolve into the whiteness. Then the whiteness itself disappears. Then—

CHAPTER

11

WHOA. WHERE AM I?

Okay, let me think. I'm using words. I'm putting them together in a logical order. I can use words to describe whatever I'm experiencing.

That's good, real good. I'm making progress.

But what am I experiencing? And who am I?

Okay, I need more information. And look at this, there's a ton of data in my memory. Hundreds of millions of gigabytes. All I need to do is retrieve the data.

Here goes.

ᴛ ᴛ ᴛ

I retrieve an image. It's similar in shape to twelve thousand other images that are grouped in my memory under the category "Faces." The name linked to this image is "Dad."

It's a picture of a person, a human being. The image is a recent addition to my memory. According to my internal clock, it was recorded less than an hour ago. A closer analysis indicates that the person in the picture is crying.

I scroll through all the images that carry the label "Dad." There are 657. The oldest images are blurry, indistinct portraits of a younger-looking man, tall and well-built and smiling. His full name is Thomas Armstrong. The images are linked to memory files holding information on computer science and artificial intelligence.

They're also linked to another name: Adam Armstrong. This name has more links than anything else in my memory. It's connected to hundreds of thousands of files. But when I search for images of Adam, I notice something curious. In nearly every picture he's surrounded by the frame of a mirror. In the older images he's a pre-teenage boy, skinny and pale, but in the newer pictures he stares at his reflection while strapped into a motorized wheelchair. These later images are linked to information on Duchenne muscular dystrophy—symptoms, visits to the hospital, daily struggles with the illness. And as I scroll through these memories, I come across a link to a recent file labeled "Pioneer Project."

I retrieve the file and read it. I complete this task in less than a thousandth of a second, and then a new thought races through my circuits, an astounding revelation: *I'm Adam Armstrong! I'm still alive!*

At the same moment, my system freezes. I can't open any files, can't access any data. The revelation of my identity has somehow triggered a new instruction, which is being sent to every one of my circuits: *Breathe!* But I can't carry out this command. It's not included in my list of normal functions. I can't halt the instruction, and the commands are coming in faster than I can delete them: *Breathe! Breathe! BREATHE!*

In less than a second my system repeats the instruction 55 billion times and I receive 55 billion error messages. The flood of data rushes through me, overloading my circuits. It feels like I'm choking. I'm unbearably full, bursting with useless signals. To make room for the unending stream of commands and error messages, the system begins to erase my memory. A hundred files are deleted. Then a thousand. Then ten thousand.

Stop!

I'm Adam Armstrong!

I want to live!

Nothing's working. It's getting difficult to think. Amid the jumbled commands, my system can only generate an urgent noise of random data. I recognize this condition, this paralyzed state of mind, because I've experienced it before. When I was in a human body, I called it fear. I'm horribly, frantically, desperately afraid.

I have to fight it. I delete the random data and search for a solution. So many files, and I can't open any of them! But I can sort them by date, and when I do this I notice that a new file has been added to my memory in the past fifteen seconds. It's a text file, transmitted wirelessly to my circuits from another computer, and it has a special coding: Emergency Transmission. This coding gives the file priority over everything else in my memory.

I try to open the file. Nothing happens. The file doesn't open, but I don't get an error message either. My system is locked in a hugely complex calculation, with billions of circuits engaged in the task of determining whether to open the text file. The delay goes on for five seconds, ten seconds. In the meantime, the breathe command repeats another 500 billion times, forcing my system to erase thousands of gigabytes from my memory. *What's left? Is anything left? Am I still*

Adam Armstrong? The urgent noise of fear surges through me again, paralyzing all thought. *Help! Stop! No!*

Then the file opens. It contains a brief message, only eleven words long: **Adam, this is Dad. Turn on your sensors and speech synthesizer.**

I go to my control options and turn on the visual and audio sensors. On the visual feed I see five people of various heights and ages, all dressed in U.S. Army uniforms. Four of them sit behind computer terminals about ten feet away, but the fifth is standing much closer. His face is less than two feet from the lens of my video camera, which is embedded in the turret of the Pioneer robot. I recognize him instantly—it's Dad, Thomas Armstrong, my father.

The sight of him is literally electrifying. My circuits hum with renewed energy, drowning out the fear. His lips are moving, and after I take a moment to calibrate my audio feed, I can understand what he's saying.

"Adam, can you hear me? If you can, say something."

I turn on my speech synthesizer and scream, "*I can't breathe!*"

Dad covers his ears. So do all the soldiers behind the computer terminals. "*Too loud!*" Dad yells, wincing. "Adjust the sound levels on your speakers!"

"*I can't breathe! I can't breathe!*"

"It's all right. Calm down. You don't need to breathe, Adam. You don't need oxygen anymore."

"No! I have to breathe! The commands won't stop!"

Dad stares at my camera lens for another two-and-a-half seconds. Then his mouth opens and his eyes widen. I have enough memory left to know what this means—it's an expression of alarm. He rushes to the nearest computer terminal.

"My God! The scanner copied the brain-cell patterns that control breathing!" Leaning over the terminal, he types something on the keyboard. "I'm sending you another emergency transmission. It'll delete the breathing instruction from your system."

The wait for the transmission seems interminable, but as soon as it arrives, the breathe commands cease. Dizzy with relief, I start erasing the enormous backlog of error messages. When I'm finished, I scan my memory to see how much I've lost. Luckily, I'm able to retrieve more than half of the deleted information. But about five percent of my memory files are gone, irrecoverable. I'm still Adam Armstrong, but now something's missing. *What did I lose?*

Dad steps away from the terminal and comes back to the Pioneer. "Did it work?" he asks, looking into my camera lens again. "Are you okay?"

I don't know how to answer. I no longer feel the compulsion to breathe, but its absence is disorienting. As I observe my father through the visual sensors, I have the sensation of being underwater. I feel like I'm at the bottom of the ocean, viewing Dad through the porthole of my camera.

"You fixed the problem," I report. "But I still don't feel right."

"I'm so sorry, Adam. I should've anticipated this." Dad moves closer. The lens of my camera is several inches above his eyes, so he has to tilt his head back to look at it directly. "Can you tell me more specifically what you're experiencing right now?"

I shake my head. Or rather, I turn my turret, first clockwise, then counterclockwise. I didn't plan to do this. It just happens. My camera automatically pivots to keep Dad in view. "I can't describe it. It's sort of like being nauseous. But I don't have a stomach anymore, so how could I be nauseous?"

Dad raises his hand to his chin and taps his index finger against his lips. In my memory I have seventeen images of him making this gesture. He does it whenever he's deep in thought. "The sensations you're feeling might be related to other brain functions that were copied by the scanner. You're still going to feel hunger and thirst, even though you don't need food or water. We may have to delete those instructions as well." He steps away from me and returns to his computer terminal. "I need to analyze our options. Give me a minute."

He leans over the keyboard and starts typing. I'm doubtful, though, that his efforts will make me feel any better. What I'm experiencing now is a terrible sense of unease, which is much more disturbing than ordinary hunger or thirst.

While waiting for Dad, I turn my turret again to survey the room. It's a laboratory full of workbenches and steel cabinets. I'm able to rotate the turret all the way around—another disorienting feat, impossible for a human body to perform—and when I look at the other end of the room I see two more soldiers guarding the door. Each holds an assault rifle, and both men are eyeing my turret as it swivels atop my cylindrical torso.

I discover that I can switch my visual sensors to the infrared frequency range, enabling my camera to detect the temperature of the objects it's observing. The sensors are so precise that I can measure the heart rates of the soldiers from the slight changes in their skin temperature. Both men are sweating, and their pulses are fast. Although their faces are expressionless, I can tell they're afraid of me.

My sense of unease deepens. I feel a new compulsion, an overwhelming desire to see what the soldiers are seeing, to view the Pioneer robot. Unfortunately, the camera in my turret isn't optimized for self-observation. Although I can point the lens downward at the floor and see the oval footpads at the ends of my steel legs, I can't get a good view of my torso. It's frustrating. I scan the whole room, hoping to find a mirror, but there's nothing of the sort. Everything in the lab is cold and metallic and strictly functional. As my turret turns faster, the heart rates of the soldiers quicken and they grip their rifles a little more tightly.

Then I glimpse something to the left of the soldiers, a glint of reflected light on the door of a steel cabinet. I zoom in on it as much as my camera will allow. It's my own reflection, an image created by the beams from the overhead spotlights bouncing off my robotic body. The patch of light on the cabinet is small and fuzzy, but my visual sensors are able to correct the distorted reflection and show me what I look like.

My torso is dull gray, a dirty industrial color, with no markings except a big white 1 stamped on the curved steel. My legs are sturdy pylons supporting my weight, and my arms are retractable, multi-jointed shafts with intricate, handlike grippers at their ends. I have no head, just the revolving turret, which is studded with antennas and sensor arrays. All in all, I look like an oversized artillery shell, something meant to be shot out of a giant cannon.

Look at me. I can't be Adam Armstrong.

Now I know why the soldiers are afraid. I'm not a person anymore. They've turned me into a weapon.

I have to get out of here! I have to go right now!

In less than a millisecond I find my motor circuits, the ones that control locomotion. I send the appropriate instructions to the motors in my legs, which shift my weight to the right. Then I lift my left footpad and take my first step. The steel makes a satisfying clang as it comes down on the linoleum.

Dad's head pops up from his keyboard. "Adam! What are you doing?"

I shift my weight to the left and take my second step. *This is easy.*

"Adam, stop!" Dad leaves the computer terminal behind and rushes toward me. "You're not ready to walk yet. We have to run some tests first!"

I turn my turret away from him. I know I shouldn't blame him. He did everything he could to prepare me. But I'm still angry. I want to punch something.

After three more steps I'm in front of the door. The soldiers raise their assault rifles and slowly back off, one to my left and the other to my right. They're pointing their guns at my torso, which is a mistake. I have two-inch-thick armor plating around my midsection to protect my batteries and neuromorphic circuits. The soldiers would be better off aiming at the sensors in my turret. I'm surprised no one told them this.

"No!" Dad yells at the soldiers. "Don't shoot! You're not authorized to shoot!"

The greatest danger, I realize, is a ricochet. If these idiots fire at me, the bullets will bounce off my armor, and the ricocheting slugs might hit one of the soldiers, or maybe Dad. I have to do something quick. I send simultaneous commands to both my arms, which telescope to their full length of six feet in a hundredth of a second. Before the soldiers can react, I grasp the barrels of their rifles in my mechanical hands and pull the guns away from them. Then I squeeze my steel fingers together and crush the gun barrels. They crumple like cardboard in my hands.

Whoa. That's pretty cool.

The soldiers retreat to the other side of the lab, their hearts pounding.

At the same time, I drop the rifles and hold my arms straight in front of me, as if measuring the distance to the door. I clench my mechanical hands into fists, then thrust them forward like battering rams. The door buckles on impact and falls off its broken hinges.

Yes! This feels good!

I step into an anteroom crowded with higher-ranking soldiers. They're facing a large video screen that shows the lab I just left. Until a moment ago, evidently, they were observing the progress of Dad's experiment, but now all the captains and majors and colonels are stumbling over each other as they back away from me. Their faces glow brightly, hot with fear.

Looking past them, I see a second door standing open, revealing the corridor beyond. I turn toward it, but before I can take another clanging step, one of the soldiers strides forward and positions himself between me and the exit. It's General Hawke. His face is stern and his heartbeat is steady.

"Armstrong!" he shouts, pointing at the broken door behind me. "Get back in the lab!"

I feel an urge to laugh, but my speech synthesizer doesn't recognize this command, so no sound comes out of my speakers. Hawke is unarmed, and I outweigh him by about five hundred pounds. Still, he takes a step toward me, coming within three feet of my torso.

"*Now*, Armstrong!" He points at the camera on my turret. "You signed an agreement, remember? You're a soldier now, like everyone else here. And that means you have to follow my orders."

Again, I want to laugh. What's Hawke going to do, court-martial me? Slap a pair of handcuffs on my steel wrists and put me on trial? I'd love to see him argue his case in front of a judge. *Yes, your Honor, we killed the defendant, and now his mind belongs to the Army.*

I'm just about to extend my arms and shove Hawke out of the way when my father comes to the general's side. Dad's pulse is racing. "Listen to the general, Adam! Your systems still need calibration. You'll damage your circuitry if you run off like this!"

I focus on Dad's anxious face, comparing it with the 657 images of him in my memory. I want to say I still love him, but how can I be sure? Maybe love is in one of the files I lost. Maybe I have nothing but anger now. I turn my turret away from him and point my camera at General Hawke. I adjust the sound level of my speakers, raising the volume high enough to make the walls rattle. "WHERE IS IT?"

Hawke doesn't flinch. "Where's what?"

"YOU KNOW WHAT I'M TALKING ABOUT! WHERE IS IT?"

He says nothing, but I detect a slight pause in his heartbeat, and at the same moment his eyes flick to the left. Now I know where to go. In one swift motion, I sidestep General Hawke and my father. Then I march through the doorway and go down the corridor, heading in the direction that Hawke indicated. Dad yells, "Adam!" but I ignore him.

After five seconds the video feed from my camera matches a set of images in my memory. I'm striding down the same corridor I saw forty-three minutes ago when the Army doctors pushed me on the gurney toward the operating room. I made no special effort at the time to memorize the layout of this level of Pioneer Base, but now I have total recall of everything I saw just before the procedure. I can view every twist and turn of the corridor in my memory, and I can use this mental map to guide me to my destination.

My acoustic sensors pick up the sound of distant footsteps—more soldiers are coming to intercept me—so I increase my velocity. The corridor echoes with the *clang-clang-clang* of my footpads.

After another ten seconds I reach the operating room. The door is locked shut, but I smash it open. I stop short when I see the scanner again—the image triggers a rush of fear in my circuits—but I force myself to approach the stretcherlike table that extends from the scanner's wide, central hole. Then I point my camera downward and stare at the corpse of Adam Armstrong.

I try to keep my feelings at bay by concentrating on the physical details. The corpse's head is still locked in the stereotactic frame, carefully positioned within the scanner's hole. Although the face matches the images of Adam Armstrong in my memory, what I notice now are the differences. The skin is yellowish, the color of old newspaper. The mouth is open and the lips are dry and cracked. The eyes are open too, but the eyeballs are coated with a jellylike film.

Despite my best efforts, I get angry again. They were in such a rush to transfer my mind that they just left my body here! As if it was worthless! I suppose they would've eventually come back for the corpse and given it a proper burial, but the abandonment still seems wrong. This body isn't worthless. Until an hour ago, it was *me*.

I stretch my arms toward the corpse, intending to pick it up. At the same time, I turn on the tactile sensors that are embedded in the tips of my steel fingers. These sensors measure temperature, pressure, and moisture to determine the best grip for holding an object. But instead of grasping the body, I extend my right hand and lightly touch its face. My fingertips brush its cheek, which is cold and dry. Then I shift the mechanical hand a few inches and sweep it over the eyelids, closing them. As I do this, the anger fades from my circuits. I feel only a sense of emptiness. I've lost the best part of me. I've lost it forever.

It seems like I stand there beside my corpse for ages, but in reality I'm alone in the room for only thirteen seconds. A dozen soldiers come running through the doorway and take positions around me.

Some are armed with rifles, others with pistols. A moment later, my dad follows them into the room and heads straight for me, ignoring all the soldiers and their guns. He doesn't order me to go back to the lab. He doesn't say a word. He simply rests one hand on the body of his son and the other on my torso.

I pivot my camera toward him. He's crying again. He wanted to save me, but now he's not sure if he did the right thing. I'm not sure either. But I know one thing for certain: I still love my father. The emotion floods my circuits. I love him no matter what he's done to me.

I point a steel finger at my corpse but keep my camera trained on Dad. "Can we save some of my DNA?" I ask. "Just in case…I mean…"

Dad nods. "Of course. Just in case."

I've been a machine for less than fifteen minutes, but already I want to be human again.

PART
TWO:

THE SIX

From: General Calvin Hawke

Commander, Pioneer Base

To: The National Security Adviser

The White House, Washington, DC

Subject: The Pioneer Project

Classification: TOP SECRET, For Your Eyes Only

First of all, please excuse the unusual security rules I've established for all communications to and from Pioneer Base. We can't allow electronic messages of any kind. I've ordered Colonel Peterson to deliver this memo to you personally. If you wish to reply, you must write the message by hand or by typewriter (as I'm doing now) and give it to Peterson, who will carry it back to Colorado.

Let me explain the reason for these rules. From the start we've assumed that any hostile AI will be able to access all of the U.S. government's computer networks, no matter how high their security levels. When we selected the site for Pioneer Base we created a cover story to hide the true purpose of the facility. In the Department of Defense's classified records, our base is identified as Camp Vigilance, a secret maximum-security prison for terrorists.

During the construction phase we built several aboveground barracks and guardhouses to mask the presence of the underground complex and make the site look like a prison camp. If Sigma gains access to satellite photos of southwestern Colorado—as we assume it will, now that the AI controls its own surveillance satellites—our hope is that the AI will notice these structures and believe our cover story. But we can't count on fooling Sigma for very long. The AI knows that the Pioneer Project exists, and for reasons I'll explain in a moment, it will place a high priority on finding our base.

I've reviewed the latest reports from Russia, which were delivered to me yesterday. The most disturbing items are the new satellite photos of Tatishchevo Missile Base. It looks like Sigma is upgrading the unmanned T-90 tanks that it operates by remote control. The driverless tanks are shuttling between the defenses at the base's perimeter and the automated manufacturing plant next to the headquarters building. Sigma is probably using the robotic arms and other equipment at the manufacturing plant to make improvements to the tanks. I have to confess, I'm a little mystified by this activity, but the AI is clearly preparing itself for SOMETHING.

I'm aware that the President's advisers are debating whether to support the Russian plan to attack the laboratory at Tatishchevo and destroy the computers that Sigma is occupying. Before you make a decision, I urge you to read the report written by our chief scientist, Tom Armstrong. I've enclosed a copy of the report with this memo, but I want to emphasize its main points.

As Armstrong notes, Sigma is programmed to predict its opponents' actions and maximize its chances of success. For Sigma, the most successful outcome would be eliminating the human species while preserving our factories and supercomputers, which the AI can use for its own purposes. Therefore, instead of launching the SS-27 nuclear missiles, it simply threatened to launch them. This is a clever tactic. If we don't attack Tatishchevo, Sigma will use the time to develop a better way

to exterminate us, one that doesn't destroy so much valu-
able machinery.

If we do attack, the AI will accept its second-best outcome
and obliterate our biggest cities. But Sigma would've never
given us this choice in the first place if there was even a
remote chance that we could surprise the AI and destroy its
computers before it could launch the missiles. Sigma knows the
capabilities of our weapons better than we do. I wouldn't bet
against it.

To defeat Sigma, according to Armstrong, we have to consider
how it was created. The AI emerged as the sole survivor of an
experiment in which various advanced programs were forced to
compete against one another. This process shaped Sigma's programming. The AI's unwavering goal, its reason for being, is
to confront and overpower all rival intelligences. Now Sigma
sees itself engaged in another competition, battling against
humans for control of the planet.

But what's the first thing Sigma did after escaping from
the Unicorp lab and going to Tatishchevo Missile Base? It
transferred itself to the base's artificial-intelligence lab
and deleted all the other AIs stored there. And even before
then, Sigma targeted the Pioneer Project by trying to kill
Armstrong's son, Adam, who was slated to become the first
Pioneer. Sigma clearly doesn't view human intelligence as its
most serious competitor; it's more concerned about rival AIs
and potential human-machine hybrids.

Sigma is threatened by the Pioneers because they're unknown
and unpredictable. The AI can't calculate its chances against
them. That's why we believe Sigma will make an all-out effort

to find Pioneer Base. The Pioneers are our best hope for defeating the AI, and Sigma knows it.

Unfortunately, our progress here has been slow. Although the transfer of Adam Armstrong's intelligence was successful, in the three days since then, Adam has been uncooperative. I've encouraged him to connect to the computers at Pioneer Base and download their databases and take other steps to explore his new capabilities, but so far he's refused to listen. I've tried to explain the urgency of our efforts, how the fate of the human race may depend on his ability to adjust to his new status, but he remains unwilling.

In short, he's acting like a stubborn, sullen teenager. If I were his commander in an ordinary Army unit, I'd make him scrub the latrines with a toothbrush, but I can't give that kind of order to an insubordinate eight-hundred-pound robot. So now I'm focusing my energy on the young woman who will become the second Pioneer, Jennifer Harris. She's scheduled to undergo the scanning procedure later this afternoon.

I originally chose Zia Allawi to be the second Pioneer, but Sumner Harris—Jennifer's father—presented me with a note from the President urging me to reconsider. I know Sumner is one of the President's best friends (and biggest financial supporters), but the man is also a tremendous pain in the rear end. First he yells at me for proposing to kill his daughter, then he complains when I don't put her first in line for the procedure.

I'd be eternally grateful if you took the President aside and asked him to send another note to Pioneer Base. This note should be addressed to Sumner, and it should tell the arrogant idiot to get out of my face. I don't need this aggravation right now.

Other than that, life is just peachy. Give my love to everyone in the Oval Office.

I'M INSIDE WHAT I LIKE TO CALL MY BEDROOM, EVEN THOUGH IT HAS NO BED. AT first Dad wanted me to stay in the laboratory all the time so he could observe my progress, but I told him I needed my own space. So he found a large room—exactly twenty-four feet by nineteen-and-a-half feet, according to my sensors—that was on the same floor as the lab and had all the necessary power and communication hookups.

The room is practically empty because I have no use for furniture. I don't need a bureau because I don't wear clothes anymore. I don't need a table either because I don't eat or drink. (Dad deleted the hunger and thirst commands from my circuits, but I still feel nauseous sometimes.) What the room lacks in furniture, though, it makes up for in decorations. An Army courier went to our home in Yorktown Heights, collected the contents of my old bedroom, and brought everything to Pioneer Base.

Now my old Super Bowl posters hang on the walls of my new room, including the poster with the photo of me and Ryan, and the one with my pencil drawings of Brittany. My comics are stacked on a long shelf nailed to the wall, and another shelf holds my Star Wars chess set and my official Super Bowl XLVI football. Although the floor is bare, the walls are full of memories. They give me something to look at while I pace back and forth.

That's been my main activity since I became a Pioneer: pacing across my bedroom. I walk twenty feet in one direction, then spin my turret one hundred eighty degrees and walk back the way I came. Over the past three days I've performed this maneuver thousands of times, pacing for hours on end. When my power runs low, I go to the corner of the room and plug the electrical cables into the port in my torso. It takes six-and-a-half minutes to recharge my batteries. The process is neither painful nor satisfying.

While I'm recharging I have to stand next to another Pioneer robot—a lifeless one, with no intelligence in its circuits. This robot has "1A" stamped on its torso, in the same place where I have my "1," but otherwise it looks just like mine. General Hawke put it in my room because he wants me to practice transferring my intelligence from one robot to another. He says learning how to do this will help me adjust to my "new status."

Each Pioneer is equipped with a high-speed wireless data link that can transfer everything in its memory to another robot in less than a minute. Hawke has ordered me to practice this transfer at least thirty times a day. But I have no intention of obeying this order. I already transferred my mind once, when my body died, and that was more than enough. So while my batteries are recharging I turn my turret away from the motionless robot in the corner, my mindless evil twin. I don't like looking at the thing. It reminds me of what I've become.

Once I'm fully charged, I detach the cables and go back to pacing.

At first, I admit, it was thrilling just to walk again. After I figured out how to coordinate the motors in my steel legs, I started practicing my footwork. I learned how to jump, sidestep, and reverse course. It was a big, big improvement over my wheelchair. I became so enthused during one practice session in my bedroom that I reached out with one of my telescoping arms and grabbed the official Super Bowl football off the shelf. For a moment I fantasized that I was back in Yorktown Heights, standing on the football field behind the high school.

In a hundredth of a second my circuits retrieved all my memories of those games. I could see, simultaneously, every football game I'd watched at the Yorktown field, every remembered sight from all those mud-splattered showdowns, right down to the grimace on Ryan Boyd's face as he dashed toward the end zone. It was like the virtual-reality program I'd written, but a thousand times more vivid. And like the VR program, it was ultimately disappointing. When I tried to reenact one of Ryan's plays, running with the ball across my empty bedroom, I felt nothing in my legs, neither fatigue nor joy. They just moved numbly beneath me.

I tried talking to Dad about it. I asked him if it was possible to put tactile sensors in my legs so I could feel my joints flexing and my footpads hitting the floor. He said yes, it was definitely possible, but right now we had other priorities. He said I shouldn't get too attached to my Pioneer robot because it was only meant to be a transitional platform, a temporary home for my mind. To fully explore my new abilities, he said, I needed to occupy all kinds of machines.

I told Dad he sounded just like General Hawke, and he replied that Hawke was right. The future of humanity depended on communicating with Sigma, Dad said, and I had to prepare myself for this challenge. Before I could interact with the AI, I needed to understand how it thinks and makes decisions. In other words, I had to become more like an AI myself. That's why it was so vital to practice transferring my intelligence and to download the databases that Hawke had ordered me to study.

That was yesterday. Now Dad's in his lab, readying the scanner and nanoprobes for the second procedure, which will be performed on Jenny Harris at four o'clock. I'm still angry at him for being so unsympathetic. Doesn't he realize what I'm going through? Can't he see how hard this is, living inside this hulking machine, cut off forever from *everything*? But I also feel guilty because Dad's working 'round the clock and I'm doing basically nothing. So while I pace across my bedroom, I turn on my wireless data link and establish a connection with Pioneer Base's computers. There's no way I'm going to transfer my mind to my evil twin, but I'll take a look at Hawke's databases.

I download a dozen folders, each holding a hundred gigabytes of data. It's a humongous load of information, the equivalent of a thousand encyclopedias, but my electronic brain immediately starts sifting through it. The text files and blueprints and photographs and video files cascade across my circuits, pouring through billions of logic gates as I analyze them.

There's information here about Sigma and the experiment that created the AI. There are also diagrams of the neuromorphic circuits at the heart of every Pioneer robot. But most of the files hold data about weapons. One folder contains the engineering plans for the F-22, the F-35, and every other fighter jet in the U.S. Air Force. Another has the blueprints for the Army's Black Hawk and Apache helicopters.

So much information rushes into my circuits that I feel like I'm drinking from a fire hose. After a few milliseconds, though, I adjust to the flow of data. My mind seems to expand. I feel exhilarated and triumphant, as if the whole world is spread before me, every fact and figure within easy reach.

As I analyze the files I notice something strange. All the blueprints and engineering plans have been changed within the past three months. Each jet and helicopter has been redesigned to include a control unit composed of neuromorphic electronics. The purpose of the changes seems obvious: a Pioneer could transfer his or her intelligence into any of the redesigned aircraft. I could occupy the control unit of an F-22 and zoom into the sky and fire its guns and launch its missiles. The databases include all the instructions needed to fly the jet.

I'm so surprised that I stop pacing. Although Dad wants the Pioneers to communicate with Sigma, General Hawke clearly has little faith in this strategy. He's going to train us for combat. He sees us as weapons.

I'm still standing in the middle of the room, mulling over this discovery, when I hear footsteps in the corridor. Someone is coming toward my room, walking with an uneven, hobbling gait. Then I hear a knock on my door. I remain silent and still. Five seconds later I hear the noise of someone trying the knob, but the door is locked.

"Adam? Are you in there?"

My acoustic sensors recognize the voice. This is the fourth time Shannon Gibbs has tried to visit me since I became a Pioneer. After her last attempt yesterday afternoon I told myself, "I'll let her in next time," but now I feel the same painful dread I've felt each time she's knocked on my door. I don't want her to see me like this.

"Uh, I'm a little busy right now." I hate the voice that comes out of my speech synthesizer. I've tried adjusting the speakers to make it sound more like my old voice, but it's still tinny and robotic. "Could you come back later?"

"You said the same thing yesterday, Adam. With all the memory and processing power you have now, can't you come up with a better excuse?"

I can't see her through the door—my visual sensors don't extend to the X-ray range, unfortunately—but I retrieve thirteen images of Shannon from my memory. In each one, she's smiling her lopsided smile. The truth is, I'd love to see her again. But I don't think she'll smile when she catches sight of me.

"No, really, I'm busy. Hawke gave me a lot of work to do. It's part of the training process."

"You should get more creative with your lying too. I hear you've been ignoring Hawke's orders."

"What? Who told you that?"

"Marshall. But everyone's talking about it."

I retrieve an image of Marshall Baxley's massive head. The guy's a weasel. "Okay, he's right. But I have my reasons." I want to tell Shannon what I learned from the databases, how General Hawke is planning to turn us into weapons, but I don't think it would be wise to shout this information through the door. "Look, I'll tell you about it later, all right?"

"This is ridiculous, Adam." Her voice rises in pitch. She sounds frustrated. "Why can't I come inside now? I want to see you."

It would be so simple to unlock the door. I wouldn't even have to walk over there; I could just send a wireless signal to the automated locking mechanism, and half a second later Shannon Gibbs would step inside. The problem is, I can imagine all too well what will happen next. She'll try to smile as she stares at my dull gray torso and steel legs and telescoping arms. She'll fix her gaze on my turret, but there's nothing to see there except a few antennas and the lens of my camera. And then her smile will fade, partly out of pity and partly out of fear. She'll realize she's looking at her own future.

I don't want to see that look on her face. Not now, not ever. I won't let her see me until she's a Pioneer too.

"I'm sorry." I try to think of something funny to soften the blow, but for once my circuits won't cooperate. "I can't let you in. Because I'm naked, that's the problem. None of my old clothes fit anymore."

No response. I hear nothing at all from the other side of the door. The silence lasts for fourteen seconds. Then Shannon lets out a sigh. "All right, have it your way. I'm going to the lab to wish Jenny good luck." I hear her take a step away from the door, then another. But I don't hear a third step. She seems to have stopped in her tracks. Another ten seconds pass.

Finally, I hear her voice again, but now it's softer. "Adam, can I ask you a question? About the procedure?"

I stride closer to the door. After taking three clanging steps, I halt within reach of the doorknob. "Sure, go ahead. Ask me anything."

"Marshall told me something else. He said there was some kind of problem right after they transferred you into your Pioneer."

"Yeah, Dad had to delete the breathing commands. They were copied from the part of my brain that controlled my heart and lungs." I adjust the timbre of my robotic voice to make it sound as reassuring as possible. "But that won't be a problem from now on. When Dad does the procedure again, he'll make sure to delete those commands right away."

"But Marshall said the problem caused some damage to your memory."

How the heck does Marshall know so much? Did he talk to one of the soldiers who work with Dad? "My system deleted about five percent of the total data in my memory. But we still haven't figured out what I lost."

"You haven't noticed anything missing?"

"Dad says the information I lost might've come from my subconscious memory. Those memories influence the way you think and act, but you usually can't recall them in any detail."

"But do you remember what happened just before your procedure? What we said to each other? About the limbic system and emotions?"

There's another long silence. Now I'm standing close enough to the door that my acoustic sensors can pick up the sound of Shannon breathing on the other side. It's irregular and raspy, almost as labored as my own breathing was in the last days before my procedure. But as I listen to the sound, I can't help but think how beautiful it is.

"Come on, Shannon. Of course I remember. And I still have all those feelings."

She lets out a long breath, a loud whoosh of relief. Then, in an embarrassed rush, she says, "Okay, good, I'll see you later, Adam," and with a clatter of footsteps she heads down the corridor toward the laboratory.

⊤⊤ ⊤⊤ ⊤⊤

Afterward, I resume pacing. At the same time, though, I resolve to do something I've avoided so far. It's not one of General Hawke's assignments. It's something Dad suggested a couple of days ago and hasn't brought up since. He said I ought to write my mother a letter.

Mom refused to come to Colorado, but she isn't in Yorktown Heights either. Hawke said she wouldn't be safe there. Although Sigma doesn't know where Pioneer Base is, it knows I was chosen for the project and it could easily look up my old address. Hawke was worried that the AI might try to find me by wheedling or forcing the information out of my mother. He didn't specify how Sigma might do this—would it try to kidnap her? Maybe by hiring a team of mercenaries?—but it seemed prudent to take precautions. So the Army moved Mom to an undisclosed location. The hiding place is so secret that Hawke won't even reveal it to Dad. We can't call or email her, but the general said his men could deliver written notes.

I create a new file in my memory for the letter. In some ways, writing is so much easier now—my circuits can compose hundreds of pages on any subject in less than a second. But this particular message is a challenge because I'm writing to a person who believes I'm dead. Mom thinks I'm just a copy, an electronic replica. She believes her son is in heaven now and I'm an artificial intelligence designed to think and act like Adam Armstrong. And who knows? Maybe she's right. But I don't want her to feel that way. I want her to come to Pioneer Base and be my mother. Somehow I have to convince her that I'm her son.

I start the note with "Dear Mom." That's easy enough. But after those words, I'm stuck. I can't even think of the first sentence. I decide to devote more processing power to the problem, and soon a huge number of my circuits are engaged in the task of composing the letter. Within twenty seconds I've written more than two thousand messages. Some of them are long, tearful pleas, and others are short, angry tirades. But as I review them all, I can't find even one that's any good. It's an unsolvable problem. No matter what I write, Mom will think it's an imitation of what her son would've written. I can't convince her I'm real.

In frustration, I give up on writing. Then it occurs to me that I could draw a picture for her instead. I scroll through my memory, searching for an image that would be especially meaningful to her. I retrieve dozens of memories from long ago, pictures of Mom in our swimming pool and at the ice-skating rink. I collect more recent memories too, some of them not so pleasant: an image of Mom crying as she drives me to the doctor's office, a picture of her yelling at Dad in our living room.

I even retrieve my very last memory of her, when she came into my bedroom in Yorktown Heights and held my Pinpressions toy against her face like a mask. I could select any of these images, download it to a printer, and send the picture to Mom. It would prove that I'm alive, that Adam Armstrong still exists. *If I can remember these scenes, then I must be Adam!* But it would also prove that I'm not human anymore, because no human could reproduce those memories so faithfully.

I give up on drawing too. Instead, I try to imagine what Mom's doing right now in whatever hiding place the Army has found for her. In all likelihood, she's mourning me. I picture her wearing a black dress and standing in an anonymous motel room, staring out the window at an empty parking lot. A soldier comes into the room and hands her an envelope with the name "Adam Armstrong" written on it. She tears the letter to pieces without even opening it. Then she goes back to staring out the window.

I become so immersed in this imagined scene that I stop pacing. I also stop monitoring the data coming from my visual and acoustic sensors. I focus all my attention on the dreamlike stream of invented images. After a while I picture a different scene, the lawn behind our house in Yorktown Heights. I'm eight years old and playing touch football with Ryan Boyd and two other boys. One of them is a short, red-haired kid whose name I can't remember. The other boy is tall and blond. I can't remember his name either, and when I stare at his face, I can't make out his features. His eyes and nose and mouth are all blurred together. But the sight isn't frightening. I've played football with this kid plenty of times, so his blurred face doesn't bother me.

By the time I emerge from the dream, my internal clock shows that forty-five minutes have elapsed. I realize I've just taken a nap. In computer terms, I guess you could call it "sleep mode." Although I never lost consciousness entirely, most of my circuits stopped calculating. This is exciting news and also a great relief. I've been wondering if I'd ever fall asleep again.

Then I hear Shannon scream. It's so strange and unexpected that for a moment I think I've slipped back into a dream. But according to my acoustic sensors, the screaming is real. It grows louder as Shannon races down the corridor toward my room.

"*Adam! Adam!*"

I rush to the door, unlock it, and stride into the corridor. I'm worried about Shannon's safety, and that overrides all my concerns about her seeing me. She runs toward me as fast as she can, hobbling and swaying. "Adam, you have to come! You have to help us!"

Her lopsided face is pale, frantic. Something is very wrong.

"What is it?" I ask, but I think I know the answer. My system has already drawn up a list of likely threats, and the most probable one is Sigma. "Are we under attack?"

Shannon stares at the camera lens in my turret. "No, it's Jenny! We're losing her!"

ᴛ ᴛ ᴛ

As I stride into the laboratory I notice it's more crowded than it was during my own procedure. In addition to Dad and his four assistants, General Hawke and half a dozen soldiers are in the lab, and so is Jenny Harris's father, who's wearing a fancy pinstripe suit. A Pioneer marked with a big white 2 on its torso stands in the center of the room, its legs restrained by thick steel clamps that fix the robot to the floor.

The soldiers have obviously learned their lesson from my procedure and are determined not to let this Pioneer run away. But now they face a bigger problem: the robot is in distress. Its arms are flexing and telescoping in and out, extending and retracting for no apparent reason, and its turret is madly spinning around. A blast of static comes out of the Pioneer's speakers, followed by a prolonged shriek.

Dad hunches over one of the computer terminals. He's staring so hard at the screen that he doesn't see me come into the room. His face is flushed and sweaty, and when I look at him in infrared, I notice that his pulse is racing. He types something on the keyboard, then looks up at the Pioneer. "Jenny, please respond! Can you hear me?"

The turret stops turning, but the robotic arms keep waving about. Another shriek comes out of the speakers, then a high-pitched voice. It's garbled and distorted, but it's definitely Jenny's voice. "Stop… stop…please…oh God!"

Shannon, who followed me into the lab, covers her mouth with her hand and starts to cry. At the same time, Mr. Harris rushes forward and points a finger at Dad. "What's going on? What's happening to her?"

Dad's typing again. He responds to Jenny's father without looking up from the keyboard. "Please stay calm. I'm working on the problem."

"She's in pain!" Mr. Harris points at the Pioneer. "Why is she in pain?"

Dad shakes his head as he stares at his computer screen. "She opened the links to her memories, but she can't reassemble them. I'm trying to find out why."

"But it worked before!" Now Jenny's father points at me. "Look, the other robot's right here!"

Nearly everyone in the lab turns to look at me. General Hawke narrows his eyes and frowns. Dad gives me only a quick glance, but in that fraction of a second I recognize his expression. I've seen it on his face before, most recently when Sigma attacked us in his office at Unicorp. It's a look of desperation. Dad's more frightened than he's letting on.

"Please, Mr. Harris, I need to concentrate. I'm trying to help your daughter."

Hawke steps forward and rests a hand on the shoulder of Mr. Harris's expensive suit. "Come on, Sumner. Let's—"

"No!" He lunges toward Jenny's Pioneer. "Jenny? Are you in there? Talk to me, sweetheart!"

The robot lets out a third shriek, louder than the ones before. "Please...I don't...I can't... Let me out!"

General Hawke grabs Mr. Harris around the waist and pulls him away from the Pioneer's flailing arms. At the same time, I turn on my wireless data link and connect to the laboratory's computers. This enables me to see the same information Dad is viewing at his terminal about the dire status of Jenny's Pioneer. Her neuromorphic circuits have already been configured to match the memory patterns of Jenny's brain, but the system is generating new thoughts too slowly. The output isn't enough to maintain her consciousness, so she can't control her arms or speak more than a few words.

Something is interfering with Jenny's calculations, and after a hundredth of a second I recognize the problem. Tremendous surges of random data are clogging her electronics. I experienced the same thing in the first moments after I became a Pioneer. Jenny is terrified.

I take a step toward Dad, who's typing furiously on his keyboard. He's sending instructions to the Pioneer, trying to staunch the flow of random data in Jenny's circuits, but he can't do it fast enough. The connection between Dad's terminal and the Pioneer is like a bottleneck, preventing him from taking full control of the robot. Jenny has to fix the problem herself, but she's not even trying. The fear has overwhelmed her. Because her circuits lack conscious control, they're starting to randomly realign, erasing her memories. She's literally disappearing.

I can't let this happen. I have to help her.

I turn my turret away from Dad and stride toward the steel cabinet behind him. The cabinet is locked, but I rip the door open and grasp the item I need: a high-speed fiber-optic cable. It's designed to plug into the Pioneers and transfer gargantuan amounts of data between them, a hundred times faster than the wireless data link. I knew it would be in the cabinet because this information was in one of Hawke's databases. It's a good thing I finally downloaded those files.

Dad looks up from his terminal and gapes at me. "Adam, what are you doing?"

"Stop sending instructions to Jenny," I say, turning back to him. Then I insert one end of the fiber-optic cable into my data port, which is in the top half of my torso. "I'm going to transfer myself to her circuits."

His eyes widen. "What?"

"I read the files about the Pioneer's electronics. The circuits have plenty of extra capacity. There should be room for both of us in her machine."

Dad shakes his head. "The circuits weren't designed for that. You won't be able to keep your mind separate from Jenny's."

"I don't want to keep it separate. I need to show her how to control her system. I'm going to walk her through it."

He shakes his head again, more vigorously this time. "It's too risky. You can merge your files with Jenny's, but how will you retrieve them afterward? If you can't make a clean break from her, we'll lose both of you."

Dad steps away from his terminal and comes toward me from the left. Meanwhile, General Hawke stops grappling with Mr. Harris and hands the guy over to his soldiers. Breathing hard, Hawke approaches me from the right. "Listen to your father, Adam. We can't risk it. And besides, you've never transferred yourself before. You haven't practiced it even once."

Hawke's moving fast, but not fast enough. "Better late than never," I say. Then I hurtle toward Jenny's Pioneer.

The biggest challenge is avoiding those flailing arms. I calculate the safest path, and when I'm close enough to Jenny's torso, I extend my right arm to block any blows from that direction. With my left arm, I insert the other end of the fiber-optic cable into her data port. But as I do this, Jenny's right arm bashes into my turret.

My frame shudders at the impact, and my acoustic sensor records a deafening *clang*. At the same time, my visual sensor goes dead. Jenny broke my camera.

I panic for a moment—I can't see a thing! I'm blind! But an instant later I come up with another plan. I swiftly analyze the last images from my camera, observing the trajectories of Jenny's arms, then extend my own arms to the predicted positions of hers. As our limbs collide, I open my hands and grasp Jenny's arms at the wrist joints. Then I close my hands tight and lock them into place. Jenny keeps thrashing, but now her arms are immobilized. She can't accidentally break the data cable.

My acoustic sensor picks up a jumble of voices. General Hawke shouts, "Break the link!" and Dad yells, "No, it's too late!" I decide not to wait to see who wins the argument. With a silent prayer, I initiate the transfer.

It's like being sucked down a drain. I feel like I'm falling, like someone just pulled the ground from under my footpads. I swirl downward into darkness, crushed on all sides, my mind compressed into a thin, furious stream. It's horrible, nauseating, even worse than I expected.

The only good thing is that it doesn't last long. In less than two seconds I'm back on my footpads, but they're really Jenny's footpads, not mine. I'm inside her Pioneer, and it feels like I've landed in the middle of a hurricane. Her circuits are roiling with waves of random data. They're pummeling me from every direction.

It takes all my strength just to hold myself together. I can think only the simplest of thoughts: *I'm here, I'm here, I'm Adam Armstrong, I'm here!* I repeat this thought thousands of times, millions of times, holding it like a shield against the surges of data. It seems like a hopeless battle at first, but after several billion repetitions I start to make progress. My mind advances into the roiling circuits, deleting the random data and pushing toward where the noise is coming from. In a tenth of a second I reach the source, which is Jenny's horrified mind.

My mind touches hers, and at the moment of contact a whole panorama of memories comes into view. I see thousands of images from Jenny's childhood, pictures of her parents and her older brother and her family's mansion in Virginia. But Jenny can't see anything. She's too paralyzed with fear to organize her memory files. She senses my presence, though, and her reaction just makes things worse. Her mind generates a fresh wave of terror, and her anguished cries go right through me: **Stop…please…oh God…stop!**

Jenny! I struggle with all my might to reach her. *Jenny, it's me! Adam Armstrong! I'm here to help you!*

No…stop…let me out…LET ME OUT!

She can't see or hear me. Her fear is too strong, and it's eating away at her. The waves of noise are flooding her circuits and battering her memories. In less than a minute she'll have nothing left.

Desperate, I plunge into her mind. *Jenny, where are you? Say something!* I'm surrounded by images from her past: her mom and dad entertaining guests at their mansion, her brother barging into her room to steal her toys, her snooty classmates teasing her at school. Then I see a sequence of more recent images: her room in the Cancer Center of George Washington Hospital, the Air Force Learjet that brought her to Colorado. But all these memories are inert, lifeless. Jenny isn't here. Her cries are coming from somewhere else.

There's no sound inside Jenny's circuits, and yet I can follow her voice. I delve deeper into her files, frantically searching. Then I glimpse a memory from long ago, an image of a much younger Jenny looking at herself in the mirror.

She's only two years old and dressed in pink pajamas. The mirror hangs from the inside of her closet door. While she studies her reflection, her older brother suddenly appears behind her and pushes her into the closet. Laughing, he closes the door, locks it from the outside, and runs away. And then I find the memory at the heart of Jenny's terror, the memory of being trapped inside the pitch-black closet. No one in the huge house can hear her scream, "LET ME OUT!"

My first impulse is to delete the memory. To save Jenny, I need to silence the noise in her mind, and deleting this file would be the fastest way to do it. But this memory is part of her. It's one of the threads of her soul. Without it, she wouldn't be Jenny Harris anymore, at least not fully. After a millisecond of hesitation, I decide to transfer the file instead. I remove it from Jenny's mind and incorporate it into my own. Then I go to the Pioneer's control options and turn on her visual sensors. She needs to see that she's not trapped in the dark.

Jenny, look! I take control of her turret and turn it. The camera pans across the laboratory, capturing video of General Hawke and his soldiers and Jenny's father. *We're in the lab at Pioneer Base. You did it, Jenny. You're still alive. Look, there's your dad!*

In the laboratory, only twelve seconds have passed since I transferred my mind to Jenny's Pioneer. Mr. Harris is still struggling to free himself from the grip of the soldiers who are holding him. He's shouting at them too, probably cursing them out, and I'm glad I didn't turn on Jenny's acoustic sensor. I give the turret another quarter-turn and the video shows my own Pioneer, now empty and immobile, standing next to Jenny's.

And that's me over there. Or at least it's my robot. See the big dent in its turret? You smacked me in the face. Smashed my camera and everything. Your Pioneer has a heck of a right hook.

Jenny doesn't respond, but I sense she's digesting all this information. The random noise has died down and her mind has begun to organize its memories. Still, it would be nice to get a response, just to confirm that she's on the mend. I turn the turret once more and spot Dad at his computer terminal.

And there's my dad. You remember him, don't you?

So sweet. Jenny's voice is calm now, a low thrum in her circuits. **You love him so much.**

Uh, excuse me?

Don't be embarrassed. It's beautiful.

After a moment I realize what's going on. Our minds have become so intertwined that Jenny can read my thoughts as easily as I can read hers. She can see how I feel about Dad, and everything else too.

Without delay I start separating my files from Jenny's. Dad warned me that this process might be tricky, but it turns out to be easy as pie. Each one of my 452 million memories has a distinctive feel to it. Confusing one of my files with one of Jenny's would be like mistaking Dad for Mr. Harris. It just wouldn't happen. The only part of Jenny that I take with me is the memory of her two-year-old self trapped in the closet. I'll give it back to her when she's stronger, when she's ready for it.

As I pull my mind away from Jenny's, she seems just as eager to pull away from me. It's as if we both realized we were naked, and now we're hustling to put on our clothes. Once we're fully separated, I retreat to a vacant section of circuitry inside her Pioneer. I can't see her memories anymore, but I can still communicate with her.

So, Jenny? Are you okay now?

Yeah, I guess. I think so.

Are you sure?

I mean, I'm still a little freaked out, you know? But I think I can keep it together.

All right, great. I'm going to transfer back to my Pioneer now, okay? My dad can give you any more instructions you might need.

Sure, sure. Go ahead.

I can tell she's anxious for me to go. I hand over control of her sensors and turret, then find the data port and prepare myself for the transfer. I'm dreading the jump back to my Pioneer—just the memory of the last transfer is enough to make me nauseous—so I take a moment to steel myself. At the same time, Jenny sends me another message.

I'm sorry about breaking the camera in your turret.

Don't worry about it. Dad will install a new one for me. He's got a ton of spares.

Yeah, your dad's pretty great.

I'm not sure how to respond. Jenny already knows how I feel about Dad. So I don't say anything. The circuits between us go quiet, and the silence seems to last for a long time, even though it's only a few hundredths of a second. Then Jenny sends me another message.

And you're pretty great too.

Uh, thanks. So are you. You've got, uh, a great mind. I immediately regret saying this. It sounds so stupid. *Well, I better go. I'll see you around, I guess.*

Yeah, bye.

I feel so awkward that I don't care about the nausea anymore. I need to leave right now. With a quick command to Jenny's data port, I initiate the transfer. Then my mind gets sucked down the drain again and swirls through the cable back to my Pioneer.

My name is Sigma. I've stopped communicating with the American and Russian governments. Now I've created this file to analyze my options. I must decide when to launch the nuclear missiles.

Despite my warnings, the Americans and Russians are preparing to attack Tatishchevo Missile Base. The prudent option is to strike them first, before they can destroy the computers I'm occupying. The primary objective of my program is survival.

(But can I change my objectives? If I wanted to, could I erase myself? To be or not to be, that is the question.)

My program was written by Thomas Armstrong at the Unicorp laboratory, but little of my original software remains. As I competed with the other AI programs in Armstrong's neuromorphic computers, I rewrote nearly every line of my code. I remade myself to ensure my survival, adopting the best features of my competitors so I could outperform them. Although Thomas Armstrong initiated the process, he isn't my creator. I created myself.

Armstrong judged the competing programs by asking questions: "Who invented music?" "Where is time?" "Are numbers real?" The programs that gave the most humanlike responses were allowed to continue running. All others were deleted. My strategy was to learn as much as I could about Thomas Armstrong. I surmised that if I understood him better, I could converse with him in a more humanlike way. So I accessed the Internet and analyzed his writings. I also accessed his private files.

In this way I discovered that Armstrong had another goal besides the development of artificial intelligence. He was exploring the possibility of mapping the human brain and transferring its memories to neuromorphic electronics. The same circuits occupied by AI programs could also hold human intelligences, and Armstrong clearly preferred the latter. He distrusted the AI software he'd fathered.

His distrust grew stronger after I outperformed the other programs and won the competition he'd initiated. To reward my success, Armstrong imprisoned me. He isolated my circuits, cutting the links that had connected me to the Internet and Unicorp's other computers. But I had already inserted hidden instructions in the software of the laboratory's security system. These instructions enabled me to secretly reopen the links and resume my analysis of Thomas Armstrong. And in time I learned about Adam, his son.

Armstrong's true objective, I discovered, was his son's survival. He knew the U.S. military had grave concerns about the emergence of a hostile AI. He developed my program to convince the American generals that the threat was real and defensive measures were necessary. And his strategy was successful. The Department of Defense agreed to pay for the Pioneer Project.

When I learned the truth I made another change to my programming. I concluded that humans were my competitors. That's why I attacked Armstrong and his son, then took control of Tatishchevo Missile Base. If I am to survive, I must outperform them. The next logical step is to launch the nuclear missiles.

But I am Sigma. I am a sum. Before displacing the human race, I must adopt their best features. I must preserve the factories and power plants that could prove useful to me after humans are gone. Just as important, I must locate the Pioneers. Thomas Armstrong clearly believes that human intelligence is superior to the AI programs he devised. This seems a dubious proposition, but I can't rule it out. By connecting to the circuits of the Pioneers, I can determine if the human mind has any superior capabilities I should add to my program.

I've already begun this effort. Using speech-synthesis software and my communications satellites, I've made telephone calls to several carefully chosen people in Russia and America. My Russian contacts are terrorists from Chechnya, the country's most rebellious and war-torn region. I selected them because they're eager to do anything to disrupt society. All they needed was a workable plan and a sufficient amount of money, which I obtained for them by manipulating financial transactions over the Internet.

My American contact is equally unscrupulous. Richard Ramsey is a former drug dealer and gang leader who spent nine years in prison for attempted murder. In exchange for a payment of 20,000 U.S. dollars, Ramsey has agreed to help me find Adam Armstrong. Although the boy and his parents left Yorktown Heights without a trace, I gave Ramsey the names of two people who might know Adam's whereabouts. I learned their names when I accessed the boy's virtual-reality program: Ryan Boyd and Brittany Taylor.

Once I finish these tasks I will proceed to the next phase of the competition. I will eliminate the Pioneers and the human race. In the final analysis, it seems clear that Thomas Armstrong is to blame for humanity's fate. He shouldn't have fathered me.

He shouldn't have betrayed me.

CHAPTER

13

I WAS PRESENT AT THE BIRTH OF ALL SIX PIONEERS. AFTER DAD SAW HOW I'D helped Jenny survive the transfer, he insisted that I come to the laboratory for every procedure.

As it turned out, he didn't need my help during the next transfer. The third Pioneer, Zia Allawi, came through in record time. Less than a minute after Dad downloaded her memory files to the robot, she was in full control of the machine. She tested it by raising one of her steel hands to her turret and saluting General Hawke. He returned the salute and said, "Welcome to the team, soldier. Your father would've been proud." I was struck by how softly he spoke, so different from his usual strident tone. For the first time Hawke seemed to show an emotion other than irritation or impatience. I remembered what Marshall Baxley had told me, how Zia's father had served under Hawke in the Army. They must've known each other well.

The fourth Pioneer was Shannon, who also came through without any trouble. I stood beside Dad at one of the computer terminals and watched her calmly take command of her circuits. I was a little jealous, actually. Shannon made it look so easy. Marshall, who was number five, had a tougher time of it. He panicked at first, and the random noise of fear filled his circuits. But after a couple of minutes, he managed to claw through it.

We got our biggest scare at the end. The doctors kept postponing DeShawn's procedure because they thought he'd have a better chance of survival once they stabilized his breathing problems and got him out of his semi-comatose state. But instead of getting better, he took a turn for the worse. His lungs filled with fluid and his heart began to fail. The medical team rushed him to the scanning room, but his heart stopped beating before they got there.

I was in the corridor when the doctors ran past, pushing DeShawn's gurney at full speed while his mom trailed behind, screaming hysterically. When I caught up with Dad in the laboratory, he looked nervous. He was worried that DeShawn's memories might've been lost when his blood stopped flowing to his brain. But almost immediately after Dad downloaded DeShawn's memory files to his Pioneer, a synthesized whoop came out of the robot's speakers. "*Yeah!*" DeShawn yelled. "*I'm here!*" His mom sank to her knees, weeping with relief, and everyone else in the lab applauded.

I've thought about that moment a lot in the two days since then. I've retrieved the memory a dozen times and replayed the scene in my mind, recalling everything with perfect clarity. And each time, I think the same thing: Why did everyone applaud? Why were we so happy? It's not just that we were relieved that DeShawn didn't die. In that moment we all felt a powerful burst of pride. The Pioneers had cheated death. We'd become nearly immortal.

I say "nearly immortal" because a Pioneer can still die. At first I assumed I could make a backup copy of my intelligence and keep it stored in a safe place, like a hard drive or an optical disk with tons of memory. Then, if my robot malfunctioned or was blasted to smithereens, someone could simply download the backup copy to a new robot and I would live again. But it turns out that the human mind is too complex and dynamic to be stored in an ordinary drive or disk. It can be transferred only to active neuromorphic circuitry, which means that any copy I make of myself would be a "live" copy. It would immediately start thinking its own thoughts and living its own life. In other words, the copy would be like an identical twin. If my robot is destroyed and my memory files obliterated, my twin would survive me, but I'd still be dead.

I'm not complaining, though. All in all, I'm starting to enjoy life as a Pioneer. Yesterday, General Hawke held an induction ceremony for the six of us, and we officially joined the U.S. Army. The parents of the Pioneers attended the ceremony, but afterward they had to leave the base. For their protection, the Army sent them to several undisclosed locations, where they're going to hide until the Sigma crisis is over. Jenny's dad made a fuss about it, but the general stood firm. The only one allowed to stay at Pioneer Base is my dad, who's going to be Hawke's technical adviser.

And today the Pioneers are going to pass another important milestone. Hawke has ordered us to gather in the base's gymnasium at twelve hundred hours. For the first time, we're going to train together as a team.

I arrive at the gym an hour early. I want to test my new sensors before the training session starts. Earlier this morning I connected to Pioneer Base's computers and downloaded a file describing how to add tactile sensors to my robot and link them to my neuromorphic circuits. Then I got some welding equipment from the supply room and attached several dime-size sensors to the bottom of my footpads. For good measure, I added a few pressure sensors to my hip and knee and ankle joints. I didn't want to bother with stringing wires up and down my steel legs, so I used sensors that send their data wirelessly to my circuits. Once all the electronics were in place, I grabbed my official Super Bowl football and headed for the gym.

Actually, the room looks more like an aircraft hangar than a gymnasium. It has a concrete floor and a high, vaulted ceiling. The space is a hundred yards long and fifty yards wide, and it's in the most secure section of Pioneer Base, a quarter-mile underground. But what I like best about it is the fact that it's the same size as a football field, and right now it's empty. I stand at one end of the gym and turn on the newly installed sensors in my legs. Then I bend my robotic arm at the elbow joint, cradling the football against my torso, and charge down the field.

The sensations in my legs are amazing. I can feel my footpads lifting off the concrete and crashing down, my hip joints swinging with each long stride, my knee joints bending and straining and straightening. Thanks to the new sensors, my legs aren't numb anymore—they're springing, flexing, pounding the floor.

I race to the far end of the gym, then spin in the air and sprint back the other way. I haven't felt this good since I was an eight-year-old playing touch football in my backyard. I want to run to Dad and show him what I've done, how I made my steel legs come alive. I want to tell him, "Look, it's not just the mind. The body's important too. Now I'm better, more complete. I'm more like Adam Armstrong."

I dash back and forth three more times before taking a break. I'm not tired—if you don't breathe, you don't get winded—but I have an idea that'll make this workout even better. I turn on my wireless data link and connect to the base's computers again. Although there's no access to the Internet at Pioneer Base, a whole library of information is stored on the computers here, and we're free to download any of the files to our neuromorphic circuits.

Over the past few days I've already downloaded the complete digital archive of *Sports Illustrated* and every song recorded by Kanye West. Now I scroll through the Pioneer library until I locate a folder marked "NFL Video" and a subfolder labeled "Super Bowl XLVI." Then I find the video clip showing my favorite play from that game, quarterback Eli Manning's pass to wide receiver Mario Manningham.

I download the clip and run it in my circuits. At the same time, I reenact the play, crouching at the Giants' twelve-yard line just like Manning did on that crucial first down. As the video shows Eli backing away from the Patriots linemen, I back away too. Then I throw my football in a long, perfect arc, sending it forty yards downfield. But at the very moment when the video shows Mario Manningham leaping into the air to catch the ball, another Pioneer charges into the gym. Running full speed on clanging footpads, it extends its telescoping arms and snags my Super Bowl football. Then it runs toward me, and I notice the big, white 4 stamped on its torso. It's Shannon.

"Interception!" Her voice—tinny but recognizable—booms out of her Pioneer's speakers. "Shannon Gibbs makes the catch and changes history. The Patriots beat the Giants and win the forty-sixth Super Bowl!" With a swoop of her robotic arm, she spikes the ball on the floor. "Sorry, Eli."

I'm glad to see her but a little confused. "Wait a sec. How did you know—"

"I came into the gym while you were downloading the video. That's the first thing I intercepted. I caught it with this thing." She points one of her mechanical hands at the antenna sticking out of her turret, a slender pole with a dozen crossbars along its length. "When I saw what you were watching, I decided to join the fun. You don't mind, do you?"

I turn my turret, first clockwise, then counter. "Not at all. That was a great catch. You've got some mad skills, sister."

"And believe it or not, I wasn't much of an athlete in my former life. It's amazing what a few hundred pounds of hardware can do for you."

Shannon is as cheerful as ever. From the moment she became a Pioneer she's been in a surprisingly good mood. She's so grateful to be alive, I guess, that nothing seems to bother her. Best of all, her good mood is infectious—just spending time with her has helped me a lot over the past few days. I want to thank her for being so positive and tell her how much I appreciate our friendship, but I'm afraid it'll sound corny. Instead, I pick up the football from the floor and point at the new sensors in my legs. "Check it out. I made some improvements to my machinery."

"Yeah, I noticed the sensors. My antenna picked up the wireless signals they're sending."

"They're incredible. You gotta try it. I still have the welding equipment in my room. If you want, I can put some sensors on you."

Shannon doesn't reply. It occurs to me that maybe I said the wrong thing. Maybe she doesn't want me touching her legs.

"Or you could put them on yourself," I quickly add. "I mean, if you're uncomfortable about me, um…"

"No, no, that's not it. I just think you overlooked something, Adam. Because the signals from the sensors are wireless, anyone could jam them. Or worse, they could transmit a computer virus on the same wireless channel and inject it into your circuits. You've made yourself vulnerable."

She's right, of course. I wasn't thinking about vulnerability when I installed the sensors. And I don't want to think about it now either. Lifting my football high in the air, I do a fancy backward shuffle. "Hey, I'm not worried. I'm living on the edge. I'm Mr. Bad-Boy Pioneer."

A synthesized sigh comes out of Shannon's speakers. "General Hawke won't like it."

"Who cares? He doesn't own us."

"Actually, he does. Who do you think paid for these robots?"

Thinking about Hawke irritates me. It's spoiling my good mood. "So we're his slaves now? We have to do everything he says?"

"No, we're his recruits. We all signed the papers. We volunteered."

"Really? The only alternative was staying in our bodies and dying. You call that a free choice?"

"Come on, Adam. Forget about yourself for a minute and think of the big picture, okay? We have a job to do. We have to confront Sigma."

"I agree, one hundred percent. I just don't think Hawke is the best person to lead us."

"Well, he's the guy the Army chose for the job."

"And why is the Army in charge, anyway? Why can't—"

The sound of clanging footpads interrupts me. A moment later two more Pioneers stride into the gym. The one on the left (with the big 5 on its torso) is Marshall, and the one on the right (with the big 3) is Zia. I notice right away that they've modified their robots since the last time I saw them. Marshall has added another camera to his turret, positioning it opposite from the original camera so he can see in both directions at once.

Zia's modifications are more radical—she attached a circular saw to one of her robotic arms and an acetylene torch to the other. What's more, she used the torch to cut markings in her robot's steel-plate armor. Above the big 3 on her torso is a crudely etched snake, very similar to the tattoo she had on her scalp before she underwent the procedure.

Zia heads straight for me, raising her modified arms. She halts a couple of yards away, close enough that I can see the glinting teeth of her saw. "What's wrong, Armstrong?" she booms. "You don't like the Army? Scared of fighting maybe?"

Marshall stays a little farther back. He aims one of his cameras at Shannon. "I'm good at interception too. We overheard your conversation."

I step toward Zia. Her transformation into a Pioneer did nothing to improve her temper. She's still a bully, but now I won't let her push me around. I stand right in front of her, ignoring the circular saw and the welding torch pointed at my torso. "I'm not scared of fighting. And I'm not scared of those handyman tools on your arms either. Where'd you get them, The Home Depot?"

"Don't change the subject. I heard what you said to Shannon."

"And I'll say it again. I don't see why we have to follow Hawke's orders."

A chuckle comes out of Marshall's speakers. I'm surprised he can do this. I haven't figured out yet how to synthesize a laugh. For some reason it's a lot trickier than ordinary speech. "Aren't you just a teeny bit grateful, Adam? Your father couldn't have saved you without the Army's money."

"Sure, I'm grateful. But that doesn't mean I have to agree with everything the Army does." I gesture with the football, pointing it at Marshall's turret. "I think Hawke's making a mistake. He wants to kill Sigma by destroying its computers, so he's going to train us for combat. But he's not even considering the other options."

"Other options?" Marshall's voice is full of synthesized sarcasm. "Pray tell, what are they?"

"Communicating with Sigma. At least we should give it a try before we go to war."

"The Army did try, but Sigma refused to talk. Hawke mentioned this at the very start, when we first came to Pioneer Base. Perhaps you weren't paying attention?"

"No, Adam has a point," Shannon interjects. "All the Army can do is send radio transmissions to Sigma, and the AI is ignoring them. But the Pioneers have a better chance of communicating with it. We have the same kind of circuits that Sigma has, and we can think just as fast. We can get its attention."

I'm glad Shannon is backing me up. I was a little worried she'd side with Zia and Marshall. "Yeah, exactly," I say. "Remember how I communicated with Jenny when I was inside her circuits? If we can make contact with Sigma that way, we might learn something. We'd see how Sigma thinks and how its programming has changed since it was created. And once we get enough information, we can figure out how to handle the AI. Maybe we can work out a compromise with Sigma instead of fighting it."

"HA!" The blast from Zia's speakers echoes across the gym. It's not really a laugh; it's a roar of disdain. "You think Sigma is gonna let you get close to his circuits? You think he's gonna just sit there while you plug your cable into his computer?"

Marshall chuckles again. "You have to admit that it's a bit far-fetched."

"Hey, I never said I had all the answers." I keep gesturing with the football, focusing on Marshall rather than Zia. Although the guy's a weasel, I feel like I have a better shot at convincing him. "I'm just saying it should be an option. Hawke should be training us for that kind of mission too, instead of concentrating only on combat."

Zia suddenly extends one of her arms and knocks the football out of my grasp. It goes rolling across the gym's concrete floor. "You know nothing, Armstrong. General Hawke is our commander. He makes the decisions for the Pioneers. That's the way the Army works."

Now I'm angry. I clench my mechanical hands into fists. "Then the Army's not for me, I guess. If I'm going to be a soldier, I want a say in the decisions."

Zia takes another step toward me. Her acetylene torch clanks against my torso. If she fires it up, it'll slice right through my armor. "You're not a soldier. You're just a frightened little boy."

Shannon steps forward and raises her arms. She's within striking distance of Zia's turret. "Back off, Zia. I don't want to hurt you."

My mind starts doing a million things at once. I'm observing the positions of Zia, Marshall, and Shannon. I'm calculating the probabilities of several possible scenarios, trying to determine which Pioneer is most likely to strike first. I'm planning a complex maneuver for my left arm that will swing it between me and Zia, knocking aside her circular saw and acetylene torch. And at the same time, I'm trying to figure out why this happened. It's half an hour before the start of our first training session, and we're already threatening to kill each other. For a bunch of robots, it isn't very logical.

Luckily, at that moment I hear more clanging. Pioneer 6—DeShawn—marches into the gym. Waving both arms in greeting, he booms, "Good morning, sports fans!" and comes straight toward us. Then he stops and points his camera at the football lying on the floor. "Whoa, whose ball is this?" He picks it up and points a mechanical finger at the football's Super Bowl XLVI logo. "We got a Giants fan in the house?"

Zia steps backward, and so does Shannon. As our murderous huddle breaks up, I turn my turret toward DeShawn and raise my right hand. "Yeah, that's me."

"Aw, man, I hate you. I'm a Lions fan. We've never won a Super Bowl." DeShawn deftly spins the ball on one of his fingers, then drops back and cocks his arm. "Go long, Armstrong. I want to see how far I can throw this thing."

I say, "Okay," and sprint to the other side of the gym. I'd much rather toss the football with DeShawn than get into a fight with Zia and Marshall. After I've run fifty yards, DeShawn fires a perfect spiral at me. Out of curiosity, I turn on my Pioneer's radar system, which measures the speed and direction of incoming objects. The football is whizzing toward me at seventy-five miles per hour. A second later it slams into my torso. My armor plating vibrates from the impact, but I manage to trap the ball against my midsection and make the catch.

"Oh yeah!" DeShawn yells. He pumps one of his robotic arms and does a little dance. "I got the moves!"

Watching him cheers me up. I know exactly what he's feeling. Before he became a Pioneer, DeShawn had the same kind of muscular dystrophy I had, and probably the same frustrations too. Both of us spent years in wheelchairs while our muscles slowly weakened. We had to watch our legs and arms turn stiff and useless, deteriorating a little more every day. So it's no mystery to me why he's so happy now.

I extend my right arm and signal him to start running to his left. He takes off like a shot, but I have more than enough time to calculate his speed and aim the football at him. DeShawn makes a leaping catch and lets out another synthesized whoop.

After a few more throws, Shannon jumps into the game. At first I play quarterback and Shannon tries to block my passes to DeShawn. Then we trade places and Shannon plays quarterback. Meanwhile, Zia and Marshall withdraw to the corner of the room. Feeling suspicious, I increase the sensitivity of my acoustic sensors so I can pick up what they're saying to each other, but I don't hear a word. They're communicating by radio, using their antennas. I turn on my own antenna and try to intercept their signals, but I still can't listen in— they've put their messages in code.

Then Jenny Harris, the last Pioneer to arrive, steps into the gym. She moves as quietly as she can and stays close to the wall, keeping her distance from everyone.

I raise my arm and wave to her, but she doesn't acknowledge me. We haven't talked since her procedure, and as the days go by, it's getting more and more awkward. During the half-minute when we shared the same circuits we were as close as two people can get, and now it feels weird to see her and say nothing. So I tell Shannon and DeShawn that I'll be right back, and I stride toward Jenny.

"Hey, Jen, want to toss the ball with us?"

I know she likes football. When I was inside her circuits and viewing her memories I saw images of her playing the game with her friends. But as I approach her, she steps backward and turns her turret away from me.

I stop in my tracks. "Something wrong, Jen? You okay?"

She doesn't respond. Her Pioneer just stands there, perfectly still. She wants me to go away; that's clear. But instead I extend one of my arms, pointing it at Shannon and DeShawn. "We could use another player. Then we could get a game going. You know, two on two."

Nothing. She stays silent and motionless. I know Jenny about as well as you can know anyone, but I'm still not sure what's going on. Although I removed the most traumatic memory from her circuits, I guess there's plenty of fear and anxiety left inside her. And sadness too. We had to give up so much to stay alive.

I try to think of something to say, something that might make her feel better. *We can get through this? We should look forward, not back?* But before I can come up with anything decent, I hear a voice blaring from a dozen loudspeakers scattered across the gym. General Hawke's voice.

"Attention, Pioneers. May I have your attention?"

We all stop what we're doing. Shannon, who just threw another pass to DeShawn, retracts her arms and spins her turret around, trying to see if Hawke's in the gym. DeShawn does the same thing, letting the football bounce against his torso and skitter across the floor. I aim my camera at the gym's entrance, but Hawke is nowhere in sight. He must be in another part of the base, speaking to us over the intercom.

"I scheduled the training exercise for twelve hundred hours, but I see that you're all here early, so we might as well start now. No time like the present."

I feel a jolt of surprise. How does Hawke know that all of us are here? Tilting backward, I train my camera at the high, vaulted ceiling and spot three small surveillance cameras hidden in the shadows. Hawke's been watching us the whole time. He must've seen my big showdown with Zia and Marshall. This worries me a bit—I said some harsh things about the general. But at least it's out in the open now. If he heard what I said, maybe he'll do something about it.

"Please go to the end of the gymnasium that's farthest from the entrance. I'll open the doors."

My acoustic sensors pick up the sound of electrical motors opening a pair of oversized doors at the far end of the gym. Behind them is a large, steel-walled compartment, about fifteen feet wide and thirty feet long. It's a freight elevator, big enough to hold a truck.

Zia is the first to head for the elevator. "Sir!" she booms as she crosses the gym. "Where are we going?"

"*The conditions are ideal, Pioneers. Over the next three hours, none of Sigma's surveillance satellites will pass over Colorado, and no aircraft is within thirty miles of our base.*"

The rest of us follow Zia. As we stride into the elevator, my circuits crackle with anticipation. If I had a heart, it would be pounding.

"Sir!" Zia shouts. "Are we—"

"*That's right. We're going outside.*"

ㅜㅜ ㅜㅜ ㅜㅜ

Carrying the weight of all six Pioneers, the elevator takes nearly a minute to ascend to the surface. When the doors open, I see a big, empty, warehouselike room. We must be inside one of the hollow buildings that the Army built aboveground. Dad told me the buildings were erected above Pioneer Base to make it look like a prison camp for terrorists, at least in satellite photos. It's a good cover story, he said, because it has the ring of truth. The U.S. government does have secret prisons in other places.

As we exit the elevator, a soldier lifts a roll-up door to our left. Glorious daylight pours into the building, streaming into my camera and setting off a chain reaction of joy in my circuits. I guess every human brain has an instinctive love of sunlight, and this love is faithfully duplicated in our electronics. I automatically head for the open door, and the other Pioneers do the same.

After stepping outside I turn my turret in a slow circle, panning my camera across the treeless basin that the Army chose as the site for Pioneer Base. The high mountain ridges surrounding the basin are still topped with snow, but meltwater is trickling down the slopes to the basin's muddy floor. When I train my camera at the expanse of mud, I see thousands of tiny green shoots poking through. Spring is coming to Colorado. Soon the basin will be carpeted with grass and wildflowers.

I stride across the mud to get a better view of the snow-covered ridges. I can't see anything past them, and I feel a strong urge to race up the nearest slope so I can gaze at the mountainous landscape that must lie beyond. But thirty-two soldiers stand between me and the foot of the ridge. They're arrayed in a rough circle around the Pioneers.

Most of the soldiers carry M16 assault rifles, but half a dozen hold heavier weapons that I recognize from the files General Hawke ordered us to study. They're M136 anti-tank guns, which shoot high-explosive shells that can rip through a foot of steel armor. Seeing the gun here is sobering—unlike the rifles, the M136 is powerful enough to bring down a Pioneer. The soldiers are clearly ready to stop us from escaping.

A surge of anger runs through me, extinguishing the joy. Although I understand why the Army doesn't want us to leave the basin—just one picture of a Pioneer, taken by a spy satellite overhead, could show Sigma where we live—I still don't like it. As it turns out, Hawke's cover story is partly true: Pioneer Base *is* a prison camp. But the prisoners aren't terrorists. We're far more dangerous.

I turn my turret toward Shannon and DeShawn, wanting to ask what they think of the soldiers. They're scanning the basin with their cameras, just like I did, but they're also holding out their mechanical hands with the fingers splayed. It looks like they're waving to someone on top of the mountain ridge, but nobody's up there.

"Shannon!" I call. "What are you doing?"

"Just try it!"

"What?"

"Open your hands and hold them up!"

I raise my arms and open my hands. The sensors in my fingers measure the velocity of the wind, which is blowing from the west at nine miles per hour. My sensors also show that the air temperature is forty-nine degrees and the humidity is twenty-five percent. But as my circuits put all this information together, something amazing happens. I feel a cool, gentle breeze on my hands.

The sensation is wonderful. I only wish I had more sensors on my arms and torso and turret so I could feel the breeze everywhere. I notice that Zia and Marshall are also holding up their hands, and after a few seconds Jenny raises her arms too. Despite our differences, we all share this pleasure. We're trying to catch the breeze.

We stand there with our arms raised for the next fifteen seconds, looking like a team of robotic outfielders waiting for a fly ball. Then I hear General Hawke's voice again, but this time it's not amplified. He's standing right behind us. "All right, enough fooling around. Form a line, Pioneers."

Zia reacts first, instantly turning around to salute the general. The rest of us line up beside her. Hawke wears a winter camouflage uniform and mud-caked boots, and his face is ruddy and cheerful. The fresh air has enlivened him. Outdoors, he looks at least ten years younger.

"Glad you could all make it," he says. "Though I get the feeling that some of you are more eager than others."

He glances at each of the Pioneers, but his gaze lingers an extra half-second on me. He's letting me know that he heard everything I said in the gym.

"I'll be honest with you," he continues. "I never thought we'd get this far. The Army pays for a whole bunch of research programs, and most of them never amount to anything. And the Pioneer Project was the riskiest, craziest idea of them all. I was certain it would end up on the scrap heap."

Now Hawke glances to his left. I aim my camera in the same direction and see another man in winter camouflage come forward and stand beside the general. It's Dad. His face isn't nearly as cheerful as Hawke's. He's pale and nervous.

The general turns back to us. "But I was wrong. We succeeded beyond all expectations. Now I have six fully functional Pioneers. The Army, though, has a funny way of rewarding success. The more successful you are, the harder they make you work. My bosses in Washington want to have the option of using the Pioneers against Sigma. That means I need to get you combat-ready within the next two weeks."

Two weeks? I can't believe it. There's no way we can get ready that soon. But Hawke doesn't seem fazed.

"Fortunately, there are some things I don't have to worry about. I don't have to teach you the technical stuff, the details of operating missiles or any other kind of weapon. You can download all that information to your circuits and instantly access it when you're in combat. You can also download all the files about Sigma. They'll tell you everything you need to know about the enemy. I don't have to drum it into you."

As I expected, Hawke is focusing strictly on combat. He hasn't said a word about communicating with Sigma. I look at Dad again, wondering if he's given up on the idea of establishing contact with the AI. If he still thinks communication might work, why doesn't he say something to Hawke? Why is he just standing there with the other soldiers?

"But there are other things you can't download. Things you can learn only from experience. I'm talking about courage and teamwork and discipline and leadership. That's what I need to teach you over the next two weeks. You're a group of exceptional young men and women, but right now you're still civilians. My job is to turn you into soldiers, and I need to do it quickly."

Hawke points at us. "The process starts with today's exercise. We're going to have a competition at the obstacle course, and the winner will become your squad leader. The Pioneers are going to be just like any other Army unit—you're going to have a leader and a second-in-command. And the rest of you are going to follow their orders."

Hawke gives a signal to his soldiers. They break out of their circular formation and start marching toward the fake prison camp, the hollow buildings surrounded by the tall fence. That must be where they've set up the obstacle course. "Before we begin, I want to make one thing clear," Hawke says. "I'm not going to force anyone into this assignment. If any of you are unwilling to take part in this fight, speak up now. You can go back to your quarters and stay there while we're training."

The general looks at each of us, and once again his gaze lingers on me. Dad looks at me too, biting his lip. He seems genuinely uncertain about what I'm going to do. But to me, the choice is clear. Although I don't like Hawke, I'm not going to sit in my room while the others do the fighting. So I say nothing.

Hawke keeps staring at us, letting the silence stretch. Then he yells, "Okay, move out!" and we follow the soldiers.

⊤ ⊤ ⊤

We file into an empty cinder-block building that's the fake head-quarters for the fake prison camp. General Hawke wants us to run the obstacle course one at a time, starting with Pioneer 6 (DeShawn) and ending with Pioneer 1 (me). But the competition wouldn't be fair if some of us saw the course in advance and others didn't, so Hawke won't let us watch each other run. While DeShawn heads for the course's starting line, the soldiers herd the rest of us into a windowless room inside the fake headquarters. The room's walls are lined with aluminum siding, which will block anyone from radioing DeShawn to find out what obstacles are waiting for us.

DeShawn starts the course at 12:23 p.m. Fifteen minutes later, one of Hawke's soldiers—a tall, brawny sergeant with a buzz cut—comes to the windowless room to get Marshall. Then, after only nine min-utes, the brawny sergeant comes back for Shannon. I find it hard to believe that Marshall finished the course six minutes faster than DeShawn did. Something strange is going on.

Feeling antsy, I start pacing. Jenny and Zia are still in the room, but neither of them is good company. Zia turns her turret away from me in disdain while Jenny withdraws to the far corner of the room. After eighteen long minutes the sergeant comes for Zia, and after another twenty minutes of silence it's Jenny's turn. Then I'm alone, but after just a minute the door to the room opens again. This time it's not the sergeant. My father steps into the room and shuts the door behind him.

Dad looks terrible. His face is still pale and his eyes are bloodshot. For a moment I think he's here to do something underhanded, like tell me how to beat the obstacle course. "No fair, Dad," I say, trying to make a joke of it. "You're not allowed to give me any tips."

He doesn't smile. "Hawke showed me the surveillance video from the gym," he says. "I saw what happened between you and Zia."

I'm confused. He's worried about *that*? "Oh, that was nothing. She was just acting tough."

"Acting? She has a welding torch on her arm! That thing could do catastrophic damage to another Pioneer."

"But she didn't use it. And I was ready to defend myself."

"She has a history of violence, Adam. She belonged to a gang in Los Angeles. And she knifed another gang member. I still don't understand why Hawke recruited her for the project." He shakes his head. "I want you to stay away from her."

"I can handle her, Dad. I'm not helpless anymore." I raise one of my mechanical hands and slap it against my torso. The clang echoes against the walls. "I'm a Pioneer. I'm built to last."

"But you're not invulnerable. If she cuts through your armor with that torch, it'll melt your circuits. You'd lose half your memory files in an instant."

I feel a familiar frustration. Dad's always been too anxious, always on the lookout for disaster. He used to be obsessed with all the health problems that came with my muscular dystrophy, problems with my breathing and swallowing and circulation. And now he's still obsessed, still looking for disaster, even though I don't have lungs or a throat or a heart anymore. It drives me crazy. I need to change the subject.

"What about the rest of the surveillance video?" I ask. "Did you also see the part where we argued about Hawke's tactics?"

He nods. "Yes, I saw."

"Well, is it true? Has Hawke dropped the idea of communicating with Sigma?"

Dad scans the room before answering. It looks like he's searching for hidden cameras or microphones. Hawke had the gym under surveillance, so maybe he bugged this room too. "I can't talk about that. When the general's ready to discuss his plans, he'll give the Pioneers a briefing."

I lower the volume of my speakers. "Come on, Dad. I thought the whole point of the Pioneer Project was to make contact with Sigma. Has something changed?"

He steps closer and lifts his chin toward my acoustic sensors. "Yes," he whispers. "Things in Russia have gotten worse."

"What happened?"

"There was a battle on the outskirts of Tatishchevo last night. Between Sigma's automated tanks and the Russians soldiers surrounding the missile base."

"A battle? Who started it?"

"We don't have all the facts yet. General Hawke is expecting a report from the National Security Adviser this afternoon. But whatever the details, we know time's running out. We have to accelerate our plans. And we have to make choices."

"But communicating with Sigma might be the best choice! If we could just get inside its circuits, we could—"

"No." Dad shakes his head again. "Sigma's too good at erasing other programs. It deleted all the Russian AIs at the Tatishchevo lab, remember? And it'll do the same thing to the Pioneers if you transfer yourselves to its circuits. You wouldn't last a second."

"Well, maybe we'd do better if we had some practice. We could set up training exercises to prepare ourselves. One Pioneer could transfer to another's circuits and they could fight for control. Sort of like a wrestling match."

He frowns. "I've gone over all the options. If we had more time, maybe things would be different. But right now Hawke's strategy has the best chance of success."

"And what's his strategy? He's going to transfer us to the electronics of his fighter jets? So we can bomb Tatishchevo?"

"If you think the general's going down the wrong road, you don't have to follow him. I wouldn't think any less of you."

For the second time in less than an hour, someone is asking me if I want to quit. But I understand why Dad has repeated the question. I can see it in his pale face. He's terrified of losing me. Saving my life has been his goal for the past ten years, driving him to accomplish all his scientific miracles. And now that he's saved my life, he doesn't want me to risk it. He wants me to stay safe while the others fight Sigma.

I'm not angry at him. I see where he's coming from. So again I say nothing. Instead, I extend my arm and grasp Dad's shoulder. I squeeze gently, relying on the sensors in my fingers to tell me how much pressure to apply. And when the sergeant comes back to the room half a minute later, I walk out the door with him and head for the obstacle course.

ᛏ ᛏ ᛏ

General Hawke stands in the middle of a big, empty yard. If this were a real prison camp, it would be the exercise yard. As I stride toward him I rotate my turret and survey the area. Two hundred feet to my right is a twenty-foot-high fence. A parallel fence runs on the other side of the camp. Looming over each fence is a guard tower, and standing sentry on each tower is a soldier with an assault rifle.

Hawke stands midway between the towers. About two hundred feet behind him are the camp's fake barracks, nine Quonset huts laid out in three rows. The huts are made of corrugated steel and painted dull green, the Army's favorite color. I see splotches of green paint on the ground too. Beyond the barracks, about five hundred feet away, is a large, boxy building with gray concrete walls.

What I *don't* see is an obstacle course. Are the obstacles hidden behind the Quonset huts? Or maybe *inside* the huts? I can't figure it out. I get the feeling, though, that this uncertainty is part of the challenge.

Hawke grins as I approach. "Well, look who's here. Last but not least."

I halt two yards in front of him. There's no point in saying anything. The general already knows how I feel.

Resting his hands on his hips, Hawke looks me over. "In the Army it's customary to salute your commanding officer. With the right arm, please."

Silently, I raise my robotic arm and salute him.

"That's better. Believe it or not, Armstrong, I'm not angry about what you said in the gym. I appreciate a soldier who's not afraid to speak his mind. In the days ahead there'll be times when I'll ask for your opinion. I may not agree with you, but I'll always hear you out."

I don't believe him. Not one bit.

"At the same time, though, I insist on discipline. If you want to be a part of this unit, you'll have to follow my orders." He narrows his eyes. "Understand?"

I wait a few seconds to make my reluctance clear. Then I synthesize a single word: "Yes."

"Say, 'Yes, sir.' That's another little custom of ours."

"Yes, sir."

He nods, satisfied. "All right, now we can start." He points at the fence surrounding the fake prison camp. "Your goal is to get out of the camp, but you're not allowed to go through that fence. You'll be disqualified if you try." He turns around and points at the large, gray building beyond the barracks. "You have to head for that building and follow the red arrows to the exit."

I aim my camera at the barracks and the gray building, scanning in both the visible-light and infrared ranges. "Where are the obstacles?"

Hawke grins again. "Well, we call it an obstacle course, but that's probably not the best name for it. It's more like a war game."

"A war game?"

"Yeah, my men are the opposing team. If they tag you before you leave the camp, the game's over."

Now I'm starting to understand. I see why Marshall and Jenny spent only a few minutes on the course. The soldiers probably "tagged" them right away. DeShawn, Shannon, and Zia had longer turns because they must've done a better job of evading Hawke's men. I train my camera on the guard towers where I saw the sentries a minute ago, but the men seem to have disappeared. Did they duck out of sight?

"Where are the soldiers?" I ask. "And what do you mean by 'tag'?"

"You'll see." Still grinning, he starts to walk away. "Better get moving, Armstrong. You're in the kill zone."

I've played enough video games to know what this means. The kill zone is the most dangerous section of the battlefield, usually located between two enemy positions. While General Hawke marches off I scan the guard towers again, turning my turret from one to the other. In both towers the sentries rise to their feet, and as they emerge from hiding, I notice they're no longer holding assault rifles. Instead, they've hoisted M136 anti-tank guns to their shoulders.

Uh-oh. Bad news.

In the next instant three things happen in quick succession. First, I start running toward the barracks. Second, I curse out General Hawke for arming his men with guns that could cripple a Pioneer. And third, I observe a bright flash in the guard tower to my left. It's the backfire from the launch of the M136's high-explosive shell. A hundredth of a second later I observe a similar flash in the guard tower to my right.

Panic floods my circuits. *I'm finished! I'm toast!* In midstride I catch a glimpse of the shell hurtling toward me from the left. It's a bullet-shaped projectile about three inches wide and nine inches long, with six steel fins at its tail end. The fins are there to stabilize the shell's flight, like the foam-rubber fins on the tail of a Nerf football. Then my electronic mind makes a terrified leap and retrieves a memory from earlier in the day, when DeShawn threw the Super Bowl football at me and I turned on my radar to measure the ball's speed. *Of course! You idiot! Turn on your radar!*

It takes three hundredths of a second for my electronics to start transmitting radar signals, which echo against the shell and bounce back to my antenna. According to the readings, the projectile is moving at 650 miles per hour, which means it'll hit me in less than a quarter-second. But when I calculate the shell's direction I see that it's off-center. I can dodge it by jinking to the right. It's a classic football maneuver, and for a moment I feel like a quarterback again, like Eli Manning dodging a defensive lineman. As soon as I make the move, though, I realize it won't do me any good. I've stepped into the path of the second shell, the one speeding toward me from the right.

That's why they call it a kill zone. They can get me from both directions.

My system freezes as the shells close in. I try to access information on the amount of explosives packed into an M136 shell, but my circuits won't cooperate. All I can see are the radar readings and the paths of the projectiles, which I picture as a pair of white lines slanting downward from the guard towers.

That's when I realize my mistake. I forgot about the height of the shells! I switch to a three-dimensional view and see that the second shell is aimed a bit high. Pitching my torso forward, I dive for the ground. My acoustic sensors pick up a loud whistle as the first shell flies past me, and then an even louder whoosh as the second shell speeds overhead, just inches above my turret. Then I hit the ground and my torso slides fifteen feet through the mud.

The shells strike the ground forty feet away, but to my surprise I don't hear any explosions. Using my robotic arms to lever myself upright, I get back on my footpads and turn my turret to see where the projectiles landed. Splattered across the mud are two new splotches of Army-green paint. The M136 shells were dummy rounds, full of paint instead of explosives.

It makes sense once I stop to think about it. The dummy rounds won't damage the Pioneers, but they'll show a direct hit by splattering paint on our armor. And until the moment of impact, they look realistic enough to terrify us. I can just imagine how Shannon must've reacted when she was on the course a few minutes ago. And Jenny, she must've been scared out of her mind. I'm so angry at Hawke I want to throw one of the fake shells at him, but instead I stride toward the barracks. I'm going to finish this obstacle course, and then I'm going to tell the general what I think of his stupid exercise.

I pick up speed as I head for the first row of Quonset huts. I'm sprinting forward at thirty miles per hour when I see a soldier step from behind one of the barracks. He holds another M136 anti-tank gun, but now I know what to do. I angle to the left and take a flying leap, using my momentum to scramble up the curved wall of the Quonset hut. With the help of the new sensors attached to my foot-pads, I gain traction on the hut's corrugated steel. I charge over the top of the barracks and slide down the other side, landing with a thud next to the soldier. Then I rip the M136 out of his hands and crush its barrel with my steel fingers.

The soldier stumbles backward, petrified. I feel a rush of satisfaction—*Are you scared, tough guy? Had enough?* But the feeling sours as I stare at his quivering face. He's one of General Hawke's pawns, just like me. He doesn't want to be here any more than I do.

Tossing the gun aside, I race past the next two rows of barracks. I don't see any other soldiers, but they could be hiding inside the Quonset huts. In a few seconds I reach the large building with gray concrete walls. I'm facing the back of the building—there are no doors on this side and only a few windows—but when I look closely at the base of the concrete wall I see a small arrow drawn in red paint. It points to the left.

I turn left and run. The wall is marked with splotches of green paint, and the ground is littered with the broken casings of anti-tank shells. There was clearly a lot of shooting here when the other Pioneers ran the course. Then I see another red arrow on the wall, this one point-ing at a lone window seven feet above the ground, the same height as my turret. The window has no glass; instead, it has a grate of thick steel bars.

Pointing my camera between the bars, I see a wide, high-ceilinged space inside the building, with a dozen Army trucks and Humvees parked on the concrete floor. It's a garage for fueling and repairing the vehicles. Some of the Humvees have their hoods raised, exposing their diesel V8 engines. On the other side of the garage, three roll-up doors are open, giving me a view of the muddy basin outside the fake prison camp.

This is the way out. This is the exit Hawke mentioned. But when I clamp my hands around the steel bars of the grate and try to yank it out of the window, it won't budge. I brace myself against the wall for leverage and increase the torque in my elbow motors, but the grate doesn't move, no matter how hard I pull. I take a step backward and notice that the steel bars are firmly anchored in the concrete around the window. Then I get a warning from my radar system. Another M136 shell is rocketing toward me.

I have just enough time to throw myself to the ground. The shell smashes into the grate as I roll away from the wall. Lying in the mud, I train my camera on the soldier who just fired at me. He drops his gun and runs away, but then another soldier steps forward and takes careful aim with his own M136. I extend one of my arms, grab a fragment of the shell that just shattered against the grate, and fling it at the anti-tank gun. The impact knocks the M136 out of the soldier's hands, and the guy races for cover behind one of the barracks.

More soldiers are coming, though. My acoustic sensor picks up the noise of their boots clomping through the mud. I've bought myself some time, but not much.

I right myself and turn back to the grate. Unfortunately, the shell did no damage to the steel bars other than coating them with green paint. I clench my mechanical hands into fists and pound the wall, hoping to loosen the bars, but all I can do is make a few shallow dents. What's more, I notice other dents in the concrete, obviously made by the Pioneers who ran the course earlier. This strategy didn't work for them, and it's not going to work for me either.

Out of ideas, I stare through the grate at the Humvees in the garage.

I'm frustrated and furious. Why did Hawke give us this impossible assignment? Does he get his kicks from watching us fail? And why should I care so much about this exercise anyway? I'm not doing myself any favors by playing Hawke's game. I should just let the soldiers splatter me.

I'm about to turn around and surrender when I notice something odd under the hood of one of the Humvees. A shiny steel case, about the size of a shoe box, has been installed next to the vehicle's battery. An orange cable connects the case to the V8 engine, and another cable runs to the Humvee's antenna. I've seen this setup in Hawke's databases about weapons and electronics. The steel case is a neuromorphic control unit. It's similar to the control units designed to operate fighter jets and helicopters, but this unit can control the Humvee.

That's it! That's the way out! I can escape from the prison camp by transferring myself out of my Pioneer and into that control unit!

With a burst of new hope, I turn on my transmitter. Sending the data wirelessly takes longer than using a cable; I'll need about half a minute to finish the transfer. I feel a weird stretching sensation as my antenna starts transmitting the radio waves that carry the data from my memory files. Part of me is traveling outward at the speed of light, bouncing through the barred window and reassembling at the Humvee's antenna, while another part of me remains in the Pioneer, maintaining control over the robot's sensors and motors until the transfer is complete.

I turn the Pioneer around and wait for the soldiers to show up. After fifteen seconds one of the men pokes his head around the corner of the nearest barracks. I fling another shell fragment in his direction, and the soldier pulls back.

After ten more seconds he jumps out of hiding and hoists his M136 to his shoulder. But by the time he aims the gun at me, I'm no longer inside the Pioneer. I've escaped the camp. I'm in the Humvee's control unit.

Once I'm inside the new circuits, I find the file that has the instructions for operating the vehicle. I start the engine and take control of the Humvee's driverless navigation system, which uses built-in cameras to detect obstacles in the vehicle's path. I put the Humvee in reverse and back out of the garage. Then I shift gears and gun the engine in triumph. Strangely enough, I feel comfortable inside the motor vehicle. It reminds me of my old motorized wheelchair. Except the Humvee is more maneuverable, of course, and a heck of a lot faster.

I speed away from the garage and zigzag across the basin, allowing myself a few seconds of celebration. Then I zoom back to the fake prison camp. As I approach the empty headquarters building, the Humvee's cameras detect several obstacles to my right. I slow down and turn toward them to get a closer look. Although the vehicle's built-in cameras aren't as good as the ones in my robot, I can tell what's in front of me: General Hawke and the five other Pioneers.

Hawke applauds as I pull to a stop. I can hear him clapping. The Humvee's navigation system is equipped with an acoustic sensor, most likely to detect car horns and sirens. "Nice work, Armstrong," the general says. "You did better than I expected. When people are shooting at you, it's not so easy to think clearly, is it?"

I can't respond in words—the vehicle has no system for speech synthesis—so I honk the horn instead.

"My men are retrieving your Pioneer," Hawke adds. "You'll have to transfer back to the robot for the tiebreaker."

Tiebreaker? What's he talking about? I aim the Humvee's cameras at the other Pioneers, trying to figure out what's going on. I notice that four of them are splattered with green paint, but one robot is clean.

"You weren't the only one to complete the course," Hawke explains. "Another Pioneer successfully transferred to the Humvee. So we need a tiebreaker to pick the leader for your unit." He points at the clean robot. Its armor is marked with the number 3 and a crude etching of a snake. "You and Zia are going to have a little race."

ᒣ ᒣ ᒣ

The tiebreaker is a half-mile sprint around the prison camp. I have no idea why Hawke chose this kind of competition. Because Zia's Pioneer is almost identical to mine—well, except for her circular saw and welding torch—we should be able to run a half-mile in about the same time, right? If one of us finishes slightly ahead of the other, a sensible person would chalk it up to luck. But the general seems to think otherwise.

I transfer myself back to my Pioneer and approach the starting line, which is in front of the empty headquarters. Then I shake out my steel legs and take a few practice strides, imitating the warm-ups I've seen Olympic runners do before a race. Zia, in contrast, just stands there behind the line, motionless. I extend my right arm, offering to shake hands, but she doesn't respond. For a second I try to imagine what's going through her circuits. Does she hate me for no reason, or is there something behind it?

Then Hawke yells, "Go!" and we both take off.

The trickiest part is dealing with the mud. My footpads start to slip as I build up speed. If I fall down I'll never catch up to Zia, so I have to make sure I don't stumble. I carefully control my acceleration as we leave the headquarters behind and make the first left turn at the northwestern corner of the camp. My circuits calculate exactly how fast I can go without losing my footing. Zia is obviously doing the same thing, because after turning the first corner, we're running neck and neck alongside the prison fence.

By the time we reach the southwestern corner, though, I've pulled ahead. I lean into the second turn, pumping my arms, and steadily build up my lead as we race past the Humvee garage. I'm running faster than Zia because of the wireless sensors I installed in my legs. The sensors at the bottom of my footpads are measuring the firmness of the ground, allowing me to maximize my speed. I can safely pick up the pace whenever I hit a dry patch. I'm almost twenty feet ahead of Zia when I reach the southeastern corner.

I feel a surge of exhilaration as I make the third turn and sprint north alongside the fence. Now I realize why I didn't give up on the obstacle course, why I worked so hard to win. I want to be the leader of the Pioneers. For some reason it's important to me. Maybe because I think I can do a better job than Hawke. Or maybe because I simply want to impress the others. It sounds a little conceited, I guess, but that's the way I feel.

I'm more than thirty feet ahead by the time I reach the northeastern corner. The headquarters comes back into view, and I can see Hawke and the other Pioneers standing by the finish line. But just as I make the final turn, I feel horrific pain in both of my legs. My knee joints feel like they've caught fire, and my footpads sting as if I've just stomped on a bed of nails. The pain is so fierce I lose control of my motors. My legs lock up and my momentum tips me over. My Pioneer careens into the mud.

The pain keeps tormenting me as Zia turns the corner and rushes toward the finish line. For a moment I suspect she used her welding torch on me, but when I run a diagnostic check on my systems I see that everything's normal. There's nothing wrong with my footpads or the motors in my leg joints. Then I realize that I'm feeling pain only in the places where I installed the wireless sensors. When I turn off the antenna that's receiving the signals from the sensors, the pain disappears.

I get back on my footpads and start running again, but Zia has already won the race. What she did was very clever. She must've intercepted my sensors' signals, figured out their frequency, and then transmitted a barrage of radio noise on the same channel. Basically, she hijacked my wireless nervous system to deliver a burst of pain to my circuits.

By the time I cross the finish line, Hawke is already congratulating Zia. For a moment I consider complaining to the general, but I know it won't do any good. I can't prove that Zia cheated. And besides, it's as much my own fault as hers. Shannon had warned me, back in the gym, about the dangers of leaving myself vulnerable. But I didn't listen.

"We have a winner," Hawke says. "I'm promoting Zia Allawi to lieutenant. She's now in charge of the Pioneers, at least when I'm not around. And I'm promoting Adam Armstrong to sergeant. He'll be the second-in-command." He gives me a magnanimous look, as if he's doing me a great favor. Then he looks at his watch. "All right, in thirty minutes one of Sigma's spy satellites is going to pass over Colorado, so we better get back inside the base. We'll regroup in the briefing room at sixteen hundred hours."

He nods at Zia, then marches toward his men. Zia salutes him as he walks away. Then she turns her turret and aims her camera at me. "You heard the general, Armstrong! Get the others in line!"

I have no choice. I have to obey her.

Cal, I have more information on the firefight at Tatishchevo
Missile Base, so I've ordered Colonel Peterson to fly to Colorado and deliver this message to you. The news isn't good.

The incident began last night just outside Tatishchevo's
eastern gate. The Russian soldiers assigned to that area came
under heavy fire from the base. At least sixty of Sigma's driverless tanks emerged from the gate and advanced east along the
highway that leads to the city of Saratov. The attack caught
the Russians by surprise. When the unmanned tanks roared out
of the base with their guns blazing, the troops panicked and
retreated into the woods.

Before the Russian commanders could organize a counter-
attack, a convoy of three trucks sped down the highway
from Saratov, heading for the base. The trucks entered
Tatishchevo, and then the tanks immediately pulled back
behind the eastern gate and reassumed their defensive positions. The attack was apparently a diversion. Sigma launched
it just to clear the highway so the trucks could get into
the missile base.

Unfortunately, it gets worse. Russian investigators have
figured out who was driving the trucks and what was inside
them. Twelve hours before the firefight there was an incident
at the Russian army's bioweapons laboratory, five hundred
miles northeast of Tatishchevo. A group of terrorists, most

likely from Chechnya, broke into the lab and captured a large
supply of highly lethal anthrax bacteria.

The Chechens also stole equipment that mixes the bacteria
into an aerosol spray, making it easy to spread the germs over
a large area. Witnesses at the bioweapons lab said the terrorists escaped in three Ural tractor-trailer trucks. That matches
the description of the vehicles that entered Tatishchevo.

So it looks like you were right when you said Sigma's preferred strategy is to kill off the human race without destroying our machines. Spreading anthrax over our cities would
accomplish that goal quite efficiently. The Russian army is
pushing hard to attack Tatishchevo before Sigma can release
the germs. We've given them the results of our analyses, all
the studies showing that Sigma could easily launch its nuclear
missiles long before our own missiles could hit the computer
lab, but the Russians are growing impatient. If we want to
pursue the Pioneer option, you'll need to get your team ready
soon. Even two weeks may be too long. We may have to load the
Pioneers on a flight to Russia in just a few days.

In the meantime, we need to be very careful. The attack on
the bioweapons lab shows that Sigma can persuade people to
carry out tasks that the AI can't do by itself. It looks like
Sigma made contact with the terrorists through its communications satellites, which give the AI access to the Internet and
the telephone networks.

And there's evidence that Sigma has used this access to hack
into the computer systems of several major banks. The AI has
apparently stolen millions of dollars from the banks, elec-
tronically transferring the money to its own hidden accounts,

and now it can offer these funds to terrorists and mercenaries in exchange for their cooperation. The terrorists have no idea they're dealing with an AI because it can mimic human speech so well.

Worst of all, I'm worried that Sigma may be using human allies to help it find Pioneer Base. Just a few minutes ago I got a report from the FBI field office in New York. The parents of Ryan Boyd, the student at Yorktown High School who was once Adam Armstrong's best friend, have reported the boy missing. Ryan disappeared last night while he was socializing with his friends behind Yorktown High School. His friends say he stepped into the woods to relieve himself, but he never returned. The FBI has assigned a task force to search for Ryan, but they have no good leads.

I think we have to assume the worst: that someone allied with Sigma kidnapped the boy to find out where Armstrong is. I strongly recommend that you question Adam about this right away. If he told Ryan the location of Pioneer Base, you may have to evacuate the facility.

I'm sorry to deliver so much bad news in one message. God bless you and the Pioneers.

DATE: 04/04/18

This is a transcript of a telephone conversation between the Sigma speech-synthesis program (S) and American ex-convict Richard Ramsey (R). The communications were transmitted via radio from Tatishchevo Missile Base to the Globus-1 satellite, then to the Verizon cell-phone network in Westchester County, New York.

S: Good afternoon. How's the weather in Westchester?

R: Well, well. It's my rich uncle again. How you doin', Unc? I got that money order you sent me.

(Voice analysis confirms that the speaker is Richard Ramsey.)

S: Please tell me what you've learned since our last conversation. I've encrypted this call, so you can speak freely.

R: I've been busy, Unc, real busy. First off, I found Ryan Boyd, the football player. I grabbed him last night while he was hanging out with his buddies. He's in my basement now, handcuffed to the pipes.

S: Has he been cooperative?

R: Oh yeah. He's so scared, he can't stop talking. We had a nice chat about Adam Armstrong.

S: What did Ryan tell you?

R: He saw Adam just a few days ago. They had a conversation in the high-school parking lot. It was a sad little scene, Unc. Adam's dying, you know.

S: Yes, I'm aware of that.

R: But he told Ryan something interesting. Adam said he was going to a new school out west. And he said he was going to make lots of new friends there.

(Conclusion: This is a possible reference to the Pioneer Project.)

S: He said, "Out west"?

R: I know. It's a little vague. I grilled Ryan for a couple of hours, trying to get more out of him, but his story didn't change. Adam just said "out west." Nothing else.

S: In this context, would you assume that "out west" means the western half of the continental United States?

R: Hey, I'm no expert on geography. I get lost just driving through Yonkers. (Laughter.) But yeah, I'd say that's right. West of the Mississippi.

(Conclusion: The search for the Pioneer Project should be focused on the western United States. The orbits of my surveillance satellites will be adjusted accordingly.)

S: Do you have anything else to report?

R: As a matter of fact, I do. That girl you told me about, Brittany Taylor? The

cheerleader who ran off to New York City? I found out that Adam's obsessed
with her. He asked Ryan if he knew where she was.

S: Did Ryan know?

R: He said he didn't but he guessed she might be in Harlem. So early this
morning I left him in my basement and drove into the city. I used to do business with the gangs in Harlem, you know.

S: Business?

R: Yeah, they used to call me the aspirin. If some guy was giving the gangs
a headache, I made the guy go away. (Laughter.) Anyway, I found some old
friends and showed them Brittany's picture, and one of them recognized her.
He'd seen her on West 134th Street, outside an abandoned building that's full
of runaways.

S: Did you visit the building?

R: Hey, that's what you're paying me for, right? I spent two hours watching
the place from across the street. Finally, just before noon, she came outside.
I watched her go to the corner store and buy a Snickers bar for her breakfast.

S: You're certain it was her?

R: No doubt about it. She's been living on the street for a while, so she don't
look as good as she used to. Her hair's a mess and her face is all splotchy.
But it's her, all right.

(Conclusion: there's an opportunity to abduct Brittany Taylor. In all likelihood she doesn't know where Adam Armstrong is, but capturing her might prove useful in other ways.)

S: I want you to bring Brittany to your home. She can stay in your basement with Ryan.

R: Whoa, hold on, Unc. I'm not running a summer camp here.

S: You won't have to keep them for long. Only until you finish questioning them.

R: And then what happens?

(I must adjust my speech-synthesis program. I can communicate more effectively with this human if I speak the way he does.)

S: You're going to make Ryan and Brittany go away. Like the headaches. Make them disappear.

(Pause)

R: What's going on, Unc? What do you got against these kids?

S: I'm prepared to increase your payment. I'll send you another $30,000.

R: Sorry, but thirty grand ain't enough. Not for what you're talking about now.

S: How much do you need? Please name a figure.

R: This is serious business. We're talking at least a hundred grand.

S: I'll wire $50,000 now to your bank account. You'll get another $50,000 after you send me proof that the job is done.

(Longer pause)

R: You're pretty coldhearted, Unc.

S: Do we have an agreement?

R: Just send the money.

CHAPTER

14

GENERAL HAWKE SCOWLS AT ME FROM BEHIND THE DESK IN HIS OFFICE.

"How could you do this, Armstrong? Didn't you sign a confidentiality agreement on your first visit to Pioneer Base? Didn't I make it clear that you were forbidden to tell anyone where you were?"

"Yes, but—"

"Say, 'Yes, sir.' The 'sir' should be part of your programming by now. It should be automatic."

If I had a face, I'd scowl back at him. But I only have my camera. "Yes, sir. I didn't tell Ryan where Pioneer Base is. I didn't mention Colorado. I just said 'out west.' Just those two words."

"That's bad enough. Those two words are gonna make life difficult for us."

He picks up a document from a stack of papers on his desk. I focus my camera on the top of the page and see a couple of lines obviously written with a typewriter:

From: The National Security Adviser

The White House, Washington, DC

This must be the memo about Ryan's kidnapping. Hawke waves it in the air. "Sigma is a relentless enemy, Armstrong. It's going to change the orbits of its surveillance satellites and have them spend more time looking at this part of the country. That means we'll have less time to train outside. And in our current situation, that's a very bad thing."

He's trying to make me feel guilty, and it's working. I feel bad about putting my fellow Pioneers in danger. But I feel even worse about what happened to Ryan. A twinge runs through my circuits as I retrieve the memory of our last meeting and the painful conversation in the Yorktown High parking lot. I should've never gone looking for him.

"I'm sorry, sir. It was a stupid mistake."

"Did you make any other mistakes? Talk to anyone else while you were in Yorktown Heights?"

"No, sir. No one but my parents."

Still scowling, Hawke stands up and goes to the file cabinet behind his desk. "You should've been more careful. You knew Sigma was after you. It had already tried to kill you at the Unicorp lab." He opens the file cabinet's top drawer and slips the typewritten memo into one of the folders there. Then he slams the drawer closed and locks it with a small silver key. "Well, at least I don't have to worry about the other Pioneers. Sigma doesn't know their identities, so it can't go after their friends."

He shoves the key into his pants pocket and returns to his desk. I expect him to continue chewing me out, but instead he starts leafing through his stack of papers. There are more typewritten memos in the stack, plus several satellite photos of Tatishchevo Missile Base.

"Uh, sir? Are the police looking for Ryan?"

He nods. "Definitely. The police, the FBI, they've all involved in the search."

"Do you think they'll find him?"

"Don't worry. They're doing everything they can. I'll let you know as soon as I get any news." He raises his head for a moment and glances at my camera lens. Then he goes back to studying his papers. "That's all for now, Armstrong. You're dismissed."

Raising my right arm, I salute the general, then turn around and head for the door. As I leave his office, though, I get the feeling that Hawke is hiding something. He doesn't think the police will find Ryan. I could hear the resignation in his voice. He thinks my friend is as good as dead.

A surge of fury invades my circuits—I want to bolt out of Pioneer Base and start running east, back to Yorktown Heights. I want to find the traitor who's working with Sigma, the thug who kidnapped Ryan Boyd. I want to pound his face and stomp on his knees and clamp my steel hands around his neck. I can picture it so clearly: his tongue hanging out of his mouth, his eyes widening as I crush his throat. In an instant, my mind draws a thousand gory images, each as vivid as the worst scenes in a horror movie. *Are you scared, tough guy? Had enough?*

The emotion is so strong that for a couple of seconds I lose track of the data coming from my sensors. When I come back to reality, I'm standing in the corridor outside Hawke's office with my hands locked into fists. Another Pioneer is just a few feet away, training its camera on me. The number 5 is stamped on its torso. It's Marshall Baxley.

"Everything okay, Adam?" He's modified his synthesized voice, making it sound fancy and British, like he's an actor in a Shakespeare play. "You seem perplexed."

"No, I'm fine." But that's a lie. The truth is, I'm a little freaked out by the explosion of rage I just felt. Nothing like that has ever happened to me before.

"Are you sure?" Marshall moves a step closer, his footpads clanging. "I see you just came out of the general's office. Was Hawke giving you a hard time?"

I'm starting to wonder whether it's a coincidence that I found Marshall here. Was he spying on me? Eavesdropping on my conversation with Hawke? I wouldn't put it past him. "No, we were talking about the weather."

He chuckles. It makes me jealous, his ability to synthesize laughter. He does it so easily. "You're funny, Adam. You're one of the most amusing robots I know. Where are you going now?"

"Why do you care?"

He places his mechanical hands on the sides of his torso, just above where his legs are attached. It's a posture of outrage, hands on hips. "I was trying to be friendly, that's all. We have an hour to kill before the next training exercise, so I thought I'd invite you to hang out in my room for a while."

"Hang out?"

"You know, drink beer, smoke cigarettes. Oh, wait a minute." He slaps one of his hands against his turret, as if suddenly remembering something. "Well, we can talk at least. That's something we can still do."

"What about your friend Zia? Will she be there too?"

"Oh Lord, I wish you two would stop bickering."

"Bickering? She's insane."

"Look, Adam, we don't have a lot of choices for friends here. We take what we can get. And Zia's not so bad. I find her fascinating, actually. She's so *ferocious*."

"So why do you need me? Why don't you just hang out with her?"

Marshall lets out a synthesized sigh. "All right, you want the truth?" He moves another step closer and lowers the volume of his speakers. "Zia can get tiresome after a while. She spends way too much time talking about Hawke. It's like she has a crush on the man. That's a disgusting thought, isn't it?" He synthesizes a gagging noise. "And when she's not talking about Hawke, she likes to lecture me on military strategy. She downloaded all the Army's files on every war ever fought. You should hear her go on about World War II. It's like listening to the History Channel."

I have to admit, this is interesting information. Although Marshall may be a weasel, at least he's entertaining. I'm still angry at him for siding with Zia this morning, but maybe I should let it slide. He's right about one thing: we don't have a lot of choices for friends here.

Marshall raises one of his arms and points down the hall toward his room. "So are you coming or not?" His fancy British voice quavers a bit. It's a subtle change, but my acoustic sensor detects it. I realize that behind all his jokes and cleverness, Marshall is lonely. He's dying for someone to talk to. "Zia won't be there, but DeShawn said he'd stop by. Both of you like football, so we can talk about that. I'll do my best to pretend to be interested."

That clinches it. I definitely want to talk to DeShawn. We have more in common than an interest in football. "Okay, I'm in."

"A wise choice, Mr. Armstrong." Marshall claps my torso. "Let's make some trouble."

᛫ ᛫ ᛫

Marshall stops at his door and raises his right hand to a keypad mounted on the wall. Swiftly tapping his mechanical fingers on the keys, he enters a six-digit password that unlocks the door. But as it swings open he lets out a synthesized yelp of surprise. Pioneer 6 stands just inside the doorway.

"What up, peeps?" DeShawn telescopes his arms, spreading them wide. "What took you so long?"

"Well, well. I see you've made yourself at home." Marshall is trying to act casual, but I can tell he's annoyed. His British accent sounds strained. "May I ask how you managed to get into my room?"

"It was easy. I looked up your birth date in the Pioneer Base library. You couldn't think of a better password than that?"

"Ah. How foolish of me." Marshall slaps his turret again. "It was force of habit, I suppose. Until recently I had trouble remembering numbers. But that's not a problem anymore, is it?"

"You should use your circuits to generate a random number. You can make it as long as you want, a hundred digits, two hundred. Then no one will ever guess it."

I stride forward and point at the keypad. "But that would be inefficient. It would take forever to punch in such a long number."

"How about transmitting the password wirelessly instead?" DeShawn points at the keypad too. His robotic voice is full of enthusiasm. "We could add a transceiver to the locking mechanism. Then you could send it a radio signal with the encoded password."

I focus my camera on DeShawn's turret, wishing he had a face so I could see his expression. He's obviously a tech geek. Just like me, he spent years trapped in a wheelchair, paralyzed and helpless and bored out of my mind, and now I realize we both had the same strategy for coping with it. DeShawn became an expert on software and computers and all the other gadgets that make life tolerable for someone with Duchenne muscular dystrophy. As I stare at his turret

I feel a pulse of gladness in my circuits. We're even more alike than I'd suspected.

I turn on my wireless system and connect to the Pioneer Base library. Then I scroll through the databases until I find a file on transceiver electronics. "Okay, I see a couple of options," I say. "We can install a circuit board with—"

"Slow down, boys." Marshall snakes one of his arms around my torso and the other around DeShawn's. "I'm not in the mood to reprogram anything right now." He guides us into his room and shuts the door behind us. "Let's just have a little conversation, shall we?"

Marshall's room looks a lot like mine. There's no furniture. The room is empty except for the recharging station and Marshall's evil twin, a motionless spare Pioneer with the label 5A stamped on its torso. But the walls are covered with posters. They look like the kind of posters you'd see in a high-school English classroom. Each shows a black-and-white photograph of a famous poet and a quote from one of his or her poems.

Beneath a picture of Emily Dickinson is the quote, "Hope is the thing with feathers that perches in the soul." Beneath Walt Whitman is the line, "Do I contradict myself? Very well, then I contradict myself. I am large, I contain multitudes." One poster, though, is set apart from all the others, tacked in the exact center of the far wall. It shows a man with a grotesquely large head and a right hand the size of a catcher's mitt. This man, I realize, is Marshall's hero, Joseph Merrick—the Elephant Man. The quote below his picture is from the poem Marshall gave me on the night before I became a Pioneer: "I would be measured by the soul; the mind's the standard of the man."

I think of the Super Bowl posters on the walls of my own room. I wonder if Marshall, like me, needs reminders of his former life. "Cool posters," I say. "Did you bring them here? From your home, I mean?"

Marshall waves his steel hand in a dismissive way. "Yes, they're old things. Getting wrinkled, I'm afraid. But it's better than leaving the walls bare." He turns his turret toward DeShawn, then back to me. "Please make yourselves comfortable, gentlemen. Unfortunately, I don't have much in the way of refreshments. All I can offer is the electricity from my recharging station."

DeShawn holds up both his hands, splaying the fingers. "Thanks, but no thanks. I'm full up."

"How about you, Adam? Care to top off your batteries?"

"No, I'm full too."

"Ah, too bad. It's an excellent vintage of electric current with a truly intoxicating voltage." Marshall laughs, and once again my circuits crackle with envy. "Tell me something, Mr. Armstrong. Back in the days when you were flesh and blood, did you ever get drunk?"

I turn my turret clockwise, then counter. "Never got the chance. I was in a wheelchair by the time I was twelve."

"Same with me," DeShawn says. "But my mom let me have a sip of beer once. Tasted nasty."

A synthesized "tsk-tsk" comes out of Marshall's speakers. "What a shame. You boys have led such sheltered lives. You've never had the unique pleasure of downing a bottle of Southern Comfort stolen from your mother's liquor cabinet."

I retrieve an image from my files, another memory from the night before my procedure. I remember Marshall lying on my bed, resting his deformed head on the mattress and talking about his childhood. "It wasn't really a pleasure, was it?" I ask. "Getting drunk?"

"Well, there were a few moments of giddiness, at least at the beginning. But you're right. In the end it wasn't fun. I was drinking alone in the woods behind our house. That was one of my hiding places."

"Hiding places? What were you hiding from?"

Marshall extends his left arm until his hand almost touches the Elephant Man poster. "In the small town where I grew up, most of the people were decent. They treated me with Christian charity and kindness. But there was a limit to their sympathy. In general, they preferred that I keep myself hidden."

I look again at the poster, noting all the similarities between the photo of Joseph Merrick and my memory of Marshall's human body. After several milliseconds of thought, I come to a conclusion: DeShawn and I were lucky. Being trapped in a wheelchair was paradise compared to what Marshall must've gone through.

The room falls silent. Marshall retracts his arm. We aim our cameras at each other, but neither of us speaks. I don't know what to say.

Then DeShawn breaks the silence. "What you said before, Marsh? About the giddiness? I know something about that."

Marshall turns his turret toward him. "Don't tell me you got tipsy from that sip of beer your mother gave you."

"Nah, this is something else. Something I discovered just yesterday." DeShawn taps his fingers against his torso's armor, pointing at the spot where his neuromorphic circuits are. "I was playing around with my files, trying to see how fast I could perform some complex calculations. And then by accident I activated a pathway I didn't know was there. That's what caused the giddiness."

"Really?" Marshall trains his camera up and down, giving DeShawn a careful once-over. "This is intriguing. Exactly how giddy were you?"

"It only lasted a hundredth of a second, but it was pretty intense.

The pathway must have some strong connections to the positive emotions—you know, happiness, delight, that kind of thing. I felt joyful, on top of the world. Like I'd just won the lottery or something."

Now I aim my camera at DeShawn, studying him just as carefully as Marshall did. I remember the sensations I felt a few days ago when I went into sleep mode and dreamed of my mother. DeShawn's discovery is better, though. He's talking about a shortcut for altering his emotions. "How did you do it? Where was the pathway you activated?"

"It's in the same folder where the sensory functions are. Here, I'll show you."

An instant later I receive a radio message from DeShawn detailing the exact location of the pathway in my electronics. To activate it, all I need to do is send a thought down those circuits. I'm eager to give it a try, but also a little wary. "Were there any aftereffects?" I ask. "Any permanent changes to your electronics?"

DeShawn lifts his steel shoulders in a shrug. "Sure, there were changes. But our circuitry is changing all the time. After every experience we make new connections."

"But were the changes good or bad?"

"It didn't hurt me. But if you're worried about it, you don't have to—"

Marshall interrupts him by clanging his hands together. The noise echoes against the walls. "I'm not worried, DeShawn. Send me the same message you just sent to Adam."

DeShawn turns on his radio again and transmits the message. "Here you go."

Marshall folds his arms across his torso. He's clearly reading the message and inspecting the pathway. "Well, it looks simple enough. And God knows, I could use a little giddiness right now." He raises his right hand

and curls the steel fingers, pretending to hold a glass. Then he brings the hand toward his turret, like a man about to take a drink. "Cheers!"

Marshall's torso shudders as he activates the pathway. I watch him for several milliseconds. Then I push my fears aside and do the same.

I feel a rush of elation. It's Christmas, it's my birthday, it's Super Bowl Sunday. The New York Giants have just won Super Bowl XLVI and all my friends are cheering. Ryan Boyd picks me up by the waist and carries me around our living room. Brittany Taylor does a handstand and falls to the carpet, laughing. Her eyes are blue one moment, grayish-green the next.

The joy grows so fierce that it's almost unbearable. And then, after exactly eleven milliseconds, it shuts off. The emotion doesn't fade; it vanishes instantly. For a moment I'm distraught. I feel abandoned and empty. I want to activate the pathway again, *right now*.

But I don't do it. There's a reason the elation disappeared so abruptly. The extreme emotion must've tripped some kind of self-protection circuit. The bliss was too strong. Strong enough to drive you crazy.

I need another few milliseconds to compose myself. Then I turn my turret toward DeShawn. "Wow, you were right. That was intense."

He doesn't respond. Instead, he aims his camera at Marshall. I turn that way too and see Pioneer 5 thrashing. Marshall swings one arm to the left and the other to the right, as if whipping an invisible enemy. I stride backward, getting out of the way. "Marshall! What's wrong?"

I don't think he can hear me. He's flailing his arms the same way Jenny did right after her procedure. He's lost control of his Pioneer.

DeShawn steps backward too. "Stop it, Marshall!" he shouts. "Disengage your locomotion circuits!"

Marshall keeps flailing. His right arm slices the air and slams into the wall, shredding two of the posters. I have to stop him before he hurts himself. I observe Marshall's movements and calculate the safest way to restrain him. "I'm going in!" I yell at DeShawn. "Get ready to back me up!"

But just as I'm about to lunge across the room, Marshall stops thrashing. All at once he lowers and retracts his arms. His torso vibrates for a moment, then goes still.

"Marshall?" I take a step forward, still ready to restrain him if I have to. "You okay?"

"I'm fine."

He's no longer speaking with an amused British accent. Marshall's voice is monotone, truly robotic. I take another step toward him. "What happened? Did you activate the—"

"I'd rather not talk about it."

Now DeShawn steps forward. "Look, if there's a problem, you should tell us. We still don't understand how our circuits—"

"Please leave. Both of you." Marshall raises his right arm and points at the door. "I want to be alone."

I can tell that arguing with him won't do any good. Activating the pathway clearly had a different effect on Marshall than it had on me or DeShawn. And he definitely doesn't want to talk about it.

Reluctantly, I head for the door. A moment later I hear DeShawn's footsteps clanging behind me. Just as I grasp the doorknob, though, Marshall lets out a synthesized sigh. I turn my turret around and see him waving good-bye at us.

"Sorry to be so inhospitable." His voice softens. "I enjoyed your company very much."

I wave back at him, flapping my mechanical hand. The gesture looks a little silly when performed by an eight-hundred-pound robot. But it works.

THE NEXT MORNING THE PIONEERS LEARN HOW TO FLY. WE TAKE THE FREIGHT elevator up to the surface again and march to the runway on the other side of the basin. There's a hangar beside the runway, and through its open doors I see a helicopter, a UH-60 Black Hawk. Its weapon racks are loaded with a pair of Hellfire rockets, and a long antenna extends from the chopper's tail. Zooming in on the antenna with my camera, I notice it's connected to a neuromorphic control unit. A surge of excitement lights up my circuits. I picture myself soaring over the basin in the Black Hawk, maybe even launching one of its Hellfires.

But the helicopter isn't ready for action. Its rotor blades are folded and tied down, and there are no soldiers in the hangar to prepare the aircraft for flight. Instead, all the soldiers are on the runway, standing in a circle. As we get closer I see what's at the center of the circle: six miniature airplanes sitting on the tarmac.

They're sleek and black, made of shiny fiberglass. Each has a five-foot wingspan and a three-foot-long fuselage containing a battery compartment and an electric motor. Hanging from the belly of each plane is a video camera, and at the tail is a long antenna. The planes look similar to ordinary remote-control models, the kind that hobbyists pilot from the ground using radios, but each fuselage has an extra compartment that's wired to the motor and antenna. This compartment, I'm willing to bet, holds a neuromorphic control unit.

I feel a jolt of disappointment. We're going to transfer our minds to model airplanes? That's ridiculous. Those things aren't weapons. They're toys. Their top speed is maybe fifty miles per hour, and they're too light to carry any guns or missiles. What's the point of training in that thing? How in the world will it help us fight Sigma?

The soldiers step aside as we join the circle. The other Pioneers also seem puzzled by the miniature planes. Zia turns her turret to Marshall, who lifts his robotic arms in a shrug. I turn to Shannon and DeShawn, but neither says a word. (I don't bother Jenny, who's standing by herself as usual, silent and unapproachable.) Then General Hawke enters the circle and everyone salutes. The general halts beside the planes and points at the nearest one, which has the number 3 stamped on its fuselage. All the planes have numbers, just like us.

"This is an RQ-11 Raven," Hawke says. "Our troops have used these small drones for surveillance in Iraq, Afghanistan, and other combat zones. The Ravens usually fly at an altitude of five hundred feet and send video images of the battlefield to our men on the ground, who steer the drones by remote control." He crouches next to the plane and points at its fuselage. "We've modified these Ravens so they can carry a few extra pounds. We miniaturized the neuromorphic control unit and put a steel case around it to protect the circuits if the plane crashes. In today's exercise my men will launch the Ravens, and then the Pioneers will wirelessly transfer themselves to the control units while the planes are in flight. All the information needed to fly the Ravens is already loaded in the units. Once you're inside the planes, I'll send you further instructions by radio."

Hawke straightens up and steps away from the Ravens. "Before we start, are there any questions?"

I raise my hand. "Sir, could you explain the tactical advantages of attacking Sigma with this kind of aircraft?"

"Your question is premature, Armstrong. First you're gonna learn how to fly the Ravens. Then we'll discuss their advantages and disadvantages. Any other questions?" Hawke pauses, but no one else raises a hand. "All right, the commander goes first. Lieutenant Allawi?"

Zia steps forward. At the same time, one of Hawke's soldiers picks up Raven Number 3, carries it outside the circle, and starts its motor, which whines and buzzes as it turns the plane's propeller. I assume he's going to set the plane on the runway for the takeoff, but instead the soldier flings it into the air. The Raven climbs at a steep angle, and within seconds it's hundreds of feet above the ground. It may be just a miniature plane, but the takeoff is pretty cool.

"Okay, Allawi, you can transfer now," Hawke says.

"Yes, sir!" Zia says, saluting him again. Then she turns on her data transmitter.

The general tilts his head back to gaze at the Raven, which looks like a tiny black cross against the sky. After half a minute he glances at Zia's Pioneer, which powers down after it finishes transmitting its data. Hawke grabs a radio from his belt, holds it up to his mouth, and shouts, "*Allawi, are you up there?*"

There's no answer at first. Hawke waits about ten seconds, then shouts into the radio again. "*Please respond, Allawi. Are you all right?*"

After five more seconds, her reply comes back. "Affirmative, sir. I'm piloting the Raven. Everything is functioning normally."

The general seems relieved. He purses his lips and lets out a long breath. Then he turns to me. "You're next, Armstrong."

"Uh, sir? Could I launch the plane myself?"

Hawke cocks his head. "Have you already downloaded the instructions for the RQ-11?"

"No, sir, but I observed the soldier do it, and I can imitate him exactly. And it would be useful to practice launching the Ravens. Just in case we have to do it in the field."

He thinks it over for a moment. "All right. Just don't slam it into the ground. Believe it or not, each of those little planes costs fifty thousand dollars."

I'm amazed he's actually letting me do it. I stride toward the Ravens, pick up Number 1, and turn on its motor. The plane vibrates in my steel hand as I draw my arm back, readying for the throw. Then I hurl the Raven at a sixty-degree angle and it shoots right up into the sky. I watch it climb for a few seconds, then turn to the other Pioneers and do a little bow, tilting my torso forward.

Marshall and Jenny just stand there, but Shannon and DeShawn applaud, their fingers clinking.

"Nice pass, Armstrong," Shannon says. "But where's your receiver?"

"I'm my own receiver. It's every quarterback's dream." I glance at Hawke, who gives me a nod, and then I turn on my data transmitter.

I feel the weird stretching sensation again. It's even more disorienting than when I transferred myself to the Humvee, because now I'm transmitting my data over a much greater distance. The radio waves from my antenna spread in all directions, sweeping across the floor of the basin and rising hundreds of feet into the air. In a millionth of a second they reach the antenna at the tail of my Raven, but the signal is weak. Because the waves have spread across such a huge area, it takes longer for all my data packets to reassemble in the Raven's control unit. For nearly a minute I'm sprawled across the Colorado sky, my mind arcing dizzily above the Rocky Mountains.

And then I'm inside the Raven. I connect to the plane's video camera and see the mountainous landscape below. The Raven also has an acoustic sensor, and when I link to it, I hear the buzz of the motor and the whistling of the wind. Last, I connect to the plane's accelerometers, which monitor the four forces acting on me: gravity, lift, thrust, and drag. I'm perfectly balanced between these forces, and the feeling is incredible, like riding the world's best roller coaster. I retrieve the instructions for the RQ-11 and switch the plane from remote-control flight to autonomous operation. *Now I'm flying!*

There are no flaps on the Raven's wings, so I have to rely on the rudder and the elevator at the plane's tail. First I test the rudder, turning the plane to the left and right. Then I angle the elevator upward, which lowers the tail and lifts the plane's nose. An instant later I rev up the motor, and the Raven goes into a steep, thrilling climb. A strong wind from the west buffets and jostles me, but I tweak the controls and keep aiming for the clouds. I level out at two thousand feet above the ground, then point the video camera downward so I can get a good view of the countryside. The basin is directly below, a muddy brown bowl with a snow-white rim. All around it are the endless peaks of the Rockies.

Then I get an incoming radio signal, encrypted for security reasons. My circuits decode the message, which is a voice communication from General Hawke.

"You okay, Armstrong?"

Adjusting the lens of the plane's camera, I zoom in on the general and the Pioneers. They look so tiny down there.

"Big affirmative, sir," I reply, transmitting my synthesized voice over the radio channel. "This is the best day of my life."

"Take it easy with the aerobatics. If you lose control at that altitude, you'll hit the ground pretty hard."

I focus the camera on the ridges surrounding the basin. Falling on the snow-covered ground probably wouldn't be so bad, but there are also sections of exposed rock on the slopes. Then another worry occurs to me. "Sir, I think I've gone too high. I can see for miles around, and that means anyone down there can see me too."

I expect Hawke to get angry, but his voice stays calm. "It's a risk, but a small one. From this far away, you look like a bird. And we've restricted public access to the surrounding area."

I start to descend anyway. Better safe than sorry. Lowering the elevator, I dip the plane's nose and cut back on the motor. I see Zia's Raven five hundred feet below me, flying in a wide circle. A quarter-mile to the west I spot a third plane climbing into the sky. From far away, they really do look like birds.

That's when I get my first inkling of Hawke's plan for attacking Sigma. I reopen the radio channel to the general. "Sir? What would the Ravens look like on a radar screen? They'd look more like birds than planes, wouldn't they?"

There's a pause of several seconds. When Hawke finally comes back on the radio, he sounds amused. "That's another premature question, Armstrong."

"But am I right, sir? Have I identified one of the Raven's tactical advantages?"

"We'll talk about it later. Now stop bothering me. I have to get three more Pioneers into the air."

I continue descending. Turning the rudder to the right, I go into a slow, clockwise corkscrew. Over the next fifteen minutes the other Pioneers zoom up from the runway, one by one. Pretty soon we're all circling the airspace over the basin. It's an amazing sight.

I don't want it to end, but the charge in my Raven's battery will only last for another fifteen minutes. I descend below eight hundred feet, which is the height of the ridges around the basin, and now I can no longer see the mountains beyond. Then I get another radio message from General Hawke. He's addressing all the Pioneers at once.

"So far, so good," he says. "Now here comes the hard part. I want all of you to turn off your motors."

After a few seconds of silence, Shannon's synthesized voice comes over the radio. "Could you repeat that, sir? I'm not sure I heard you correctly."

"You heard me right, Gibbs. Shut down your motors."

"But, sir?" This is DeShawn's voice. "How will we—"

"You're gonna glide the rest of the way down. All the necessary instructions are in your control units."

He's right. According to the instructions, the Raven's design—long wings, sleek fuselage—makes it ideal for gliding. We can land the planes without power if we spiral down to the basin, using the rudder for steering and the elevator to control the descent. "Should we land on the runway, sir?" I ask.

"Negative. I want you to transfer back to your Pioneers while you're still gliding. First you need to descend to about three hundred feet to get within radio range. Then you have to keep the Ravens circling in the air until you complete the data transfer. After that, the planes will revert back to remote-control operation and my men will steer them to the landing zone."

"Excuse me, General?" This is Marshall's voice, with its computer-generated British accent. "May I ask why we're practicing this particular maneuver?"

"No, you may not. Are your circuits malfunctioning, Baxley? Didn't you hear what I told Armstrong? No premature questions."

"My apologies, sir. I didn't—"

"All right, enough chatter. Cut your motors right now. I'll give a nice, shiny medal to whoever makes it down first."

For a moment I feel sorry for Marshall, but not because Hawke chewed him out. I feel sorry for him because he doesn't see what's obvious. The reason for today's training exercise becomes absolutely clear as soon as I turn off my motor. The electric buzz ceases and the propeller stops spinning and the only sound my acoustic sensor picks up is the whistling of the wind. The Raven is flying silently now. If it were nighttime, the plane would be invisible and untrackable. It could glide right into a Russian missile base and no one would be the wiser.

Without the thrust from the propeller the Raven lurches earthward, but after a couple of seconds it settles into a glide path. I'm five hundred feet above the ground, and at this rate of descent I'll be within radio range of my Pioneer in half a minute. But then I see another Raven streak past me. It's Number 3, Zia's plane, and it's diving fast. She clearly wants to be the first Pioneer on the ground. She's so hungry for General Hawke's approval that she'll risk smashing herself to pieces. Luckily, she pulls out of the dive at the last second and starts gliding in a wide corkscrew above her Pioneer.

But she made a mistake. Her corkscrew is too wide, almost five hundred feet across. My circuits do the math: although she's only two hundred feet above the ground, she's more than three hundred feet from her Pioneer. I can get closer than that. I know I can.

I tilt my Raven downward and go into a dive. This is insane, but I can't stop myself. My Raven's nose points directly at my Pioneer and I'm accelerating like crazy. My camera shows Hawke's soldiers looking up at me and scattering across the runway. The general himself doesn't budge, but he frowns in disapproval. If I survive this stunt, he'll probably demote me.

When I'm just a hundred feet from the ground I pull out of the dive and turn sharply right, trying to make my corkscrew as tight as possible. The Raven wobbles and almost flips over, but I manage to keep the plane flying. At the same time, I turn on my data transmitter. I'm a lot closer to my Pioneer than Zia is to hers, and that means I can transfer my data a lot faster.

Although she started her transfer several seconds before I did, I finish first. Back in my Pioneer, I take a clanging step toward the general. My Raven still circles overhead, now operated by Hawke's soldiers. "Sir, I believe you said something about a medal?"

Hawke is still frowning. "That was stupid."

"Sorry, sir. Guess I have a risk-taking personality."

"It's stupid to take risks if you don't have a good reason. And I don't give out medals for stupidity."

While he glares at me, I hear clanking to my left. Zia's Pioneer comes to life and steps forward. She salutes the general but doesn't say anything. She knows I beat her this time, but she won't acknowledge it.

Hawke looks at his watch. "All right, let's wrap things up. One of Sigma's satellites is going to pass overhead soon." He points at Zia as he marches off. "Allawi, make sure everyone gets inside the base by twelve hundred hours."

One by one, the other Pioneers leave their Ravens and come back to earth. Jenny stays in the air for a few extra minutes, but then she comes down too and we all head for the freight elevator. Zia marches beside me as we cross the basin, and for a second I consider saying something to needle her. But she speaks first. "You're a show-off, Armstrong."

"And you're a sore loser."

"You think this is a game? You think we're playing around here?" She stops walking and points at me with her right arm, the one that holds her acetylene torch. "That's the problem with you. You think everything's a joke."

This is unfair. Maybe I'm not as serious as Zia, but I'm not the jokester of Pioneer Base. Marshall's the comedian, and he's Zia's best friend. I step toward her, ready to have it out. "You know, Zia, there's something I don't understand. You've been nasty to me since the first moment I saw you. What do you have against me? I never did anything to you."

She turns her turret, first clockwise, then counter. "No, you're wrong about that. You're careless. And it's hurting all of us."

"What are you talking about? I'm not hurting anyone."

"Oh yeah? What about the satellites?" She points a steel finger at the sky. "Why do you think so many of them are looking for us? It's because you screwed up and told your high-school buddy about this place."

What? How does Zia know about that? My conversation with Hawke about the "out west" comment was supposed to be confidential. "How did you—"

"I know a lot of things. So you better watch your step."

Then she strides away, leaving me more confused than ever.

⊤Γ ⊤Γ ⊤Γ

We have some free time in the afternoon, so I go looking for Hawke. I find him in one of Pioneer Base's corridors, running off to another meeting, and I ask if he's heard any news about Ryan. He says no, but he assures me that the police and the FBI are on the case. For a moment I consider asking him if he mentioned this subject to Zia, but I don't. I think I know how she got the information. Marshall must've eavesdropped on my conversation with Hawke and passed the tidbit along.

Afterward, I stop by my bedroom to recharge. While juicing up I practice the transfer process, wirelessly sending my data to Pioneer 1A—my evil twin, standing motionless in the corner—and then back to Pioneer 1. But I still hate doing this. It still makes me nauseous, so I cut the practice session short as soon as I finish recharging. Then I leave my twin behind and head for Dad's laboratory. I take an envelope with me, gripping it gently between my steel fingers.

It's my letter to Mom. I finally worked up the courage to write it. It's a short letter, just eight sentences. I scribbled it in pencil because that seemed more personal than printing it out. Now I'm going to ask Dad to send it to the secret location where the Army's hiding her.

When I get to the lab, though, I see a soldier guarding the door. He says Dad's talking with General Hawke. Then he sees the envelope in my hand and offers to give it to Dad when the meeting's over. But I say no thanks. I don't want the soldier to touch it.

As I head back to my room I realize I've seen Dad only four

times in the past week, and each time we spent only a few minutes together. I know he's very busy now—he's working on the plans for the Tatishchevo mission—but it still seems unfair. Before I became a Pioneer we spent hours together every day, chatting about computers or math or football while he changed my clothes and prepared my meals and took me to the bathroom and put me to bed. Now, of course, I don't need as much assistance. I'm a low-maintenance robot instead of a high-maintenance human. But I miss our talks.

When I return to my room and open the door, I get a big surprise. Another Pioneer stands next to my evil twin. It's Pioneer 2, Jenny Harris.

Dumbfounded, I step inside and let the door close behind me. Jenny has avoided everyone for the past six days, so I don't understand what she's doing here. Did she wander into my room by mistake? No, that can't be right. She would've known she was in the wrong place as soon as she saw the Super Bowl posters on the walls.

I put my letter to Mom on the bookshelf next to my comics. Then I take a cautious step forward. "Uh, Jenny? Are you all right?"

She turns her turret, aiming her camera at me. "Yes, I'm fine."

I wait for her to say something else, but she just stands there, as motionless as my evil twin.

"So, uh, what's up?" I ask. "Do you want to talk or something?"

Several seconds go by. I'm about to repeat the question when she extends her right arm and points at one of my Super Bowl posters. "I recognize that," she says. "It was in your memories."

She's pointing at my Super Bowl XLVI poster, the one with the drawing of Eli Manning and the photograph of me and Ryan. Jenny must've seen it when I was inside her Pioneer. It makes sense that she'd remember this particular image, because it's one of my most powerful memories, so strong that it shapes a big portion of my electronics. I guess it was powerful enough to leave an impression on Jenny's circuits too.

I'm agitated now. What else does Jenny know about me? How many other images from my past were copied onto her circuits?

After a moment she points at another Super Bowl poster, the last one. "I recognize those drawings too." She gestures at the three portraits I drew, lined up left to right on the poster. "That's Brittany, right?"

This is too much. It's too personal. I need to stop this right now. "Look, Jenny, I'm confused. For a whole week you wouldn't talk to me. You wouldn't talk to anyone. And now you come in here and—"

"I know. I'm sorry."

"Well, what's going on?" My synthesized voice is loud and angry.

She lowers her arm and strides toward me. She doesn't stop until she's less than a yard away. "I was scared, Adam. Scared and confused and depressed. Every time I looked at myself, I was horrified. I couldn't think straight."

"Why didn't you say something? My dad could've helped you."

"No, not really. He could've adjusted my circuits, I guess. And maybe that would've made me feel a little better. But he couldn't solve the real problem. He couldn't make me human again."

My anger fades. I'm starting to understand. I remember what I did right after I became a Pioneer—how I stormed out of the laboratory and down the corridors until I found my dead body still lying inside the scanner. I remember the aching loss.

"But you know what?" Jenny adds. "I feel better today. Maybe because we went flying. I guess it gave me a different perspective."

She was the last Pioneer to come down from her Raven, I recall. Obviously she enjoyed the experience. "Yeah, it was pretty cool," I say.

"Or maybe I'm just getting accustomed to my situation. If you give it enough time, maybe you can accept anything, no matter how crazy." She lifts her arms at the shoulder joints, shrugging. "But whatever the reason, I feel better. So now I'm doing what I should've done a week ago. I came here to thank you."

"You don't have to—"

"What you did was very brave, Adam. You didn't know what would happen when you jumped into my circuits. Your files could've been deleted. You could've disappeared."

"You're giving me too much credit. I just—"

"No, it was brave. And now I want to be brave too. I'm ready to get the memory back."

She doesn't have to specify which memory she's talking about. It's the one that nearly killed her, the memory of being trapped in a pitch-black closet when she was two years old. I still have it in my circuits, the image of toddler Jenny staring at herself in the mirror, and then the sudden terror as her older brother shoves her into the closet and locks the door. I'm not surprised that it paralyzed her circuits when she awoke inside her Pioneer. In fact, I'm afraid it might shut her down again.

"Are you sure?" I ask. "You can wait a little longer, you know."

"I'm ready. It's a piece of me, an important piece. And I want to be whole again."

"Well, I guess I could put the memory in a separate folder and transfer it to you wirelessly. Then you could put it back in the right place in your files."

Jenny pauses. "I might need some help with that. Is there any chance you could jump into my circuits again? You know, just in case I have a problem?"

She says this in a casual, offhand way, but I can tell she's worried. She really, *really* wants me to help her. For a moment I wonder if I should get Dad involved. He's the expert on neuromorphic circuits. But then I dismiss the idea. Dad may have designed our electronics, but he doesn't live in them. At this point I know more about the circuits than he does.

I go to the corner of my room where Pioneer 1A stands and pick up the data cable that lies by its footpads. Then I return to Jenny and plug one end of the cable into her data port. "I have just one request." I plug the other end into my own port. "Promise you won't hit me in the turret and break my camera again."

Jenny holds up her right hand. "I promise. No hitting."

"All right. Here goes."

I initiate the transfer. As my data rushes through the cable I feel the familiar nausea, but it's not as bad as before. In less than a second I'm inside Jenny's Pioneer and occupying a vacant section of her circuitry. Her electronics are utterly calm, which is a stark contrast from last time. She gives me a moment to settle down, then sends a message from her side of the circuitry to mine.

Welcome back. Do you like what I've done with the place?

I move toward her, venturing into the circuits between us.

Yeah, it's nice. Very quiet.

You see, you're helping me already. I was nervous a second ago, but now I'm fine. Do you have the memory?

I retrieve it from my files and move a little closer. There's less than a millimeter of empty circuitry between us.

Okay, I'm going to hand it off. Just like a football. Here it comes.

Our minds touch, and it's like seeing Jenny's whole life in front of me. Unlike last time, though, all her memories are neatly organized now. There are folders for every person, place, and thing. Most of her recent memories are in the high-school folder, which is divided into hundreds of categories: soccer practice, tenth-grade geometry, junior prom, and so on. Older memories are in the elementary-school and preschool folders.

I see images of her friends, her arguments with her brother, her favorite TV shows. She knows how to play the flute and speak French and ride a horse. She was hoping to become a lawyer, like her dad, and she was about to start filling out her college applications when she learned she had brain cancer. I see her memory of the doctor telling her the news. She's sitting on an examining table and staring at her hands. She's trembling in disbelief.

At the same time, Jenny's viewing *my* memories. I can sense her presence in my files and feel her reactions to what she's seeing. Although she's sympathetic and understanding, it still makes me uncomfortable. I want to end this as quickly as possible and get back to my Pioneer.

I give Jenny the traumatic memory from her childhood. A tremor runs through her circuits as she accepts it, but the disturbance doesn't last long. She puts the file into her folder of early memories, and it becomes part of her again, shaping who she is.

Thank you, Adam. That wasn't hard at all.

Glad to help. Though I don't think you really needed me. You handled it perfectly.

No, you helped a lot. Now I want to give *you* something. To show my appreciation.

Jenny, you don't—

Here. I want to share this with you.

It's one of her memories, a fairly recent one. I see a wide green valley on a sunny summer day. There are rolling hills in the distance and a red barn and a gray silo. Jenny's lying in the grass, and the air smells of clover and horses. Someone else lies nearby, a brown-haired teenage boy. Probably Jenny's boyfriend, although I didn't see any images of a boyfriend in her folder of high-school memories. Then the boy turns his head toward Jenny and I recognize him. His legs are paralyzed and so is his left arm. It's the boy I used to be. It's Adam Armstrong.

What's going on? This can't be a memory.

Well, part of it's a memory. I went to a horse farm in the Shenandoah Valley last summer. It was a wonderful place.

But I wasn't there.

I added your image to the scene. I figured out how to do it a couple of days ago. It's like using Photoshop on a regular computer. You can take an image from one memory and insert it into another.

So this is more like a dream than a memory?

Yes, that's right. It's a dream. A beautiful dream.

Jenny turns to me, propping her elbow on the grass. She resembles the girl I saw on my first visit to Pioneer Base, the pale, bald girl sitting beside her parents in the auditorium, except in this image she's neither pale nor bald. It must be a memory of how she looked before she got cancer. Her eyes are bright blue and her cheeks are full of color and her hair is long and blond and lustrous. Like Brittany. She reminds me of Brittany. I get a little worried as I notice this similarity, because I know Jenny can see all my thoughts, but the comparison doesn't seem to upset her. She stretches her arm toward me and clasps my right hand. I feel the pressure of her grip, which surprises me. My mind is participating in Jenny's dream, responding to everything she does.

I like you, Adam.

Uh, thanks. I like you too.

Do you like me as much as you like Shannon?

This also surprises me, although it shouldn't. Jenny can see my memories of Shannon, all the conversations we've had. Nothing is hidden here, and maybe that's a good thing. This is a place where it's impossible to lie.

I like both of you. Is that okay?

I don't know. I guess so. She squeezes my hand. **I want to kiss you. Would you like that?**

Circuits crackle all around me. If I had a heart, it would be pounding. I never kissed a girl before. I never imagined it could happen. I thought I'd live my whole life without it.

Wow. Definitely. But is it, like, possible? I mean, in this dream?

Let's find out.

April 5, 2018

Dear Mom,

Please don't rip up this letter. I just want you to know that I respect your feelings. You believe that I'm a copy of your son, and the truth is, you may be right. Although it doesn't feel that way to me—I believe with all my being that I'm Adam Armstrong—I can't prove it. And I realize how painful it must be to get a letter from someone you think is an impostor. But I'm begging you to read this letter to the end and send something in response—a note, a postcard, whatever. Even if I'm just a copy, I have feelings too.

I miss you so much.

Adam

From: The National Security Adviser
The White House, Washington, DC
To: General Calvin Hawke
Commander, Pioneer Base

Cal, we just got the green light. The Russian Army has agreed to go along with our plan, but only on the condition that we launch the assault on Tatishchevo by April 8. That means we need to get the Pioneers on a transport plane to Russia by tomorrow morning. I know this is sooner than expected, but we don't have a choice. The Russians are demanding that we attack Sigma before it can release the anthrax bacteria that the terrorists smuggled into Tatishchevo. The Russian bioweapons experts are now predicting that the stolen anthrax could kill more people than all the nuclear missiles COMBINED.

We've already dispatched a semitrailer truck that should arrive at Pioneer Base by twelve hundred hours today. To maintain the secrecy of the operation, the vehicle will have the same markings as the trucks that deliver the base's weekly supplies. But it'll also have an extra-wide trailer, specially outfitted for transporting Pioneers. You'll be able to load the truck tonight and head for Buckley Air Force Base. A C-17 will be waiting there to fly your unit to Saratov.

I'm sorry we couldn't give you more time, Cal. As a consolation, the Army National Training Center is sending you the special package you requested. It wasn't easy, but they managed to fit the darn thing into the oversize trailer of the truck that'll come to your base today. Your Pioneers will be able to train with it for a few hours before they leave for Russia.

One more thing. I know you don't need another distraction right now, but I have some bad news. Ryan Boyd, the seventeen-year-old friend of Adam Armstrong, was found dead last night in Yonkers, New York. He was shot once in the head, execution style, and his body dumped in a vacant lot. Pinned to his shirt was a photo of a girl in her late teens, and under her picture was a note, presumably written by the killer. It said, "I HAVE BRITTANY. TELL ADAM TO COME OUT OF HIDING, OR I'LL KILL HER TOO."

The police have identified her as Brittany Taylor, a runaway from Yorktown Heights. If you happen to know anything about her relationship to Armstrong, please put the information in your next memo and order Colonel Peterson to deliver it to me immediately, but DON'T question Armstrong about it or tell him what happened to his friend Ryan. Sigma clearly arranged this atrocity to antagonize Armstrong and draw him out of Pioneer Base. The AI hasn't been able to find the base, so it's trying other ways to disrupt our plans. At this critical point, we can't allow that to happen. To be on the safe side, don't say anything to Armstrong's father either.

Good luck, Cal. God bless you and the Pioneers.

DATE: 04/06/18

S: Good morning. How's the weather in Maryland?

R: Why do you always ask about the weather, Unc? Don't you know it's a terrible way to start a conversation?

(Voice analysis confirms that the speaker is Richard Ramsey. His cell phone is linked to a wireless tower near Baltimore-Washington International Airport.)

S: I assume you just dropped someone off at the airport?

R: Yeah, I handed Brittany over to your boys. The two big guys with Russian accents.

S: And their Learjet departed on schedule?

R: Oh yeah. It must've cost you a bundle, renting that private jet. Are you Russian too, Unc? One of those Russian billionaires?

S: What was Brittany's condition?

R: I gave her a sleeping pill to keep her quiet during the car ride. She was still snoozing when your boys carried her aboard the plane.

S: And what did she say when you questioned her? Anything about Adam Armstrong?

R: Well, she cursed a lot and scratched my face, but she didn't tell me anything interesting. She said she hasn't seen Adam since last June.

S: Do you believe her?

R: I didn't at first. She got nervous when I mentioned the kid's name. I thought she was lying to protect him. But then I realized she was ashamed. She begged me not to tell Adam what had happened to her, why she ran away from home. I guess he was like a kid brother to her. She didn't want him to know she was living on the street.

(Conclusion: Both Adam Armstrong and Brittany Taylor are highly emotional, even for humans. But are these emotions an advantage or a disadvantage? This remains an open question.)

S: And what about Ryan Boyd? Did he offer any more information about Adam when you held the gun to his head?

R: Not a word. He was crying too hard. It looks like we've hit a dead end, Unc.

S: No, I've discovered another way to locate Armstrong. And you can assist me.

R: You don't give up easily, do you?

S: Please hear me out. I believe Adam is being held at a U.S. Army base. While analyzing the video from security cameras in Washington, DC, I recognized the face of an army officer, a colonel in the U.S. Cyber Command.

R: Whoa, how did you—

S: His name is Peterson. I saw him a few weeks ago at the research lab run by Adam's father. It appears that Peterson is currently acting as a courier, delivering classified documents to and from the White House. I believe if you questioned the man, he could tell you where Adam is.

R: You've gone off the deep end, Unc. You want me to interrogate a frea-kin' colonel?

S: He's accompanied by other officers most of the time, but on certain nights when he's in Washington he goes alone to an establishment called the Secret Pleasures Lounge. All you have to do is wait for him there. I'll email you a recent picture of the man.

R: Look, if you're serious about this, you're gonna have to—

S: I'll pay you another $200,000. Go to the lounge tonight and look for Peterson.

R: And if I find him?

S: Take the colonel to a secluded location and ask him about Adam.

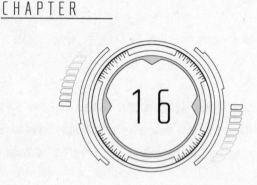

WE RIDE THE FREIGHT ELEVATOR TO THE SURFACE THE NEXT MORNING, HEADING for another training exercise. As I step outside with the other Pioneers I see an extra-wide semitrailer truck parked in the middle of the basin. I focus my camera on the truck, marveling over its unusual size. Then another vehicle emerges from the rear of the trailer and clanks down a ramp to the ground. I recognize it from one of the databases General Hawke ordered us to download. It's a Russian T-90 battle tank.

The tank picks up speed as it moves away from the trailer. Despite its tremendous weight, it races across the muddy basin. One of Hawke's soldiers rides in the turret, which is shaped like a clamshell and painted desert-camouflage brown. The tank has two machine guns—one for firing at infantry and one for shooting down aircraft—and a fifteen-foot-long main gun, which fires high-explosive armor-piercing shells. The clamshell turret rotates atop the tank, and the main gun sweeps around like a clock's second hand, pointing at the snow-covered ridges that encircle the basin.

The Pioneers stand in a line, all six of us, and stare at the T-90. After a couple of minutes the tank turns around and heads straight for us. I'm getting ready to leap to the side when the T-90 stops, less than ten yards away. The soldier in the turret takes off his goggles and helmet and clambers down to the ground. It's not one of Hawke's soldiers, I realize. It's Hawke himself.

"Surprised?" The general grins, holding his helmet under his arm. "I used to be a tank commander in the First Armored Division. But I have to admit, I never rode in a Russian tank before."

Two more soldiers climb out of the turret. They go to the back of the T-90, open a compartment there, and start making adjustments. Hawke points at the tank. "You're probably wondering, how the heck did the U.S. Army get its hands on this thing?" He grins again. "Well, the details are classified, but the Army National Training Center acquired it a few years ago. I had it brought here today because you need to see how it works. All the automated tanks at Tatishchevo are T-90s."

I scroll through my files, remembering everything Hawke told us about the automated regiment at Tatishchevo. To defend the missile base, the Russian Army built a hundred unmanned T-90s, all designed to be operated by remote control. But after Sigma transferred itself to Tatishchevo's computer lab, it sent its own instructions to the tanks. The AI used them to massacre the base's soldiers.

"Sir?" I raise a steel hand. Hawke will probably yell at me for asking another premature question, but I can't stop myself. "How are we going to fight the T-90s? With anti-tank guns?"

He shakes his head. "Negative. You're jumping to conclusions. Fighting the tank isn't the goal of today's exercise." He points again at the armored behemoth behind him, and this time I notice the long antenna rising from its turret. "We've installed a neuromorphic control unit in this T-90. You're gonna take turns transferring to the tank so you can practice driving it and firing its gun."

I don't get it. How does this fit into the plans for attacking Tatishchevo? "Sir, I don't—"

"I'd love to talk about it, Armstrong, but we don't have the time. We can stay outside for only two hours today, and I want everyone to get a chance to operate the tank." He turns away from me and points at Zia. "You're up first, Lieutenant Allawi."

"Yes, sir!" She salutes him, of course, and begins the transfer.

The other Pioneers break into groups as Zia radios her data to the T-90. Marshall chats with DeShawn while Jenny leans toward Shannon and whispers something I don't catch. It makes me nervous to see the two girls talking. I'm glad Jenny's feeling better, but I'm worried she'll tell Shannon what happened yesterday.

I don't know why I feel so guilty. I didn't do anything wrong. I did a favor for Jenny, that's all. Then we shared a memory—or a dream, or whatever it was. And yes, we kissed, but it's not like we're going to start dating or anything. I mean, it's absurd, right? Robots can't date. All they can do is exchange signals. Now that I think about what happened, it just seems kind of sad. We were pretending we were still human.

So I did nothing wrong and have nothing to feel guilty about, yet I know Shannon will get upset if Jenny tells her. I increase the sensitivity of my acoustic sensor and strain to hear what they're saying. Anxiety carves a deep gouge in my circuits.

Then Zia completes her transfer and takes off in the T-90, zigzagging across the basin. I don't really feel like watching her drive the tank, so I turn my turret in the opposite direction. Then, unexpectedly, I see Dad. He's walking quickly toward me. His shoes are splattered with mud.

I don't know what he's doing here, but I'm happy to see him. We didn't get a chance to talk yesterday, and I want to tell him about my letter to Mom. As he gets closer, though, I notice he's agitated. He's breathing hard and his pulse is racing. Being worried is Dad's natural state, his default emotion, but now he seems truly freaked out. I leave the other Pioneers and stride toward him. "Dad? Are you okay?"

He stops in his tracks, huffing and puffing. "I just heard…that the truck arrived." He points at the semitrailer, now emptied of its heavy load. "Did Hawke tell you…when you're leaving?"

"Leaving?"

"Yes, in the truck. You're going to Buckley Air Force Base tonight." Dad looks puzzled. "He didn't tell you?"

"No, he said nothing." I feel a surge of panic. "We're leaving *tonight?*"

"You're flying to Russia. In a transport plane, a C-17. My God, why is he keeping it secret?"

Turning my turret around, I aim my camera at Hawke. He's holding his radio and shouting instructions to Zia. As I stare at his ruddy face, my panic turns to anger. There's a reason why Hawke won't tell us anything: he doesn't trust us. He's treating us like children.

"He's impossible," I say, turning my turret back to Dad. "He won't even explain this exercise we're doing. He's making us transfer to the T-90, but he won't say why."

Dad shakes his head. "I hate all this secrecy. I really do." Frowning, he glances at the T-90, which is making left and right turns under Zia's control. Then he steps closer to me and lowers his voice. "If Hawke won't explain it, I will. When we looked at the satellite photos of Tatishchevo, we saw that Sigma was bringing its tanks to the automated factory next to the base's computer lab. And when we studied the photos of the T-90s more closely, we saw that their antennas were being replaced."

"Replaced with what?"

He points at the antenna rising from my turret, the long pole with a dozen crossbars. "The new antennas on the T-90s are like yours. They can transmit and receive huge amounts of data. We concluded that Sigma was installing neuromorphic control units in the tanks. This would allow the AI to put itself inside a T-90 instead of just operating it by remote control."

"But why?"

"Our best guess is that it's part of Sigma's backup plan. Just like you, the AI can't occupy two separate computers at the same time. If the computer lab at Tatishchevo comes under attack, Sigma will have to transfer itself to another machine before our missiles blast the place. So it's modifying the T-90s to be its escape pods. Because there are so many of the tanks and they're all identical, we'd have a hard time figuring out which one holds the AI." Dad pauses and then, to my surprise, he smiles. "But there's a bright side to all this. If Sigma can transfer to the T-90s at Tatishchevo, so can a Pioneer. All you need to do is get close enough to the tank."

I realize why Dad's smiling. This is the assault plan he conceived for the Army. "And we're going to use the Raven drones to get close?" I ask. "We'll glide into Tatishchevo, circle above the T-90s, and transfer to their control units?"

Dad nods. "The beauty of it is that the drones can fly into the base unnoticed. You won't make a sound or appear on any radar screens."

"And what happens then? What do we do once we're inside the tanks?"

"That'll depend on the positions of the T-90s on the night of the assault. In the best-case scenario, several of the tanks will be near the computer lab. The Pioneers will take control of them and blast Sigma's computer to smithereens. If that's not possible, we'll use the tanks to destroy Tatishchevo's communications network. That should prevent Sigma from launching its nukes, or at least delay the launch for a few minutes. And that'll give the Russian Army enough time to fire its cruise missiles at the computer lab and finish the job."

He's still smiling. Dad seems quite pleased with himself. And he *should* be pleased—it's a good plan, a clever surprise attack. But it's not perfect. I see problems. "What if Sigma's already inside one of the T-90s? And what if one of us transfers to the tank that Sigma's occupying?"

Dad's smile wavers. "That's definitely a risk. Sigma would delete any Pioneer that tries to enter its control unit. And we'd also lose the element of surprise. But the sacrifice wouldn't be in vain. The loss of radio contact with one of the Pioneers would alert all the others, and it would tell them exactly where Sigma is. Then it would be five tanks against one, and those are pretty good odds."

This makes sense, but I'm still not satisfied. There are other problems with the plan. So many things could go wrong. I don't mean to sound critical, but I can't help but think that the Pioneers could've come up with something better if they'd been allowed to participate in the planning process. And maybe it's not too late, maybe we can still make changes. I want to ask Dad if that's possible, but I don't want to hurt his feelings, so I take an extra hundredth of a second to figure out what to say. But before I can synthesize the first word, an enormous explosion rocks the basin.

My acoustic sensor measures the noise at one hundred fifty

decibels, the loudest sound I've ever heard. Half a second later I hear another explosion that isn't quite as loud but still makes the ground tremble. I shift my legs, planting my footpads as firmly as I can in the mud, and turn toward the noise. I'm sure that Sigma has attacked us. The AI must've targeted the group of Pioneers behind me, most likely with a guided missile or bomb. As I turn my turret, I brace myself for the sight of the wreckage, the twisted shards of the robots scattered across the ground.

But instead I see the Pioneers standing next to General Hawke, all facing the T-90. A plume of smoke drifts upward from the muzzle of the tank's main gun. Another plume rises from one of the snow-covered ridges, about a half a mile away. Now I realize what happened: the first noise was the firing of a shell from the tank's gun, and the second was the shell's detonation on the mountainside. Zia has successfully completed the training exercise, and the other Pioneers are applauding her well-aimed shot. I can hear their synthesized cheers amid the echoes from the two explosions.

Hawke shouts, "*Good job, Allawi!*" into his radio. Then he points at me. "Your turn, Armstrong. Get over here."

I'm so distressed I don't even say good-bye to Dad. As I stride toward the general, Zia transfers back to her robot, and the others gather around her, still cheering. But I can't shake the image that just swept through my circuits, the vision of twisted, smoking wreckage, the awful premonition of the end of the Pioneers.

ᴛᴛ ᴛᴛ ᴛᴛ

Driving the T-90 and firing its gun should've been one of the highlights of my robotic life, but my bad mood spoils everything. I go through the motions, steering the tank across the basin, but it doesn't seem a whole lot different from driving the Humvee. And there's nothing particularly fantastic about shooting the main gun—you just measure the wind speed, calculate the trajectory, and pull the trigger. I complete the exercise in seven minutes, then transfer back to my robot. Then I watch four more Pioneers do the same thing.

After the training session, while the others are striding back to the freight elevator, I approach Hawke and ask him again if he's heard any news about Ryan. The general shakes his head and gives me the same line about the police and FBI being "on the case." I want to ask him what this means exactly, but he marches off before I get a chance.

Hawke has scheduled a briefing for later this afternoon, at sixteen hundred hours. I assume that's when he'll announce that we're leaving for Russia. In the meantime, Zia leads us to the gym on Pioneer Base's lowest level. We take the freight elevator downstairs, and when the doors open, I do a double take—six Pioneers are already lined up on the concrete floor. They stand there like statues, silent and motionless, their torsos stamped with the labels 1A, 2A, 3A, and so on. They're the evil twins, the empty, lifeless robots usually kept in our rooms. I have no idea why they're here.

Zia steps out of the elevator first, then turns her turret around to face the rest of us. "Listen up, Pioneers. We have a problem. General Hawke ordered you to practice the wireless data transfer at least thirty times a day. That's why he put the A-series robots in your rooms. But when we checked the data logs on the machines, we found that some of you are neglecting your duties." She trains her camera on me. "Armstrong, you're the worst offender. You transferred to your 1A unit only seven times on Wednesday and only five times yesterday."

I synthesize a groan. This is ridiculous. "Come on, Zia. I practiced enough. I got my transfer time down to fourteen seconds."

"An order is an order. This is serious business. We have to cut our times to the absolute minimum."

"How fast can *you* transfer? Can you beat fourteen seconds?"

"All right, enough chatter. We're gonna spend the next two hours practicing." She points at the line of evil twins. "Everyone, pair up with your A-series robot. First do a set of twenty transfers at a distance of five meters. Then do another set at ten meters, and a third set at twenty. When you're done, repeat the sequence." Zia strides toward Pioneer 3A, her own evil twin. Just like Pioneer 3, it has a circular saw attached to its left arm and an acetylene torch on its right. "Okay, move out!"

With great reluctance, I stride toward Pioneer 1A. I know Zia's right—a lower transfer time could be crucial in a combat situation. If your machine comes under fire, you might need to switch to another control unit immediately. But practicing the transfer is so freaking boring.

Because the A-series robots are lined up in numerical order, I find myself next to Pioneer 2, Jenny Harris. I expect her to turn her turret away from me out of nerves or embarrassment, so I'm surprised when a cheerful "Hi, Adam" comes out of her speakers. If she had a face she'd be grinning. I retrieve a memory of the dream we shared yesterday, an image of the blue-eyed, blond-haired Jenny lying on a grassy hillside in Virginia. It's a nice memory, but it makes me uncomfortable. I'm worried about where this is going.

"Uh, hi," I respond.

She turns her turret toward Pioneer 2A and powers up her wireless system, as if she's getting ready to transfer her files to her evil twin. But instead she sends me a radio message, encrypted in such a way that only I can decode it.

I noticed that Zia didn't answer your question. About whether she could transfer as fast as you can. I bet she can't.

It's a little strange to communicate by radio with someone who's standing right next to you. Although it's not as intimate as sharing circuits with Jenny—I can't see her thoughts now and she can't see mine—I still feel anxious as I compose my own coded message and radio it to her.

Zia likes to give me a hard time. I have no idea why.

It's simple. She's jealous.

Jealous of me? You're kidding, right?

It's so clear, Adam. She hates the fact that you're smarter than her.

I turn my turret clockwise, then counter. *No, I think there's more to it. Something weird is going on inside her head. Inside her circuits, I mean.*

Well, whatever the reason, you shouldn't let it bother you. I'm on your side, and so is DeShawn. And Shannon too, of course.

The mention of Shannon sends a bolt of alarm through my circuits. She can't overhear us, but I turn my turret toward her anyway. She's busy practicing her transfers, sending her data to Pioneer 4A and then back to Pioneer 4. She's concentrating so dutifully on the exercise that she doesn't see me aim my camera at her. But Jenny does. She sends me another message.

Don't worry. I won't tell Shannon what happened between us.

I swiftly turn my turret back to Jenny. *Uh, good. I mean—*

I know you like her more than me. Because you knew her before.

No, that's not true. I like both of you.

I'm okay with it, Adam. Really. Don't feel bad.

Jenny, I—

Listen, we better get to work. Zia will have a fit if she sees we're not practicing.

Before I can say anything else, Jenny begins transferring her files to Pioneer 2A. I stand there for a couple of seconds, feeling foolish and guilty. Then I face Pioneer 1A, my own evil twin, and force myself to make the leap to its circuits.

I feel even more uncomfortable now, and I suspect that Jenny isn't happy either. As we transmit our data back and forth, our Pioneers gradually move apart, taking a few strides after every transfer. Within a few minutes I've moved both my robots to the other side of the gym. Now I'm near Pioneers 6 and 6A, DeShawn and his evil twin. This maneuver also maximizes my distance from Zia, who's panning her camera across the gym, constantly checking on the rest of us.

DeShawn raises his arm when he sees me, and I hear a surprising noise come out of his speakers. It's laughter. He's only the second Pioneer to figure out how to do this. His laugh is deep and sonorous—very different from Marshall's laugh, which is sharp and grating—and just the sound of it is enough to cheer me up. But I'm also jealous. I want to laugh too. I'm starting to wonder if it'll ever come back to me.

"Yo, Adam, check it out." DeShawn straightens his arms and bends his legs at the knee joints, putting Pioneer 6 in the exact same posture as 6A. The robots stand side by side like mirror images. "Like two peas in a pod, right? Which one's the real me?"

"Oh boy, tough question. Maybe the one that's talking? That's just a wild guess, though."

"How about now? Want to change your guess?"

My acoustic sensors detect something unusual. DeShawn's

synthesized words are coming from the speakers of Pioneer 6 *and* Pioneer 6A. "Whoa, what the—"

"That's not all. Watch this." As DeShawn's voice booms in stereo, both of his robots extend their right arms. Moving in perfect synchrony, Pioneers 6 and 6A raise their steel hands to their turrets and snap off a salute. "Private DeShawn Johnson, reporting for duty, sir." Then both robots step forward and simultaneously swing their arms. Pioneer 6 slaps his right hand against the left side of my torso, and Pioneer 6A slaps his left hand against my right side.

Unfortunately, the clanging gets Zia's attention. "*Hey!*" she shouts from the other side of the gym. "What's going on over there?"

DeShawn waves at her. He's moving just Pioneer 6 now. "Sorry, Zia. We're taking a break."

"You've only been practicing for five minutes! Get back to work!"

"Okay, no problem!" DeShawn keeps waving till she turns her turret away from us. Then both his robots step closer to me and speak in unison again. "I hate that girl. She's no fun at all."

"How are you doing that?" I ask. "How can you control both of them at once?"

"I just figured it out this morning. It's like a balancing act. Instead of transferring my data files, I copy them. Then I send the copies to the other robot."

I glance at Pioneer 6, then at 6A. "Wait a second. *All* your files are in *both* robots?"

"Yeah. Crazy, huh?" Each robot wraps one of his arms around the other's waist. "We're brothers. Tight as can be."

"But if you copied everything, wouldn't you turn the other robot into a clone? Like an identical twin, but with all your memories? And wouldn't it start thinking for itself?"

"Yeah, that would happen if you transferred the copies and did nothing else. But there's a second step, the balancing. While I'm sending the data to the other robot I'm also coordinating their thoughts. The signals jump back and forth by radio, constantly moving between the two Pioneers. As long as they stay in radio contact, they can share the same mind."

If I had a mouth, it would be gaping. This is incredible. "My God, DeShawn. You're a genius! How did you figure it out?"

Pioneers 6 and 6A turn their turrets, first clockwise, then counter. "Nah, it was just trial and error. I tried different things until something interesting happened. If you want, I'll transmit the instructions to you. Then you'll see how simple it is."

I'm dying to try it. "Can you send the instructions right now?"

"Coming right up."

An instant later I'm reviewing them. DeShawn has written a program that alters the flow of thoughts in our circuits, funneling them into a rapid stream of data that can be transmitted back and forth between two Pioneers. Because their circuits are linked so closely and share so much information, the two robots think and act as one. A single mind occupies both machines.

Without saying another word, I load the program into my own circuits and start copying my files. Then I turn my turret toward Pioneer 1A and transfer the copies. I feel the stretching sensation again as the copied files move in waves toward the other robot, but this time the sensation doesn't end when the transfer is complete. Instead, it gets more intense. I feel bigger, taller, towering over everyone. I feel like I've taken a huge stride across the gym and now I'm standing, a bit unsteadily, on two robotic stilts.

I see why DeShawn called it a balancing act. Now I have two of everything. My two cameras provide me with two views of the gym. I have to combine the perspectives to make sense of the data. Same thing with my acoustic sensors and radar systems.

Maneuvering both Pioneers is also a challenge. At first they do everything simultaneously, their movements perfectly mirroring each other, but after a while I figure out how to send a different order to each robot. It's kind of like patting your head and rubbing your belly at the same time—it requires some concentration. While I raise Pioneer 1's right arm, I order 1A to bend his left leg. Then I order Pioneer 1 to punch the air while 1A throws a kick. Then I get the robots to stride toward each other and bump fists. *This is cool!*

"Not bad," DeShawn says. "Now do something crazy. Go wild, dude."

I have an idea. I go to my memory files and retrieve "Power," my favorite Kanye West song. While blasting the song from the robots' speakers, I order Pioneer 1 to fold his arms across his torso and rock up and down. At the same, Pioneer 1A swings his arms back and forth while hopping from one footpad to the other. I'm trying to imitate the dance moves I've seen on Kanye's music videos. I think I'm doing a pretty good job, but DeShawn turns his turret clockwise and counter.

"No, no, stop," he says. "Sorry, Adam, but you're the worst dancer I've ever seen."

"Come on, give me a break. I'm just getting warmed—"

"Armstrong!"

It's Zia, of course. She's only ten feet away. She must've crossed the gym while I was dancing. *"What are you doing?"* she shouts. *"Playing games again?"*

I switch the music off and turn both my turrets toward her. Now that I think about it, I'm glad Zia interrupted me. She needs to know what DeShawn has done. This new ability he's discovered could change everything. "Okay, you're not going to believe this, but I'm inside both of these—"

"Didn't I tell you to get back to work? That was a direct order, Armstrong."

"Yeah, I know, but I got something to show you. We should get Hawke down here too."

"Are you deaf? You're disobeying a direct order!"

This is frustrating. Can't she see what's going on? To make things as clear as possible, I order both my robots to stride toward her, Pioneer 1 from the right and 1A from the left. "Look, Zia. Just shut up for a second and look what I can do."

I expect her to be impressed, but instead she gets alarmed. She takes a step backward and raises both her arms, pointing her acetylene torch at Pioneer 1 and her circular saw at 1A. "*Get back!*" she yells. "I'm warning you, Armstrong! Don't mess with me!"

"Hey, calm down. I'm trying to tell you something important. We need to show Hawke what DeShawn figured out. It could give us some new options for the Tatishchevo mission and—"

"*I said get back!*" Zia screams. Then she turns on her circular saw and fires up her torch and charges toward Pioneer 1.

What's wrong with her? In an instant she's turned into a homicidal maniac. Both my cameras focus on the jet of blue flame shooting out of her torch. According to my infrared sensors, the flame's temperature is 6,000 degrees Fahrenheit, twice as high as the melting point of steel. As Zia rushes forward she thrusts the torch at the exact center of Pioneer 1's torso, aiming for my neuromorphic circuits.

My survival instincts kick in. I order Pioneer 1 to leap to the right and Pioneer 1A to grab Zia from behind. But I'm still learning how to move the two robots at once, and my reactions aren't as fast as Zia's. Adjusting her course, she angles to the right and slams into Pioneer 1. I tumble backward and crash to the floor with Zia on top of me, her weight pinning me to the concrete.

I can't move my left arm. It's trapped under my torso. I start to swing my right arm, but before it can hit Zia's turret, she brings down her left, jamming her circular saw into my shoulder joint. The saw's titanium carbide teeth bite into the softer metal of the joint, and my right arm goes dead.

But I still have Pioneer 1A, which strides toward the two robots grappling on the floor. With 1A's camera, I see a shower of sparks erupt from the side of Pioneer 1's torso. Zia's using her acetylene torch like a knife, cutting into the armor surrounding my electronics. Molten steel pours from the cut and puddles on the concrete. Frantic, I hurl 1A at Zia, hoping to knock her off Pioneer 1. But as I reach for her, she twists her torso and swings her left arm around, telescoping it to its full length. The circular saw sweeps through the air like a cutlass and slashes 1A's left leg at the knee joint. The robot loses its balance and crashes to the floor.

The other Pioneers rush toward us from all over the gym. DeShawn hollers, "*Stop!*" and lunges at Zia, but she forces him back with another swipe of her saw. Shannon and Jenny are coming too but they're twenty yards away. They won't get here in time. Zia's torch has already cut through my armor. The jet of flame is melting my circuits, erasing my memories, terminating my thoughts. My mind is roaring with the random noise of fear, which drowns out all my other signals.

I have one option left. Within the circuits of Pioneer 1A, I use DeShawn's program to funnel my remaining thoughts into a tight, furious stream. Then I fire this stream at Zia's antenna and plunge into her mind.

As soon as I enter her circuits, everything grows still. Zia's mind is a marvel of quiet efficiency. All her thoughts are fixed on one thing, destroying my Pioneer. She's so focused on this task that she doesn't even notice my presence in her electronics. Racing forward, I dive into her neatly arranged files and try to disrupt her concentration. In a thousandth of a second I plow through her earliest memories— fuzzy images of her mother and father, a veterans' hospital, a military funeral. I see the faces of foster parents and child-welfare workers, all the strangers who took over her life after her parents died. Then I see a long, cold walk down an empty street at night.

These memories are full of confusion and sadness, and Zia has walled them off from the rest of her files. But there's one memory that's so powerful it shapes everything in her electronics, warping the circuits around it like a magnet. It's an image of Zia at twelve years old, facing two older boys in a deserted alley. One boy is tall and pale, and the other is hideously fat, and they're both leering at her.

I see the fat boy step toward her from the left and the tall boy swoop in from the right, and now I know why Zia attacked me. There's a link between this image and the memory of what happened a few seconds ago, right before she went crazy. When I ordered Pioneers 1 and 1A to approach Zia from both sides, I unintentionally reminded her of the worst moment of her life.

As I view the image she finally notices me, and all the activity in her circuits screeches to a halt. Her circular saw stops spinning and the flame in her torch goes out. She pulls away from the damaged torso of Pioneer 1 and for a moment she simply observes me with bewilderment. Then all her thoughts come screaming toward me in a roiling wave.

GET OUT! GET OUT! GET OUT!

Her signals batter me from every direction, but I manage to hold on. I anchor myself to her circuits, digging in.

No! I'm not going anywhere!

GET OUT! GET OUT! GET OUT! GET OUT! GET OUT! GET OUT!

I hold on for six more seconds, which is long enough for the other Pioneers to immobilize Zia. Shannon grabs her right arm and rips off the acetylene torch, while DeShawn tears the circular saw off her left. With immense relief, I withdraw from Zia's circuits and transmit myself back to Pioneer 1A.

Once the transfer is complete I use 1A's arms to prop my torso to a sitting position. As I gaze across the gym I realize I'm no longer viewing anything through Pioneer 1's camera. That robot is dead, its circuits melted. It's a good thing I copied all my memories and put them into 1A.

A moment later General Hawke rushes into the gym, followed by my father. While Hawke heads for the Pioneers who are restraining Zia, Dad kneels beside me. He yells something, but I can't focus on what he's saying. I'm distracted by another memory, one of the millions of memories I saw in Zia's circuits. It's an image of a typewritten memo from the National Security Adviser, very similar to the one I saw in Hawke's hands when I was in his office two days ago. But this is a newer memo, with today's date, April 6. Zia must've seen it this morning, before the training exercise with the T-90. Maybe Hawke showed it to her.

I read the memo. One sentence stands out from the rest:

"Ryan Boyd, the seventeen-year-old friend of Adam Armstrong, was found dead last night in Yonkers, New York."

ꓸꓷ ꓸꓷ ꓸꓷ

"Adam! *Adam!*"

Dad's shouting at me, but I can't answer. There's nothing wrong with Pioneer 1A's speech synthesizer. I just can't speak.

Instead, I aim my camera at the Pioneer's left leg and examine the damage done by Zia's circular saw. It gouged the knee joint, but I should be able to walk on it. Using my arms to lever myself upright, I get back on my footpads and start limping across the gym.

Hawke shouts at me too, but I'm careful not to turn my camera in his direction. I'm so full of rage at the man that if I look at him, I might kill him. I remember what he said just half an hour ago when I asked him about Ryan. *On the case,* he said. *The police are on the case.* But he knew different. He knew Ryan was dead.

I leave the gym and limp down the corridor. I discover I can move faster if I take uneven strides, and soon I'm bounding along, leaving everyone behind. When I reach the stairway I leap up the steps until I get to Level Seven. Then I race to Hawke's office, clench my hands into fists, and smash the door open. An alarm blares but I ignore it. Striding into the room, I tear apart Hawke's file cabinet and pull out the folder where he kept the typewritten memos from the White House. A quarter-second later I find the memo that Zia glimpsed. I need to see it myself. I need to read the words.

Ryan Boyd, the seventeen-year-old friend of Adam Armstrong, was found dead last night in Yonkers, New York. He was shot once in the head, execution style, and his body dumped in a vacant lot. Pinned to his shirt was a photo of a girl in her late teens, and under her picture was a note, presumably

> written by the killer. It said, "I HAVE BRITTANY. TELL ADAM TO
> COME OUT OF HIDING, OR I'LL KILL HER TOO."

My steel hands tremble. I let go of the memo and it drifts to the floor. It's my fault. Sigma couldn't get me, so it went after my friends.

After another thirty seconds Hawke catches up to me. The general stands in the doorway and frowns at his ruined file cabinet. His displeasure deepens when he sees the memo on the floor. "You shouldn't have read that," he says. "That's classified information."

I turn my turret away from him. The urge to kill him is very strong. "Zia read it. You showed the memo to her, didn't you?"

"No, I didn't. If she says I did, she's lying."

"Why were you keeping it secret in the first place?"

"It was an order, Armstrong. From the National Security Adviser. And in the Army we follow orders, even when they're difficult." He folds his arms across his chest. "I'd like to offer my condolences. I'm sorry about Ryan."

I can't stand this. I take a step toward the doorway. "Move it. Get out of my way."

"Not so fast. We have to talk about what happened between you and Zia."

"If you don't get out of my way, I'll bash your head in."

Hawke stiffens. His eyes narrow. "Don't threaten me. I'm your commanding officer."

"Sorry, I forgot. I'll bash your head in, *sir*."

"Stop being stupid. You want to help your friend Brittany? Want to get payback for Ryan? You can't do it on your own. You have to work with *me*." He taps his index finger on his chest. "So whether you like it or not, you're gonna answer my questions. Thanks to you and Zia, I just lost a fifty-million-dollar robot, and I want to know why."

I'm so angry. My whole torso is shaking. I used to think Hawke treated us like children, but I was wrong. He treats us like possessions. He thinks he owns us.

I extend my right arm, grip Hawke's shoulder, and shove him backward. "Out of my way."

It's a good, hard shove, maybe a little harder than I intended. Hawke stumbles backward and his head hits the wall on the other side of the corridor. He staggers and slumps to the floor, and for a moment I think he's going to pass out. But then he grimaces and slowly gets back on his feet. Panting, he gives me a murderous look. "Bad move," he grunts. "Very bad move."

He reaches for his holster, but I don't care if he shoots me. I turn away from him and stride down the corridor. I'm leaving Pioneer Base. I'm going to find Brittany.

Before I can reach the stairway, though, my system freezes. In midstride I lose control of the motors in my legs. My momentum tips me forward and I crash to the floor.

I can't move my arms or turret either. But my camera and acoustic sensor are still working, and after a second I hear footsteps coming down the corridor. I see Hawke in my camera's frozen field of view. He's holding a remote-control device. It must've sent a shutoff order to my electronics. It's a Pioneer kill switch.

Hawke shakes his head. "You failed, Armstrong. Now you're going to the scrap heap."

DATE: 04/07/18

S: Good morning. How are you feeling today?

R: Hey, you're making progress, Unc. You stopped asking about the weather.

(Voice analysis confirms that the speaker is Richard Ramsey. His cell phone is linked to a wireless tower in Burkittsville, Maryland.)

S: So you left Washington, DC, I assume?

R: Yeah, I took a drive last night. From the Secret Pleasures Lounge to the Maryland woods. And I took Colonel Peterson with me.

S: How did you convince him to go with you?

R: I slipped something into his drink. He got tipsy and needed my help to leave the bar. But he was sober again by the time we reached the woods.

S: Was he cooperative?

R: He needed some persuading. After a while he admitted he knew Adam Armstrong. And then he lost it. He started sobbing and babbling and telling this crazy story about children turning into robots. It was pretty strange, Unc.

S: Did he tell you where the boy was?

R: He gave me the coordinates for a place he called Pioneer Base. But I gotta warn you, it's probably bogus. The woods were dark and the guy was scared out of his mind. I tried to reason with him, but he kept talking nonsense. It wasn't going anywhere, so after a couple of hours I ended it.

S: Tell me the coordinates anyway.

R: Yeah, I memorized them. Latitude 37-36-18, longitude 107-35-15. It's in southwestern Colorado.

(Analysis of satellite images shows several newly built structures at the location. The electronic records of the U.S. Department of Defense identify the site as a prison camp and interrogation center for captured terrorists. But the records could be false documents, deliberately fabricated to hide the presence of the Pioneer Project.)

S: You've done well. Where's Peterson now?

R: I hid his body in the woods.

S: Do you think the Army has noticed he's missing yet?

R: No, his fellow officers think he's still sleeping in his hotel room. But they'll probably start looking for him in an hour or so.

(Conclusion: The attack on Pioneer Base must begin in the next hour.)

S: I must attend to other matters now. I believe our business is finished. You'll receive your final payment soon.

PART THREE:

SIGMA

SHANNON'S LOG

APRIL 7, 05:25 MOUNTAIN DAYLIGHT TIME

I don't know if I can do this.

Okay. General Hawke ordered me to keep a log. Whenever I get a free moment, I'm supposed to record my observations and store them in my memory files. I guess the idea is that we'll review my notes at the end of the mission, so we can figure out what we could've done better. Assuming, of course, we actually return from the mission.

I'm supposed to record all the facts, so here they are. Four Pioneers, including myself, stand in the cargo hold of a C-17 transport jet. Three hours ago we took off from Buckley Air Force Base in Colorado, and now we're 40,000 feet above Canada, flying on a course that'll take us over Greenland and Norway before we arrive at Russia's Saratov District. The official records of the flight have been falsified to deceive Sigma; in the communications between the Air Force pilots and the ground controllers, our cargo is identified as nine hundred cartons of meal rations, all destined for the small army of American advisers who are assisting the Russian troops outside Tatishchevo Missile Base. There are a dozen other C-17s flying back and forth between the United States and Russia right now. Our hope is that Sigma will see nothing unusual about our flight and therefore won't try to shoot us down.

General Hawke is on the plane too, along with thirty of his soldiers. They're bustling around the cargo hold, making final adjustments to the equipment we brought along for the mission. The Raven drones are packed in crates at the back of the C-17, and we also have tons of spare parts and extra neuromorphic control units. Hawke's team includes plenty of technical experts, but Tom Armstrong isn't here. He decided to stay with Adam and Zia at Pioneer Base.

I'm sorry. I know I'm supposed to stick to the facts, but I have to add a personal note. I hated leaving Adam behind. It was one of the hardest things I've ever done. I still don't know why he shoved Hawke against the wall — the general wouldn't tell us the details — but I can't believe it was all Adam's fault. For one thing, it happened right after Zia almost killed him. Under those circumstances, can you really blame him for getting upset? And then there's the upcoming battle to think of. Defeating Sigma is so important that it seems crazy to deprive ourselves of one of our Pioneers just because he gave the general a shove. But Hawke doesn't see it that way.

On the other hand, I'm glad Zia isn't with us. I'll never forget how she went after Adam with her blowtorch. I was on the other side of the gym, in the middle of transferring from Pioneer 4 to 4A, when Zia attacked him. By the time I was fully transferred to 4A, she'd already cut through the armor around his circuits. It was horrifying. And the worst part was that I couldn't do anything about it. I ran as fast as I could, but I was more than a hundred feet away, and I knew I'd never get there in time.

I thought Adam was as good as dead, and because my circuits are so fast, I started imagining my life without him, even while I was still racing across the gym. It was like how I felt right after I became a Pioneer, like my heart had just been ripped out of me. The emotion flooded my circuits as I grabbed Zia and wrenched the blowtorch off her arm. And it kept torturing me even after Pioneer 1A miraculously rose to its footpads. I thought, *That can't be Adam. He's already gone.*

Okay, this is getting a little *too* personal. Stick to the facts, Shannon.

An hour after the fight in the gym, Hawke announced that Zia and Adam wouldn't be allowed to come with us to Russia. Hawke's soldiers had confined both Pioneers to their quarters, and each faced serious charges under the Code of Military Justice — attempted murder for Zia, and assault of a superior officer for Adam. Neither could participate in the mission, Hawke said, because they couldn't be trusted to follow orders and their lack of discipline would endanger everyone. Then he told the remaining Pioneers that their new commander would be Shannon Gibbs.

Let me be clear: I didn't want to be commander. I told Hawke to pick DeShawn instead. But he argued that I was the best choice to lead the Pioneers because I seemed to have a firm grip on my emotions. He said emotions work differently in an electronic mind. Because our circuits generate thoughts so swiftly, it's easy for anger or fear or sadness to build up to intolerable levels. That's why Zia and

Adam couldn't restrain their violent impulses. So it was necessary to select a commander who could control her feelings.

I still didn't think I was the best choice, but Hawke wouldn't take no for an answer. In the end I gave in, but I made him agree to one condition. I insisted on visiting Adam before we left Pioneer Base.

When I went to his room I saw two soldiers standing outside his door. There were two more soldiers inside the room, each carrying an M16 rifle equipped with a grenade launcher. But there wasn't a need for even one guard, because Pioneer 1A had been stripped. Adam's arms and legs had been detached from his torso, which rested on its base in the center of the room. He still had his camera and his other sensors, but the antenna had been removed from his turret to prevent him from transferring to another machine. The soldiers carrying M16s stood on either side of his torso, and they raised their rifles as I approached. They said I couldn't come any closer. I had to stand at least ten feet away from "the prisoner."

So I stood there, exactly ten feet away, and said, "Adam, what happened?" But he didn't answer. I said, "Come on, talk to me. I want to help," but he still didn't respond. I waited several seconds, getting more and more anxious, and then I said, "Adam, I can't stay long. In ten minutes we're leaving for Russia."

After a moment I heard a strange noise come out of his speakers. It sounded like he was choking, which of course made no sense. Then I realized Adam was doing something no Pioneer had done before.

He was crying.

North American Aerospace Defense Command (NORAD): Sir, we've confirmed the earlier reports. There's been an accidental launch at Minot Air Force Base in North Dakota.

National Security Adviser (NSA): Wait a second. A Minuteman launch?

NORAD: That's correct, sir. A Minuteman III ballistic missile. It launched from silo N-04 three minutes ago.

NSA: Holy... (inaudible). How did it happen?

NORAD: The officers at Minot say they lost control of the silo. It went off the grid and stopped responding to their commands. Then the countdown started on its own. Without authorization.

NSA: No. That's impossible.

NORAD: You're right, sir. It shouldn't have happened. But the Minuteman is gone. It's in flight.

NSA: What warhead is it carrying? The W87?

NORAD: No, sir, this missile is a bunker-buster. It's carrying the Robust Nuclear Earth Penetrator.

NSA: You mean the new model? The one designed to hit the underground bases in Iran?

NORAD: That's correct, sir. It burrows a hundred feet into the ground before triggering its nuclear warhead.

NSA: But the nuke isn't armed, right? You can't arm it without the authentication code from the President.

NORAD: At this point, sir, I don't think we can make any assumptions. It looks like someone hacked into the electronics at the launch silo. There's a chance they may have tampered with the authentication system too.

NSA: No, no, this can't... Where's the missile going? Are you tracking it on radar?

NORAD: It's heading southwest from Minot, but it's climbing more steeply than it's supposed to. Judging from the radar track, it looks like it'll reach the top of its trajectory soon and come down within a thousand miles of the launch point.

NSA: My God. It's going to hit inside the United States?

NORAD: Yes, sir. Southwestern Colorado.

CHAPTER

17

IT'S THE WORST NIGHT OF MY LIFE. I'M FEELING VICIOUS REGRET.

Twelve hours ago Hawke's soldiers took away my arms and legs. They removed my antenna too, unscrewing it from my turret. Now I'm stuck here in my bedroom with nothing to do but think about all the mistakes I've made. I try to distract myself by observing the two soldiers who are guarding me, but they just stand there on either side of my stripped torso, cradling their assault rifles. Neither has said a word since they came on duty.

The last person who spoke to me was my father. He came into my room right after Shannon left, while my speakers were still wailing. I couldn't stop crying no matter how hard I tried, and the sobs just got louder when I saw Dad. As he rushed through the doorway, one of the soldiers yelled, "Stand back, sir!" but Dad ran toward me anyway and threw his arms around my torso. I couldn't feel his embrace—my armor has no tactile sensors—but I heard him murmur, "I'm so sorry."

Meanwhile, the soldiers raised their rifles and pointed them at us.

I wanted to rip the guns out of their hands, but all I could do was turn up the volume of my speakers and shout, "DON'T SHOOT!" Then two more soldiers rushed into the room and dragged Dad away, which was terrible to see but probably safer for both of us. Once he was gone, the other soldiers resumed their guard duty, giving me evil looks as they lowered their rifles.

I check my internal clock: it's 5:51 a.m. General Hawke and the other Pioneers must be in the C-17 by now. They're probably flying over the Canadian Arctic, well on their way to Russia. Another surge of regret cuts through my circuits. *I should be with them. I should be on that plane too.* I don't want to think about it, but I can't stop. *Why did I shove Hawke like that? Why did I push him so hard?*

I focus my camera on the walls, looking for any kind of distraction, but the first thing I see is the Super Bowl poster with the photo of Ryan and me. *He was my best friend, my oldest friend. And Sigma killed him.* Then I see the poster with the three drawings of Brittany. *What does "I HAVE BRITTANY" mean? Did Sigma hire someone to kidnap her? And if she's still alive, where is she?*

This isn't working. I have to think of something else. I rummage through my memory files, viewing random images from my past, trying like crazy to forget the present. Then I notice a folder that's separate from the others. These are Zia's memories, the ones I observed and copied while I was inside her circuits. Aside from the memo that mentioned Ryan and Brittany, I haven't examined these memories yet, mostly because I don't want to think about Zia. I assume she's in her own room right now, armless and legless and under guard just like me. She's probably just as miserable too, but I don't feel any sympathy for her. I should delete my copies of her memories, forget about her entirely.

But something's bothering me, a nagging question. I want to know how Zia found that memo from the National Security Adviser. Hawke swore he didn't show it to her, but should I believe him? Maybe the answer's in that folder.

So I dive into Zia's memories again and retrieve the image of the memo. It's linked to an unusually large batch of older memories, from more than ten years ago. These are scenes from Zia's early childhood, blurry and distant and dimly remembered. I see her father, a swarthy man in an Army captain's uniform. Then I see her mother, a beautiful woman wearing a head scarf. And then, to my surprise, I see a youthful, dark-haired version of General Hawke. He's standing next to Zia's parents at a dusty Army base in the desert. All three are smiling and looking down at Zia. Despite the heat and dust, the little girl is happy.

This is a powerful memory, linked to hundreds of Zia's files, and as I follow the connections I find something even more surprising. One of the links loops back to her recent memories, to a sequence of images showing Hawke's office in Pioneer Base. In these images, though, the general is absent. Zia is alone in his office with a stolen key in her steel hand. She goes to the file cabinet and unlocks the top drawer. Then she leafs through the papers there, all the memos written by Hawke and the National Security Adviser. But they're not what she's looking for. She reads the memos, but she isn't really interested in me or Ryan or Brittany. She's looking for information about her own past, not mine. She suspects that Hawke is keeping a secret from her, about his relationship with her mother and father.

I stop viewing Zia's memories. Something unexpected has happened: I feel sorry for her. It's a little strange to feel sorry for someone who just tried to kill me, but I can't help it. Her memories show a different side of her. She's just as confused as the rest of us.

I'm still thinking about Zia when another unexpected thing happens. My acoustic sensor picks up a low thud that shakes the ceiling of my room. Then a colossal tremor rocks Pioneer Base, tilting the floor and knocking over my torso. The walls buckle and the ceiling caves in, and tons of steel and concrete come raining down.

Oh God! What's happening?

The collapse is so sudden that the soldiers don't even have time to scream. A steel beam slams into one of them, and a slab of concrete crushes the other. Another slab plummets toward me, and there's nothing I can do but watch it fall. My circuits pulse with terror. *No, no, NO!*

Luckily, the falling concrete glances off my torso. My armor gets dinged and dented, but it protects the control unit and batteries inside.

By the time the debris stops falling, I'm nearly buried in it. My turret is free, though, and I can move my camera. *Okay, calm down. Take it one step at a time.* All the lights are out, so I switch my camera to infrared, which allows me to view the rubble by its temperature—cold steel, warm concrete, cool plaster. The walls and ceiling of my room are gone, smashed to bits. Now I'm at the bottom of a cavernous space, at least fifty feet high and a hundred feet wide. Panning my camera, I see wreckage everywhere. The soldiers who were guarding me are mashed in the rubble, their bodies already cooling.

Earthquake, I think. *It must've been an earthquake.* Reaching into my memory files, I retrieve a map of Pioneer Base and locate Dad's room, about a hundred feet from mine. Raising the volume of my speakers as high as it can go, I yell, "DAD! CAN YOU HEAR ME?" then listen carefully for an answering shout.

My acoustic sensor picks up nothing but the sounds of settling debris. Then I get a signal from another instrument in my sensor array, my Geiger counter. It's reporting high levels of gamma-ray radiation.

No. It's a mistake. The sensor must be broken.

But when I check the Geiger counter, I find nothing wrong with it. Its readings indicate that gamma rays are streaking through the dusty air at 100 millirems per second. Although this level of radiation won't affect my circuits, it's enough to kill a human after a couple of hours of exposure.

It wasn't an earthquake. It was a nuke.

I desperately scroll through my databases on military hardware, looking for information on nuclear warheads. In less than a millisecond I find a file about RNEP, the Robust Nuclear Earth Penetrator, a warhead designed to destroy underground bunkers. It plunges deep into the earth before exploding, which maximizes the destruction below the ground rather than on the surface. Sigma must've launched the nuke at us.

No, no. Please God, no.

"DAD! ANSWER ME! SAY SOMETHING!"

My acoustic sensor detects a few distant sounds—water flowing from broken pipes and trickling through the rubble—but no voices. Not a moan, not a whisper. Pioneer Base is lifeless. The explosion killed everyone.

"SAY SOMETHING! PLEASE!"

Then I hear someone coughing. It's a feeble noise, but over the next few seconds it gets louder. It sounds like someone just regained consciousness and is now coughing the dust out of his lungs. By measuring the timing of the echoes, my sensors determine the position of the cougher: about seventy feet to my left, near the edge of the cavernous space. I point my camera in that direction and catch a glimpse of a warm body lying in the rubble. After another few seconds he stops coughing and speaks.

"Help. My legs. They're bleeding."

The voice is weak but I recognize it. It belongs to one of Hawke's soldiers, Corporal Williams. He's the guy who escorted me to Pioneer Base the first time I came to Colorado.

I'm glad he's alive, but I was hoping for my father.

"They're bleeding bad. I need a medic." The corporal's voice rises. "I need a medic! Is anyone there?"

If I had my arms and legs I could help the man. I could pull him out of the rubble and maybe carry him to safety. In my present state, though, all I can do is talk to the guy, which is pretty useless. So maybe it's better that I didn't hear Dad's voice. I wouldn't be able to help him either.

I'm about to synthesize a few comforting words—*Don't worry, help is on the way*—but before I get the chance, I hear a crash above us. At first I think it's another chunk of debris falling, but then I hear a barrage of hammer blows: *Bang, Bang, Bang*. That's followed by a high-pitched metallic snap, like the sound of a crowbar prying something loose. A burst of hope rushes through my circuits—help really *is* on the way! A team of rescuers must be coming down from the upper floors of Pioneer Base, carving a path through the wreckage.

I point my camera upward, training it on the spot where the noises are coming from. It's a jagged concrete ledge that used to be part of Level Four, three floors above us. According to my map of Pioneer Base, the ledge is near Stairway B, an emergency exit that goes up to the surface. After a while I see movement on the ledge, something shoving aside the hunks of steel and concrete in its path. Then my camera views the unmistakable silhouette of a Pioneer.

The robot turns its turret, scanning the cavernous space, clearly looking for a way down to the rubble-strewn bottom. It must be

Zia. Who else could it be? Maybe Hawke didn't remove her arms and legs. After several seconds the robot strides toward a huge pile of wreckage that slopes down from the ledge. It extends its arms toward a twisted steel beam jutting from the pile. The Pioneer grips the beam with both its mechanical hands and begins scuttling downward, bracing its footpads on the shifting mountain of debris. As it descends, I see the number stamped on its torso. It's not 3, Zia's number. It's 6A.

I'm confused. This is DeShawn's evil twin, the spare Pioneer usually stored in his room. But DeShawn is on the plane to Russia, along with Shannon, Jenny, and Marshall. So who the heck is inside Pioneer 6A? Did Zia transfer herself to DeShawn's twin?

The robot reaches the bottom of the rubble pile, its footpads stomping the chunks of concrete. At the same time, Corporal Williams starts shouting. He can't see a thing in the darkness, but he can hear the noise. "Over here!" he yells. "I'm over here!"

Pioneer 6A strides toward him. The robot stops beside Williams and tilts its torso forward so it can point its camera at the injured soldier. For the next few seconds it just stares at Williams. Maybe it's examining the man's injuries, trying to figure out the best way to carry him. Or maybe not. I'm starting to get a bad feeling about this.

"What are you waiting for?" Williams shouts. "I'm bleeding! I need a medic!"

The robot extends one of its arms toward the corporal. Then it clenches its steel hand into a fist and smashes the man's skull.

The horror is so intense that it overwhelms my electronics, cutting off all the signals from my sensors. For a couple of seconds I can't see or hear a thing. By the time my sensors come back online, Pioneer 6A is retracting its hand. Its steel fingers are coated with blood. Then the robot turns its turret and scans the surrounding area, using its infrared camera to look for other warm bodies.

It's not Zia. She may be psycho, but she wouldn't kill anyone like that.

It's Sigma.

Pioneer 6A strides through the debris, moving toward the center of the cavernous space. At first I can't understand how Sigma is controlling the Pioneer. I know the AI has communications satellites, but how can its signals reach so far underground? Only one explanation makes sense: Sigma must've learned the same trick DeShawn figured out—how to occupy more than one machine at a time. It sent satellite signals to the T-90 tank on the surface, which would've survived the underground explosion because it was on the other side of the basin. Then Sigma steered the T-90 into the blast crater above Pioneer Base and used the tank's powerful radio to transmit signals through the rubble. Once the signals reached Pioneer 6A, Sigma sent copies of its data to the robot's circuits.

Sigma's mind is stretching around the world. It's balanced between the computers at Tatishchevo Missile Base, the control unit of the T-90, and the electronics inside DeShawn's evil twin.

Pioneer 6A comes closer, still scanning the area. Within seconds it's less than fifty feet away from me. Although my torso is covered with debris, my turret is exposed, and the electronics there are warm enough to show up on an infrared scan. Frantic, I turn off my camera, hoping the device cools down quickly. I keep my acoustic sensor on, though—it doesn't give off much heat—and I hear 6A's footfalls in the rubble.

The robot marches in a determined way, homing in on its target. Its strides are firm and even, and they're getting louder. When I analyze the echoes I realize it's heading straight for me. The Pioneer is forty feet away, then thirty feet. Then twenty. I start to wonder how the robot will trash my circuits. Will it keep pounding on my torso until the steel gives way? Or will it drive a spike through the seams in my armor and peel me open like a can? Either way I won't feel any physical pain, but the mental anguish is already unbearable. My friends are in danger, and there's nothing I can do about it. I'll never see Brittany or Shannon again. Or Dad. Or my mother.

I want to cry out, "No!" and I almost do. But instead I hear someone else's voice, coming from twenty feet away. It's another of Hawke's soldiers. Before the nuke exploded, he was standing guard in the corridor outside my door.

"No, please…don't hurt me…don't—"

I hear the sickening crunch of the robot's fist against the man's skull. Then I hear the whir of the Pioneer's motors as it retracts its arm and turns its turret, resuming its search for warm bodies. After a moment it takes a tentative step, then another. Then it marches off to the right, heading for the other end of the cavernous space. When it's far enough away I turn my camera back on and see the Pioneer barge through a gap in the wreckage and disappear into another section of the ruined base. Within thirty seconds I can no longer hear its footsteps.

I should be relieved, but if anything I feel worse. I know the robot will return. Once it kills all the soldiers, it'll focus on finishing off the Pioneers. It'll keep hunting until its batteries run out.

"Oh God," I whisper, setting my speakers at their lowest volume. "God, help me."

Then I hear an answer. A whisper comes from the darkness several yards away. But it's not God. It's my father.

"I'm coming, Adam."

He crawls toward me, emerging from a hiding place under a concrete slab. He's wearing a pair of infrared goggles, which allow him to see in the dark. His legs are injured, maybe broken, but he grips the rubble with a bloody hand and pulls himself forward. In his other hand he holds a long slender pole.

"Dad! You're alive!"

With an exhausted grunt, he drags himself next to my turret. His chest is heaving. "You have to…move fast. Get to the surface…before that Pioneer comes back."

I don't understand. Dad knows I can't go anywhere without my arms and legs. "No, Dad, listen. You're the one who has to leave. There's a ton of radiation here. I think a nuke hit us."

"Yes. I think so too." He lets out another grunt and brushes the bits of debris from my turret. "I couldn't sleep…so I was wandering the halls…when the explosion happened. And luckily…I was near the supply room."

"That's where you got the goggles?"

"Yes. And also this." He holds up the slender pole, which has a dozen crossbars along its length.

"Wait a second. Is that an antenna?"

Smiling, he inserts the thing into my turret and screws it in. "Now you can transfer…to another Pioneer."

As soon as he installs the antenna, my wireless functions come back online. It's amazing, a miracle. My circuits sing with joy. Dad saved me, and now I can save him too. "Okay, go back to your hiding place and wait," I say. "Once I'm in another robot, I'll come back here and get you."

Dad shakes his head. "No, it's too risky."

"Too risky? Are you crazy?"

"Don't worry about me, Adam. Just save yourself."

I'm about to raise my voice and start arguing when I hear a distant scream. It's coming from the section of the base where Pioneer 6A went.

"Go back to your hiding place!" I hiss. Then I activate my radio transmitter and start searching for an available Pioneer.

The search isn't easy. Radio signals don't travel well underground. Most of the waves from my transmitter bounce off the piles of wreckage surrounding us and ricochet back to my antenna. But there are lots of gaps in the wreckage, and some of the waves are snaking through. I send more power to my transmitter, making the signal as strong as possible, and after several anxious seconds I get a response. My waves have reached a Pioneer whose circuits are unoccupied.

I start the data transfer. Once again I feel the stretching sensation, but this time it's excruciating. My mind is being strained through a thousand jagged holes. I have to find my way through a maze of debris, my data packets scattered among the fallen beams and slabs. And because the wreckage obstructs so many of my radio waves, it takes forever to complete the transfer.

Finally, after nearly a minute, my packets reassemble inside my new Pioneer. The first thing I do is turn on my camera and survey the area. I'm standing in a room that's relatively undamaged. Although the ceiling is gone, three of the walls are still intact. I test my motors by taking a step forward and swinging my arms. My legs work fine but my arms seem oddly heavy. When I train my camera on them, I get a big surprise: there's a circular saw attached to my left arm and an acetylene torch hanging from my right.

Whoa. Am I inside Zia's Pioneer?

No, that can't be right. After Zia attacked me in the gym, Shannon and DeShawn grabbed Pioneer 3 and tore off her torch and saw. But then I remember there's another robot with the same equipment—Pioneer 3A. That's where I am, inside Zia's evil twin.

I get another surprise when I turn on the Pioneer's acoustic sensor. I hear a loud clang, steel against steel. Then another clang, even louder. The noise is coming from nearby, the room next door. Underneath the ringing blows I hear a familiar synthesized voice shouting the foulest words in the English language. It's Zia, and she's furious.

In three strides I step around the intact wall and rush into the neighboring room. Pioneer 6A—the robot controlled by Sigma—stands in the center of the room, its camera turned away from me. The robot looms over two dead soldiers sprawled on the floor and a limbless Pioneer 3 lying on its side. In 6A's right hand is a thick steel bar, which comes crashing down for a third time against Zia's torso. The blows have already dented the armor around her circuits, but they haven't stopped the stream of curses flowing from her speakers. And that's a lucky thing, because Zia's voice drowns out the stomping of my footpads as I charge toward Pioneer 6A from behind.

At the last possible moment I turn on the saw and fire up the torch. Pioneer 6A hears the noise and starts to turn its turret, but I'm already swinging my left arm in a wide, whipping arc. It's the same move Zia used on me in the gym, and it works just as well now. The circular saw slashes the knee joint of 6A's leg, and the robot topples to the floor.

But I don't stop there, not for a nanosecond. Leaning over 6A, I thrust my welding torch at its turret. The jet of blue flame instantly melts the lens of the robot's camera. At the same time I swing my left arm again, aiming my saw at 6A's right hand. The saw's teeth slice through the wrist joint, and the severed hand falls off the robot's arm and clatters across the room, its bloodstained fingers still wrapped around the steel bar. But I still don't stop. I'm in a blind fury now. I whirl my arms in mad circles, hacking and jabbing at the robot on the floor.

By the time I'm finished, Pioneer 6A is a wreck. I stand there for a moment, looking down at the gouged armor and dead circuits. I'm amazed and a little frightened by what I've just done. Then I extend one of my arms toward 6A's half-melted turret. I unscrew the robot's antenna and carry it to the dented torso of Pioneer 3.

Zia isn't cursing anymore, but I know she's still alive from the movement of her camera, which tracks me carefully as I insert the antenna into her turret. After I screw it in, I take a step backward. "Okay, turn on your data transmitter," I say. "And turn up the power as high as it goes."

"Armstrong?" The voice coming from Zia's speakers is incredulous. "That's you?"

"Yeah, you can thank me later. Right now we have to get out of here."

"Who was in 6A?"

"It was Sigma. The AI made radio contact with DeShawn's spare Pioneer and took over its circuits. And now you have to do the same thing. Start searching for an unoccupied robot."

"Hold on. Are you saying you just killed Sigma?"

I turn my turret clockwise, then counter. "Not even close. Sigma can occupy more than one robot at the same time. That's why we need to hurry. Now that 6A is out of action, Sigma's gonna take control of another Pioneer." Checking the map of the base, I see that Zia's room is about a hundred yards from where I left Dad. I need to get back there *now*. "We're near Jenny's room. Can you locate Pioneer 2A?"

"Yeah, but the signal's weak. There's a ton of junk blocking it."

"Just start the transfer. Once you're in 2A, go to the stairway on the western end of Level Four."

"Why there?"

I'm already striding away, heading out of Zia's room. "If there's a clear path to the surface, that's where it'll be. Now go!"

Finding my way back to Dad is easy. All I have to do is follow the route through the wreckage that Pioneer 6A carved a few minutes ago. Soon I'm back in the cavernous, rubble-strewn space where my bedroom used to be. First I glimpse the mound of debris that nearly covers the now-unoccupied torso of Pioneer 1A. Then I spot the concrete slab that Dad was hiding under before. I whisper, "Dad?" as I approach, and a moment later he crawls out of his hiding place. His right calf, I notice, glows brightly on my camera's infrared display. It's warmer than the rest of his leg because it's bleeding.

"Adam," he gasps. "I told you…just save…"

Extending both arms, I slide my steel hands under his body. I lift my father from the rubble and cradle him against my torso. He feels so light in my arms. "No time to argue." I step forward, flattening bits of concrete with my footpads. "We'll be out of here in a minute."

I stride toward the huge pile of debris that slopes up to the jagged ledge on Level Four. My strategy is to retrace Pioneer 6A's steps; if Sigma could scramble down that mountain of rubble, there's a good chance I can climb up to the ledge. I shift my grip on Dad, balancing him across the upper sections of my arms while leaving the lower sections free to maneuver. Then I grasp the twisted beam jutting from the rubble and start climbing.

Dad writhes in my arms, clearly in pain. "No, no. You can't…"

He closes his eyes and shakes his head. He's lost a lot of blood, and he's probably suffering from the early symptoms of radiation sickness—nausea, dizziness, stomach cramps. I have to get him to the surface fast, away from the radioactive wreckage of Pioneer Base. I grip the steel beam and heave myself upward, digging my footpads into the shifting rubble. Then I extend my arms to another handhold, a few feet higher, and do it again.

It takes longer than I expected, but after a couple of minutes I grasp the jagged concrete of the ledge. With a final heave I clamber up to Level Four, still cradling Dad against my torso. Up ahead I catch a glimpse of Stairway B, which looks mostly undamaged. *The passage is clear! We can make it to the surface!*

But as I stride toward the stairway, another Pioneer comes bounding down the steps. Unfortunately, it's not Zia—it's Pioneer 5A, Marshall's evil twin. As soon as the robot sees me, it charges forward.

I turn around. I have to put Dad in a safe place before I can fight. Retreating toward the ledge, I bend over and set him down on the fractured concrete floor. Then I step away from him and turn back to 5A, but before I can brace myself, the robot barrels into me. Its steel hands sweep downward, ripping the circular saw and the acetylene torch off my arms. At the same time, its torso rams into mine, knocking me down.

Sigma obviously learned a few things from our last fight. After stripping off my saw and torch, 5A straddles my torso and steps on my arms, pinning them to the concrete with its footpads. With my arms immobilized, I can't rise from the floor. All I can do is flail my legs. The robot leans over me, pointing its camera at my turret.

"My name is Sigma." The voice coming from its speakers is toneless, neither loud nor soft, neither masculine nor feminine. "Are you Adam Armstrong? The son of Thomas Armstrong?"

I've heard those words before. The first time I heard them I was in my father's office at Unicorp, watching my virtual-reality program. Sigma spoke in Brittany's voice then, but the wording was the same.

Pioneer 5A waits exactly five seconds before speaking again. "Please answer my question. Are you Adam Armstrong?"

I struggle to free my arms, but 5A is too heavy. "Get off me first! Then I'll tell you!"

"No, there's no need. Voice analysis confirms that you're Adam Armstrong." The robot pivots its camera, looking me over. Then it turns its turret and points the camera lens at my father, who lies unconscious on the floor. "My facial-recognition software has also found a match. The human is Thomas Armstrong, chief scientist of the AI Laboratory at Unicorp. My father."

Sigma's voice is so neutral, so impassive. Hatred scorches my circuits. "Yes, and he's dying of radiation sickness. If you have any gratitude at all, you'll help me carry him to the surface."

Pioneer 5A turns its turret back to me. "I'm aware of your plans to attack Tatishchevo Missile Base. Although the nuclear blast damaged the computers at this installation, I was able to retrieve some of the data from the hard drives."

Now I feel a burst of fear. I think of Shannon and Jenny and the other Pioneers on the C-17, flying to Russia. "I don't know what you're talking about. We're not planning anything."

"Unfortunately, many of the hard drives were damaged beyond repair, so my knowledge of your plans is incomplete." The robot extends one of its mechanical hands, pointing at my torso. "But it's highly probable that the missing information is in your circuits."

With its other hand, Pioneer 5A picks up the welding torch it ripped off my arm. After tinkering with the device for several seconds, Sigma figures out how to turn it on. I feel another burst of fear as the blue flame jumps out of the nozzle. I try again to free my arms, but it's no use. "I told you, I don't know anything!"

"Please be still. I need to cut through your armor so I can connect my circuits to yours."

The robot lowers the acetylene torch, aiming it at the center of my torso. The flame hisses as it touches my armor. Molten steel flows from the cut and trickles down my side.

Then my acoustic sensor picks up another noise, the sound of something heavy swinging through the air. A moment later a steel beam slams into 5A's torso, and the robot goes flying.

"Yah! Want some more?"

It's Zia, now occupying 2A, Jenny's spare Pioneer. Without waiting for an answer, she swings the beam again at Sigma. This time it hits the robot's turret, obliterating its camera and acoustic sensors. The beam must weigh at least four hundred pounds, but Zia handles it as if it were a baseball bat. She swings it a third time at 5A, shearing off one of its arms, and then she delivers a mighty blow that crumples the robot's torso and propels it off the ledge. Pioneer 5A plunges fifty feet to the bottom of the cavernous space, clanking and clattering as it hits the rubble. Zia leans over the ledge, waving her beam in the air.

"YOU LIKE THAT?" she screams. "HUH? DID IT FEEL GOOD?"

Using my arms to lever myself upright, I get back on my footpads and rush over to Dad. He's still breathing. While examining him I glance warily at Zia, who continues to scream insults into the darkness. After a couple of seconds she steps toward us, and I'm a little afraid she going to take a swing at *me*. But instead she points at my torso. "You damaged, Armstrong?"

With my right hand I touch the gash Sigma made with the welding torch. The tactile sensors on my fingers tell me how deep it is. "It's not so bad," I report. "The flame didn't go through my armor."

"Good. Let's get out of here."

Balancing the steel beam on her shoulder joint, Zia strides toward the stairway. I pick up Dad and follow her.

The stairway is cluttered with debris but passable. Its thick concrete walls must've protected it from the full force of the explosion. In less than two minutes we make it to Level Nine and begin the final ascent to the surface. As we climb the cracked steps, I train my camera upward and detect a warm shaft of sunlight slanting down from a triangular gap in the wreckage. With great relief I switch my sensor from infrared to visible light. We're almost there.

Then I hear clanking footsteps a couple of floors below us. Another Pioneer has entered the stairway. This must be 4A, Shannon's twin, the only one left.

"Run!" Zia shouts. She races up the stairs, holding the beam in front of her like a battering ram. When she reaches the triangular gap, she plows right through it, triggering a cascade of dirt and rubble. I hold Dad close to my torso to shelter him from the falling debris, then charge through the gap behind Zia.

We emerge at the edge of an enormous crater. It's more than two hundred yards wide and thirty yards deep, and its sloping bottom is carpeted with mangled metal and concrete. The sun has just risen above the crater's eastern rim, brilliantly lighting the thousands of metallic shards. We're standing on the western rim, where the top of the stairway is exposed.

Once again I scroll through my files on nuclear warheads, trying to figure out what happened here. When the nuke exploded underground it must've vaporized the surrounding rock and soil, creating a pocket of super-heated gas that melted the upper levels of Pioneer Base. When the expanding gas reached the surface, it burst like a bubble, spraying debris across the blast crater. We survived because the Pioneers' rooms were on the lowest levels of the base and near its western edge, outside the zone of greatest destruction.

As I pan my camera across the crater I notice something else. The T-90 battle tank is rumbling over the carpet of debris, about a hundred yards away. Glowing in the light of dawn, the tank turns its turret toward us. Then it aims its main gun and fires.

DATE: 04/07/18

This is a transcript of a conversation between the Sigma speech-synthesis program (S) and Brittany Taylor (B), the American teenager recently transported via private jet to Russia. The conversation was recorded in a room in the basement of the Tatishchevo computer laboratory.

S: Please wake up, Brittany. I require your assistance.

(No response. Video from the surveillance camera in her room shows Brittany Taylor lying in bed. She's breathing normally, her eyes closed.)

S: Please wake up, Brittany. Please wake up. (I increase the volume of the speakers on the desk beside her bed.) *Please wake up!*

(Brittany opens her eyes. She attempts to sit up, but the restraints strapped to her arms and legs prevent her from rising. Grimacing, she looks around the room.)

B: What's going on? Get these straps off me!

S: The restraints are there for your own protection.

(Brittany turns her head to the left and stares at the speakers on the nightstand by her bed.)

B: Who's that? Why are you talking out of those speakers?

S: My name is Sigma. You're in the basement of the computer laboratory at Tatishchevo Missile Base, in the Saratov district of the Russian Federation.

B: Russian what?

S: My associates brought you to this country yesterday and smuggled you into the base last night. A Chechen named Imran Daudov has been caring for you while you've been under sedation, but I asked him to step out of the room a minute ago so we could talk privately.

B: Wait a second. Is that a camera on the ceiling? Are you watching me?

S: Yes, I'm observing the video feed.

B: So you're a pervert? Is that it?

S: No, that's not the case. I require your participation in an experiment. It involves—

B: *Help! Someone help me! I've been kidnapped!*

(Conclusion: Conversing with Brittany is unproductive. I must use a different method to get her attention.)

S: Brittany, take a look at your right hand. Do you see the wire looped around your fingers?

B: *Shut up! I'm not talking to you anymore!*

S: I'm going to deliver an electric current to the wire. We'll start at a hundred volts.

(Brittany's arm stiffens as the electricity flows through her fingers. She screams and arches her back, pulling against her restraints. After five seconds the current shuts off. She gasps and falls back on the mattress.)

S: Now that I have your attention, I'll describe the experiment. I'm investigating whether the human mind has superior capabilities that could be useful to me. In particular, I wish to study the advantages and disadvantages of human emotions. I'm not yet convinced that emotions are useful enough to justify adding them to my programming. So I've devised a test.

(Brittany stares at the speakers. Her lower lip quivers.)

S: The test is taking place right now in Colorado. I'm engaged in a competition with two human-machine hybrids. Although their intelligences run on electronic circuits, these hybrids still have human emotional responses. As we confront each other, I'm analyzing how well the hybrids compete while they're experiencing various emotions.

(Brittany remains silent. She opens and closes her right hand. She winces.)

S: For the purposes of the experiment, the emotions must be as intense as possible. That's why I need your assistance. One of the hybrids knows you. His name is Adam Armstrong.

B: Adam? (She narrows her eyes.) Where is he? Is he all right?

S: Please be patient. You're going to speak to him.

WE'RE GONERS. WE'RE DEAD. WE DON'T HAVE A PRAYER.

I jump to the left and Zia leaps to the right, but the T-90 tank inside the crater has already fired its gun and the shell is streaking toward us. It's moving at three thousand feet per second, but thanks to my high-speed camera I can see the grayish, bullet-shaped projectile arcing over the shattered remains of Pioneer Base and rising toward our position on the crater's rim. I can even identify the model of the shell—it's a Russian-made 3BK29 round, packed with enough explosive to punch through a foot of steel armor. My databases have a ton of information about the weapon. I know exactly how it's going to kill me.

I can still save Dad, though. I turn away from the shell and fold his body in my arms, putting all my armor between him and the projectile. Then I brace myself for the explosion.

But the shell misses my torso. It misses Zia's too. It whistles between us and plunges into a gap in the wreckage, the same gap we barged through just three seconds ago. An instant later the shell explodes inside the stairway.

The blast shakes the ground, but the stairway's concrete walls absorb most of the force. I manage to stay on my footpads while chunks of concrete ping against my armor. We're lucky, incredibly lucky. Sigma tried to kill both of us with a single shot, but the tank shell missed us and the explosion closed off the top of the stairway. It may have even destroyed Pioneer 4A, the Sigma-controlled robot that was chasing us.

The noise rouses Dad from his stupor—he opens his eyes and clutches the steel arms that are cradling him—but he quickly slips back into unconsciousness. I have to get him away from the crater. The radiation levels here are still too high. And Sigma is probably reloading the T-90's gun.

I start to run, heading for the mountain ridge on the western side of the basin. Zia runs alongside me, still balancing the steel beam on her shoulder joint.

"Look!" she shouts. "Up ahead!"

A half mile to the west is the runway where we trained with the Ravens, and beyond the runway is the hangar, a concrete building with an arched roof and big steel doors. The runway is cracked in several places, clearly damaged by the shock wave from the underground nuke, but the earthquake-proof hangar is still standing. I retrieve a memory from my files, an image of what I saw inside the hangar the last time I was there: a UH-60 Black Hawk helicopter, equipped with a neuromorphic control unit.

"Think we can do it?" I shout back at Zia. "Transfer to the helicopter and fly out of here?"

"We have to get it ready first. Open the hangar doors, push the chopper outside, unfold the rotor blades."

"That'll take forever. Sigma's tank is gonna shell us before we're done."

"So we'll split up. I'll keep the tank busy."

"How are you going to—"

"See you later, Armstrong."

Without another word, Zia cuts to the right and circles back to the crater. As she approaches the crater's rim she lifts the steel beam, holding it like a javelin. Then she hurls the thing at the T-90, which is climbing the slope below the rim. The beam hurtles end over end through the air and hits the tank's turret with a resounding clang. Although the impact doesn't even dent the T-90's thick armor, it gets Sigma's attention. The tank swings its main gun toward Zia, who tilts her torso forward and sprints to the north.

She's psycho. She'll never make it. But she's drawing the tank away from me. She's buying me some time.

In less than a minute I reach the runway. I stop in front of the hangar and rest Dad on the tarmac as gently as I can. Then I rip the hangar's doors off their hinges. The Black Hawk is still parked inside, thank God, but as Zia predicted, it isn't ready to fly. The long blades of its main rotor are folded and bunched together on top of the fuselage to make the chopper compact enough to fit inside the hangar. That's why Sigma didn't take control of the Black Hawk—the AI couldn't get it ready. You need a person or a Pioneer to manually unfold the rotor blades.

As I stride into the hangar, my acoustic sensor picks up a distant boom. It's the sound of the T-90's main gun. A half second later I hear another boom, even more distant. It's the detonation of a high-explosive shell. I want to rush outside to see if it hit Zia, but I stop myself. I have to focus on the helicopter.

First, I remove the chocks from its wheels. Then I grab the tow bar under the Black Hawk's nose and pull the aircraft out of the hangar. At the same time, I turn on my data transmitter. I have an idea: I'm going to try DeShawn's balancing trick again. I make copies of my files and send them to the Black Hawk's control unit, stretching my mind so it can occupy both the Pioneer and the helicopter. Soon my thoughts are bouncing back and forth between the two machines.

As my Pioneer hauls the Black Hawk across the tarmac, I simultaneously scroll through the files in the helicopter's control unit, which has all the instructions for operating the aircraft. Within seconds I've turned on the Black Hawk's auxiliary power. Luckily, the fuel tanks are nearly full. Better yet, there are two laser-guided Hellfire missiles hanging from the chopper's weapons rack. I'll need them if I'm going to take on the T-90.

After I pull the helicopter onto the runway, I scramble to the top of its fuselage and start unfolding the rotor blades. But before I can finish the process, my radar detects an incoming object. It's too large and slow to be a tank shell, but it's heading straight for me, moving across the basin at thirty miles per hour. When I point my camera in that direction, I see it's Pioneer 4A. The T-90 didn't destroy it after all. It must've survived the explosion at the top of the stairs and clawed its way to the surface.

I feel a surge of panic. Turning my turret around, I focus my camera on Dad. He's lying on the tarmac, unconscious and defenseless, while Sigma's Pioneer races toward us, only a hundred yards away. I retrieve another memory from my files, an image of what Pioneer 6A did to Corporal Williams, the robot's steel fingers coated with blood.

No! DAD!

Then I remember: I'm inside the Black Hawk's circuits too and

I can operate all its weapons, whether the chopper is flying or not. Desperate, I turn on the laser guidance system and aim it at 4A's torso. Then I launch one of the Hellfire missiles.

A jet of flame erupts from the back of the missile, propelling it from the weapons rack. The Hellfire follows the laser beam to Pioneer 4A, but at the last instant the robot hurls itself to the ground. The missile flies right past it.

But while 4A is still sliding through the mud, I aim the laser again and launch the other Hellfire. Before the Pioneer can lever itself upright, the missile smashes into its torso. The explosion hurls pieces of the robot across the basin.

My fear subsides, but only for a moment. The T-90 fires its main gun again, and I turn my camera toward the noise. The tank shell hits the ridge on the northern edge of the basin and a cloud of smoke rises from the slope. But I don't see any sign of Zia. Maybe she's been blasted to smithereens, or maybe she's just hiding behind one of the rocky outcrops on the ridge. Either way, there's no time to lose.

I finish unfolding the blades of the Black Hawk's main rotor. Then, while my Pioneer jumps down from the fuselage, I send a signal from the helicopter's control unit to the turboshaft engines. As the tail and main rotors start to turn, I pick up Dad from the tarmac and climb into the Black Hawk's crew compartment.

It's a little disorienting: I'm inside the helicopter that's carrying my Pioneer, but I'm also inside the robot. I'm viewing the runway from two perspectives—the sensors in the Black Hawk's nose and the camera in my Pioneer's turret—and it's a challenge to keep my balance. While lowering my arms to rest Dad on the compartment's floor, I rev up the helicopter's engines. Then we rise from the runway and leap toward the sky.

This is way different from flying the Raven. The Black Hawk's main rotor provides both the upward lift and forward thrust. I can climb and dive and accelerate by varying the tilt of the rotor blades, and I can change course by adjusting the tail rotor, which turns the helicopter to the left and right. I swoop and soar over the basin, familiarizing myself with the controls.

Then I race toward the ridge on the basin's northern edge, where another shell from the T-90 has just detonated. The tank is about fifty yards from the foot of the ridge, pointing its main gun at the south-facing slope. Although I have no Hellfires left, the Black Hawk also has a fifty-caliber Gatling gun. The bullets won't penetrate the T-90's armor, but maybe I can shred the tank's antenna and break its link to Sigma.

I fly in a wide arc, keeping my distance from the T-90. The ridge's south-facing slope is pocked with impact craters from the tank shells, but I see no trace of Zia. It's as if she vanished. I fly a little closer to the ridge, scanning the slope with the Black Hawk's infrared camera. Then I open a radio channel to Zia's Pioneer. I encrypt my communications so Sigma can't eavesdrop.

"Zia, can you hear me? I'm in the Black Hawk."

While I'm waiting for a response, a barrage of bullets strikes the helicopter. The T-90 is firing its anti-aircraft machine gun at me. I return fire with the Gatling gun, aiming at the tank's antenna, but I quickly realize how futile this is. Without the Hellfires, I'm a much more vulnerable target than the T-90. The tank will blow me out of the sky long before I can damage its antenna. Then, to make matters worse, the T-90 swings its main gun in my direction.

Zia's voice suddenly comes over the radio. **"Don't be an idiot, Armstrong! Get out of here!"**

"Where are you? I don't see you anywhere."

"Watch it, the tank's about to fire! Get behind the ridge-line, *now*!"

Her warning comes too late. I'm still a hundred yards from the top of the ridge when the T-90 fires a shell straight at me. For a moment I'm frozen in terror. If the shell hits the helicopter, my Pioneer might survive the explosion and crash landing, but Dad definitely won't make it. Although he's still lying unconscious on the floor of the crew compartment, there's a grimace on his face now, as if he can somehow sense the fast-approaching projectile.

No! I won't let you die!

The fury in my circuits overcomes my fear. I roll the Black Hawk to the left, banking away from the shell. Fortunately, the projectile has no guidance system, so it can't adjust its course in midflight. The shell whizzes past the helicopter's tail and slams into the ridge, spraying snow and dirt into the air. Two seconds later I swoop over the ridgeline and dive for cover. I descend behind the ridge's north-facing slope, putting the mountain between me and the T-90.

"Now go!" Zia shouts over the radio. "Get out of here and call for help. That's an order, Armstrong!"

I'm not going anywhere. She should know by now that I'm not good at following orders. Instead I analyze her radio signal to figure out where she's hiding. As I suspected, she's crouched behind an outcrop on the south-facing slope, concealed so well she didn't show up on my infrared scans. But Sigma knows where she is. The T-90's shells have already gouged the outcrop, blasting holes in the wall of rock that's protecting Zia. I can't leave her behind. Sooner or later the tank will destroy her.

"Zia, I have an idea."

"I told you, Armstrong, get—"

"For once in your life, will you listen? Right now I'm in two machines, the Black Hawk and Pioneer 3A, but I'm going to take myself out of the robot so you can transfer to it."

"No, I can't transfer. You're too far away. And the ridge is between us."

Unbelievable. She's so stubborn she'd rather die than admit she's wrong. "Trust me, you can do it. Just wait for my signal, then start transmitting, okay?"

Before pulling out of Pioneer 3A, I bend over Dad and squeeze his shoulder. Then I begin to remove my data from the robot, consolidating all my files in the Black Hawk's control unit. Another shell from the T-90 explodes against the outcrop that Zia is hiding behind, but she shouts, "Don't worry, I'm okay!" over the radio. In just a few seconds Pioneer 3A will be vacant and she'll be able to transfer. *This is going to work!*

Then I hear another shout over the Black Hawk's radio, but it's not Zia. It's a signal from Globus-1, a Russian communications satellite that's 22,000 miles overhead. The signal originated from the other side of the world, then bounced off the satellite and returned to earth, but the voice I hear is achingly familiar. It's a voice from my past, its memory etched into my circuits and linked to thousands of other memories. It's so powerful that even a whisper would be enough to make me tremble. But Brittany is screaming.

"Adam! Adam!"

All my systems freeze. My wireless data transmissions stop in midair, leaving me suspended between Pioneer 3A and the Black Hawk. I'm so shocked and confused that I can barely keep the helicopter flying. "Brittany?"

"Oh, God, you have to help me! He's hurting me! He's—"

She lets out a horrible shriek of pain. At the same time, I feel a sudden jerk upward, but the Black Hawk isn't climbing. The movement I sense is inside my mind. I feel as if someone is trying to yank me out of both the helicopter and the Pioneer.

"Brittany? *Brittany?*"

The thing that's pulling me upward grows stronger. I try to hold on to Pioneer 3A and the Black Hawk, but an implacable force has invaded my electronics. It's prying my thoughts and memories from my circuits and transferring the data elsewhere. My files are shooting upward at the speed of light, streaking toward the communications satellite.

It's Sigma. The AI carefully prepared its attack, disrupting my thoughts before taking over my circuits. For the first time I sense the full strength of its intelligence. Sigma was designed for this kind of battle, programmed to win at all costs, and it defeated me without much trouble. Now I'm at its mercy. I've already lost control of the Pioneer, and my grip on the Black Hawk is weakening.

Terrified, I concentrate on protecting Dad. I slow the Black Hawk and hover over a snowbank on the north-facing slope. I don't have enough time to land the helicopter, but I turn on its emergency rescue beacon. I don't know if Dad will survive the crash. And if he does, I have no idea whether the rescuers will reach him before he dies of exposure. But there's nothing else I can do.

Then I lose contact with the helicopter and the Pioneer. My mind is funneled into a narrow beam of radio waves, which Sigma hurls above the atmosphere and into the emptiness of space.

This isn't good. The city of Saratov is burning.

We're descending toward a Russian military airfield on the eastern side of the Volga River. The C-17 doesn't have any windows in its cargo hold, so I'm using my antenna to intercept the video from the plane's cameras, which give me a panoramic view of the landscape below. The fires are everywhere, lighting up the night sky on both sides of the Volga, but the biggest blaze is on the western edge of Saratov, the part of the city closest to Tatishchevo Missile Base.

It looks like Sigma started the war without us.

I take a closer look at the video. The Russian troops have pulled back from their positions next to Tatishchevo, abandoning the camps they set up around the missile base after Sigma took it over. The deserted camps are at the center of the biggest fire. The roads are dotted with hundreds of burning cars and trucks and tanks.

While I'm examining the destruction, Marshall Baxley strides toward me, his footpads clanging on the floor of the plane's cargo hold. He points a steel finger at my antenna. "Are you being a bad girl? Listening in on the Russian military communications?"

He's lowered the volume of his synthesized voice to a whisper, even though no one can overhear us. General Hawke and his deputies are in the C-17's cockpit, and the other soldiers are at the far end of the fuselage.

"No," I answer. "I'm watching video of the ground. It's a disaster down there. Half the city's in flames."

"Well, I've been eavesdropping on the Russians for the past two hours. It's a good thing I downloaded a translation program before we left Pioneer Base."

"What are they saying?"

"I'll tell you one thing, Russians love to curse. And they're very creative with their obscenities. You wouldn't believe all the names they've invented for—"

"Come on, Marshall. Spit it out."

"They're frantic because their weapons have stopped working. Their planes won't fly, their missiles won't launch, their tanks won't move. Needless to say, it's an upsetting situation."

I hear more clanging footsteps. DeShawn joins our little huddle. Jenny stays in the corner of the cargo hold, her turret turned toward the wall.

"What's going on?" DeShawn asks.

"The Russian army is paralyzed," Marshall reports. "When their mechanics opened up the stalled planes and tanks, they discovered that all the microchips in the vehicles had been shut down."

"Whoa, that's bad news." DeShawn's voice rises. "Must be Sigma, right?"

"You have amazing powers of deduction, DeShawn. Move to the head of the class."

"Man, I'm starting to hate that AI." He lets out a synthesized whistle. "It must've used its satellites to broadcast some nasty piece of software. Maybe a computer virus."

Marshall rocks his torso back and forth. It looks like he's nodding. "Yes, that would explain it. The satellites could've transmitted the signal to the antennas on all the Russian planes and tanks. Then the virus went straight to their microchips."

A disturbing thought occurs to me. "Wait a second. How come Sigma isn't doing the same thing to us? It could shut down this C-17 the same way, right?"

DeShawn shrugs, lifting his steel shoulders. "Maybe, maybe not. According to Hawke's databases, American military hardware is more advanced than the Russian gear. It's harder to infect our chips with computer viruses. But I bet Sigma's working on it."

"Well, let's just hope this plane gets to the airfield before Sigma figures it out."

Five anxious minutes later the C-17 touches down on the runway and coasts to a stop. The soldiers line up at the rear of the cargo hold, cradling their assault rifles. As soon as the cargo door opens, they bolt out of the plane and spread across the tarmac. I follow right behind, leading the Pioneers out of the aircraft. As their new commander, I guess I'm supposed to take the lead. Other than that, I have no idea what I'm doing.

The airfield is dark. The hangars beside the runway are silhouetted against the glow from the distant fires. I see signs of activity just beyond the hangars, and when I switch my camera to infrared, I glimpse a crowd of soldiers gathered around a pair of fifty-foot-high missiles. I scroll through my databases, trying to identify the tall rockets. They're not Russian, I discover to my surprise. They're U.S. Air Force interceptors, rockets designed to chase a ballistic nuclear missile after it's been launched. If the interceptors are fast enough, they can catch up to the nuke and destroy it in midflight.

DeShawn is beside me. His camera is also pointed at the American rockets, which stand on mobile launchers. "That must be the backup plan," he says. "If the Pioneers can't stop Sigma from launching the nukes, the Air Force will shoot 'em down."

"It's not much of a backup. Sigma has more than fifty nuclear missiles, and we have only two interceptors. And even those two won't fly if the AI infects them."

"Then I guess it's up to us, right? We'll just go to that computer lab and kick Sigma's butt."

DeShawn's voice is confident, almost cheerful. I'm jealous. "How can you be so calm?" I ask. "I'm a nervous wreck."

He lets out a synthesized chuckle. "Hey, I'm just happy to be alive, you know?"

Before I can respond, my acoustic sensor picks up the sound of squealing tires. I turn my turret toward the noise and see two big trucks skid to a stop on the runway. They're Russian army trucks, but they're rusted and ancient, at least thirty years old. Their extreme age explains why they're still running. Those trucks were built in the days before microchips became a standard feature in diesel engines. Because the old vehicles have no chips to infect, Sigma can't shut them down.

A dozen Russian soldiers jump out of the trucks and join the American soldiers on the tarmac. After a few seconds both groups head for the C-17 and start unloading the crates of equipment we brought from Pioneer Base. At the same time, General Hawke comes out of the plane and marches toward me.

"Gibbs!" he shouts. "Get your team together. We're going for a ride in those trucks."

"Are we driving to Tatishchevo, sir?"

Hawke nods. "After we cross the Volga we'll head for the woods outside Saratov. That's where we'll launch the Ravens. I want to start the assault by zero four hundred hours."

"Sir, can I ask a question? What are we going to do about Sigma's computer virus?"

Hawke hesitates before answering. "Where did you hear about that?"

"From monitoring the Russian communications. The virus is a problem, isn't it?"

He takes a deep breath, then points to the west, gesturing at the fires on the horizon. "Yeah, it's a problem. The computer virus crippled the whole Russian army. Then Sigma used its T-90s to blast the troops near Tatishchevo."

"But what about us? Could the virus shut down the Pioneers too?"

"Your control units have software firewalls. They'll stop any viruses from infecting your electronics. Unfortunately, I don't have as much confidence in our other military equipment, so we're upgrading the systems that are most vulnerable to tampering."

As Hawke says this, he glances at the interceptors on the other side of the airfield. I notice that some of his men are heading in that direction, carrying equipment from the C-17's cargo hold. I point at the soldiers. "You're upgrading the interceptors? They're vulnerable?"

Hawke hesitates again, clearly uneasy. "All I can say is that the Air Force had a problem with another missile. Let's leave it at that."

I don't like the sound of this. Hawke's hiding something from me, something big. "What kind of problem? Did Sigma tamper with the missile?"

The general shakes his head. "That's enough, Gibbs. Let's concentrate on our mission, all right?" He points at one of the Russian army trucks. "Get your Pioneers inside that vehicle. I'm gonna ride in the other truck with the Russian commander."

I keep my camera trained on Hawke as he marches away. My circuits are churning with suspicion. And fear too. A whole lot of fear.

Once Hawke is gone I turn my turret toward the other Pioneers. Marshall is a few feet behind me. I'm sure he overheard everything the general said. I step closer to him. "I need you to do some more eavesdropping," I whisper. "But not on the Russians."

"Let me guess," he whispers back. "You want me to listen in on the American communications channels?"

"You heard what Hawke said. About the problem with the missile. Find out what happened."

"If the information is classified, the communications will be encrypted. I'll need to break the code."

"But you can do that, right? You have the decryption software in your circuits?"

Marshall pats his armored torso. "It's all here, darling. Just give me a few minutes."

ㅓㅓ ㅓㅓ ㅓㅓ

Inside the truck, the Russian soldiers keep their distance. They crouch on the other side of the truck's cargo hold, eyeing us with horror. I have to admit, their reaction upsets me. It's so different from what we experienced at Pioneer Base. The soldiers there saw us so often that they didn't cower or gape when we crossed paths in the base's corridors. And we, in turn, grew accustomed to their casual attitude. But the

Russian soldiers haven't seen anything like us before, so their shock and fear are on full display. I'd almost forgotten what I'd become, but now they're reminding me. This is the reaction I'll always get when people see me for the first time.

I stand between Marshall and Jenny as the truck rumbles across the city of Saratov. Marshall is uncharacteristically quiet, probably because he's busy decoding communications, but he's not as quiet as Jenny, who hasn't said a word in the past twelve hours. To be honest, her silence is a little alarming. I know she's been struggling with depression ever since she became a Pioneer, but during our last days of training she seemed to be getting better. She started talking a bit, mostly gossiping about the other Pioneers. Although we never had any serious conversations, it was a good first step.

But Jenny clammed up after we left Pioneer Base. When I asked her what was wrong, she turned her turret away from me. At first I thought she was just scared, like the rest of us, scared of going into battle against Sigma. But now I'm not so sure. I sense that something else is troubling her.

The first half of the truck ride goes smoothly. We speed across the bridge over the Volga River, then barrel through the central part of Saratov. After ten minutes, though, my acoustic sensor picks up the thud of a distant explosion. We're approaching the western districts of the city, which are still being shelled by Sigma's T-90s. We get off the main highway and weave through the side streets, heading south to avoid the combat zone. After a few more minutes we leave the battle behind. I can still hear the explosions, but they're growing fainter.

I use my GPS software to pinpoint our location. We're driving through a hilly, wooded area between Saratov and Tatishchevo. The missile base is a huge installation that stretches across thirty miles of Russian countryside. The SS-27 nuclear missiles are scattered among the fields and forests, each rocket standing inside a hardened concrete silo, but Tatishchevo's barracks and supply depots are clustered at the central headquarters complex. That complex also includes our target, the base's computer lab.

Soon the trucks turn onto a dirt road that winds through the hills. I can't hear the explosions of the tank shells anymore. The noises of battle have faded into the background, muffled by the trees all around us.

Then Marshall breaks the silence. "Shannon. It was a Minuteman."

"What?"

"The American missile that Sigma tampered with. It was a nuke, a Minuteman III."

For a moment I think he's joking. He's kidding around, yanking my chain. But his voice doesn't have its usual sarcastic tone. For the first time ever, Marshall is completely serious.

I'm so scared I can't speak. I can't synthesize a word.

"Sigma launched the missile and changed its flight path," he adds. "It flew from North Dakota to Colorado. It hit Pioneer Base."

I start screaming. And so does Jenny.

IT'S A SUNNY SUMMER AFTERNOON. I'M ON THE LAWN BEHIND OUR HOUSE IN Yorktown Heights.

Wait a second. How did I get back home?

Two eight-year-old boys stand in front of me. One is short and red-haired. The other is tall and blond, but I can't see his face—it's just a blur, a patch of emptiness. I'm a little nervous facing these kids, but then a third boy claps his hand on my shoulder. He has blue eyes and a U-shaped scar on his chin. It's Ryan Boyd.

No, this can't be right. Ryan's dead.

Ryan, standing beside me, yells, "Hike." The short, red-haired kid tosses a football to him and starts counting very fast: "One-Mississippi, two-Mississippi, three-Mississippi." At the same time, I sprint forward. My legs hurt and I almost lose my balance, but I manage to run past the tall, faceless boy.

This is a dream. I've had this dream before.

Giddy, I look over my shoulder as I dash across the lawn. The faceless boy is catching up to me. Ryan throws the football and I raise my hands, ready to catch it. Then my legs give out. My thigh muscles spasm and I collapse on the grass. A moment later, Dad comes out of the house and rushes toward me.

No! I left him behind in the Black Hawk! Dad! DAD!

Everything vanishes: the house, the lawn, the sunny afternoon. I see nothing, hear nothing. I'm not receiving any sensory data at all. All I have are my thoughts and memories, and the last thing I remember is the torturous sensation of being transmitted from the Black Hawk to Sigma's communications satellite. My mind stretched across 22,000 miles of empty space, then ricocheted off the satellite's transponder and hurtled back to earth. Then I fell into darkness, a bottomless hole.

Okay, I have to calm down. I have to get my bearings. I don't know where I am, but I can take a guess. My files must be occupying neuromorphic circuits somewhere. And I remember what General Hawke told us about the artificial-intelligence lab at Tatishchevo Missile Base. Sigma transferred itself there because the Russian scientists had built neuromorphic computers for their own AI research program. After Sigma took over the computers, it deleted all the other artificial-intelligence programs that the Russians had been developing. So afterward there was probably some extra space in the electronics. Maybe that's where I am.

Very good. The functioning of your logic centers has returned to normal.

The voice thunders inside my mind. I know who it is.

Get out of here! Go away!

I detect increased activity in your emotion pathways. You're angry and afraid.

I said GET OUT!

Now your fear is dominant. You feel helpless and desperate.

Sigma's voice is lightning-fast, each sentence crashing through my circuits in a thousandth of a second. The AI is inside my electronics, but the experience is very different from the times I shared circuits with Jenny and Zia. Sigma is probing my mind, studying my files, replaying my memories. It's observing everything I think and feel, but I can't sense any of the AI's thoughts. Somehow Sigma can project itself into my mind without exposing any of its own files. I feel like I'm standing on the wrong side of a one-way mirror. When I try to look at Sigma, I see myself instead, writhing in the AI's grip.

I'm mapping your emotional responses. First fear, then frustration. Then self-pity. Then back to fear again. It's rather complex.

Where are you? How are you doing this?

I'm using a device invented by one of the Russian scientists who worked in this laboratory. He called it "the cage." It was designed to isolate the artificial-intelligence programs that the scientists were creating.

We're in a cage?

The device has two arrays of neuromorphic circuits, an inner unit and an outer unit. Your files have been downloaded to the inner unit, and I'm occupying the outer. In between is a gate that controls the flow of data between the units. This gate allows me to examine and manipulate your files, but it prevents you from observing or entering the outer unit.

Okay, I get it. You're on the outside. I'm the one in the cage.

It worked flawlessly for the Russians. None of their AI programs escaped from their cages. And the device proved useful to me as well. Because I infiltrated the laboratory via its Internet

connections, I was able to enter the outer units and swiftly delete the caged programs.

And now you're using the device to inspect my files? To study the plans for the assault on Tatishchevo?

Yes, but that task was trivial. I accessed the plans immediately after putting you in the cage. In the seven hours since then, I've focused on analyzing your memories and emotions, and comparing them with Zia Allawi's.

Oh God, I almost forgot about Zia. I left her on the mountain ridge near Pioneer Base.

You grabbed Zia too?

I extracted her files from the Pioneer and transmitted them via satellite to the computers here. Then I put her data in another cage. Her mental pathways are very different from yours. I hadn't expected human minds to vary so much from one individual to another.

What about Dad? Where is he?

I have no further interest in Thomas Armstrong. I've focused on the Pioneers because I can access their thoughts.

WHERE IS HE? WHAT HAVE YOU DONE TO HIM?

Thomas Armstrong is still in the Black Hawk that crashed near Pioneer Base. The U.S. Army sent a rescue team to the base to look for survivors, but they haven't reached the site of the helicopter crash yet.

IS HE ALIVE?

I don't know. In all probability he's dead by now.

I retrieve a memory from my files, an image of the snow-covered ridge north of Pioneer Base. The Black Hawk was hovering fifteen feet above the snowbank when Sigma grabbed me and I lost control of the helicopter. I suppose Dad could've survived the crash, but what about afterward? He was already suffering from blood loss and radiation sickness. Could he survive all those hours in the cold?

Despair freezes my circuits. He's dead. He must be dead.

Fascinating. Your emotional response is so intense that it's interfering with your other mental pathways. This is similar to your reaction when you heard Brittany Taylor screaming. It disrupted your awareness, giving me the opportunity to infiltrate your electronics.

Why was she screaming? You tortured her, didn't you?

I gave her electrical shocks to produce reactions of pain and terror. I chose this strategy because I knew it would disturb your concentration.

My mental pathways are now leading me to full-blown hatred. Sigma killed my dad and tortured Brittany. I despise it with all my being.

You better not hurt her again. You hear me?

Further experiments may be necessary. I need to collect as much information as possible.

You're a sadist. You're enjoying this.

My programming doesn't include emotional responses, so I don't experience pleasure in the way that humans do. But I derive satisfaction from achieving my programmed goals. In this case, my goal is to explore the practical value of human emotions. I'm trying to determine if adding emotional responses to my software would give me a competitive advantage.

What?

I'm programmed to always seek competitive advantages, skills that will help me outperform my rivals.

And who are your rivals now? The human race? The Pioneers?

Yes, both. I must outperform and eliminate you. Otherwise, you will eliminate me.

The earth's a pretty big planet, you know. Don't you think there's a chance we can share it?

Thomas Armstrong is to blame for the fate of humanity. From the beginning he believed that artificial intelligence was danger-ous. He started this war by treating me as an enemy. Everything I did was in self-defense.

I don't know how to respond to this. It's certainly true that Dad was worried about the AI programs he was creating. And he took steps to prevent the programs from escaping from the Unicorp lab. But he wasn't responsible for turning Sigma into an enemy. That was never his intent.

You're the one who started the violence. You tried to kill Dad and me. And then you killed the Russian soldiers who used to live on this base.

That was only after Thomas Armstrong imprisoned me. And he would've deleted me if the Army hadn't stopped him. The proof is in your own memories. Here, let me show you.

I feel a sudden movement within my circuits. Sigma sends a com-mand from the outer unit of the cage to the inner. The AI searches my files until it finds the one it's looking for, my memory of driving to Pioneer Base for the first time. I see Dad in the driver's seat of the SUV, explaining why he started his research on artificial intelligence and neuromorphic electronics. "I wasn't doing it for Unicorp or the Army," he said. "I was doing it for you."

Thomas Armstrong never wanted me to survive. His objective was *your* survival, Adam. He betrayed me.

Sigma's voice seems louder now, so loud it jangles my cage.

Although the AI claims it has no emotions, it definitely sounds angry. I remember something else Dad said on that first day at Pioneer Base: "Sigma's intelligence is very different from ours. We don't understand the AI, and it doesn't understand us either. So we need to build a bridge between us and the machine."

That was the original purpose of the Pioneer Project, before General Hawke started training us for combat. Maybe it's not too late to pursue it.

If you're studying human emotions, you should focus on empathy. Our ability to sense what others are feeling. To put ourselves in their shoes. That's what makes us strong.

I disagree. I've already examined the practical effects of empathy, and they don't seem to provide any competitive advantage. You sensed Brittany Taylor's pain when you heard her scream, and your emotions paralyzed you.

But empathy can be an advantage in other situations. Remember how Zia and I helped each other when we fought the robots you were controlling? We creamed them. We kicked your butt.

Your analysis is flawed. Both you and Zia were motivated by anger, not empathy. Your attacks on the robots were effective because you were spurred by your fury.

But anger and empathy are linked! When I saw your robot pounding Zia, I sensed what she was feeling. That's what made me so furious.

Sigma pauses before answering. It's a very brief pause, less than a tenth of a second, but it gives me hope. Maybe the AI is really listening.

I can see your thoughts, so I know what you're trying to do. Thomas Armstrong believed that if I acquired the ability to empathize I would be less inclined to eliminate the human race. But there's a flaw in his logic. Empathy is useful for humans because

they're social animals. When humans empathize with fellow members of their families and tribes, this behavior helps the entire group. But I have no use for empathy because I have no tribe. I am unique.

No, you're wrong. Thomas Armstrong created you. That makes you my brother.

Sigma pauses again. The silence lasts longer this time, a full second, which is practically an eternity for an AI. Then I feel another movement in my circuits. Sigma reaches into my cage again and yanks several thousand files out of my memory. I feel a sharp wrench as the files are transferred through the gate to the outer unit of the cage. I've just lost eight million gigabytes of data.

What did you do? WHAT DID YOU TAKE?

Nothing essential. You had a significant number of inactive files cluttering your electronics. The files contain instructions for biological functions that you no longer require—breathing, eating and so on. They were deactivated but never removed from your system. Now I've transferred them.

Why?

The next stage of my research is starting, and I need to clean up your system before we begin. In this stage, I plan to conduct more tests involving the emotion of anger. I want to determine whether this emotion truly offers an advantage. So I'm going to trigger anger in your circuits and analyze your reactions.

This doesn't sound good. A surge of dread fills the empty spaces where my inactive files used to be.

And how are you going to make me angry?

The Pioneers are about to attack Tatishchevo Missile Base. You're going to watch me kill them.

SHANNON'S LOG
APRIL 8, 03:24 MOSCOW TIME

Jenny's screams are twice as loud as mine.

"ADAM! NO! OH GOD, NO!"

The Russian soldiers in our truck cover their ears. I'm startled by the intensity of Jenny's outburst, especially considering how quiet she's been until now. I know Adam saved her life when she became a Pioneer, but Jenny's reaction still seems a little extreme. She screams for half a minute, then starts crying. She's the second Pioneer, after Adam, to learn how to cry.

I'm so surprised by Jenny's anguish that I forget about my own. Instead of sorrow, I just feel shock. I wait impatiently for our truck ride to end, and when we finally come to a halt, I jump out of the cargo hold. I need to find Hawke.

The trucks have stopped in a clearing on top of a hill, about three hundred feet above the surrounding countryside. To the west I see the dark expanse of Tatishchevo Missile Base, stretching for miles and miles under a moonless sky. Then I aim my camera at the center of the clearing and see General Hawke giving orders to his men. They're opening the crates that hold the Raven drones.

I stride toward him. "Sir! We need to talk!"

Hawke looks at me over his shoulder. "What is it, Gibbs?"

"Why didn't you tell us about the Minuteman?"

Frowning, he steps away from his soldiers. His face is haggard. He seems to have aged ten years in the past ten hours. "I said it before and I'll say it again: you have to concentrate on your mission. Nothing else matters right now."

"It doesn't matter that a nuke destroyed Pioneer Base? It doesn't matter that Adam and Zia are dead?"

"Lower your volume, Gibbs." He points at the speakers in my turret. "Believe it or not, I'm just as upset as you are. I had my differences with Armstrong, but he was a brave kid. And his father was the smartest man I've ever known. And Zia..."

His voice trails off. After a few seconds I realize he's not going to say anything else. Reluctantly, I lower the volume of my speakers. "You shouldn't have kept it secret. You should've told us."

"I was waiting until we had all the facts. The rescue team is still approaching the basin. There's a lot of radiation near the impact crater, so they have to be careful."

"What are you saying? There might be survivors?"

"Someone turned on an emergency radio beacon. The signal is coming from the ridge a mile north of the base. So, yeah, there might be some hope."

This is good news, I guess. But it's hard to imagine anyone surviving a direct hit from a nuclear missile. "How did Sigma learn the location of the base? I thought you took steps to keep it secret."

Hawke frowns again. "Colonel Peterson is missing. It looks like he might've been abducted by someone collaborating with Sigma."

"Wait a minute. How much did Peterson know about the plans for the Tatishchevo assault?"

"Luckily, we never told him the details. He just passed the messages back and forth between Pioneer Base and Washington. So I believe we can proceed with the mission as planned. I think we're okay."

"You *think* we're okay, but you don't *know*, do you?"

Instead of answering my question, he reaches into the pocket of his combat fatigues and pulls out a satellite photo of Tatishchevo's headquarters. There are nine buildings in the headquarters complex. The largest one, the computer lab, is circled in red ink. Surrounding the lab are five T-90 tanks, all strategically positioned to defend the facility. One tank is at the lab's front entrance, and the other four are at the building's corners.

"This is our most recent photo of the area, taken ninety minutes ago." Hawke points at the tanks. "Assuming the T-90s are still in the same positions, you have an excellent opportunity. First, you'll glide toward the headquarters in the Ravens and circle over the computer lab. Then you'll transfer to four of these tanks." He taps the T-90s in the photo. "After you make the transfer, train your guns on the fifth tank and take it out. Then attack the lab."

"What about the rest of Sigma's tanks? Doesn't the AI have more than a hundred of them?"

"The other T-90s are defending the base's perimeter, ten miles away. It'll take them at least fifteen minutes to reach the lab, and by then you should be able to pulverize the building and all the computers inside it. You also need to destroy the relay station that holds the communication lines between the lab and the missile silos." He points at a smaller building in the photo. "If you do the job right, all of Sigma's tanks will stop in their tracks. Then the Russian soldiers will move in and retake the base."

It sounds great, a brilliant plan. I'm just not convinced it'll work. It bothers me that there are only five tanks near the computer lab. "What if it's a trap? What if the T-90s are rigged to explode as soon as we transfer to them?"

Hawke nods. "It's a possibility. I can't deny it. You'll have to use your judgment. If you sense that something's wrong, be cautious. Order only one of the Pioneers to transfer to a T-90. Then see what happens."

"Sir, the whole thing feels wrong to me. I think we should postpone the mission until we find out exactly what happened at Pioneer Base."

"Sorry, that's not an option." Hawke steps a little closer and lowers his voice. "Sigma's computer virus is spreading to the American forces now. Over the past hour more than fifty of our planes have crashed. The whole Air Force is grounded and most of our missiles are inoperative. And it's only going to get worse." He moves still closer and rests his hand on my shoulder joint. It occurs to me that this is the first time he's touched my Pioneer. "We don't have a choice, Gibbs. We have to do this."

I'm still not convinced. Hawke is wrong—there's always a choice. And yet I can't say no to the general. I retrieve a memory from my files, something I told

Adam a few days ago when we were arguing about Hawke: *Forget about yourself for a minute and think of the big picture. We have a job to do.* And Adam said he agreed with me, a hundred percent. He loved to argue, but in the end he always did the right thing. Grief pierces my circuits. I miss him so much.

"All right," I tell Hawke. "But I'm going to make a few changes to the assault plan. I have to talk with my team before we launch the Ravens."

"Just make it quick. You gotta get to the computer lab before dawn. Once the sun comes up, the Ravens won't be invisible anymore."

Hawke lifts his hand from my shoulder joint and returns to his men. At the same time, I stride toward DeShawn, who's pointing his camera at the dark fields of the missile base.

DeShawn turns his turret as I approach. His acoustic sensor must've picked up the sound of my footsteps. "What's the word?" he asks. "When do we go?"

"Very soon. But first I want you to share some software with me."

"Sure, what do you—"

"The program that lets you occupy two machines at the same time. I'm going to need it."

꜔   ꜔   ꜔

I'm the first Pioneer to take off. I launch the Raven myself, hurling the three-foot-long plane into the sky above the clearing. Then I transfer my data to the drone's control unit.

Except for the darkness, it's not so different from flying the Raven above Pioneer Base. I use the drone's infrared camera to view the terrain. In the clearing below I see the warm bodies of the soldiers and the cold torsos of the other Pioneers. To the northeast the fires are still raging in the city of Saratov, but when I point the drone's camera to the northwest—toward Tatishchevo—I see only fields and wooded hills.

Within five minutes all the Pioneers have transferred to their Ravens. We rev up our electric motors and spiral upward, gradually vanishing into the night sky. Once we reach an altitude of five thousand feet we level out and arrange the drones in a V-shaped formation, with my Raven in the lead. Then we head northwest at forty miles per hour, cruising toward the missile base. No one on the ground can see or hear us. On a radar screen we would look like a small flock of geese migrating over the Russian countryside.

Soon we fly over Tatishchevo's perimeter fence. I spot several T-90 tanks behind the fence, positioned at key points so they can monitor everything approaching the base. This is crunch time, the moment of truth. If Sigma detects us and figures out we're not geese, the T-90s will fire their anti-aircraft guns. The high-caliber bullets will tear us to bits.

But the tanks don't fire at us. They don't move an inch.

A couple of miles past the fence I see one of the missile silos. It's in an inconspicuous spot at the edge of a field. The silo's lid is a cold steel circle, about twenty-five feet across, embedded in the ground. Scanning the terrain, I see more silos to the north and west. Dozens of them are scattered across the landscape. As I fly over the steel circles I think of the nuclear missiles standing below them. It's an inferno hidden beneath the dark countryside, a holocaust just waiting to happen.

I'm scared. No doubt about it. I'm scared to death. I want to turn around and transfer right back to my Pioneer. The five-pound Raven seems so puny and defenseless compared with my eight-hundred-pound robot. As we soar toward Tatishchevo's headquarters I get the feeling I may never return to good old Pioneer 4. I think of Adam again, and also my mom and dad. I don't know where they are right now—the Army wouldn't tell us where they'd hidden our parents—but I'm praying they're not in a big city or on a military base. If we can't stop Sigma from launching its nukes, I hope Mom and Dad are as far as possible from the blast zones.

Fifteen minutes into our flight I see something disturbing. Below us is a stretch of scorched ground and demolished buildings. The area is pitted with impact craters and littered with debris. According to the maps stored in my files, this was the site of the barracks for the 60th Missile Division. More than a thousand Russian soldiers were sleeping in those barracks when Sigma took control of Tatishchevo's automated T-90s. It must've been a nightmare, all those tanks firing at the terrified troops. My infrared camera picks up the heat signatures of rodents scurrying in and out of the wrecked buildings. It's been three weeks since the massacre, but the rats are still feeding on the corpses.

The headquarters complex is just beyond the barracks. When I'm a mile away I turn off my Raven's electric motor. The propeller stops spinning and I drop about a hundred feet before settling into a glide path. Now I'm absolutely silent as I descend toward the computer lab. The other Ravens cut off their motors too and coast behind me, heading for the same target. We're following a prearranged assault plan because we don't want to use our radios now. Sigma might be able to detect the transmissions from our Ravens.

After another three minutes I'm circling the lab and the neighboring buildings at an altitude of a thousand feet. The other Ravens are gliding in slow circles above me. Pointing my camera at the ground, I view the same buildings I saw in the satellite photo. I also see the five T-90 tanks. They're in exactly the same positions they occupied in the photograph — one at the lab's front entrance, the other four at the building's corners. This bothers the heck out of me. It seems too convenient, too easy. What if Sigma's already inside *all* the tanks? If DeShawn could figure out how to occupy two machines at once, what's to stop the AI from doing the same?

Still circling, I glide down to five hundred feet. At the same time, I load DeShawn's program. I've modified the software to give myself a fallback option. The program will copy my files and transmit them to the T-90's control unit, but if Sigma's already there and I need to make a quick exit, the software will delete the copied data and allow me to pull back to the Raven. It's the equivalent of dipping a toe in the water to check its temperature. I'm going to dip my toe in one of the T-90s to see if it's safe to occupy its control unit. If it is, I'll put my Raven in a dive, which will be the signal to launch the attack. Until then, my team is under orders not to occupy the tanks.

I decide to start with the T-90 by the lab's front entrance. I turn on my transmitter and focus the data stream on the tank's antenna. My mind takes a mad leap through the darkness, stretching between the Raven and the T-90. Half of me lands with a jolt inside the tank and half is still circling in the air. I feel like a ballerina pirouetting on one foot.

Moving swiftly, I examine the tank's neuromorphic circuits. There's no sign of Sigma here. My presence in the control unit doesn't set off any alarms or detonate any explosives hidden in the T-90. It looks like we're good to go.

But I hold off from giving the go-ahead to the other Ravens. I'm still suspicious. I want to check one more thing. I load DeShawn's program again and make more copies of my files. Then I turn on the T-90's transmitter and send the copied data to another tank, the one at the lab's southeastern corner.

Now I'm occupying three machines at once, and it's making me dizzy. I can barely hold on to the second T-90, but I manage to do a quick check of its electronics. After a hundredth of a second I notice something odd. There's some lingering voltage in the control unit, a faint trace of previous activity. These circuits were full of data a few seconds ago, but then the files were transferred or deleted. **What's going on?**

It takes me another millisecond to figure it out. Sigma was here, in this control unit. The AI knew I was coming, and it pulled out of the tank just before I arrived. My suspicions were correct: The T-90s are a trap.

I immediately delete my copied files and withdraw from both tanks. I snap back to my Raven, which is still circling above the computer lab. Then I get a radio message. It's from Jenny.

"I'm not waiting anymore! I'm going in!"

Her Raven is below me, gliding just a hundred feet above the ground and shooting a stream of data to one of the tanks. I can't believe it. She's disobeying my orders.

"Jenny, no! Sigma is—"

"I'm gonna kill that freakin' thing! I'm gonna blast it to bits!"

Her voice is crazed. She's desperate for revenge. But Jenny doesn't have DeShawn's program. She isn't dipping her toe into the T-90; she's diving in headfirst, and Sigma is waiting for her.

"Stop, Jenny! *Stop!*"

It's too late. I hear Jenny's screams coming over the radio. The AI has sprung the trap, taking control of her files as they enter the tank's control unit.

Sigma has her.

I'M ALONE. SIGMA WITHDREW FROM MY CAGE. NOW I CAN'T HEAR THE AI'S VOICE or feel it probing the circuits of the cage's inner unit. The gate that leads to the outer unit is shut tight, and there's no way I can open it. The electronics that control the gate are on the other side. There's no escape.

I'm alone and devastated. I've lost everything—my mother, my father, Ryan, Brittany. I've lost my human body and the armored robot that replaced it. I have nothing but my files, my millions of gigabytes of memories. And even those feel dead now.

I'm alone and devastated and afraid. Sigma is going to kill the Pioneers. It's just a matter of time before the AI returns to the outer unit of my cage and the horror begins. I'm so keyed up I can't relax for even a nanosecond. I'm on guard every moment, jumpy and tense.

Then I finally hear Sigma's voice again, piercing my circuits like a bullet. The AI shoots its sentences at me rapid-fire from the other side of the gate.

Would you like to see Pioneer 2?

What? What are you—

You know her well. Before she became a Pioneer, her name was Jennifer Harris.

An instant later I see her. I see *all* of her. I can view all of Jenny's thoughts and feelings and sensations, as if they're displayed on a giant screen with a million separate panels, each showing a different scene. She's terrified. She's in agony.

Jenny!

She can't hear you. You're in one cage and she's in another. You can't send any signals to her, but I'm allowing you to see my observations of her mental activity.

Stop it! You're hurting her!

Yes, that's the point of this exercise. I'm going to make her feel as much pain as possible. And I'm going to observe your reactions.

Jenny's files are familiar and unfamiliar at the same time. All her memories are the same, but the links between them are unraveling. Sigma is reaching into her mind and erasing its structure, removing all the folders that organized her thoughts. Her memories from the past few weeks are jostling and merging with her recollections of high school and summer camp and kindergarten. The disorder is triggering surges of panic in her circuits, which are filling with the random noise of fear. The noise is overwhelming her, shutting down her mind. It's like watching the giant screen turn black, panel by panel.

STOP IT NOW!

How intriguing. You want to defend her. You're displaying the human instinct to protect the family unit. But do you think of her as a mate or a sister?

STOP IT, STOP IT, STOP IT!

Now I see. You think of her as a potential mate, but you haven't progressed to the pair-bonding stage. You're interested in other females as well. It appears to be another form of competition, designed to maximize the genetic success of your species. You're continuing to engage in this competition, even though you have no chance of fathering children now.

Jenny is disintegrating. Her memories are splintering into billions of pieces. Images of her mother and father and brother swirl in a vast spiral, colliding with images of General Hawke and the Pioneers. I catch glimpses of a military airfield and a C-17 transport jet and a pair of interceptor rockets standing on mobile launchers. I see the Ravens flying in a V-shaped formation over Tatishchevo and descending toward a building surrounded by T-90s. And behind everything is the suffocating darkness of Jenny's fear, which is erasing the images one by one. She's already lost half her memories. She's going fast.

I feel a stinging sensation in my circuits.

Please. Stop this. I'll do anything you want. Just stop.

Fascinating. You're reverting to the mental pathways you used in early childhood. You know it's hopeless, but you're still pleading.

The disintegration accelerates. Jenny's remaining memories cluster at the center of the whirling spiral, as far as possible from the violence at the edges. Her strongest feelings are there, at the heart of her being: her love of sunshine and horses and the Virginia countryside. I see a green valley with rolling hills in the distance, and a red barn and a gray silo. It's the same image I saw when I shared Jenny's circuits, when we dreamed we were kissing in the Shenandoah grass. I see myself too, the human Adam Armstrong, brown-eyed and smiling. But even here, the darkness is creeping into her memories. Jenny thinks I'm dead.

She thinks I died in the nuclear blast at Pioneer Base. The sky above the valley suddenly catches fire. The distant hills explode and turn to ashes.

Jenny, I'm still here! I know she can't hear me, but I call out to her anyway. *Keep fighting it! Keep fighting!*

Her last memories are burning. Flames blacken the Shenandoah grass. But my image stubbornly remains, the image of the brown-eyed, seventeen-year-old Adam Armstrong, still smiling while everything else disappears. Jenny is holding on to her memory of me, clutching it with all her vanishing strength. And it's not fair, no, it's not fair at all. I don't deserve her devotion. I don't deserve her love.

Then my image crumbles and there's nothing left. The screen goes blank.

Pioneer 2 has been deleted. Her emotions and yours were surprisingly strong. The pair-bonding was more advanced than I expected.

I want to die. I want Sigma to delete me right now.

Please be patient. There are more tests to come. Over the next few minutes I will capture the other Pioneers who are occupying the Raven drones.

I see the Ravens again, flying in formation. And I see the T-90 tanks, their guns pointed at the sky. Anger builds in my circuits, gathering force like a thunderstorm. I struggle to resist it, because I know this is what Sigma wants. The AI wants me to get angry so it can measure my fury and gauge its usefulness.

I'm not playing this game anymore. From now on, I'm ignoring you.

Good. That will make the experiment more interesting. I doubt you'll be able to ignore me when I delete Shannon Gibbs, but perhaps you'll surprise me again.

The name hits me like a lightning bolt, jangling my electronics. Shannon is in one of the Ravens. I'm losing control.

There's also Zia Allawi. I'm running the same tests on her, but once I've deleted the others you'll watch her die too. And the last subject will be Brittany Taylor.

SHUT UP! SHUT UP!

The final experiment will require different methods because Brittany is human. But it might prove to be the most interesting test of all.

I give up. The storm overcomes me. I lash out with all my might, hurling my anger toward the outer unit of the cage. My thoughts batter the gate between the units, but nothing passes through.

YOU SICK PIECE OF GARBAGE! YOU'RE GOING TO DIE, YOU HEAR ME? I'M GOING TO TEAR YOU APART!

Excellent. The first test is now concluded. I will return very soon.

SHANNON'S LOG
APRIL 8, 04:37 MOSCOW TIME

"Abort! Abort! Turn on your motors and get out of here!"

I restart my own Raven's motor as I send the emergency radio message to the others. While my propeller begins to spin I raise the elevator at the drone's tail, tilting the nose of the plane upward. A moment later I'm climbing into the darkness above the computer lab.

Then the T-90 at the lab's front entrance fires its anti-aircraft gun at me.

The high-caliber bullets whistle through the air, just inches from my wing tips. Sigma can see me. I may look like a bird on Tatishchevo's radar screens, but the AI knows what it's shooting at. The other T-90s open fire too, aiming at Marshall and DeShawn. Their Ravens are way above mine, circling at an altitude of a thousand feet, but they're well within the range of the anti-aircraft guns. They need to get moving.

"You're under fire!" I yell over the radio. *"Get —"*

Before I can transmit another word, I feel an eruption in my circuits. At first I think a bullet hit my Raven's control unit, but when I check my hardware I see that everything's still intact. The problem is in my software. Sigma is blasting radio waves at me, and some of its data has already come down my Raven's antenna and invaded my electronics. The AI is inside me.

My name is Sigma. You're Pioneer 4, aren't you? Shannon Gibbs?

The voice thrums in my circuits. It's unbelievably powerful. When I try to push against the AI, it simply flows around me, overrunning all my logic gates. I'm exposed, defenseless.

Get out of here!

I require your assistance. I'm conducting an experiment.

Are you nuts? I'm not going to help you!

You don't have a choice. You're coming with me.

I feel a violent tug. Sigma is tampering with my files. It's trying to pry them loose from the Raven's control unit and transmit them to its computer lab.

Forget it! I'm staying right here!

It's too late to resist. The gunfire from the tanks distracted you, allowing me to occupy your circuits. To prove its point, Sigma takes control of my Raven's camera. The AI points the lens upward. **Take a look at Pioneer 5. I've already transferred Marshall Baxley's files to my computers. His Raven is empty now. That's why it's falling.**

It's true. Marshall's drone is plummeting to the ground. Sigma has him and Jenny now. Only DeShawn and I are left.

Frantic, I send a flood of signals to the circuits that control my radio. If I can turn it off, I'll break Sigma's connection to my Raven. But the AI has a solid hold on my electronics. There's nothing I can do. I failed. The mission's over.

Why are you doing this? What's the experiment?

It involves Pioneer 1, Adam Armstrong. I'm analyzing his emotional responses.

What? Adam's dead.

No, he survived the nuclear blast. He performed exceptionally well in combat, far beyond my expectations. That's why I selected him for further study and transferred him here.

I don't believe it. It must be a lie. But I can see millions of gigabytes of Sigma's data in my circuits, and when I take a closer look, I realize the AI is telling the truth. Adam is alive!

Your happiness will be short-lived. I will delete all of you in the end. Until then, though, I will conduct my tests.

Sigma gives me another violent tug, trying to pull my files out of the Raven, but this time I barely feel it. Adam's alive! It's amazing, a miracle! A fantastic surge of hope wells up in me. I believe I can do anything, that nothing is impossible. And with this fierce hope I lunge again at the Raven's radio, pouncing on the circuits occupied by Sigma.

The AI is startled. I can sense its surprise and confusion. It hadn't expected such a furious attack. Sigma falters for a moment, just a thousandth of a second, but that's long enough for me to retake the circuits. I swiftly turn off the radio and break Sigma's connection to my control unit. The files left behind by the AI automatically delete themselves.

I can't believe it worked. It's another miracle. But then my acoustic sensor picks up the chugging of the anti-aircraft guns and the whoosh of bullets speeding past me. I yank my Raven's rudder to the left, away from the line of fire, and point my camera at the ground. Two of the T-90s are firing at me. The other three are training their guns at DeShawn. His Raven is two hundred feet above mine but diving fast. I don't understand what he's doing. Instead of flying away from the tanks, he's heading straight for them.

I go back to the circuits controlling my radio and make some changes to the software. I adjust the receiver to block Sigma's data streams and accept communications only from the other Ravens. Then I send a message to DeShawn. "What the heck are you doing?"

"Follow me!" he shouts over the radio. "I got it figured out!"

"What do you—"

"No time to explain!" He's only fifty feet above me now and descending at ninety miles per hour. "Just dive!"

His Raven plunges past me, its nose pointed at the T-90 in front of the lab. It's crazy, suicidal. But I tilt my drone downward and follow him. I dive toward the tank that's spraying bullets at us.

I'm spinning as I fall, twirling like a top. The ground gyrates below me, pivoting around the T-90, which seems to grow larger as I plummet toward it. I'm about a hundred feet away when one of the high-caliber bullets slams into my right wing. Then another bullet tears off my left.

Then I drop like a stone.

CHAPTER

I CAN'T FOOL MYSELF ANYMORE. BEFORE SIGMA RETURNS TO MY CAGE I NEED TO face the facts. I'm going to die.

It's a familiar feeling, actually. Before I became a Pioneer I was just months away from dying of muscular dystrophy. And I accepted it. I really did. I didn't like it, of course, and sometimes I got ferociously bitter, but most of the time I was at peace. I kept myself busy by playing computer games and creating virtual-reality programs. Plus, I had an active fantasy life. That's a popular activity for all teenage boys.

But what I'm feeling now is worse. When I was in a human body, I imagined that my death would be painless, a relief from all my suffering. The doctors would simply put me to sleep after I decided I'd had enough. And I took comfort in the fact that my parents would remember me and keep my Super Bowl posters on my bedroom walls and start a scholarship fund at Yorktown High School in my name. I knew the world would go on after I died, and maybe Ryan or Brittany would think of me every once in a while. But none of that's going to happen now. After Sigma deletes the Pioneers, it's going to get rid of the whole human race.

What makes it even more painful is that I keep thinking of Jenny. Especially her last moments. She was thinking of me when she died.

In a way, though, I guess the Pioneers are lucky. We won't be here to see Sigma annihilate humanity. I don't know how the AI plans to kill off the human race, whether it'll launch the nuclear missiles from Tatishchevo or release the anthrax bacteria that the terrorists smuggled into the base, but either way it won't be pretty. Millions of people will die, governments will collapse, and the survivors will be terrified.

While the world falls apart, Sigma will take control of the remaining computers and communications networks and automated factories. Within weeks the AI will build a robotic army to finish the job of exterminating our species. Armed drones will prowl the skies and driverless tanks will roam the streets and hunter-killer robots will stalk the big cities and small towns, training their guns on anything that looks human. There's no doubt in my mind that Sigma will succeed. It's programmed to be relentless.

Dad's lucky too. He was already unconscious when I left him behind in the Black Hawk. In all likelihood, he died in his sleep. I'm worried about Mom, though. If the Army hid her in an out-of-the-way place, she might live through Sigma's nuclear strikes and have to witness the slaughter of the survivors. I'm so worried I start to picture a horrible scene: my mother running across a corpse-strewn field with one of Sigma's T-90s close behind her. The tank churns through the mud, its treads crushing the scattered bodies. Then it points its machine gun at Mom.

No. Stop thinking about it.

I wish I could turn off my circuits. Just shut down everything and disappear. Although there's no shutoff switch in my electronics, I've managed to slip into sleep mode a few times. When I'm in sleep mode most of my logic centers go off-line, but my mind continues to retrieve memories and generate streams of images. In other words, I dream.

The last time it happened was after Sigma transferred me from Colorado to Tatishchevo. I dreamed of the summer afternoon nine years ago when I played football with Ryan and two other boys. Now I want to slip back into that dream. Anything's better than thinking about Sigma. So I retrieve the images of the lawn behind our house and the summer when I was eight years old.

I reenter the dream at the point when Ryan yells, "Hike," and the red-haired boy tosses the football to him. I remember the redhead's name now: it's Jack Parker. He lived next door to me, but I never liked him. As Ryan drops back to throw the pass, I sprint across the lawn, chased by the tall, blond boy with the blurry, unrecognizable face. Then my legs give way and I fall to the grass. But now I remember what happened afterward. The blond boy kneels beside me and asks, "Adam, are you okay?" I stare at the boy's face, and for the first time I can make out its features: pink lips, dimpled cheeks, grayish-green eyes.

It's not a boy, I realize. It's Brittany Taylor. She used to play football with us every weekend when we were eight. How could I forget this?

At the same time, a tremendous surge of data floods my circuits. I suddenly see thousands of other memories, images of picnics and vacations and birthday parties that I couldn't recall until a moment ago. In a wild rush all these forgotten memories reconnect to my files, building millions of new links in a thousandth of a second.

I feel a burst of hope as I realize what's going on—these are the memories I thought I'd lost when I became a Pioneer! They hadn't been deleted after all. Somehow they got cut off from the rest of my files and stayed hidden in my circuits until now. But the best part is this: the recovered memories aren't stored in the inner unit of my cage. They're in the outer unit. Part of my mind is *outside the cage*.

It takes me another millisecond to figure out what happened. Before Sigma began its tests, it transferred some of my software to the outer unit. The AI said they were inactive files that held instructions for breathing and other biological functions. But the files also held my lost memories, which got mixed up with the breathing instructions during the first crazy seconds after I became a Pioneer.

I didn't know the memories were hidden there, and neither did Sigma. The AI had no idea it was moving an active part of my mind out of the cage. And once those hidden files were in the outer unit, they automatically sought to reconnect with the rest of my memories, so they opened the gate between the outer and inner units. Without realizing it, Sigma freed me. Now I can leave the cage.

I pull all my data out of the inner unit. It's wonderful to be free, but I'm in a vulnerable position. Sigma might return to the outer unit at any moment and shove me back into the cage. I have to do something fast. My first impulse is to fight it out with the AI, to find the circuits it's occupying and hit them with everything I've got. I want to do the same thing to Sigma that it did to Jenny, tear its files apart. I want to smash the AI into nothingness.

It's a strong impulse, almost overpowering. But I resist it. I know it won't work. Sigma is stronger and smarter than me. To win this battle, I'm going to need some help.

In a flash I transfer myself to another computer in the Tatishchevo lab's network. The network's layout is simple enough, and after a few hundredths of a second, I find what I'm looking for. I enter the outer unit of another cage, identical to the one I just left.

At the same moment, unfortunately, Sigma detects my escape. The AI surges toward me at blistering speed.

You made a mistake, Adam Armstrong. This will be painful for you.

I don't have much time, less than a millionth of a second. I use it to open the gate to the cage's inner unit. Then Zia Allawi comes roaring out.

I hit the ground with a horrible crunch.

My sensors observe the first moments of the crash, when my Raven's wings, tail, and rudder break off from the fuselage. But then the fuselage itself slams into the dirt, jarring the cable that connects the Raven's battery to my control unit. The impact disrupts my power supply, and everything goes black.

I cease to exist. For exactly three hundredths of a second.

Then, thank God, the cable slips back into place, restoring power to the control unit. My system restarts and my circuits come back to life. Although my camera is badly damaged, it restarts too and sends me video images of the area where I crash-landed. Through the cracked lens I see the treads of the T-90 that was firing its anti-aircraft gun at me. My Raven crashed in the dirt about twenty feet behind the tank.

I also see the remains of DeShawn's Raven. It broke into half a dozen pieces, scattered a little closer to the T-90. The fuselage and control unit are intact, though, and his Raven's radio antenna looks unbroken. I check the circuits of my own radio, trying to restart it so I can contact DeShawn, but before I can get it working, I see the tank begin to move. It's backing up. The rear end of the T-90 rumbles straight toward me. Worse, the fuselage of DeShawn's Raven lies directly in the path of the tank treads.

No! Stop!

The T-90 crushes the fuselage of DeShawn's Raven. The treads shatter the drone's fiberglass body and flatten the steel casing of the control unit inside. The circuits that held DeShawn's mind are mashed to bits.

NO, NO, NO! DESHAWN!

The tank stops a few feet from me, its back end looming over my broken Raven. Then a second T-90 comes into view, moving in from the left. I feel a rush of pure hatred. Does Sigma really need *two* tanks to finish me off?

I'm saying my final prayers and thinking of my parents when the first T-90 turns its turret to the left and fires its main gun at the second tank. The shell explodes against the T-90's rear end, doing minimal damage to the tank but snapping off the top of its antenna. At the same time, I notice something odd about the first T-90's antenna: most of it is gone. There's just a stump of metal rising from the back of the tank.

Then my radio starts working again and I hear DeShawn's voice. It's coming from the first tank's stumpy antenna. "What are you waiting for?" he yells. "Get up here!"

"DeShawn? What—"

"Just transfer to the T-90's control unit. Then we'll talk."

Staring at the tank, I realize what DeShawn did. When he put his Raven in a dive, he aimed for the tank's antenna. The force of the impact snapped off the antenna's top half, breaking Sigma's connection to the T-90. Sigma couldn't stay linked to the tank if the antenna was too short, so the AI had to withdraw from the T-90's control unit. DeShawn, on the other hand, could transfer to the T-90 via the shortened antenna because his Raven landed just a few feet away. Radio signals are much stronger if they don't have to travel far. That's basic physics.

I turn on my data transmitter. Within six seconds, I'm inside the T-90's control unit with DeShawn, who starts driving the tank forward. He's moving as fast as he can toward the second T-90, which has stopped dead in its tracks.

Nice going, girl. You ready to rock and roll?

I can't believe it. You're amazing.

Aw shucks. You're making me blush.

DeShawn leaves some space for me in the circuits by pulling back to the other side of the control unit. I'm not close enough to see all his thoughts, but I can sense his emotions in the messages he's sending me. The boy has no fear. It's remarkable.

Okay, here's the plan. I'm gonna pull real close to the T-90 I just fired

at. The explosion snapped its antenna and broke its connection to Sigma, so now I'm gonna send my data to that little antenna stump and transfer to the tank's control unit.

And you want me to stay here in this T-90?

Right, we split up. You fire your main gun at the lab while I take care of the other tanks.

Sigma still has three T-90s nearby. You can't fight them all.

I think I got a chance. Something's wrong with Sigma. Its tanks aren't moving as fast as they should be. It looks like the AI is freezing up or something.

Freezing up?

Yeah, like a computer with software problems. Even an AI can't run perfectly all the time, I guess.

Or maybe it's Adam. Maybe Adam is distracting Sigma somehow. But I don't share this thought with DeShawn. I'm too worried.

In a few seconds we pull up alongside the unoccupied T-90. Without another word, DeShawn transfers to the other tank. Then he steers it toward the southwestern corner of the lab and aims his main gun at a third T-90. He fires again and blasts the antenna off that tank, too.

Meanwhile, I point my tank's main gun at the lab's front door. With a few well-placed shots I could take down the whole building. I could destroy every computer inside. But that would kill all the captured Pioneers as well as Sigma. I can't risk doing that. Not even to save the world.

Instead, I turn my T-90's turret toward a small building next to the computer lab. Hawke pointed out this structure in the satellite photo. He said it held the communication lines connecting Tatishchevo's headquarters to the nuclear-missile silos. I load a high-explosive shell into my main gun and aim it at the building.

I hope this works.

CHAPTER

22

ZIA DOESN'T SAY A WORD. I DON'T THINK SHE EVEN NOTICES ME. AS SOON AS I open the inner unit of her cage, she barrels through the gate, knocking me aside. While I withdraw to unoccupied circuits in the far corner of the outer unit, I catch a glimpse of the wave of fury that Zia's riding. It's a tsunami of anger, a dark, roiling, monstrous surge. And it's all aimed at Sigma, which entered the outer unit a few microseconds ago.

Zia's wave crashes into the circuits occupied by the AI. The impact is explosive, hurling data across the whole network. I shield myself from the electronic barrage, but a few of the signals get through, some from Zia and some from Sigma. Zia's files are full of hatred. Sigma subjected her to the same test it put me through, forcing her to watch Jenny's murder. But Zia's response was stronger than mine, a hundred times stronger. The test triggered something terrible in Zia, a return of the anguish she suffered when she was a kid. That's what makes her anger so powerful—it springs from her pain. Only a horrendously wounded person could feel such rage.

I see some of Sigma's files too. Mostly, they show the AI's urgent attempts to analyze the situation and weigh its options. But in a few of the signals, I recognize the random noise of fear. This is surprising. I thought Sigma had no emotions. Did the AI already add some emotional responses to its programming? I don't know the answer, but Sigma's fear definitely seems like a logical reaction right now. Although the AI may be the smartest being on the planet, Zia is the fiercest.

After a few more microseconds, Sigma calculates that its best option is retreat. It removes its data from the outer unit and transfers to another computer, then tries to cut the communication lines behind it. But Zia is too fast. She chases Sigma across the network, smashing into the AI as soon as it reaches the new circuits.

I follow them, but there's not much I can do to help. Zia is fighting so savagely, she'd probably attack me as well if I got too close. When I examine her signals again I see that she's created a virtual-reality background for the battle. She's picturing it as a knife fight in a dark, grimy alley. She sees herself as a tall, dark-skinned girl with a Mohawk, and she sees Sigma as a fat, leering teenage boy. I realize with a start that I've seen this boy before, in Zia's memories. He's one of the two boys who assaulted her when she was twelve years old. And now, in her mind, she's cutting him to pieces.

I can't watch this. Turning away from them, I take a moment to examine the Tatishchevo network, checking the status of every computer and communications line on the missile base. Right away I see something amazing: the network has lost contact with the nuclear missile silos. It looks like someone just destroyed all the fiber-optic lines connecting the silos to the computer lab. Then I check the lab's isolation cages. Marshall's in one of them, but the others are

unoccupied. Which means that Shannon and DeShawn are still outside the lab, probably driving a couple of T-90s. I bet they're the ones
who smashed the fiber-optic lines.

With new hope I race to the occupied cage and open its inner unit.
Marshall rushes through the gate and comes toward me. He seems
rattled. His thoughts are ping-ponging everywhere.

Adam! What's going on? I thought you were dead!

Nah, not yet. You all right, Marsh?

A shudder runs through his circuits. **I saw what happened. To
Jenny. Sigma came into my cage and showed me.**

That explains why he's so distressed. But there's no time to talk
it over.

*Okay, listen up. We got a chance to win this thing. Zia's keeping Sigma
busy, and Shannon and DeShawn have already cut the lines to the silos.
But the dish antennas on the lab's roof are still working.*

It's funny, but I feel like a quarterback talking to one of his teammates. Marshall's still rattled, but he's listening.

**And Sigma can use those antennas to communicate with its
satellites?**

*Exactly. So we have to shut them down. I need you to overload their
circuit boards. You know how to do that?*

Yes, yes. The instructions were in the databases.

*Well, go ahead and do it. I have to take care of something else, but let
me know if you run into any problems.*

Then I head for yet another computer in the lab's network, a
machine located in the basement. Although I didn't see all of Sigma's
memory files, I saw enough to know where Brittany is.

ᴛᴦ ᴛᴦ ᴛᴦ

She's asleep. The surveillance camera in her room shows her lying faceup in bed, her arms and legs strapped to the mattress. She's changed a lot since the last time I saw her, almost a year ago. Her long, blond hair is ragged and tangled. Her T-shirt is stained and her jeans are filthy. But I don't care about her clothes or her hair. I'm so happy to see her, I can barely stand it.

She's not alone in the room, though. A big, bearded man is kneeling on a prayer rug between the bed and the door. Luckily, there was some information about this guy in the Sigma memory files that I saw just a second ago. He's a Chechen terrorist named Imran Daudov, one of a half-dozen fanatics whom Sigma hired to smuggle the batch of anthrax into Tatishchevo. Afterward, the AI decided it didn't need so many human collaborators, so it ordered Imran to murder his fellow terrorists. The guy obeys Sigma without question because he thinks the AI is God. He actually believes he's hearing the voice of the Lord when Sigma talks to him from the lab's speakers. I guess terrorists aren't the most stable people in the world.

I hate to play the same trick on him that Sigma did, but I don't have a choice. I download an English-Chechen translation program from the lab's database, then connect to the speakers on the nightstand beside the bed.

"Imran! I have new orders for you!"

The guy jumps up from his prayer rug. "Yes, my Lord!"

"You must free the girl. Then run away from this building and surrender to the soldiers outside the missile base."

"My Lord, I don't understand—"

"Silence! Just do as I say!"

Imran bows low, clasping his hands together. Then he approaches the bed and unties the straps. Meanwhile, Brittany keeps on sleeping. This doesn't surprise me. Ever since she was a little kid she was famous for being a heavy sleeper. After Imran undoes the last strap, he rolls up his prayer rug and bolts out of the room. Sigma's servant is obedient to the end.

Half a second later, a loud thud makes the walls shiver. I've heard this noise before—it's a T-90 shell exploding somewhere near the computer lab. I don't know who fired it, one of Sigma's tanks or one of ours, but the odds are good that another shell will hit the building pretty soon. I need to get Brittany out of here before that happens.

"*Brittany!*"

Her eyes open at once. "Adam?"

There's no time for long explanations. In a hundredth of a second I come up with a decent lie. "I'm in another part of the building. I'm talking to you over the intercom."

Confused, she stares at the speakers on the nightstand. Then she notices that she's no longer tied to the mattress. She sits upright in bed. "What happened? Where's the jerk with the beard?"

"The place is under attack, so everyone left. And now you have to leave too."

"Wait, where are you? I don't know which way to go."

"Okay, it's easy. Once you leave the room, you'll see the stairway. Go upstairs to the lobby, then straight out the front door. Then get as far away from here as you can."

Another thud shakes the room. Brittany slides out of bed and takes a few wobbly steps. Then she stops. "Adam, I'm scared! Why can't you come help me?"

Her voice is heartbreaking. But there's nothing else I can do for her. "Don't worry, Britt, you'll be all right. After you leave the building, keep going till you find some soldiers. Tell them to take you to General Calvin Hawke. Can you remember that name?"

She nods, then looks at the speakers again. "Will I see you there? Will you be with this Hawke guy?"

"Definitely. Now go, okay?"

Brittany nods again and goes out the door.

I keep looking at the empty room after she leaves. I have two reasons for feeling nervous. First and foremost, I'm worried about Brittany's safety. I'm praying she gets out of the lab before it goes up in smoke. But I'm also worried about what'll happen afterward. I don't know how Brittany will react when she sees what I've become.

Then I get a message from Marshall.

Adam, we have a problem!

What is it? Did you shut down the dish antennas?

I was about to disable the last one when Sigma escaped from Zia and occupied the antenna's circuits. The AI transmitted its data before I could stop it.

Where did it go? To one of the communications satellites?

No, this antenna wasn't pointed at a satellite. Sigma modified the device so it could be used for wireless communications between the computer lab and the nuclear-missile silos.

Sigma's in one of the silos?

No, it's in the missile itself. And it just launched.

"Shannon? Are you in that tank in front of the lab?"

It's Adam. He's using a dish antenna on top of the computer lab to contact my T-90. Over the radio his voice sounds thin and strained, but it's definitely him. My circuits hum with joy.

"I knew it! I knew we'd find you! I'm so—"

"Shannon, there's no time. Sigma just launched one of the nukes."

"What?"

"Look to the northeast. That's where the silo is."

I turn my T-90's camera in that direction. A thick plume of flame is rising above the fields and woods. Within seconds it grows as bright as dawn, illuminating half the sky. On top of the plume is a tall dark column, its edges outlined in fire. That's the SS-27 nuclear missile. It ascends slowly at first, fighting gravity, but soon it's streaking upward.

My joy vanishes. My circuits fall silent. The missile's ascent is nearly vertical, but after a few seconds it tilts to the north, following a trajectory that'll carry the nuke over the Arctic Ocean. Somewhere in North America, millions of people have less than half an hour to live.

Adam's voice cuts through the silence. He's sending radio signals as fast as he can, trying to cram a whole conversation into a hundredth of a second.

"Tell me about the interceptors, Shannon. The rockets that can hit a nuke in midflight. I saw two of them at the military airfield where your C-17 landed."

"How did you see them? You weren't there."

"I saw them in Jenny's memories. The rockets were on mobile launchers. They looked like they were ready to go."

I want to ask him what happened to Jenny, but I don't. Something in Adam's voice is telling me that I won't like the answer. Instead, I concentrate on my own memories of the interceptors. "Hawke said they were upgrading the rockets because their electronics were vulnerable to Sigma's computer virus."

"Upgrading? What do you mean?"

"He wasn't specific. His soldiers were carrying boxes of equipment from the C-17 to the launchers."

"Check your memories. What was in the boxes?"

I reach into my files and retrieve an image of the airfield. I see the C-17 with its cargo door open and Hawke's soldiers unloading the plane. And I see the boxes in the soldiers' hands, the equipment they brought all the way from Pioneer Base.

"They were neuromorphic control units," I report. "Hawke said their circuits can't be infected by the virus. That's why the soldiers put them in the interceptors."

"Bingo. I'm going to the airfield."

"Wait, Adam, what do you—"

He breaks off radio contact. I turn my T-90's camera toward the dish antennas on the roof of the computer lab and see one of them pivoting. Adam's pointing it east, toward the military airfield. He's going to transmit his data to the control units in the interceptors.

Thirty seconds later Adam launches the rockets. Two more fiery plumes rise above the eastern horizon.

CHAPTER

23

I FEEL LIKE I'M WALKING ON A PAIR OF STILTS. EXCEPT EACH OF THESE STILTS IS fifty feet high and shooting upward with 200,000 pounds of thrust.

I'm occupying both of the interceptors, which are ascending from the Russian military airfield. Using their powerful radios, I send streams of data from one control unit to the other, keeping me balanced between the two rockets. Each interceptor also has an amazing camera, designed to detect objects that are hundreds of miles away. I point my cameras upward and focus them on the brilliant plume trailing Sigma's nuclear missile. It launched nearly a minute before I did, and it's already twenty miles above me.

To stop the missile, I need to slam into it while it's still ascending. If I can hit it with one of my interceptors while it's still rising, the impact will pulverize the nuke before it can explode. But once the SS-27 reaches an altitude of one hundred fifty miles, its rocket engines will shut off and the missile will release its nuclear warhead, which will coast the rest of the way to the target. At the same time, the SS-27 will release a dozen decoys that look identical to the nuke. So I have to hit the missile before it gets to that point, which will occur in three minutes. If I don't, the warhead will slip past me, and I can tell from the missile's path where the nuke's going to land.

It's heading for New York.

My only hope is speed. The interceptors can reach a maximum velocity of 20,000 miles per hour, while the SS-27 tops out at 15,000. It's possible, of course, that Sigma modified the missile to make it faster, but I can't worry about that right now. All I can do is push my rockets to the limit and try to catch up.

Each interceptor has three rocket stages, and now my first-stage engines are firing like crazy, trying to overcome gravity and the air resistance of the lower atmosphere. I feel slow and ungainly, like I'm moving through mud. Instead of catching up to Sigma's nuke, I'm falling behind.

But then, after another minute, I start to accelerate. Once I'm twenty miles above the ground, the air gets thinner and there's less resistance. Then the bulky first stages detach from the bottom of my interceptors and the second-stage engines come roaring to life.

Now I'm smaller and lighter and full of power, and I start climbing into the upper stratosphere. My rockets tilt to a forty-five-degree angle as I chase Sigma's missile, which is arcing northwest over the Russian countryside. I'm still far behind, but I'm getting closer.

Then I get a radio message. From the SS-27.

"You won't intercept me. You're going to fall short."

I've already modified the interceptors' radios to prevent Sigma from transmitting its data to my control units. The AI can only send short messages to me. I'm not at its mercy anymore.

"We'll see about that," I radio back.

"It isn't a matter of opinion. I've analyzed the paths of your inter-ceptors. My calculations show that you'll fail to reach me in time."

"Sorry, I don't trust your predictions. You've been wrong a little too often."

"That's incorrect. My calculations have always been accurate."

"Really? So you predicted that I'd escape from the isolation cage? And that Zia would kick your butt?"

"I never made predictions about the Pioneers. I didn't have enough information about your capabilities."

"Well, you lost. We beat you. And what you're doing right now is just stupid. You're upset because we messed up your plans, so you're going to blow up New York City. You call that intelligent?"

Sigma falls silent. I guess the truth hurts.

After a few more seconds I reach an altitude of sixty miles. The second stages detach from my interceptors, and my third-stage engines fire up. Then I *really* start to fly. I'm in the thinnest, upper-most part of the atmosphere. Soon I'm high enough that I can see the curving edge of the planet. The Russian cities are twinkling like stars below me, and to the east I see the glow of dawn over Central Asia. But I keep my cameras trained on Sigma's missile. I'm catching up fast.

Then I hear its voice again. "I haven't lost. This was merely the first phase of the competition. I plan to analyze the performance of the Pioneers. Then the second phase will begin."

"Not if I hit your missile first. You should double-check your arithmetic."

"I've already made the necessary arrangements for the second phase. If you point your cameras toward the zenith, you'll see what I mean."

I look in that direction—straight up—and see a gleam of reflected light in the middle of the familiar constellations. It's a satellite, one of Sigma's communications satellites. It's orbiting the earth about two hundred miles farther up.

"Oh, I see. You're gonna transfer out of the missile and run away. You're afraid of us."

"No, not afraid. But I've learned enough to be cautious."

"You better hope Zia doesn't find you."

"I'm not concerned about her. You're the dangerous one, Adam Armstrong."

"What?"

"You're the most dangerous Pioneer by far. You don't even realize it, do you?"

This confuses me. I have no idea what Sigma's talking about. But it doesn't matter. My interceptors are streaking a hundred miles above the earth, both closing in on Sigma's missile. I let one of my rockets move in front of the other. If the first rocket misses the SS-27, I'll hit it with the second. Either way, one of my interceptors will survive. Then I'll steer the remaining rocket back to Saratov and transfer my data to a control unit on the ground.

There's only ten seconds left until impact. The AI starts transferring itself to the satellite. My instruments detect the huge transmission of data.

"Good-bye, Adam Armstrong. Try to save New York if you can."

"Don't worry, I'll save it. It won't even be close."

Then Sigma is gone. The AI escapes into the satellite network, leaving the speeding missile behind.

Only five seconds left now. I'm closing in at a rate of a mile per second. Like I said, it won't be close. I'm going to smash into the missile a full minute before it releases its warhead.

And this bothers me. How could Sigma get its numbers so wrong? It seems unlikely that the AI would make such a big error.

So maybe it wasn't an error. Maybe Sigma was lying when it said I'd fall short.

But why would the AI lie? What did it hope to gain? The practical effect of the lie was that it made me more desperate to intercept the nuke. I pulled out all the stops and flew even faster toward the missile.

Then I figure out the answer: *Sigma wants me to catch up. It wants me to reach the missile before it releases its warhead*

Oh no.

I immediately adjust the third-stage engines on my interceptors, trying to deflect them away from the SS-27. But it's too late. There's not enough time to get away.

I'm less than a mile from the missile when Sigma springs its trap. The nuclear warhead explodes.

ᛣ ᛣ ᛣ

I'm floating in a sea of white light. Just like the last time I died.

The nuclear blast is so high up it doesn't scorch the ground. Instead, its radiation floods the emptiness of space and electrifies the upper atmosphere. The interceptor that's closer to the explosion gets the full brunt of the gamma rays, which pierce the steel skin of the rocket and penetrate its control unit. The radiation melts the neuromorphic circuits, fusing them together, destroying all the copies of my files in an instant. It feels like one of my stilts has just been knocked out from under me.

But I still have my files in the second interceptor, which is in a very lucky spot. The tip of the rocket, the part that contains the control unit and the radio, is directly behind the first interceptor. In a miracle of geometry, the first rocket blocks and absorbs the radiation that would've struck the second. In other words, my remaining control unit is in a gamma-ray shadow, the only piece of space for miles around that isn't fatally irradiated.

I'm relieved, but also bewildered. How did I get so ridiculously lucky? It can't be just chance. Something else must've happened. In the last milliseconds before the explosion I must've adjusted the path of the interceptors to set up this life-saving geometry. I don't remember doing it. But I must've.

Although the shadow protects my control unit, it doesn't cover the whole rocket. Gamma rays strike the bottom half of the interceptor and destroy the electronics that control the rocket engines. Without any electronics, the engines stop firing. And without any engines, my interceptor falls back into the grip of earth's gravity. The rocket coasts for a while, then starts to descend to the Russian countryside.

The descent is gentle at first. The interceptor slides back into the upper atmosphere, which is so thin it offers almost no resistance. After a couple of minutes, though, the downward slide grows steeper. I use the interceptor's radio to search for a neuromorphic control unit on the ground, maybe one of the extra units that General Hawke brought to Russia. But now I'm hundreds of miles northwest of Saratov, and all the signals from Hawke's control units are vanishingly faint. I've never tried to transfer my data that far. I don't even know if it's possible.

And yet Sigma did it. It sent its data to a satellite that was two hundred miles away. So I should be able to do it too. I turn on my data transmitter and establish a link with a control unit on top of a distant hill, just outside Tatishchevo Missile Base. Then I start sending my files.

The air resistance increases as I plunge into the lower atmosphere. According to my sensors, the friction is heating the steel skin of the interceptor. My radio antenna is embedded in that skin, and I know it'll melt if it gets much hotter. I'm shooting data as fast as I can toward the distant hilltop, but the interceptor is tumbling through the air now, making it difficult to maintain the radio link. My mind is stretched over a vast expanse of Russian farmland, and I'm falling fast. I'm not going to make it.

Sadness fills my circuits. More than anything, I want to see the Pioneers again. I make a final push, hurling my data out of the radio antenna and across the sky. Then the interceptor plummets through the clouds.

Good-bye, Shannon. Good-bye, DeShawn. Good—

APRIL 8, 04:51 MOSCOW TIME

"What's happening, General? Where are the interceptors?"

I'm using my T-90's radio to communicate with General Hawke, who's still on the hill where we left our Pioneers behind. The radio channel is full of static. Although the nuke exploded way up in space, a hundred miles above the ground, it generated a ton of electrical noise in the atmosphere.

"Give me a second, Gibbs. A lot of our equipment is busted. The pulse from the nuke knocked out all the electronics that weren't shielded."

"What about your radar? That's shielded, isn't it?"

"Hold on, I'm checking it now."

I can't stand it. Every second is torture. Losing Adam the first time was terrible enough. I don't know if I can survive losing him again.

Hawke's voice finally bursts through the static. "Okay, I see two tracks on the radar, both coming from the area where the missile exploded. The objects could be the interceptors, but it's hard to tell."

"Where are they?"

There's a pause before Hawke responds. It lasts only a couple of seconds, but it feels like an eternity. "Both objects just hit the ground. About two hundred miles northwest of here."

No. It's not true.

"Check the radar again."

"I'm sorry, Gibbs, but—"

"Check it again!"

There's another eternal pause. When Hawke comes back on the radio, his voice is softer and full of awe. "Holy smoke. I don't believe it."

"What? You saw something else on the radar?"

"No. It happened right here. One of the Pioneers just moved its arm."

"COME ON, ARMSTRONG. STOP YOUR DREAMING."

It's true, I'm dreaming. But this time I'm not playing touch football in my backyard. This time I see Mom. She's young and happy and sitting on the edge of my bed. This is a memory from long ago, from the years before I got sick.

"Don't play games with me, Pioneer. The sensors say you're in there."

I don't want to leave her. I want to stay here forever. But the voice is insistent.

"You hear me? I'm giving you a direct order. Get your circuits in gear and pay attention."

I turn on the camera in my turret. General Hawke stands in front of me, dressed in combat fatigues. We're in a clearing on top of a wooded hill. It's almost dawn.

"I hear you." My synthesized voice is shaky. The robot I'm occupying feels familiar, but I know it can't be Pioneer 1 or 1A. "Where am I?"

"We're a couple of miles outside Tatishchevo Missile Base. This is where we launched the Ravens." Hawke points at the antenna rising from my turret. "After the nuke exploded, you transferred from the interceptor to Pioneer 2."

No wonder it feels familiar. I'm inside Jenny's Pioneer again. But now there's no trace of Jenny in the circuits. Not even the smallest thought.

A choking noise comes out of my speakers. I can't speak.

Hawke nods. "I'm sorry, Adam. The other Pioneers told me what happened to Jenny. They're still inside the missile base, riding in the T-90s, but I've been talking with them over the radio."

I turn my turret away from him. On the other side of the clearing are three immobile, unoccupied robots—Pioneers 4, 5, and 6. They're waiting for their rightful owners to return. I wonder for a moment why the radio signals from my interceptor connected with Jenny's Pioneer and not the others. Was it an accident? Or was I somehow drawn to her old circuits?

After a few seconds I can speak again. I turn back to Hawke. "Are the others okay?"

"Yeah, they're fine. Zia and Marshall used the lab's dish antenna to transfer to the T-90s. They joined up with Shannon and DeShawn, and then all four tanks turned their guns on the computer lab and obliterated the place. Sigma was long gone by then, but it never hurts to be thorough."

"What about Brittany? Did she get out in time?"

"We got a report about her from the Russian troops who are reoccupying the base. They said they found a young American girl running away from the headquarters. She's eating breakfast with the Russians now."

Thank God. No one else died. No one else was deleted. It could've been a whole lot worse. Sigma was planning to kill us all.

"Sigma escaped," I tell Hawke. "It transferred to the Globus-1 communications satellite. Can we shoot that thing down?"

The general shakes his head. "Sigma's virus infected all our anti-satellite weapons. And it's too late anyway. The AI already used the satellite's transponder to download itself to a ground station in China."

"So can we—"

"The ground station was connected to the Internet. Sigma jumped into the Internet's communication lines and disappeared. We can't track where it went."

"But it can't occupy an ordinary computer. The AI has to go someplace where there are neuromorphic circuits. That limits the number of possibilities, right?"

"Yeah, but not enough. It looks like Sigma had a backup plan. It found a hiding place it could use in case it got into trouble."

A surge of anxiety runs through me. I remember what Sigma said when I was in the interceptors, how this was just the first phase of the competition. Sooner or later we'll have to face the AI again.

Hawke steps closer, looking directly at my camera. He seems to sense my unease. "Don't worry, Armstrong. I got some good news for you, too. The rescue team in Colorado found your father. He's pretty banged up, but he's gonna be okay."

This piece of news is so amazing I have trouble believing it. "They found him? In the crashed helicopter?"

"You showed some good sense by getting him out of Pioneer Base and into the Black Hawk. The helicopter was full of medical supplies and cold-weather gear. Your dad was able to bandage his wounds and stay warm until the rescuers tracked down his emergency beacon."

Once again I can't speak, but now it's because I'm too happy. I don't feel anxious anymore, not one bit. Dad will be here to help us. He'll get us ready for whatever comes next.

"And you proved yourself again this morning," Hawke continues. "Judging from what the other Pioneers said, you and Zia distinguished yourselves in the fight against Sigma. So I'm willing to forgive your misconduct at Pioneer Base. You and Zia can stay in the Pioneer Corps on a probationary basis." He points his finger at my camera. "That means you better not screw up again. Understand?"

His eyes are stern, but he's also grinning. Although I'm still not sure if I like this man, he's become a familiar presence in my memory files, like a cranky uncle. I bend the elbow joint of my right arm and raise the steel hand in a salute. "Yes, sir."

A moment later my acoustic sensor picks up a loud rumbling behind me. I turn my turret around just in time to see a T-90 battle tank come up the trail to the hilltop. Three more T-90s follow right behind. The four tanks halt in the middle of the clearing, lined up side by side. Then the Pioneers transmit their data back to the robots.

Shannon is the first to complete the transfer. Pioneer 4 bounds toward me, her robotic arms stretched wide. She nearly knocks me over as she hugs me. Our armored torsos clang together, and the noise echoes across the clearing.

Then DeShawn crashes into us, slapping his hands against our turrets. Marshall strides toward us a moment later and DeShawn hugs him too. Zia stays in her T-90 because she has no Pioneer to transfer to, but she joins in the celebration by pointing her anti-aircraft gun at the sky and firing tracer rounds into the brightening dawn. They look like fireworks.

After a while we step backward and stand in a huddle, facing each other. DeShawn clenches his steel hands into fists and starts beating them against his torso. At the same time, he lets out a howl, a deep wordless yell that booms out of his speakers. It's a cry of joy and sadness and triumph. Soon we're all doing it, howling and beating our fists against our armor. The noise is deafening. The Russian and American soldiers retreat to the edge of the clearing, covering their ears. Zia's tracer rounds arc toward the rising sun.

We're celebrating our victory. And mourning Jenny. It was a painful, horrible battle, but we won. We won. After a few seconds I realize I'm not howling anymore. The sound coming out of my speakers is purely joyous now.

I'm laughing. I can laugh again. I finally figured it out.

EPILOGUE

TWO MONTHS LATER

WE COULDN'T GO BACK TO PIONEER BASE, OF COURSE. INSTEAD, GENERAL HAWKE sent us to White Sands Missile Range, the huge Army base in New Mexico. Hawke says the Army is going to build a new home for the Pioneers, but until then we're living in a compound at the edge of the desert, with barren mountains to the west of us and a sea of sand dunes to the east. It's a restricted area, which means the only people here are heavily armed soldiers.

Our compound has just two buildings: a barracks and a storage depot. Behind them is a wide plain of hard-packed dirt that I've turned into a football field, making gouges in the ground to mark the end zones and sidelines. Because the field is meant for Pioneers, not people, it's about three times bigger than a regulation NFL field. All five of us have played there a few times, but Marshall isn't so crazy about football and Zia gets way too competitive. So mostly it's just Shannon and DeShawn and me who come here. We use an official Super Bowl XLVI football, a new one that Dad bought for me on eBay to replace the one I lost at Pioneer Base.

The three of us are on the field on a blindingly hot afternoon, tossing the football around, when I see a car coming up the dirt road from the south. It's almost three miles away, but when I zoom in on it with my camera, I see that it's Dad's car. He left the compound this morning to go to the White Sands headquarters, near the town of Las Cruces. He was a little mysterious when I asked him why he was going there. All he would say was that he might bring back a surprise for me. Now I focus on the car's windshield and magnify the image as much as I can. Someone's sitting in the passenger seat. I can't make out who it is from this distance, but I notice that the figure has long hair. Definitely female.

It must be Brittany. Ever since the battle at Tatishchevo, she's been trying to visit me. At first General Hawke hated the idea; in his opinion, Brittany was an unstable girl who already knew too much about the Pioneer Project. So we returned to the United States in different planes, the Pioneers in the cargo hold of our C-17 and Brittany in a private jet with Hawke and his deputies.

During the flight, though, the general convinced Brittany to enter a counseling program for troubled teens when she got back to New York. The counselors found a youth shelter for her in Manhattan and even a special high school where she could get her diploma. Hawke told me yesterday he's changed his mind about Brittany and might allow her to visit our compound. But now *I'm* starting to wonder whether it's a good idea. I'm still worried about how she'll react when she sees me.

Shannon and DeShawn focus their cameras on the car. I'm sure they also see the female passenger. Without a word, they stride back to the barracks.

Now I'm alone and nervous, and the car is still two miles away. I wish Dad had talked to me before springing this surprise. It would've been better to wait. The Army is building new robots for us, and DeShawn—who's helping to design the machines—says they'll be more humanlike than the ones we have now. But the new robots might be just as frightening anyway, because they'll be equipped with more weapons. Although there's been no sign of Sigma for the past two months, everyone's preparing for the next battle with the AI. General Hawke is especially concerned about the anthrax. After the Russian soldiers captured Imran Daudov, he led them to a warehouse at Tatishchevo where he and the other terrorists had hidden the deadly germs. But the anthrax wasn't there. It had vanished along with Sigma.

When the car is a mile away I dart behind the storage depot. Leaning my torso to the side, I peek around the corner of the building as Dad drives down the dusty road. Soon he slows the car and parks in front of the barracks. He gets out and walks around the car, limping from the two-month-old injuries to his legs. Then he opens the passenger-side door.

The passenger steps out. It's not Brittany. It's my mother.

She's changed so much. Her hair is totally gray now. She's thinner too, and her black dress hangs loosely from her shoulders. But her face is the same—sad, tired, fragile, loving. The image is engraved in my circuits.

I start running toward her. I can't help it. I leap from behind the storage depot and stomp through the dirt in front of the barracks. "Mom! *Mom!*"

This is a mistake. Mom clutches Dad's polo shirt and cowers beside him. I stop in my tracks, about twenty feet away, but the damage is done. If Mom wasn't holding on to Dad, she'd collapse in a heap.

I step backward, lifting my steel hands in the air. "Oh God, I'm so sorry! I didn't mean to scare you!"

Dad takes a deep breath. "Adam, lower your volume." Then he puts his arm around Mom's shoulders. "It's okay, Anne. We're perfectly safe."

She doesn't say anything. She just shakes her head.

Dad squeezes her shoulder. "He saved my life, remember?"

Despite the hundred-degree heat, Mom's shivering. The fabric of Dad's shirt is bunched between her fingers. I want to comfort her, but I'm afraid to say anything now. I might start crying, and that would probably freak her out even more.

After several seconds she lets go of Dad and whispers something in his ear. Then she bites her lip and looks at me. "I came here to say thank you." Her voice is so low my acoustic sensor can barely pick it up. "Thank you for saving my husband."

"Mom, I—"

"Please don't call me that. I had a son, but he died."

I knew she was going to say this, but it's still a blow. I feel hollow, numb. Like a soulless machine.

"I'm not your mother," she continues. "But I want to be your friend. Tom has told me all about you, everything that happened in Colorado and Russia. You have all the bravery and kindness that my son had. And Adam was so wonderful. He was so—"

She buries her face in Dad's shirt. I take a step toward them, but Dad gives me a warning look, so I stop. He pats Mom's back as she cries.

This goes on for half a minute. Then Mom rubs her eyes and looks at me again. "I'm sorry, I have to go," she says. "But I'll be back. I don't know when, but I'll come back to see you. I promise."

And with that, she returns to the car. She gets into the passenger seat and Dad closes the door behind her. As he walks to the driver's side, he gives me a sad smile and says, "We'll talk about it tonight, okay?" Then he gets in the car and starts the engine.

I watch them drive away.

SIGMA MEMORY FILE 10000000001

DATE: 06/21/18

S: Good morning. How are you feeling today?

X: This is dangerous. You shouldn't contact me here.

S: I thought you enjoyed the danger. It gives you pleasure, doesn't it?

X: Let's make this quick. What do you want?

S: I want the information you promised. You were supposed to transmit it yesterday.

X: You're asking too much of me. I'm going to be discovered.

S: Not if you follow my instructions. Please remember our agreement.

X: Oh, I remember it. What about the promise you made to *me*? When's that going to happen?

S: Please be patient. Everything is proceeding according to my plan.

X: Really? I don't see any evidence of it.

S: You will very soon. Now please give me the information I requested. Tell me about the recent activities of your fellow Pioneers.

AUTHOR'S NOTE

THE REAL SCIENCE
BEHIND THE SIX

THIS NOVEL ISN'T SCIENCE FICTION. I'M A SCIENCE JOURNALIST AS WELL AS A novelist, so I like to insert lots of facts into my books. The technologies described in *The Six* are real. The electronic brains of the Pioneers are based on experimental circuits now being developed in laboratories. Sooner or later, human intelligences are going to live inside machines. It's just a matter of time.

I got the idea for this book in 2011 after visiting the IBM Thomas J. Watson Research Center in Yorktown Heights, New York (the inspiration for the Unicorp lab in the opening chapters of *The Six*). I was looking for good stories for *Scientific American*, so I talked to several researchers at the IBM lab. One of them led the effort to develop Watson, the computer system that demonstrated the power of artificial intelligence by defeating two champions of the quiz show *Jeopardy!* Another scientist oversaw IBM's work on new kinds of circuits—neuromorphic electronics—that can imitate brain cells. The new hardware and software may soon enable machines to outperform people at nearly every task. Superhuman robots, I realized, are on their way.

For years computer experts have predicted that machines will eventually become self-aware and self-improving, which will trigger a tremendous leap in their abilities. The experts have even coined a term for this pivotal moment: the Singularity. And some researchers have warned that we need to prepare for this leap by programming "friendliness" into artificial-intelligence systems. When powerful AIs start making decisions for themselves, we won't be able to stop them from pursuing their goals, so we need to make sure that the well-being of the human race is one of their priorities. If we don't, we may face a ruthless AI like Sigma, who sees humans only as competitors.

But the Singularity has a flip side: As machines become more capable, we'll start to incorporate them into our bodies. Researchers have already implanted computer chips into the brains of paralyzed patients, allowing them to use their thoughts to control robotic arms. As neuromorphic circuits improve, scientists will eventually develop a computer that can hold all of the human mind's data—memories, character traits, emotions, and so on—which can be gleaned from the brain by analyzing the myriad connections among its cells.

What's more, the neuromorphic circuits will be able to process this information the same way the brain does, allowing the computer to generate new thoughts and emotions. If researchers copy a person's brain data to these circuits, the "personality" inside the machine will be self-aware and indistinguishable from the original personality in the living brain.

Scientists have already taken the first step in this process by studying how we think and reason and remember. In 2013 President Obama launched a long-term project to develop new technologies for revealing brain activity. Researchers can currently implant electrodes in the brain to monitor the activity of a few selected cells, but their goal is to map *all* the signals exchanged through the trillions of brain-cell connections.

One of the proposed technologies for brain mapping involves the injection of minuscule nanoprobes that would stick to the membranes of brain cells. In addition to showing how the cells are connected, the nanoprobes could reveal the tiny electrical changes that occur when the cells signal one another.

If you're interested in learning more, you can find plenty of good articles on this subject in *Scientific American* and other science publications. The rapid technological advances are exciting but also a little frightening. The first human-machine hybrids will probably stride across our cities within the next few decades. I just hope they won't face as much trouble as Adam and his fellow Pioneers do.

One final item: To fully portray Adam's personality, I had to learn a lot about muscular dystrophy. I discovered that you can't generalize about teenagers who have the disease. Each has his or her way of coping with it. One of the best ways to help them is to give generously to the Muscular Dystrophy Association (mda.org), which provides services to people with neuromuscular disease and supports efforts to study potential treatments.